DIVIDING ILLUMINATION

THE WEBS OF FATE
BOOK TWO

C J WALLINGSFORD

Dividing Illumination
Book Two of The Webs of Fate
Copyright © {2025} Courtney J Wallingsford

First edition 2025
Print ISBN: 978-1-954426-09-2
Ebook ISBN: 978-1-954426-08-5
Cover design by CJ Wallingsford
Interior Artwork CoverCraft by Julie
Chapter Header design by CJ Wallingsford
Editing by KillingItWrite (Gina)

For more information: cjwallingsford@outlook.com

TRIGGER WARNING

This book is intended for mature audiences. This series will contain explicit content and dark elements that may be triggering to some. It will include a magical race of beings known as the Seraphinus that has two factions with extreme prejudice against each other.

Additional warnings:
Violence / Mature Language
Contracted Servitude
Emotional / physical abuse
Substance abuse / addiction
Sexually explicit scenes*

*While not included in this book, this series will feature a MMF relationship

For anyone who has been in a bad place
and stuck in a bad relationship.

RUNE DIAL

The Continents Calendar

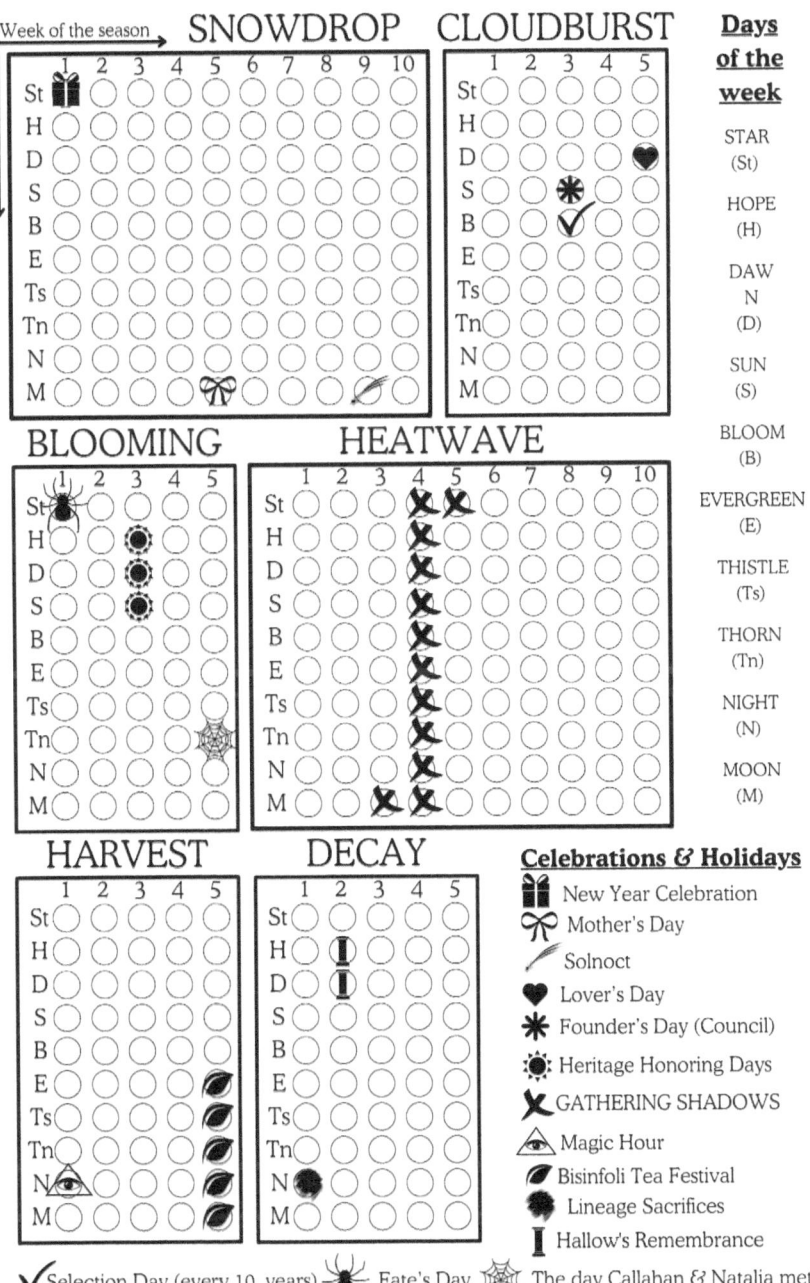

Week of the season →

Day of the week

SNOWDROP
CLOUDBURST
BLOOMING
HEATWAVE
HARVEST
DECAY

St
H
D
S
B
E
Ts
Tn
N
M

Days of the week

STAR (St)

HOPE (H)

DAWN (D)

SUN (S)

BLOOM (B)

EVERGREEN (E)

THISTLE (Ts)

THORN (Tn)

NIGHT (N)

MOON (M)

Celebrations & Holidays

New Year Celebration

Mother's Day

Solnoct

Lover's Day

Founder's Day (Council)

Heritage Honoring Days

GATHERING SHADOWS

Magic Hour

Bisinfoli Tea Festival

Lineage Sacrifices

Hallow's Remembrance

✓ Selection Day (every 10 years)   Fate's Day   The day Callahan & Natalia met

Do use these fifty days to your advantage.
Think long and think hard about your actions.
Consider wisely how you will present yourself and conduct
your business in the future. If you cannot be civilized,
I will be forced to abide by our laws.
A reckless abandon will not be suffered.
Your Light will be destroyed.

CHAPTER I

NATALIA

FIFTH'S SUN DAY, WARMWAVE, 4049 6TH
MILLENNIUM

"Look what I found!"

Ness's shrill exclamation rakes across my brain as I lay in the grass with my eyes closed, soaking up the warmth of both suns on this cloudless morning.

I squint through my eyelashes at the sky in the throes of a hangover and exhaustion. My head is pounding, but the fifteen bottles of vodka I consumed last night were a necessity. I survived Gathering Shadows and needed to celebrate with Ness.

For twelve days, the Dark gathers the most powerful of their kind to compete for the right to take part in the contest for the throne. It is a brutal set of scenarios designed to test strengths and the prowess to dominate. The Dark calls them games, but the trials are deadly and painful experiences.

Groaning, I curl into a sitting position, one eye closed, the other trying to focus on Ness in the bright illumination of the suns. I have no idea how she is so perky after drinking nearly twelve bottles of vodka herself. She's pristine with her radiant, medium-brown skin and perfect makeup, giving her eyes a

1

feline-like flare while I feel like a creature slithering in the mud of a riverbank.

Ness steps forward, her long black hair braided over one shoulder. Her legs are unfairly long and toned and perfect. I focus on the small snake hoisted in her hand. The tail is wrapped around her wrist, and she's grinning from ear to ear across her diamond-shaped face.

I smile. "He's cute."

She comes to a stop, turning to display her enthusiasm for the creature to Massimo and lifting the snake toward him. "See how adorable?"

Massimo's black eyes widen to the size of a gold coin, and his cool brown skin goes ashen. For a man who is ripped with muscles on top of muscles, the fear glazing his large features looks odd. "What are you doing, you crazy woman? Put that thing down." He points away from his broad chest.

"Aw, you're just an adorable cutie, isn't that right?" she coos at the serpent, putting her face closer to the head, the thin pink tongue licking out toward her.

Massimo takes a giant step away, giving her a frosted glare that scrunches his face, causing the scar that runs from his temple to his chin to wrinkle. "Now," he orders, his arms flailing as he tries to get further away from the spot as Ness crouches to lower the snake. "Not here, you daft woman. Wherever you found it."

Ness stops and gives him a dumbfounded glance. Her grin turns to a flinch of confusion. "It's a baby garter snake, not a king cobra."

"Get rid of it. Somewhere over there." He points to the far end of the yard. "Away from the house, back in the brush."

I smirk. "Mass, it's harmless."

"Both of you have lost your minds. I've been dosed by

Vypers, and that scaly worm is a relation. I don't care what kind it is. Get rid of it."

Ness blinks her wide-set, brown eyes. "Are you telling us you're afraid of fun noodles? You? A big, bad, Dark Seraphinus, better known as a Darkling to us Magia, with ultimate power, like, the total badass, fine-ass package, is scared of this little guy?" She hoists the snake, the tiny spaghetti body weaving between her fingers as the snake slithers around her limbs.

He gapes with horror. "Fun...noodles?"

"Yeah." Ness moves the snake closer to Massimo's face. "Massimo, meet Mr. Cutest Little Fun Noodle Ever."

She gets closer still, and Massimo back peddles, swatting at her hand and the snake with indignation. "Fucking burning afters, I don't get nearly enough to deal with you." He points a finger at her but jerks away as the snake flicks its tongue an inch from his gesturing hand. He damn near yelps as he jumps backward. "Get rid of that thing, or I will."

Ness huffs. "Jeez." She turns to me. "You'd think it was some kind of Light attack dog."

Grinning, I say, "Maybe put Mr. Cutest Fun Noodle Ever back in the brush before he becomes Mr. Dead Fun Noodle."

"Well, that's not very nice, is it? No. That's okay, we'll find you a nice new home, won't we? Yes. Don't worry, I won't let the big, bad Darkling hurt you." Ness turns and walks away, continuing to babble in baby talk to the snake as she goes.

The shirt she wears has an open back with a strap across the shoulders, displaying the marks of her Magia training down her spine. I have all those same marks and even more from the base of my neck to the small of my back. Unlike Ness, I completed the training required to hit pinnacle status, whereas Ness quit after basic healing and defense. Her marks stop between her shoulder blades, appearing black on her brown skin, but on my pale skin, the ink stands out as much truer to the jade color used.

Massimo drags his hand down his face. "She's insane. She has to be."

I shrug and stretch my arms over my head. "She likes fun noodles, more commonly known as snakes. Her idea of romance is a man taking her to the reptile house. She's planning to propose to the first man who doesn't get freaked out after a couple of runes."

"Runes?" He blinks at me. As a Darkling, his eyes are completely black, a foggy ring of smoke for irises in the center. I used to find those Darkling eyes eerie, but I've grown accustomed to their sinister appearance in the time I've spent staring into them. He turns his head to glance at Ness. "She wants to spend runes looking at snakes?"

"Yes." I snicker at his dazed expression. "Closest she ever came to true love was the guy who owned Nella, but I'm pretty sure Ness was just there for the fun noodle. I heard more about Nella than the guy."

He gapes at Ness's back. "There's definitely something wrong with her. What happened with the guy? Get rid of the snake?"

I drop my arms, roll my neck, and pull my head to the side to stretch further. "He cheated. Invited her over and, in the meantime, got high, and his other girl showed up. He forgot Ness was coming over, and he and the other girl started fucking, then Ness arrived. He actually told her he forgot she was coming over. It was a great time. We spent the same on vodka that month as we paid in rent and Seraphinus tax."

Massimo frowns. "You mean living taxes?"

"*Seraphinus*," I stress. "You lot own everything, and I had to pay tax for the land I was living on, tax for the building on the land, tax for buying anything. So you lot got your cut of profits from any sales made *and* a living tax. What the fuck is wrong with you Darklings? Don't you have enough?"

He swings his arms together and smacks a closed fist to an open palm. "Humans are annoying, so you pay tithes to us to compensate us."

I roll to my feet, breathing out and rubbing my face. "In other words, you're selfish assholes." Dropping my hands, I see Ness has started back toward us.

Massimo curls his lip, his voice tight. "Give me an address for the shitty guy. I'll take of it."

I sigh with a smile. The idea of Massimo descending on that asshole with all the glory of an offended Darkling sounds like just rewards. Humans have died for lesser offenses. "Don't have one, or I would. I'm going to..." I gesture toward the mansion.

Bobbing his head, Massimo says. "I'm going to keep an eye on the crazy one and make sure she doesn't bring anything slimy and legless into Cal's house."

I turn and head back into the house. It's massive and gorgeous, done up in minimalism and dark shades of grays, blacks, sleek silvers, and metal. The style reflects its owner, Callahan, who may be the most impressive badass Darkling in the world.

The house isn't the only thing Cal owns, though. He owns the surrounding city, the land, Massimo, Ness, and nearly three hundred other souls, including me.

I absently rub the contract written in his Dark magic on my forearm as I walk through the hallways, soaking in the comfort they offer. Up two flights of stairs, I retreat to my designated room.

Inside, I close the door and lean against it, strumming my fingers against the mahogany wood. The windows across the way overlook the yard, giving me a beautiful view. The thought that I live in such a grand place is nice, but that's it. I live here. It isn't home.

Ness and Massimo are visible in the yard below. Ness is laughing at something while Massimo scowls. He claims Cal and I are going to kill each other, but my coin is on Massimo killing Ness first. He twitches and sneers whenever he's around her.

I push off the door and head for the bathroom. At least I have my own space back. During Gathering Shadows, I shared a room, a bathroom, and even a closet with Cal in Ilbuio. I had been tethered to Cal, holding his hand and fighting at his side through the games. Every day could have meant death, and I came close a few times, surviving only by my Magia healing skills using Ki.

In the bathroom, I remove my clothes and start the shower, waiting for the water to warm up. I glance at the mirror. I'm thin, almost shapeless. I don't have the curves Ness does. She's gorgeous and feminine, tall too, with long legs.

I cup my breasts, trying to push them higher and together to make it look like I have big boobs. It's a daydream. I'm not built like her. I'm slender, with barely a curve at my waist. My ribs and hip bones are visible. My abdomen is shadowed with lean muscle, but even that's subtle. There isn't a single asset of my figure that's extreme.

Sighing, I check my face, drawing my fingertips along my jawbone. My face is angular, my eyes too big and wide set from my slender nose. I stare at myself, puff up my cheeks, toss my straight, shoulder-length, white-blonde hair and then turn away from the mirror. I don't like reflective surfaces. They always tell the truth, and I'm not the gorgeous woman I want to be. Not like Ness. Not like my sister Sasha was.

Stepping into the massive waterfall shower of black marble, I soak in the steam and hot water, recalling the days.

I'd met Cal's ex-girlfriend, Telra, who formed a hatred of me of massive proportions, but some of the Seraphinus I met were nice. Mostly, it was a constant fight, and not just in the games, but with Cal.

I'd accepted his contract to avoid Tony, to avoid being a breeder and popping kids out to further the Magia bloodlines, but my reasons were a lot more complicated. Cal wants to own me, body and soul, and use me for his gains, but I was dangerously close to believing he also *wanted* me. It's a fantasy, one I long for and shouldn't.

He'd almost killed me for trying to shield myself. Or his contract had, but he could have stopped it. He didn't, forcing me to hand over a part of myself I had no interest in relinquishing.

I haven't wrapped my head around a lot of this yet.

The sex with Cal had been incredible. The way he makes me laugh at times and how he touches me with gentle caresses and little brushes of his lips makes it hard to remember I'm a contracted vassal rather than his girlfriend.

I try to process it while I get dressed before I grab my guitar and pluck the strings, tuning it by ear.

I fiddle with the knobs as I strum notes. It soothes the raging chaos within me the same way Cal taking my hand does. Music has always been my comfort, but Cal is new. It scares me the easy peace that comes to me when I'm with him.

CHAPTER 2
NATALIA

I play through a couple songs, humming lyrics rather than outright singing. A lace of silver Light illuminates my hands, and I frown at the subtle defense my magic weaves against its proximity to the Dark. I shift, turning toward the door, and wait for the inevitable knock. I might not be able to see another soul, but my Light knows the presence of the Dark, two natural enemies.

"Yes?" I lean on the guitar, hugging it close. Of all the expensive things Cal has given me, the instrument is by far my favorite. It's no Dragola, but it's higher quality than I ever could have hoped to afford.

The door opens to reveal Cal. Framed by the doorway, his warm, medium-brown skin carries a red tinge, highlighted by the mahogany wood. I stare, drinking in the calming sight of him.

All Seraphinus are alluring. It's part of what they are. I've never seen one that's unattractive, but Cal is the prettiest of them all.

He kicks a box into the room. It slides over the hardwood

until it hits the rug under the bed. "Everything I don't tell you is in those books."

That's funny. Cal doesn't tell me anything. Ever. When I first signed his contract, I thought he was hiding things. He's not. He answers me in detailed honesty when I ask specific questions. He just doesn't explain things.

I bob my head, dropping my gaze from his lean body to the box. "Okay."

"Read them."

"Okay."

He leans against the door frame and crosses his arms. His shoulders are broad, his hips narrow. While he lacks significant bulk, there's nothing weak about him. "No sass?"

"Don't have a lot to work with here."

"Are you all right, Little Star?" He takes a step into the room.

I try to smile. "I'm dandy like you're a dandy."

"Hmm." He moves inside and sits on the edge of the bed. "I have to go answer the Council, so I'll be gone a day or two."

Focusing on the guitar, I hum at him. He's headed to see the Council because of me, because of my contract. He's been accused of breaking the accords between Dark and Light, illegally coercing me, the Light, into the service of him, the Dark. While the allegations aren't false, they aren't necessarily true. He had tried to manipulate me in ignorance.

Although I carry the Light in me, I am not a Seraphinus but a Magia, a blend of both Light and Dark in a human body. For a few millennia, the Magia have been breeding for power, and I am a result. I never needed Cal and agreed to the contract for my own reasons.

I nod a few times, running my thumb over the strings of my guitar. "Duly noted."

He grasps the neck, his large hand with five lines of script over the back, wrapping around it. I peer at the script. The contract is illegible to me, Dark shifting and blurring to obscure the words. There used to be four, but a new line has been added to his contract with Massimo.

He pulls the guitar away from me, setting it to the side with care. "Talk to me, Little Star."

"Hmm?" I lift my eyes to his and blink.

His eyes are full black, his nose straight on his face. It's a beautiful face with chiseled features and a square jaw. As pretty as he is, Cal is just as deadly.

He frowns, features pinching with concern. "What's wrong?"

I force a faux yawn. "Nothing. Tired."

"Too much vodka?"

A real yawn takes over me, and I give in, covering my mouth and shuddering. Smiling, I shake my head. "No, there's no such thing. I'm just tired. That's all."

"More nightmares?"

I lift and drop one shoulder. The nightmares were frequent over the last two nights since the maze. Terrible, horrifying dreams that felt too real, plaguing me in the night. At least in Ilbuio, Cal and I shared a bed, and when I woke in a panic, he was there to soothe me.

Last night, I had been alone, laying in fear, soaked in sweat, heart racing for runes until the suns rose. I would have run for Cal and sought comfort in all his beauty and strength if not for Ness snoring next to me in the bed.

He says, "It gets better."

I nod.

Cal rubs his face, giving me a half smile, a dimple forming. "You've been half dead with more sass."

I drop my eyes, staring at the bedspread between us. It seems as expansive as the ocean between the two continents.

All I want is to fall into him, but I won't allow myself that weakness. "It's not my fault. It's a default setting, but the switch must have gotten shorted out. It just needs a reset."

"You would tell me if there was a problem?"

I smile. "Sure."

The weight of his eyes bore into me. I don't move, staring at the duvet.

I ran from the Magia straight to Cal's contracted service, signing away my life before I knew it, losing everything I knew in a fraction of a rune. We returned yesterday from Ilbuio, and I been out of bed for a mere three runes since. Now, I have a reading list.

I'm still trying to figure out what happened. The last couple of weeks are all a blur in my recall banks. I'm dazed and out of sorts from Gathering Shadows. I need to catch my breath, and most of all, I need to patch the wall Cal almost knocked down in my head that reads, "Warning: Do not trust.'"

I look to my forearm, the contract we share in my pale skin created by Cal's black, Dark magic.

'Stand at my side. Watch my back and protect my blind spot. Take my hand when it is offered. Be the star that guides me. Callahan Matteo Barraco.'

There's not much I understand about the magic of contracts other than there are two types: written and worn. My contract is worn, like Massimo's, embedded in our skin by a piece of Cal's magic. It spells out expectations, and if I disobey, the contract will turn on me with searing retribution. It's a brutal agony that should be reserved for the worst afters imaginable.

I let my eyes fall to his forearm, where the contract is less stark against his warm, tawny skin. His reads differently, both of us bound by separate commitments.

'Stand at my side. Watch my back. Protect me always and keep me safe. Be my home. Natalia Serena Swan.'

My name sparkles in my silver Light magic like a beautiful brilliance against the blackness of his magic.

His hand slides along my jaw to lift my head, drawing my attention to him. My brain doesn't want to focus, not even on his face, no matter how gorgeous.

He whispers, "Little Star."

It breaks my trance. "That's me."

"You told me the only time you didn't sass was when you were dead."

I curl my lip. "Do you even know what a joke is?"

"Maybe not?" He flashes his teeth in a wide grin, too flashy and quick to be real.

"You must have a depressing life. You should probably fix that."

Chuckling, he says, "I did. I contracted someone who tells jokes."

I perk up. "Oh, you own a comedian now?"

"Sometimes. She's a bit bland at the moment."

I roll my eyes. "Put it in her contract. She'll have to be funny then."

"You'd think, but she's stubborn. It might kill her if I forced it."

"She sounds like a pain in the ass. You could do better."

"No." He laughs. "Her uses far outweigh any annoyances."

Glaring at the ceiling, I huff. "I'll work on the annoying bit then and try harder."

He throws himself at me, and I have enough time to sit up straighter, eyes widening before I'm flat on my back beneath him. He smiles, wrapping his hands around my wrists as I press my palms to his sculpted chest, needing to feel his strength.

"Someday, you're going to give in."

"And on that day," I say, trying for a deep, dramatic voice, "the laws of physics will change, fish will sprout wings and fly away, the burning afters will freeze over, and the Ancients will walk the earth again."

"On that day, huh?" He smirks, pinning my hands over my head.

I allow it, closing my eyes and relaxing beneath his weight, my lips curling upward in humor. "Yes. So, never, ever gonna happen."

"Careful, Little Star." His nose finds my ear, his other hand sliding under my shirt to wrap around my waist. "There are rumors of an Ancient walking this world. You may be close to the day."

I jerk a bit, but he holds me still, pulling back to meet my eyes. I jut my head forward, widening my eyes. "Wait. What?"

"For now, I don't have a use for you, so I'm done with you," he says, pulling his hand from beneath my shirt. Instead, he reaches into his pocket and then rolls so I'm on top, straddling his narrow hips.

I wrinkle my nose in disgust despite my wonderful seat. "That's nice."

Cal sits up. "Hand," he says, holding an open silver cuff in his palm.

Rolling my eyes and fluttering my lashes, I stick my hand out. The cool metal clicks as he closes it around my wrist. It fits snugly, and I lift it for inspection. Plain silver encases me. I drop my hand. The thought to tease him that I expected his name engraved in the silver to mark me as owned crosses my mind, but I withhold the retort.

A male voice at the open door says, "Sir? The car is here."

Cal nods. "Thank you, Thomas."

There's no response, and I don't have to look to know that

Thomas has left. That's how it works. Provide your usefulness and then leave.

"Bye, Master-Owner-Boss," I say, trying to get off his lap.

He catches me with firm hands on my hips. "The car is for you, not me."

"Oh. You, like, really meant it. You're done with me." I cave in on myself, unsure of how I feel. Disbelief, confusion, dejection, and heartbreak flitter through my chest. Callahan cups the side of my face, and I try to turn my head away. "I'm in shock. Give me a fraction, and I'll jump for joy."

He kisses my cheek. "While I'm gone, I'm sending you to a spa." He grips my face, forcing me to meet his eyes. "I will collect you when I'm ready."

"So...you're *not* done with me?"

"The cuff is linked to my accounts. Use it to pay for whatever you want. Rest, sleep, and center," he says. "It also has a tracker. You're allowed here or at the spa, and if I catch you anywhere else, I'm going to inflict punishment. Do you understand me?"

I sigh. "And by that, you mean severe physical pain again. Goody. Got it."

"No, I don't like hurting you. Take Ness with you. Spend as much as you want, and relax," he says, sliding his hand along my jaw and around to hold the back of my neck. "I need you back to you again."

I frown. "I am me."

"You're rather subdued."

"I'm being a good vassal. Sit. Stay. Don't speak. Good girl."

His eyes sparkle, a sharp intake of air flaring his nostrils. "Don't tease me."

I nod. "Right."

He buries his hands in my loose, damp hair, strands pulling tight as he draws me closer. He kisses the side of my head. "If I didn't have to face the Council, I wouldn't leave you."

Resting my forehead on his shoulder, I close my eyes and nod, inhaling his scent of bourbon and honey with a hint of cloves. Part of my brain sobs, begging for me to make him stay.

"You got dosed with nightmare toxin, and that amount is going to linger. It'll take time to clear out of your system."

I hum. "I'm fine."

"Good." His lips graze down my neck. "I need my little star."

I snort with humor through my nose. "Fucking liar."

He grins, opening his mouth against my neck, dragging his teeth closed against the thin skin. My body shivers, tickling hairs standing up, and a tingle echoes out from my spine, making me squirm.

His voice rumbles, "The Dark never lies. I have to go. Pack a bag, you'll go for the few days I'm gone, and when I collect you I expect sass."

"I'll crank the dial to eleven."

He holds me close, one arm slipping around me to force me tighter against his solid torso. "This is temporary. You're still under contract. You still belong to me."

I relax into him with a hum. I don't want to go. I don't want him to go. I don't even want to move. All I want is to sit here, straddling his hips in his lap with my face in the crook of his neck, safe in his arms.

"I'm telling you this, so you understand that if you're not there when I come to collect you, you're in trouble—a lot of trouble, the kind of trouble where if I'm not using you, you'll be tied up in my room waiting for me to decide to use you."

I shiver at the implication, recalling the way he thrust into me like a machine, and tension coils tighter in my lower stomach.

"Kinky." I lean back smiling.

I press my hands to his chest, no give to the muscles beneath my palms. His entire torso is sculpted and cut into precision, radiating strength in subtle carvings without flagrant display. I want to trace the dips and bulges, to learn every inch of the machine his body is.

"If you keep drooling like you want to eat me, I'm going to let you." His voice is a husky growl, his eyelids half closed.

I lick my lips, tantalized at the offer. "Would you? Or would you eat *me*?"

He growls low in the back of his throat, lifting his hips to shove his half-hard dick into me. "Don't tease me right now."

"You're the one who likes anticipation."

He shoves us over, pinning me under him. My ankles lock behind his back, and one of his hands slides along my thigh to my hip.

"You're mine," he snarls in a guttural grumble that leaves me breathless. The sheer possessiveness in his tone sets me on fire with need. "If you ever try to leave, I will hunt you down. I'll find you. I'll drag you kicking and screaming back to me, and kinky will be the last word on your mind."

"I mean," I pant, "you really don't know what my kinks are so..."

His lips whisper over my jaw to mine, pressing against them. The hand in my hair tightens and yanks my head to the side as he kisses me with brutal desire. His tongue glides across mine, and I lose my breath to him, tightening my legs around his hips.

He is rough, with jagged edges that cut, but he offers me so much more than his wicked demands. He is freedom, even if it means serving him. It is an odd balance to be tied to this gorgeous man and have independence.

Cal pulls back, lips curving against mine. "Little Star, if I'm late for this summons, there will be consequences."

"You can handle it." I jerk my head up to kiss him. Cal can handle anything.

He grips my hair, his other hand running along my leg to my butt, squeezing it hard. My fingers curl into the front of his dress shirt to pull him closer. He's arrogant, but deservingly so for his beauty and power, two things I want to taste.

Our clothes come off, one article at a time. His hands and magic slither over me everywhere, a cool kiss of the Dark soothing my skin burning with longing to be touched, contrasting the demanding rough warmth of his hands answering the searing desire within me. I pant for air as he rolls me over to my stomach beneath him.

He knocks my legs open with his knees, and I squeeze my eyes shut as I stretch my arms out before me, gripping the duvet in my fingers. Both suns are up in the sky, shining, illuminating the room through the windows, and I am shining with them. There is nothing he isn't going to see.

His hand presses me down between my shoulders as he pulls upward on my hip, forcing my body to where he wants. "Now, you see." He leans forward, mouth next to my ear, his hard body pressing along mine. "As much as I want to tell you to sit on my face, I don't get to because you've decided to be difficult, and you need to be put in your place."

My body betrays me and shivers, my chest tightening with anticipation. I ask, a bit breathless, "Is this how you put Massimo in his place, too?"

He bites my earlobe hard. I try to jerk away but am pinned under the weight of him and his hands, I can't escape.

I whimper, "Cal."

He grasps my wrists, pulling back. With a chuckle, he twists my arms behind me. "No."

"Oh," I nod. I know I shouldn't. I know he's going to get cranky, but I laugh as I ask, "So, just your girlfriend, Telra, then?"

"We're going to play a game."

"The games you play suck."

His dark coils around my arms, binding them tightly. I try to roll over, but he presses his hand between my shoulder blades again, adjusting on his knees between my legs. "It's called Helpless Little Star, and you're not going to like it."

His fingers slide between my legs, and I bite my lower lip. My body pulsates with an ache demanding to be filled, and a rush of heat creeps through me even as I arch into his touch. "Not seeing a downside here."

"No?"

He teases me to the edge and then stops. I gasp and grind my teeth, but he starts again. I'm almost there, my body tense and ready to burst, but he stops again.

"Kind of seeing a downside now." I try to get my arms free, but his magic tightens around me. Any little twitch I make sends his magic slithering further to hold me in place. He starts toying with my clit again, and I groan. "Oh, you fuck," I moan, pressing my forehead into the bed.

"Who's in charge?"

I almost sob. "This game sucks. I want to play a different one."

He chuckles. "Are you sure about that?"

A response of little ripples of awareness crawls down my spine at his silky whisper. There is a heat to his words, making seductive promises. I clench my hands. "Yes."

He keeps rubbing my clit in little soft circles, and his other hand leaves me. I make another futile attempt to rip my arms free, not wanting to be bound up. His magic lashes further around me, up my forearms and biceps, slithering across my upper back to connect across.

He pushes into me, and I arch, sinking deep into the position and groan. It's a short-lived relief as he rocks in and out with slow, short strokes, barely giving me anything. It's not his full length, not the deep and hard strokes I want. It kicks up the ache in me to a full, burning need.

I groan again. "This anticipation shit fucking blows."

His hand tangles in my hair, pressing my head into the mattress, his other hand gripping my hip and forcing me into a deeper stretch. It's hard to breathe, and my arms are going numb. My body throbs in ecstasy, but my mind thrashes out at the restriction.

I pant and try to squirm. It's futile, though. His magic has me lashed down, wrapped around my legs and arms, bound tight for his amusements. Cal chuckles, returning to his delicious torture, barely rocking and his hand between my legs. My body responds, muscles clamping down with greed, threatening to snap.

"Who's in charge, Little Star?"

I hiss and struggle against his magic, binding me. "I hate this game."

"Play along, and it gets better. Who's in charge?"

Torn, I clench my jaw and fingers. The answer is him, but I'm not ready to give in. "No idea what you mean."

He pinches my clit, rolling it between his fingers. "Wrong answer. Try again."

CHAPTER 3
CALLAHAN

This woman could make an Ancient crazy. She's doing a fine job at driving me insane. My balls are about to explode, but I'm on top, in charge, even if she won't admit it. I use my magic to spread her legs wider and slide out, almost, and then give a little push back in.

Natalia's breath hitches, and she moans, long and slow. If this were any other person, I might be concerned I would break something if I stretched their body this far, but I've watched her put herself in weirder positions.

I find her clit again and circle it with the tip of my finger. "Who is in charge?"

"The Council?"

I almost curse at her but shove the fury to the back of my mind. She's going to learn her place here and now. "Who, Talia?"

"Um..." she breathes out. She's struggling, but pulled and bent, she lacks leverage. Even if she had it, she's not strong enough to break free. I have her wrapped up and tied tight in the Dark right where I want. "Dammit."

"Who?" My voice is deep and thick with desire. I'm going to lose it as soon as she cooperates, but that could be five fractions, five runes, or five days. I never can tell with her.

She squirms in a useless attempt again as I remind her I'm still playing. I give her another couple half strokes in and out as I play with her clit. She pulses around me, her muscles begging in twitches and tense quivers. Natalia has the will of immovable object to still refuse to give in.

"Fuck," she almost sobs. "I hate this fucking game. I quit."

I'm half-crazed, and I've teased her worse, threatening to let her come and pulling back half a dozen times, but she's still holding back, fighting. She knows the answer. She knows what to say to get what she wants. I know she does.

"Not an option. Tell me who's in charge."

She tries to break her arms free to no avail and relaxes. "Damn you, you're the fucking worst asshole ever."

I grin. As frustrating as she is, I'm enjoying this. Watching her squirm, hearing her delectable, little breathless mewls. This woman is going to bend to my will, and when she does, I'll make her my queen.

She whimpers. "I hate you."

I would care if I thought she honestly meant it. It would fracture me, leaving deep cracks in my core if I even questioned if it was true. It's not, though. She's on edge, struggling to hold back. "Who is—"

"I say you, and then you stop torturing me, right?"

My little star is a little too smart for how stubborn she is. It's a dangerous combination. I stroke her clit, giving her short, slow thrusts of my hips, sliding in and out and watching her writhe. "Answer the question."

"You," she grinds out, the word a twisted snarl.

My grin widens. "How bad did that hurt for you to say? Worse or better than getting stabbed in the heart?"

21

"Worse, asshole. Way worse."

I shake with contained laughter and hum, pushing her body toward an orgasm. She tenses, breathing hard, and I stop to run my hands up her sides as I lean over her. She's warm and soft and growling at me.

I chuckle as I nip her ear. "Who's in charge?"

"You."

I flick her earlobe with my tongue. "Say it, Little Star." I nip her neck as she mutters under her breath. "Louder."

"You're in charge." It comes out as a defeated whisper but audible and discernible this time.

"Which means who's not in charge?"

She squirms. The woman is full of sass and power. It's incredible as much as it's astounding. I love that about her, but not when it's directed at me.

I pull back, teasing her again. The throb beneath my fingertips and her shudder let me know it's working. "Who's not in charge, Little Star?"

She whimpers, trying again to move. She's not going anywhere, and each attempt only sends my magic wrapping further around her. It's a beautiful sight, her bound up in my Dark and on display, squirming under me and glittering with a lace of silver Light over her skin.

I keep teasing her, rocking my hips. She has to break soon, or I might. "Who?"

"Me."

I thrust harder, pushing deeper to encourage her. My magic tightens as it hisses in my mind, wanting us to give in and fuck her. I grab the back of her hair, my fingers catching and pulling as I lift her face from the bed. "Say it."

"I'm not in charge," she manages, her voice twisted with need.

22

I thrust all the way back in, and she lets out a muffled scream. I let go of her hair, and her head falls forward as I wrap my hands around her hips, lifting her, forcing myself deeper. She mewls, her body responding and stretching to accommodate me, warm and wet.

I grit my teeth, balls ready to burst, almost losing control of myself to give us both what we want. I grip her hips harder and clamp down on my self-control. "You're mine, Little Star, in every possible way." I breathe out through my nose in relief, cock throbbing. "Which makes me your alpha. You answer to me, obey me."

She pants, "*Mhm.*"

It's an adorable little pant, and it's an agreement. I pull back and slam into her, then drop one hand, finding her clit again. "So, when I tell you to come for me, you come, and you say my name."

She whimpers.

"Come for me, my little star," I say, working her clit. It slips under my fingers, slick with her arousal, but she does, clamping down with a breathless cry.

"Cal," she says, almost a sob as she comes hard.

My eyes close and cross as I lose myself in her for the moment, riding out her pleasure, soaking in it for my own. She sags, limp and whimpering with soft noises, still pulsing around me. I push her legs further apart, opening her to me and latch onto her hips.

I'm not done with her yet. I want to feel that again, hear her call my name. I'm not letting her go. She belongs to me. All her power, her body, the sass and jokes, and her heart. It's all mine, and I'm never letting her out of my Dark.

Our contract catches my eye as I adjust my grip, ready to burst and focus on what we both really want. Her name sparkles next to my Dark, spelling out the servitude. I belong to her as much as she belongs to me.

A skip of my heart sends something glittering and warm through my veins, unfamiliar to me, and yet I know what it is.

"Come for me again, Little Star."

CHAPTER 4

NATALIA

I come to, groggy and unsure of where I am. My limbs feel like heavy rubber, but every cell of my being hums with contentment. Basking in the afterglow, swaddled up in sheets, I smile until consciousness interrupts my blush haze.

I'm alone in bed.

I break out of the cocoon, searching for Cal.

The light of the day is dwindling, the orange hue cast on the lawn outside letting me know that one of the suns has already disappeared beneath the horizon. I slump in dejection at Cal's absence.

He has a good reason for leaving, though, reporting to the Council to prove he's done nothing illegal. Still, I wish he were here, that I could curl up against him and soak in his strength as I coast in bliss.

I eye the box of books he delivered, and decide to ignore them. I have questions, yes, but I won't find those answers in books. The only question I want to ask only Cal can answer, and when he gets back I'm going to finally ask him what this is, if I'm a pining fool.

There's a knock on my door, and I run a hand down my face as I adjust the sheet to cover me. "Yes?"

Ness opens the door and waltzes in. "Hello to you, too. Where have you been all day? You missed dinner. Mass and I— Are you naked?" Her lips peel apart with shock.

I glance at myself and shove fingers through my hair, pushing the white-blonde strands from my face. I clear my throat, still half dead to the world, my brain steeped in post-orgasmic chemicals to the point of failure.

"Uh, yeah."

"Have you been sleeping all day? Are you sick or some-thing? You don't look sick. You look like you— Oh freaking Mother." Her voice upticks to a shrill scream. "You did not! No—wait–you totally did. You got laid!"

I ignore the embarrassment creeping across my face. "Yeah."

Her jaw drops. "What the fuck did I miss?" She jumps to the bed, kneeling on the mattress to clasp her hands on my shoulders. "Cal? It's got to be, right? Yes! Tell me."

I try to laugh, but I'm too lethargic. "Yes, Cal, but calm down."

"I will not."

"Seriously, stop yelling." I wince, rubbing the space between my eyes. "It's not as charming as you think."

Ness stares. "Tell me you sat on his face."

My chest dissolves into butterflies as I consider what Cal did to me. "No."

"Dammit." Ness throws her hands up. "I really thought he'd do that."

Grinning, I say, "Oh, he does."

Ness squeals and bounces. She freezes, her face scrunching in confusion. "Wait, what?"

"Not today, but he has."

"Not today?" Ness yells. She grabs a pillow and hits me in the shoulder with it. "Start talking."

"We shared a room in Ilbuio— Uh-uh." I hold a finger up. "Am I talking, or are you yelling?"

Ness tosses the pillow back toward the headboard and lays next to me. "Yes."

"He fucked me in Ilbuio–twice–and I didn't sit on his face, but close enough."

"Finally," Ness says with laughter. "Good for you, babe."

"Pretty sure the first time was an adrenaline rush we had after surviving a hunt, but yeah, it happened again the last night, too."

Cal had shredded a sheer black dress from me and damn near devoured me after the farewell dinner. I'd lost count of the orgasms, lost the functionality to comprehend anything but him. I'd been delirious in pleasure long before he'd finished.

Ness perks up, head tilted. "What the fuck is a hunt?"

Twisting my lips to the side, I consider while staring at the ceiling. "It's a game. We were prey, and about a hundred other Seraphinus were hunters, and we all got set loose, and they were trying to kill us."

"Crappy game."

"That's what I said." I snicker. "A lot. The games were not games. They were death traps of torturous agonies."

Ness nudges me. "And today?"

The humor in me dies, and I squeeze my eyes shut. "That was fucking me into submission. It worked, too, okay? Busy telling the man he's in charge."

"What?" She busts up, chortling and flushing red as she tries to keep hold of herself.

"He tied me up in his magic, made me crazy, made me tell him he's in charge before he'd get me off. He got me there and stopped until I said he was in charge."

27

Ness fans herself. "And that face? That body?"

"Yeah, the man is physically flawless," I say with a grumble, but I can't stop my grin. I don't remember another time I've ever been so aroused.

"Yeah, a badass, hot as fuck man going all dominant male on you in bed. Such a turnoff."

I tip my head back against the pillows. "All right, it was hot. So, so hot, and I had tons of orgasms, but I'm trying to believe he only did it to make a point."

"He can make a point to me anytime. Think I could take a turn on Mass?"

I snicker. "Feel free. I don't care."

"But you care if it's Cal."

Shrugging, I sink lower against the pillows with an empty feeling crawling through my chest. "I'm not laying claim, babe. It's not like that. Cal will throw you or us out if you piss him off. I'm not sure if you piss Massimo off that we're safe, but it's the safer option." I curl to my side and lean my head on Ness's shoulder. "I'm not too sure what happens if we piss them off. Best case, they toss us, and I don't know what that means for us. The Magia... I've been accused of betraying them, and they were ready to kill you for that."

"Babe, I'm going with you if you get tossed, and we could figure it out. I'm smart. You're badass. We'd manage."

"The Magia would hunt us down, and best case, we'd get dragged before the Assembly and punished."

"Maybe you, babe," Ness retorts with a sneer. "They'd kill me."

"Let's not get thrown out, okay? We both turned our backs on the Magia—betrayed everything they stand for."

There is a knock on the door again, and I elbow Ness. "You get that."

Ness groans but sits up. Answering the door, she says, "Oh,

hey, Mass." She clears her throat. "What's up? Oh, quick question, if I were to, let's say, piss you off, would I and or I and Tallie get chucked out the front door?"

"You already annoy me, but piss me off?" There's a pause. "Fuck up enough, and yes, I'd take great delight in throwing you out. Where's Tallie?"

Ness sighs, opening the door wider. "She's here, hanging out in bed. You know, sleeping off whatever you assholes did to her over."

"After you've been attached to me all day, I'm so glad I don't have to deal with you for the next few days. Tallie, your car is still waiting for you."

I frown, "What? What car?"

Ness juts her chin forward. "Hey." She pokes him in the shoulder. "We had fun. It was a great time."

Massimo frowns, fixating on me. "Cal was supposed to see you before he left. He was going to—"

"Oh, yeah." I hold up my wrist, eyeing the silver bracelet. "I was sleeping. Never mind. I'll be down in a few minutes."

He shrugs and turns to leave. "You can make the driver wait through the night if you want. It's here for you, and that human won't dare to leave without you. It looks scared out of its mind just being on Cal's property."

Scoffing, Ness says, "Maybe because you lot kill humans on the slightest whim?"

"Your point?" Massimo crosses his arms. "The lot of them are animated clay pots." He waves a hand, saying, "Literally. The Ancients made their kind out of mud, breathed life into them. They're fragile, annoying pests."

I lift an eyebrow, but Ness swells with indignation. "So, what? What are we to you? A bunch of ants trying to steal discarded and forgotten crumbs from your floor?"

He considers her, eyebrows lifting and pushing together.

"Humans? Yes, ants. You two?" He points a finger at Ness then moves to me. "Aren't human, especially Talia. You don't break when we just look at you like they do."

"Huh." Ness cocks a hip, her hand resting on it as she inspects Massimo. "So that's it? They're just animated pottery to you, so you can send them to the afters whenever you get annoyed because who cares?"

Blinking, Massimo stares with confusion. "What part of being a god walking amongst mud vessels don't you understand?"

I clear my throat. "That they are living beings? That they don't deserve to get crushed to dust just for existing?"

Giggling, Ness covers her mouth. "It's cute that you think you're a god, though."

Glaring upward, Massimo turns around. "I'm walking away now."

Ness watches him go, leaning back and cocking her head to the side before she closes the door and leans against it. "How do I some of that?"

I roll my eyes. "Is he really your type?"

"Cause Cal is really yours?"

I shake my head. "I'm trying to not go down that road. I'm his contracted vassal, not his girlfriend. I'm trying not to think about the fact that Cal's gorgeous and great at fucking me, and I really like him, and you're going to help me not get those ideas, m'kay babe?"

"Sure." Ness steps away from the door and holds her hands up. "I just want to see you happy."

"I know, and I love you for that. But I need to focus on the fact that Cal's the guy who holds our contracts, and we're responsible for being useful." With a sigh, I say. "We need to pack a bag."

"Why? What's with the car?" Her eyes get wide. "Oh shit, did you piss him off? Are we getting thrown out? Did I do it?"

I smile with pressed lips. "We're going to a spa since he doesn't have a use for me right now while he's reporting to the Council."

"That's a perk to the job I didn't expect. He's busy, so we get to go to a spa?"

"Yeah, definitely won't complain about this part. Go pack so we can leave."

CHAPTER 5
CALLAHAN
FIFTH BLOOM'S DAY, WARMWAVE, 4049 6TH MILLENNIUM A.I.

I step into the hearing chamber, a big, round room constructed of volcanic black rock and opal marble with a glass-domed ceiling three stories above me. I come to a halt a pace inside the room and glance around.

The chamber is vacant, and I tip my head back to glare at the ring of one-way tinted gold windows that circle the second story. It provides anonymity for the Council members who will preside over the dispute as they watch on from the other side.

A disembodied female voice snaps, "You are late, Callahan. You were to present at Thistle's rune for judgment."

I glance at my watch, noting it's half past Star's rune. I should have been here about four runes ago, but it's Natalia's fault. Fighting my glee, I struggle to stop from grinning but fail.

Out of sight, the female drawls with a lack of humor, "Is something funny, Callahan?"

"My apologies. I was..." I hesitate, searching for the appropriate language. I can't tell the Council I was fucking Natalia into a comatose oblivion. "I was managing a contracted. I was uncomfortable neglecting my duties and therefore delayed."

I'd fallen out of consciousness with Natalia for a while, and it had been hard to pry myself away and leave her. This annoyance has elevated to aggravating, but a summons to the Council is not to be ignored.

Silence rings in my ears as I wait for a response. This time, it comes from a calmer and deeper male voice. "Tending to contracted is the obligation of a contractor and cannot be held against you. We will proceed. Take your position as the accused, please, Callahan."

I stride to the middle of the room onto a circle grooved into the white floor. Slipping my hands into my front pockets, I turn to the door as it opens. Pierre steps into the room, his Light presenting in golden coils around him, a subtle defense at being near my Dark. It wraps around his broad shoulders in thick ropes of golden Light.

On the threshold, he pauses to tuck a loose strand of his long blond hair behind his ear, smoothing the hair along the side of his head, where the rest is pulled back into a knot at the base of his skull. "Callahan."

With a hiss, my Dark slides around me, warning Pierre's Light that it's present and alert and will protect me from its enemy. I lift my chin, narrowing my eyes against the glow of his magic as I seethe. He's as tall as I am, but his nose is in the air like every other Light Seraphinus. It's a straight nose in a square face, his features regal. It's a face I abhor with vile passion.

He steps into one of the circles along the outer edge of the room, a second man following him. He's a bit shorter than Pierre and me, with average features, and his hair is a shade like bland mud in the glow from Pierre.

I pull my ears back, realizing Pierre brought Tony, a Magia

male I've encountered before. The male who was going to union with Natalia. I'd broken their planned union with glee, claiming my little star for my own, but Tony's presence will complicate this trial.

He steps into a ring next to Pierre, a position that indicates his allegiance in the hearing.

I frown at them both, Pierre staring back with a straight face while Tony smirks. It's irritating, the smug expression making my Dark rabid. It wants to rip his head off.

The female voice returns. "We are convened."

The ring I stand within illuminates as a brilliant blue, and my shoulders twitch, my Dark twisting around me in protection. While I'm not imprisoned by a physical cage, crossing the ring will cause instant death. I hate enclosed spaces, a result of being buried alive.

Pierre remains aloof, nonchalant about the glow around his feet, but Tony drops his chin toward his chest to gape at the illumination encircling his feet. "What the fuck is this?"

The male voice ignores the question, saying instead, "The investigation will commence. Callahan, you stand accused of breaking the accords. Guilt of a crime this high will result in death. How do you plead?"

I shrug. "Not guilty. This is a waste of time."

"Your decree has been recorded," the male voice states.

"Your opinions on the matter are irrelevant," the female voice retorts, picking up his words with hers full of disdain. "You will stand trial for the illegal contract of a Light coerced into service of the Dark."

I roll to the balls of my feet, shaking my head. Natalia has the Light within her. I cannot deny that, but she does. I can leverage that. "The contract in question is for a Magia."

"Falsehood," Pierre says. "Natalia Swan is a Light Seraphim."

I rock on my heels, uncomfortable with my current predicament of being enclosed, and lift my eyebrows. "Foundation of claim?"

Pierre lifts his chin, his features hardening. "Natalia Swan is my daughter."

The air is forced from my chest as if I'd been punched. The room spins in a blur, and I try to recover my wits. I'd suspected that she was a Light Seraphim, not Magia as she claimed, but Pierre's claim is like a blade shoved under my ribs. The man murdered my father, and I fucked his daughter.

Tony laughs. "You should see your face. Not so tough now, are you, Darkling bitch?"

Gripping my fists, I snarl, "Shut up, inconsequential, animated clay pot." I catch the moment and my breath, steadying and squaring my shoulders. "Proof?"

"Her mother, Annika and I had an affair. She had a previous daughter, which was used as leverage to force her to end our relationship, and she returned to her husband. When I encountered Natalia in Ilbuio, I left to track down Annika to confirm my suspicions that Natalia is my child. Annika confirmed that she had been pregnant when she dissolved our relationship and that Natalia is indeed my daughter."

"Hearsay," I argue. "There is no proof she is what you claim, and Natalia herself claims to be Magia. My contract stands therein between the Dark and a Magia."

Pierre draws a hand down his chest, rolling his broad shoulders back. "What she claims to be does not negate the truth. She is my daughter. I will remind you the circle does not allow an individual within to lie."

"Questionable founding on desirous belief," I counter, my stomach churning. "The circle prevents an individual from *knowingly* stating false information. If you believe you are stating the truth, it will allow it. Under no circumstances is your claim proven, and so the word of the individual holds no power."

Pierre laughs. "You can deny my claim, but you cannot deny what she is. She has the Light. It is a continuation of my heritage seed."

I can't refute that statement, but I can circumvent it. "Natalia holds the magic of the Magia."

Pierre gestures to Tony. "Allow the accuser's witness to speak. He can clarify as he is Magia. Are the Magia able to generate Light or Dark magic?"

Tony grins. "Nope. Nat's always been different. She generates the Light."

"Biased source of information. The boy has already attempted to interfere—"

"Fuck you," Tony snaps, interrupting me.

It's a bad idea. The glowing ring around him brightens and buzzes, a zap render through the air. He yells, his head tipped back as he seizes. He tips forward, hands on his knees to brace himself, gasping for air.

I smile as he sways and falters, crouching low to brace himself with one hand on the floor. Shrugging, I say, "The rules of the Council indicate a speaker is to be granted the ability to finish before another begins."

Pierre turns to him. "Young man, do try to contain yourself, or you will be zapped again in increasing capacity until death is achieved."

Standing, Tony glares at me. "I am a man, you useless Darkling piece of shit, and I am here to corroborate. I am an unbiased source of information."

I chuckle at him opening that door. "I am calling your previous relationship with Natalia Swan into question. You may attempt to manipulate this inquiry to regain a woman as a man in love may be inclined to do."

Tony smirks and opens his mouth, but Pierre holds his hand out. "I recommend against responding to that, boy."

The smirk Tony wears twists to a sneer. "Man. I am a man."

Pierre shrugs and crosses his arms. "I am nearly halfway through my ninth century, and Callahan," he turns and frowns, peering, "is in his third century?"

"Fourth," I correct him. I am closing in on entering my fifth. It is a matter of pride that I've lasted this long, and that isn't something I'll let Pierre diminish.

"You look young, but I digress. The fact remains, Natalia Swan is a Light Seraphim and my daughter."

"Natalia informed me she was Magia. Any interactions I made were based upon that claim made by her."

Pierre clicks his tongue. "She presented with the Light, and as you say you are in your fourth century, you would know what that means regardless of her claim."

"The Magia are breeding for power and are a blend of Light and Dark. There was no certainty that she was born of a Seraphinus given the history of the Magia."

"You either believe us to be fools without wit, or you are an idiot. I cannot say which, and it matters little. No words you spout will deviate the course of this hearing from your illegal coercion of Light into a contract of servitude to the Dark."

"I acted based upon the knowledge I possessed from the individual."

Pierre lifts an eyebrow. "Callahan Barraco, you are a Mandolux, yes?"

I grip my fists. He knows what I am, what my father was. It's why he killed my father. "Your point?"

"Did you feed upon the magic as a Mandolux?"

I am backed into an irrefutable corner. "Yes."

A chuckle wafts through the air from an unknown source. "Callahan, if you fed upon the Light, then you have no stance to argue the magic of the individual," the Council says, a second male voice this time. "Natalia Swan is a Light Seraphim. Callahan, you will be judged on the validity of how she came under contract."

I narrow my eyes. I'm going to have to play the game after all and subterfuge this inquiry another way. "There is nothing illegal about Natalia's contract."

Pierre holds a hand up with two fingers extended. "I request that statement be struck from the records and not used in this trial. The contract in question no longer exists, and the current contract could be legal."

The Council answers, "Stricken."

I grip my fists. "I object to the statement being removed from this trial. Pierre is correct. There was a prior contractual arrangement. The Council should know that Pierre came into Ilbuio to claim Natalia as the Light and remove her from Ilbuio. She told him she was fine where she was and that she was Magia."

"Her claims are irrelevant," the female voice says in a sour tone.

I tip my head back and smirk. "Natalia decided on her own to renounce his claims to her. There was no clause in her contract to make her speak in such a manner. I want it on record that the aforementioned interaction was prior to Pierre learning of her heritage. On Pierre's second visit to Ilbuio, he presented me with this farce of an accusation that Natalia had been coerced into her contract, attempted to take charge of her, and she again told him she was freely serving. She twice informed him there was no coercion and did so of her own volition."

The deeper male voice asks, "Pierre report. Are these claims true?"

"You are blatantly ignoring his confession of refusing to

comply with the Council's decree that I was to take charge of Natalia."

I shrug, rolling my shoulder blades together to stretch out some of the mounting tension. "The accused has the right to defend themselves before judgment is proclaimed. I had no ability to defend. Therefore, any decree would have been a stern suggestion at best if not a laughable overreaching of power, something this Council was born to deter."

"Subsection D of that same ruling states an exception for when a life is threatened."

I open my mouth to state that her life was not at risk, but stop. Natalia's life had been at risk, both from herself in contempt of the contract as well as the games of Gathering Shadows.

Across the way, Pierre smiles with knowing glee.

I frown. "Natalia's life was never under threat from *me*."

Laughing, Pierre looks upward, hands on his hips. "My son—"

"I am not your fucking son," I yell and brace. The ring buzzes, and stinging pain ripples over my skin. It was worth it. Two-fold for the way I show Tony I don't even flinch and am better than him.

"No," Pierre drawls, smiling wider. "But you will have to excuse my use of the phrase."

I ball my fingers into tight fists, Dark tendrils wrapping around my wrists and stretching up my forearms. "To the point at hand, Natalia's contract was not issued in coercion. She freely accepted a contract with me."

Tony bursts into laughter. "Yeah, because there wasn't a dragon trying to kill us. You took advantage of her, offering to save her if she would take a contract."

"If you knew Natalia, you would know she can manage a single smoragon and did not require my services. I believe you yourself declared that she was powerful enough to handle it without my help. Strange you should now recant."

"You said that if she accepted your help, it was an immediate agreement to the new contract."

Pierre turns murderous eyes on Tony, but I grin. The wording is going to work in my favor. "On record, the source stated *new* contract."

The Council male voice booms, "Recorded and noted, Callahan."

I relax with a smile, pressing my hands together and pressing through my fingers to crack my knuckles. "Yes, she accepted my help in exchange for agreeing to a new contract. We had previously come to an agreement on a contract which is separate from the agreement you bore witness to." I lift a hand to eye level. "Establishing timeline."

"Granted," the female voice says.

I pivot to square up to Tony. "My acquaintance with Natalia began sooner than you realize. I was present during your dinner arrangement at The Gardens. You can corroborate these facts as I met Vanessa on the very same night. Did you not interrupt a phone call between Vanessa and me?" I chuckle. "For clarification, I am programmed into her phone as 'Tallie's Sexy Darkling.'"

Tony turns red and leans forward. "Yes, I did interrupt that call. It was right before she threw Ki-cha at me. Tell my girl that hurt."

"Yes, well, I do believe you were there to hurt her, speaking of coercion of a Light Seraphim." I snicker. "I will pass your message along to Vanessa."

"We both know that wasn't Ness's blood, and she's not my girl," Tony says, low, voice rippling with heat.

"That's right. Your girl is dead."

Tony vibrates with rage, a vein throbbing in his forehead. "I can't wait for them to kill you."

Lifting my eyebrows, I rock on my heels. "You'll be waiting a long time."

Pierre sighs and rubs his face. "We are off topic. Natalia's coerced contract should remain our focus. Have you finished establishing your timeline, Callahan?"

"Natalia's contract has not been coerced. Not the first offer nor the last, and your claims that she was are weak at best, if not altogether abhorrent twists of the facts as you know them. Yes, I have finished establishing that I was in contact with Natalia prior to her acceptance of the new contract."

Pierre shrugs. "I will establish a fact relevant to my next point."

"Confirmed," the female Council member states.

"Callahan, please confirm that Massimo Verta is your contracted man."

I scowl, unease sliding through my gut at the realization of where this line of facts is leading, but incline my head. "Yes, Massimo Verta is my contracted."

"You have already stated you were aware of the dinner at The Gardens by your own testimony while establishing a time-line. Why did Massimo draw a Light avenger to The Gardens during such time?"

My heart beats twice, a steady pulse like hammer strikes against my sternum. That is a problem, and I need to word my response with care. "Massimo was less inclined to believe in what Natalia could do."

"Allow me to rephrase." Pierre smirks. "Why did you instruct Massimo to bring a Light avenger to The Gardens where you were watching Natalia?"

"Speculation. You have no evidence to support that I instructed my man to do anything."

Pierre's grin grows. "Did you instruct Massimo Verta to bring a Light avenger to The Gardens?"

There are two general cautions of reporting to the Council my father warned me to adhere to. The first is patience. The second is that words are fickle. Both things are the best ally one has when on trial.

I smile. "No."

The expression on Pierre's face turns putrid. We are both aware I cannot lie in the circle of inquisition. I rub the back of my hand with Massimo's contract, a rush of excitement spurning through me. It's rare that I give Massimo direct orders. We often decide things together, which helps to negate the use of our contract in Council hearings.

Pierre lifts his chin, murder in his blank, white eyes. "Did you intend to use an avenger to scare Natalia into a contract?"

"Yes." I shrug. "I wanted her to agree to a new contract and had intended to attempt to use an avenger to further my goals, but the plan was horribly derailed by others."

Pierre lifts his hand. "This trial should be concluded. On record, Callahan has admitted to collusion to coerce Natalia."

"Intentions or desires and actions are separate," I say. "I could want to kill you but walk out of here. Would I be on trial for your murder?"

"Strike from the record," Pierre growls. "No relevant bearing to the confessed collusion."

The air crackles, the speakers for the Council clicking on to indicate a response from the Council. "Denied," The male voice states from overhead with a smile in his tone. "Intentions and thoughts are excluded from punishable offenses."

I grin, but Pierre crosses his arms, his legs apart in an aggressive stance, betraying his annoyance. "The avenger arrived, and you gained Natalia's contract as you *intended*."

"The avenger is not why Natalia accepted the *new* contract. You still have failed to prove I coerced her."

Tony yells, "It might not have been the avenger, but it sure fucking was the dragon, and you used the situation to make her accept the contract. She was scared, and you leveraged that. You've confessed you colluded to scare her, and whether your plans did it or not, you achieved what you intended. The contract is illegal."

Shaking my head, I pivot to Tony. I know why Natalia accepted my contract, and my intentions had nothing to do with her acceptance. "It wasn't the avenger." My voice is low but razor-sharp as I say, "It wasn't the smoragon. I did nothing that forced Natalia's actions."

"You're a fucking liar."

I bare my teeth in a silent warning, wrestling with my Dark to keep it restrained. "I explained this to you once. I see you weren't listening, so I will repeat myself for the benefit of Pierre and the Council. Natalia accepted my contract for her own reasons. Nothing I did had any bearing on her decision. Natalia wanted to be free of you and the Magia." I twist my head to Pierre. "I will remind you again: Natalia has informed you twice that she is voluntarily under contract. She refuted you twice, once after she burned out my contract with no motives other than her own."

Pierre purses his lips, but Tony slashes at the air. "Bullshit. Utter fucking bullish. Nat wouldn't do that. She's known since the day she was born that she has a duty. She's questioned the Magia, but she'd never turn her back on us."

I chuckle under my breath, lifting pressed hands, fingers in a steeple and the forefingers press to my lips. I consider my next words. I've made my point, and Pierre knows there are no grounds for this hearing to continue, but I can solidify my innocence.

"I will establish a foundation of evidence with facts to oppose the witness's ideals."

"Confirmed," the female voice says in a sour tone.

I nod, dropping my hands to my hips. "Natalia, or Tallie as she prefers, has spoken to me of her duty. She spoke in length about her sister's relationship with you and then of the arrangement of your sister and her brother. She never expected to serve the duty you refer to, citing your relationship and her brethren's as a means to an end that left her without those expectations. To be clear for the Council, the duty referenced is union and production of children to further the Magia agenda."

I cross my arms and lift my chin and voice. "Your continual insistence to call her Nat, the same nickname you used for her older sister whom you were to union with, supposedly deeply in love with, and had planned a life with until her demise is revolting. It irks Natalia, and the thought of conceiving children with you is repulsive to her, given the rather active sexual relationship you shared with her sister. You treated Tallie poorly, made attempts to control her when you are not dominant enough to do so, and the same could be said of the Magia, who are also responsible for the death of her siblings. Should I go on? There are other facts I can share if the Council deems it necessary."

"There is no need," the deeper male voice answers.

Pierre frowns, eyes pinching. He remains silent, watching, no doubt absorbing information. He is waiting for me to slip up, to say the wrong word, one that he can twist. I incline my head, not speaking. They cannot hold me accountable for anything, regardless of the validity of their concerns.

The rings go out around us, and the second male Council member says, "Callahan, you are cleared of charges."

A slow smile curls my lips at Pierre. I take a step backward, eyes on Pierre's. I chuckle. "The things I'm going to do to her just for being your daughter."

Tony lurches toward me. "You sick fuck."

Pierre throws out a hand, Light tendrils racing through the air and wrapping around Tony, stopping him short.

He puffs up his chest, making pathetic attempts to break free. "I'm going to fucking kill you if you touch her."

I lean in close, my voice low and warped with glee. "I already have. I've tasted her, fucked her, broken bones..." I trail off as Tony thrashes. I lift my eyes to Pierre once more. "She's bled for me, and she'll bleed again. I always intended to keep her, use her, but now? Now I think I'll enjoy hurting her."

Pierre's face is tight, but his features twitch, the slightest betrayal of rage. He shrugs. "Like father, like son."

Tensing, I fight not to react to his quip. It's rather bold of him to mention that here before the Council when he damn knows what transpired would spell death to the both of us. On stiff knees, I walk out of the hearing chamber, wrangling with my Dark to keep it under control.

One day, I will have the chance to rip his head off, and I will with joy, but not here, not now.

CHAPTER 6
CALLAHAN

Flying over Narwal, I stare down across the world at my city, one of dozens that belongs to my lineage. Buildings glitter in under the early morning, the smaller red sun already rising. The second, larger yellow sun will follow soon, bringing a balance to the red hue and warmth. I want to be home before then, forcing my aching muscles to push harder, flapping my wings faster.

Natalia is synonymous with pain in the ass. I have no idea what to do with her now. There's too much temptation to dose her with the nightmare again and again, to keep her high on the venom that draws out her fears while I inflict pain, using what she's most afraid of while she's drugged and watch her mind tear apart.

I've seen it done before. The individual becomes a drooling, rapid mess, terrified of everything, reduced to a broken, vacant shell. I could destroy her, then give her to Pierre. She'd be nothing but a breathing, terrified corpse. As my contracted, I have full rights to do it without legal hassles from the Council.

I consider fetching her from the spa but decide against it.

46

Banking, I turn and head home. I need my conscience to decide my course of action rather than acting rashly. Natalia is my contracted for a reason. It's a reason I'm having trouble recalling.

I want to tear her Light out, leaving her as a husk, destroyed beyond repair and drop her into the capital of the Light for Pierre to find.

Landing in the yard, I force my magic within me to retract my wings, my shoulders aching with discomfort. Rolling and stretching the burn away, I go in search of Massimo.

As I enter my office, I find Massimo sitting behind the desk, scowling at a computer screen, documents and parchment filled with Dark magic scattered on the surface. He's reviewing contracts–my contracted.

I scowl. "Did someone leave?"

"The acquisition of Agra means restructure." He lifts a mug from a coaster and takes a drink. "You're back sooner than I expected. Things went well then?"

"No," I snap. "What the fuck is Agra?"

He stares at me, lines deepening in his square face. "The liquor company you purchased in Blooming as your birthday gift to yourself?"

I'd forgotten about that. It's irrelevant. "Where are you on setting up a meeting with the Magia?"

"Established a contact but waiting on information. Agra doesn't need much. It's a popular brand with several expensive options. Your new century-aged blend was started last week."

"Move faster. I want to talk to Natalia's mother."

Massimo drains his mug and stands. "I'll make it a priority over this mess. What happened?"

I grip my fists. "Pierre Bordeaux claims Natalia is his daughter."

Massimo's face screws up as he shies away. "Fuck."

Leaning over, I spread my sweating hands flat against the cool surface of the desk. I splay my fingers and try to contain the quelling rage that has my hands trembling. "I am trying very hard to remember why she is contracted, and every time I do, all I can think is that Dark Contractual Law allows me to do anything I want with a contracted, and I go in circles because I want to rip her pretty little body to pieces and feed them to that Light fuck."

Massimo nods and sighs. "She is an unlimited supply of Light for you to use as a weapon and sustains you as a food source. She's good in a fight, capable of healing herself, you, me, anyone, and you want her to be your queen."

"That's never going to happen." I shove the desk as I roar, kicking at it. The contents fall to disarray, the table lifting and slamming into the wall, and I round on him. "That bitch is Pierre's seed and—"

Massimo grabs my shoulders. "Cal, you need reason. She's Natalia–it's Natalia. Talia, your unlimited source to feed on, to wield, your star."

My heart slams against my rib cage as adrenaline courses through me, muscles coiling tight and vibrating. "Find her. Tell her to stay away," I grind out. "If she comes near me, I'm going to kill her."

Nodding, Massimo steps back. "I will."

I curl my lip. "Put her somewhere I don't know."

He keeps nodding. "I can do that. I'll turn the tracker off so you can't find her right now, and then I'll set up the meeting with the Magia."

"Yes. I want to know if that cunt knew. If she's just played stupid this whole time–been in contact with him–if he's using her for something..."

"All right." Massimo chuckles. "But she's been adamant on

48

the fact that she's not the Light from the start. She told him to go to the afters twice in front of you."

"It could have been staged, a game she was playing. The Light lies."

"She's been against the fact that she's the Light. She has no wing scars, didn't know a damned thing about the Light in her or how to use it, and she's always told you she's Magia."

"Lies," Callahan growls. "She's been lying this whole time. I'm a fool. I believed her, trusted her, but it's the fucking Light."

"Cal." He tips his head back and laughs. "She went through the games with you. If she wanted you dead, that would have been easy to do."

"She's Pierre's fucking daughter." My Dark bursts free, sharp needle-like tendrils racing toward Massimo.

He tucks and rolls to dodge the attack and then stands, gaping at me.

I grip my fists, reminding my Dark that Massimo is important, valuable, and our contracted. We do not hurt our contracted without due cause. "She's the gods damned Light, and she's his fucking seed, and I fucked her, protected her, I—" I bite the words off before I say something I regret or will make me hurl.

Giving me a melancholic stare, Massimo softens. "She has no idea, and she's proven loyal. She turned him down. She could have been free of you, gone with him to Izul. She didn't."

"It could be a ploy. Until I know she didn't know, I don't trust her."

Massimo puts a hand to his jaw and cracks his neck. "I presume you would like me to not tell her why she's banished, then?"

"No. Don't tell her a fucking thing. I don't need her running to him."

"Positive sides," Massimo begins with a smile on his face as he ticks them off. "You have Pierre's daughter under contract, and that is clearly upsetting him. She's under contract, so she's easy to destroy if necessary. She's Pierre Bordeaux's daughter, so her heritage is powerful, and she might even be developing still. She's a Seraphim—"

"She calls firelight and smites. That's not Seraphim skills, that's full-blooded Seraphinus."

"Then why bother talking to the Magia at all?"

I open my mouth, some logic returning. "She's not wholly Seraphinus. Pierre said he had an affair with Annika, her mother."

"Which means she's better than a Seraphim with that Magia shit, maybe that's why she's not like the rest. She'll have a lot longer life span. So ultimately, you could use her, and when the dust settles after you're king, you'll still have time to kill her for your pleasure."

"I don't need her."

"Need is a debatable word choice, but right now, all you're smelling is blood."

"He killed my father," I seethe.

Massimo frowns. "You killed mine."

"That was the games," I snap. "There's no similarity. If I hadn't killed him, he would have killed me."

"I was watching," he whispers, eyes gazing and going out of focus. "I know what happened."

"He was a mean prick of a bastard, and if memory serves right, you weren't too upset he was dead."

"I wasn't, but when you offered me my contract, I still wanted to rip your fucking spine out," Massimo says with a huff. "You say I'm your voice of reason, so listen to me. Natalia may be Pierre's daughter, but that doesn't change anything. I'll hide her away, and until I decide you're calm enough to deal with this rationally, she'll stay there. Got it? She's contracted for a reason. You need a Light source, and you're never going to find a replacement. She's useful."

I can't breathe. My knees are weak and wobbling. "Get out," I snarl. "Go fucking hide her from me before I lose my self-control."

Massimo leaves, and I falter into the wall, turning to press my back against it. I slide down the smooth painted surface and slump on the floor, gripping my fists and gritting my teeth.

Natalia is Pierre's seed. I fucked her and claimed her. The acid boiling in my stomach burns my throat as I exhale. I'm the Dark. She's the Light. That was sick enough, but I enjoyed the taste of her, the daughter of Pierre.

Pierre. He killed the contender list to carry out his vendetta against my father. He'd hid behind politics for his personal gain as a coward, and I was falling in love with his daughter.

Tipping my head back, I blink at the ceiling, my Dark wrapping around me in a possessive hunger. I'd promised myself revenge on Pierre, and a painful demise of his heritage seed by my hand would be justified. A dozen different ways to kill Natalia and deliver her mutilated corpse to Pierre tumble through my mind, but my Dark hisses and my gut squirms.

Dropping my face into my hands, I clamp my jaw, shaking with fury. "Fuck," I grunt, picking my head up to stare at the mess in my office. My eyes haze over as I stare at the desk. The day I sat opposite Natalia and grinned at pressing her contract into my flesh replays, and I bare my teeth.

I'd intended to put her at my side as my queen, but that is over. There isn't a single reason I contracted her that seems to be of any importance in comparison to what she is.

Massimo can hide her away for now until I get control of

my temper. Pierre wants Natalia out of the service of the Dark, and I'll give him what he wants. She'll be dead, of service to no one and nothing at all.

CHAPTER 7

NATALIA

I sit here, eating room service with Ness, as I scan the service menu to put together a plan for the day. Yesterday, I'd taken my time, but I might only have one or two more days before I'm called back to Cal's house. I'll have books to read, training to do, and uses to provide for Cal.

The door opens without so much as a knock, and I sit straighter in excitement until I see Massimo stalking forward. He glares at me with one eye flinching shut.

Ness perks up like a dog, seeing its owner come home. "Hey, Mass. Want some? Pull up a pillow." She tosses one to the foot of the bed with a wide grin.

Massimo stares at her, then turns to me. "I'm not here for breakfast."

Excitement rushes through me like my lungs dissolving into butterflies. Cal said a few days, but maybe he's back already and wants me to come home. "Do I have a use?"

Massimo shakes his head, his features pulling together in a sad scowl. An unease sparks in me.

His eyes flicker to Ness, and he crosses his arms. "You've been banished."

Ness shifts, and I exchange a glance with her. "Um..." I lick my lips, shifting with nerves. "Okay, this sounds bad. Is this bad?"

Massimo seems like he's trying to smile, but it's a joke of an attempt. "Yes. This is bad."

I swallow hard. "What does that even mean? Banished?"

His features soften. "A banished contract is still a contract. They're not free to sign with anyone else, are cut off financially, and become outcasts. Anyone contracted or another contractor will never aid a banished contracted. It's bad." He bobs his head but holds a hand up. "Normally. For now, you just stay put. Stay here. Don't come back until Cal or I come get you. That's all it means for you. You still have the cuff for finances. Stay here, go nowhere else."

I pull a pillow into my lap, cross my arms around it and hunker down, cuddling it for comfort against the slippery dejection squirming through my stomach to mix with my half-eaten breakfast. "Sure, okay, but, like, why?"

"He doesn't want to see you, and if he does, your life is forfeited."

I nod, my eyes beginning to burn, the food turning to rotten pulp in my belly. "Why? What did I do?"

Massimo shakes his head. "This is where you shut your mouth. Don't ask questions. Do what you're told."

Ness sneers, her hackles raising. "This is a fucking joke, right? Like, you two seriously aren't—"

"*You* are highly expendable," Massimo says. "If I were you, I would shut my mouth."

I blindly reach out, latching onto Ness's arm while a lump lodges in my throat. "No, I need her."

"Right here, babe," Ness puts her hand over mine.

Massimo sighs, rubbing his face. When he drops his hand, he appears haggard and melancholy. "Stay put. I'll take care of the arrangements for you to remain here. The cuff will remain activated. Just keep doing whatever it is that you do here. Do not leave this place ever, and under no circumstances are you to come back or find me or Callahan. Nod and answer me if you understand."

I nod, Ness mirroring the motion. "Yes."

"Understood."

Massimo turns his back, and I clear my throat, tightening my grip on Ness as I ask, "How long?"

He stops but doesn't turn around. "For the sake of your life, just do what you're told." Massimo walks out, and the door shuts with a soft click behind him.

I turn to Ness, blinking eyes too tight in my head that sting and my sight goes blurry. "I'm sorry. I'm so sorry, babe. I don't know what I did."

Ness pries my fingers loose and pulls me close. I fall into her, dragging in a ragged breath as she whispers, "Nothing. You didn't do anything. You're always beautiful and incredible."

"Maybe I was supposed to...?"

"No, babe, no." Ness smooths my hair back. "I don't know what happened, but it's not your fault. You're perfect. You're always so badass *and* have a great ass."

"Then why are we banished?" I try to breathe in, but it catches in my throat, a sob ripping out of my chest. "I can be useful. I wasn't fighting."

Ness wraps me in closer and hushes me. "He's a fucking moron, him and Mass both, and you know what? Fuck 'em. Let's spend all his money and pamper ourselves because we're awesome, and we deserve this shit."

I nod against her shoulder, staring through unshed tears.

Ness grasps my head between both hands and forces me to gape at her. She grins. "I want a girl like you."

I do my best to smile, pulling away to an upright position and run fingers under my eyes, blinking away the wet at the song reference. "Yeah," I sigh, snatching up the booklet with all the services offered. "Fuck him. We should find the most expensive shit on here."

Ness nods once. "You know it. He wants to be a dick? Fine, we'll spend all his money."

I curl against the pillows at the headboard, and Ness follows, cuddling on her side and with her head on my shoulder. We flip through the book, and my eyes scan words that filter through my brain without registering.

The food is trying to come back out the way it went in, my stomach lurching. Everyone always wants to use me, and for the first time ever, I had been accepting of it. I wanted to be useful to Cal. But now he doesn't want to use me—he doesn't even want to see me. It breaks something loose in my chest.

Ness sits up. "Manicure, pedicure, seaweed wraps, facial, wax, and I'm getting all the add-ons," Ness says. "What about you?"

I nod. "Maybe the sauna, heat soak. Swim a bit."

"Really? That's it?"

I shrug, trying to force my brain to function. "Today. No need to rush through anything now, right?"

"True," Ness drawls. "All right, sauna it is."

Forcing a smile, I say, "Do whatever you want. Go wild. Fuck 'em remember? Get a manicure every day so the polish matches your mood. Why not? It's his coin, and we're banished."

Ness laughs. "Fuck it. Yeah, I'm doing that."

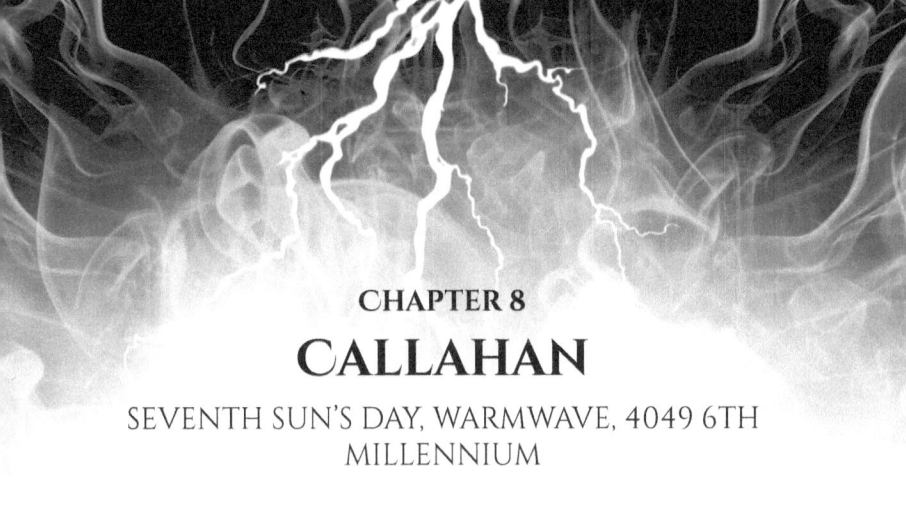

CHAPTER 8

CALLAHAN

It's been two weeks, almost to the rune, since I left Natalia in bed and reported to the Council, learning the truth about her heritage. The contract I share with her burns, a constant dull ache I don't understand. I trace the lines, the angry, red-lined letters raised as tiny ridges beneath my fingers.

'Stand at my side. Watch my back. Protect me always and keep me safe. Be my home. Natalia Serena Swan.'

Her name glitters in my tawny skin, dazzling silver, a reminder of what she is. Curling my lip at my forearm, I stand at the counter as my cappuccino cools. The large yellow sun has set, the smaller red still sinking low.

The song by Dark Marrow, "I'll Stay," inspired the line about being her home. Natalia claimed I wasn't going to be her home, and I'd said I was, but I have no idea what that means to her. Drawing a finger over the words, I remove the line from the contract, and the irritation ceases, my magic settling.

That's one problem solved.

Massimo walks into the kitchen. I scowl at him, cocking my jaw. He lifts his eyebrows, and I ask, "Where is she?"

Cocking his head, Massimo studies me. "She's Pierre's daughter."

I sneer, my lip curling back, hands clenching. We've had this same exchange a hundred times already. He always has the same response, and I'm getting better at not reacting with violence to the statement.

"I know what she is, but I want that woman where I can keep an eye on her. She'll make a mistake, and I'll catch her in a lie." Turmoil rolls through me, my magic hissing and curling around me in rage.

Shrugging, Massimo says, "No."

"I've calmed down."

"No."

"That was our agreement," I snap. "Until I calmed down. I have. I'm not going to rip her head off."

"You've declined to utilize logic."

"How?"

"You could change her contract, add a clause to prevent her from lying, then ask her if she knows her father is Pierre. You won't."

"I don't want that bitch to know she's his seed if she doesn't already know."

"I've offered to take Thomas with me to ask her if she's aware of her origins in vague questions. Thomas would know if she's lying, and I wouldn't need to reveal the truth to her."

"She's intelligent enough to ask questions. I don't want her to know that fuck is her father. If she finds out, it might change things."

"She doesn't know. You know it. I know it. You're being irrational because of your delicate feelings."

"Delicate?" I widen my eyes in indignation.

"He killed your father, yes. He killed five of the strongest Dark." Massimo opens the fridge. He pulls out a beer, cracks off the top and throws it on the counter. It clinks in the silence as he takes a drink. "I know more than most, but there's more to the story than even what I know. You don't talk about it, but I pick up on things."

"Stay out of it." I point a warning finger at him.

Shrugging, he leans against the counter. "I'm not asking. I'm telling you. Whatever secrets you have, they eat their way out in ways you don't intend."

I scowl, pressing my fingers to the porcelain of my cup to test the temperature. Pierre gathered the five contestants for the Dark Throne and dosed them with nightmare until they were broken, drooling bodies. Their minds were destroyed. But that's not even the whole story. My hatred was woven by the webs of fate, inescapable and inexcusable. What he did, what I did, what my father did, it's all interwoven in the webs, sowing vehemence and acrimony with dazzling ferocity.

"The Magia's city council is meeting tonight, Park and Twelfth. They call it the Assembly."

I take a sip of my cappuccino. "Time?"

"My source didn't give one. He said he didn't know, and he died while I was trying to believe he didn't know."

"One less rat in my city," I say with a shrug. "Go get Thomas."

Massimo chugs his beer and sets the empty bottle next to the cap before leaving with a knock on the counter. I lift my chin as he turns away and then consume my beverage in a single breath. The cup clinks as I replace it on the small plate.

Bracing on the counter, I cock my jaw at the slate surface as I wait, breathing hard, my Dark snarling in my head. Nothing about Natalia makes sense, not her origins, not her actions, not my desire for her, nothing.

I snatch the cup and hurl it against the wall, the porcelain shattering. Shards fly in different directions as I scream, "Fuck!"

Massimo returns with Thomas in tow. He raises an eyebrow at the shards of porcelain.

I frown at Thomas, the only other Seraphim I have contracted. I raised him after I sent his father to the afters for his treatment of human women, but I usually leave him out of business, trying to keep him sheltered from the miseries of this life.

"How squeamish are you, kid?"

Thomas inclines his head. "I'm ready for whatever you need."

"We're going to see the Magia. I have questions. I will be getting answers. You're there to make sure I'm getting the truth."

Smirking, Thomas nods. "I can do that."

"Good."

I DRIVE out of the underground garage and off my property, speeding through the city. I park at the corner Massimo indicated and turn to him. "You're clean up if anyone runs."

"Always am," he says, getting out.

I turn over my shoulder to Thomas in the backseat. His lineage is lowbred but incredibly useful. "Just tell me when something's a lie, and you shouldn't have to, but if you do fight, do not use your magic. They can absorb it and send it back."

Thomas inclines his head. "Understood."

We get out to meet Massimo on the sidewalk, and he leads

us to a brick building. He moves past the stairs leading up the main entrance, around the side to the ally. At the back, there are a set of steps that lead down.

Massimo goes first, trying the handle. He rocks back and throws his shoulder into it, the latch breaking with metal sheering. Inside, we head down the hallway as my heart rate picks up. I need answers about my little star, but I suspect I won't like what I hear.

We move into an open room befitting the leaders of a cockroach infestation. It's lit by fluorescent box lights, with no windows in the cinder block walls painted white, but the paint is old, yellowing and chipping away. My right shoulder rolls in a twitch at the confined space with a low ceiling.

There are seven people sitting around a round table in blood-red cloaks, the hoods pulled up. They cease talking as I approach them in the middle of the room. Stopping, I pull my eyebrows together and cross my arms. "You look like a bunch of fucking idiots."

Next to me, Massimo laughs. "Like a low-budget, shitty entertainment picture about a cult."

None of the red hoods say anything or move as bulbs overhead flicker. I scoff. "Is this really the best the Magia have to offer?"

One lifts from its seat, tall, with wide shoulders. A male voice floats from beneath the hood. "Leave now, Darkling. If you run, you and yours may keep your life."

I blink, a bit stunned. "Did you just...threaten me?" The table remains silent, and I check my surroundings, meeting Massimo's eyes with disbelief before turning back to the one who spoke. "Moving on, I have a few questions."

"We do not answer to you."

"Mmm," I chuckle. "This is my city. You answer to my whims and rules."

"No."

I consider killing one to make a point, but until I know which is the Magia I seek, I hesitate. I don't want to kill the wrong one. "Annika," I say, watching for a reaction.

The one standing says, "There is no Annika here."

From behind me, Thomas clears his throat. "That's a lie."

At least that assures me this is the right room. It's laughable that this setup is the elite Magia. The man standing drops his shoulders. "Whatever information you sourced is incorrect."

I smile. "Faelings can discern a lie simply by hearing it, so I'll ask one more time: which one of you is Annika?" The table remains still and silent. I narrow my eyes. "You can talk to me, or I start delivering pieces of Natalia. I'll cut her apart piece by piece, fingers, toes, hands, feet. She'll survive it, and I'll keep going until I get what I want."

Another stands, pulling back the hood to reveal a woman with blonde hair and similar features to Natalia. "I am Annika."

I drop my arms and step to the table. In haste, I grab one hood and snap the head all the way around, bones crunching in the stagnant air. The lifeless body crumples, slipping from the chair to the floor.

"I don't like repeating myself," I say, grabbing the shoulder of the individual next to the dead one and forcing them back down in their seat. "I suggest you avoid making me do so in the future. You're a nest of rats that I tolerate living in my city. Don't piss me off, or I stop being tolerant."

Annika rolls her shoulders back, eyes hardening. "What have you done with my daughter?"

"Do you know who her father is?"

Her lips pinch with fury. "What are you implying about me?"

"You either had an affair, or you were raped by a Seraphi-nus. It's common enough," I say, glancing back at Thomas.

He winces and shuffles his feet in place, head low. As revolting as his father was, I love Thomas like a son and harbor no ill will toward him for the sins of his father.

I face forward again, meeting Annika's eyes. They're the same as Natalia's, gray but set closer to her nose.

Her eyes soften. "Have you hurt her?"

"Yes, but she healed. Magia are pesky like that." I indicate the corpse growing cold at my feet. "I have to kill you quick, or you get back up. Tell me about her father."

She sighs, leaning back and lifting her chin, head to the side. Annika stares at the ceiling. "I attempted to save a human who had incurred his wrath simply for existing, it seemed."

I bob my head. "Humans are annoying."

"I engaged in a fight, which he found amusing. He decided that if I bought him a drink for his troubles, he would allow the human to live. Unorthodox though it may be, I saw this as a duty, and so I did."

"A drink doesn't usually get you pregnant."

"Tony has reported to us your knowledge of how we oper-ate. The Assembly helps to arrange marriages. I was an heiress like my daughter, a bloodline to be bred for purity's sake."

"Cut the shit, you're breeding for power."

She shakes her head. "The Magia serve to balance your kind. We protect humans from you and your wars. We need to maintain our bloodlines and power to perform our duties."

"Get to the fucking point. Who is her father?"

Annika shifts. "A drink led to conversation. He was charm-ing. It resulted in an affair. The Assembly became aware of it," she says, gesturing at the surrounding hoods, "and I was given a choice: to kill him and return, or they would kill me and my daughter."

I mock a frown. "How does killing the child they had bred make sense?"

"I chose to do as they asked, but I was pregnant. I did my best to convince everyone the child belonged to my husband."

I breathe easier. "I don't care about any of that. I want to know if her father was a Light Seraphinus." Annika inclines her head, so I press her, "Is he dead?"

Her eyes flicker past me and then return to mine. "Yes. I killed him."

Thomas calls out, "Lie. Twice."

Gripping my fists, I grind my teeth as my magic slips free, curling around my arms. The other standing figure turns and throws a hand toward Annika. "Deceit," he yells, the air shimmering before his hand. "You will pay for this treachery."

Annika jerks backward, tripping over her chair and hitting the floor. I move, grabbing Annika under the arm and pulling her to her feet, snarling at the attacker. "Do anything to her before I have my answers, and you will all die." I turn my acrimony on her. "Who is Natalia's father?"

She wipes blood from her mouth. "Pierre Bordeaux."

I grip harder, causing her to wince. "Does Natalia know?"

"No," Annika says, voice tight.

I glance at Thomas. He shrugs. It was the truth.

The hooded man speaks again. "Leave, Darkling. We grant mercy for exposing this betrayal. Annika Swan, you are found guilty of betraying the Magia and this Assembly for the second time. We granted leniency once, yet you have proved untrustworthy."

She squares her shoulders but stays focused on me. "They already killed two of my children, manipulated their initiation trials—"

"Silence," the man roars. "You are sentenced to death for your crimes."

Two hooded figures pop up, and I grab one by the shoulder, kicking the knee sideways. The body breaks as the man groans with pain. I shove it away, turning to Annika as she puts the second on the floor. "Natalia said it didn't make sense."

"They were meant to die and force her to breed." Annika shoves her hand flat against a third figure's chest, and it crumples. "If Tallie returns, they'll breed her and then kill her. Promise me you won't let them. Promise me you'll take care of her."

Smirking, I shake my head. All the remaining figures are on their feet, closing in on Annika as she backs away. I eye them, lifting an eyebrow. "Natalia doesn't need me."

Annika directs her gaze to the figures encircling her but lifts her voice. "She doesn't know any of this or what she is." She counters a strike, ducks another, and drops a hooded figure. Grabbing another and breaking the arm. "Tallie needs your protection. I do not."

I grab a figure from behind, take it down and slam my fist through the rib cage. Grunting, I withdraw my bloody fist, "They'll kill you."

She yells with laughter in her voice, "Do you think she inherited all her power from her father?"

I wipe away the gore with the robe as I deliberate. I have Pierre's daughter, but his old lover could prove useful as an alternative to hurting him. "Does he still care for you?"

"I'll die before I hurt him." She kicks but gets taken down.

Massimo steps next to me. "Your decision?"

"Let them deal with this in their own way. I have my answers. What does my conscience say?"

"She is Natalia's mother."

Thomas steps next to me on my other side, watching the hooded figures fighting. "Are we doing something else?"

I pivot my head toward the boy. "You're doing nothing. If you die, that's a waste of my last century."

Thomas laughs.

Rubbing my mouth, I curse under my breath, then let my Dark loose, tendrils racing out and grabbing figures, throwing them away from Annika. The strange sense of my power rushing warns me one of the Magia has siphoned the Dark. Natalia's done that enough, so I know the sensation and what follows.

A figure gets up, splaying an open hand at me.

I shove Thomas out of the way and dodge the bolt of Dark thrown back at me. Upright, I check to be sure Thomas isn't bleeding.

Massimo picks up a couple of bodies, throwing them into the wall. They crumple on the floor where they lay, unmoving as Massimo approaches the hooded figure who dared to fight back. He grabs the individual, the hood falling back to expose a delicate female face.

She bares her teeth. "Darkling piece of shit."

Massimo twists her and bends her backward. She screams and goes limp. He drops her as I pull my magic back in while surveying the bodies around the room. Most are grumbling and shifting, bones snapping as they begin to regain their feet. Magia are as stubborn as they are hard to kill.

Annika lowers her hands, eyes hard. "I won't help you."

"This wasn't for you," I tell her, turning. "Right now, you can run and save yourself. My conscience is clear. What happens from here is not my concern."

I head for the door, stalking back the way we entered, grabbing Thomas by the shoulders and pushing him ahead of me for safekeeping. By the time I reach the door, Massimo has caught up, and I slam the door open so hard it snaps off the hinges.

Annika darts past me, calling out, "They will kill her if they can't use her," her voice fading as she sprints up the hallway.

Sneering, I head out into the night. Annika is long gone, but at the top of the stairs, I turn to Massimo. "Where is she?"

"She's Pierre's daughter."

"She doesn't know that."

Massimo smiles. "You aren't going to kill her or destroy her to retaliate against Pierre?"

I hesitate in my response, still weak with temptation at the sound of that name. It's a mistake.

Shaking his head, Massimo's grin widens. "You're getting there." He pats me on the shoulder as he moves past.

I grunt and flick my gaze to Thomas, scanning for signs of damage. Relief washes over me at the lack of blood, and I incline my head. "You were useful."

The boy laughs. "It was fun. Nice to get out and flex my power."

I wave him up the steps. "Go, follow Mass."

He's still chortling as he moves past me. "Yeah, sure thing, *Dad*." He rolls his eyes. "I know I'm a fragile flower that needs protection."

One Dark tendril twists free of me, tripping him up. "As a Seraphim, you're weaker." I extend a hand to help him to his feet, smiling at him as I give him a nudge to start moving. "However, Magia are capable of taking down Seraphinus, and I don't want you dead."

Thomas hesitates, so he falls in step with me. "In case I haven't mentioned it lately, I appreciate you for taking me in, raising me, and giving me my contract."

I check that we aren't being followed as we enter the street, heading toward Massimo, waiting by my car. The weight depressing my lungs is lifting, and I tap a closed fist against

Thomas' shoulder. "Then don't call me dad. It makes me feel old."

Thomas laughs. "Sure thing, sir."

"Knock that shit off."

He slides into the back seat when Massimo opens the door for him. "Thanks, Mass."

"Anytime, kid." Massimo shuts the door, shaking his head with a grin as he meets my eyes over the roof of the car. "Love that boy. He's one of the best choices you ever made."

"I'm aware," I say, climbing behind the wheel. I glance at him in the backseat via the rear-view mirror. He's grinning ear to ear, twiddling his thumbs.

My heart soars to see him so cheerful. His father might have been a waste of space, but Thomas is anything but, even if, by Dark standards, he's low-born and deemed too weak to be of service.

Thomas leans forward between the two front seats, "Um, while we're out, can we get ice cream like we used to? Cause that would be cool." He adds quickly, "If you've got time."

Massimo chuckles. "Ice cream sounds good."

I do a quick sweep of the area as I start driving. "For you, I'll always have time. Where do you want it from, kid?"

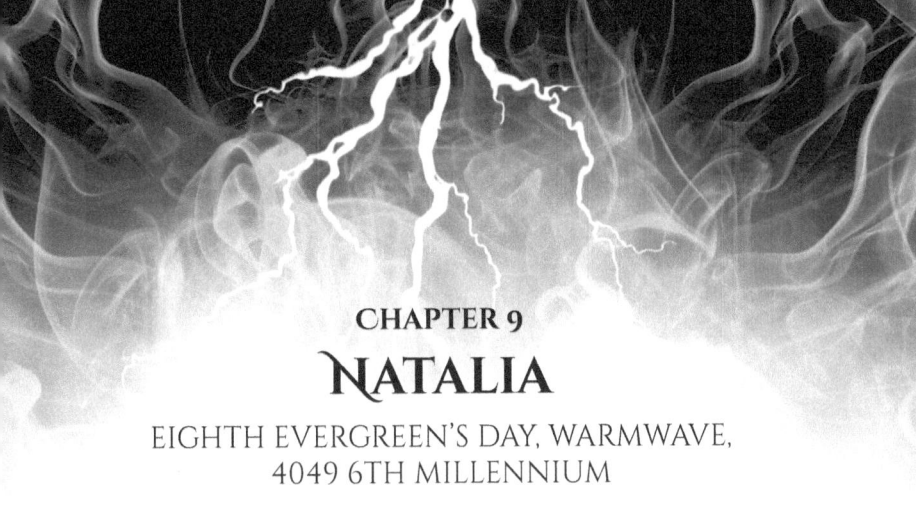

CHAPTER 9

NATALIA

EIGHTH EVERGREEN'S DAY, WARMWAVE, 4049 6TH MILLENNIUM

Scrubs, facials, massages, wraps, manicures, pedicures, sweating it out in the sauna, fancy water infused with cucumber, every treatment in the services menu booklet has been checked off, and I've started to repeat them. The resort has laundry services, which is a blessing because I only intended to be here a few days. At least the resort is luxurious, and there are open garden areas to accommodate stretching exercises, but it's closing in on four weeks, two-thirds of the way through Warmwave.

Restless, I lean a shoulder against the wall and stare out at the suns sinking low over the grounds. The resort is beautiful–built for serenity. If I had to pick a place to be banished to, there are worse. I fiddle with the silver cuff around my wrist, the scent of mango heavy from my skin, and I sigh, wishing for the fancy sugar scrub Cal bought me. I should have packed it. Nothing smells better than that.

Ness calls out from the bed. "Babe, are you hungry? I'm getting hungry, and this shit has given me a headache, so I'm done for the day."

I turn so both my shoulders are flat to the wall and raise an eyebrow. "Sure, call for dinner. No idea why you're still screwing with that nasty book, though. We're banished, remember? We aren't providing usefulness."

She flips the cover shut, and I frown at the clicking scales. At least the mango scent covers the foul stench it emits, and as we're banished, Cal doesn't have to know that Ness is in contempt for bringing that thing with her and letting me near it.

"It's a Dark Codex," she says with narrowed eyes as if I've insulted her character. "It's older than every Seraphinus in existence presently, older than just about everything in existence."

"Uh-huh." I roll my eyes. "I remember."

She picks it up, cuddling it against her chest. "It's so, so cool. It's this complicated little baby full of magic and secrets. Cal gave it to me."

"I'm fairly certain he expects it back."

"Maybe," she rolls her lower lip out. "But I'm Cal's thing for the rest of my life, so maybe he'll let me keep it once he gets the translations I'm putting together."

I don't bother reminding her that we're banished, not really Cal's anything. He doesn't want to see me. I'll spare her the bubble burst.

Shoving it into her bag, she says, "Besides, I'm almost done, and it's something to do. I'm kind of sick of the whole pampering thing, which is surprising and depressing. I think this has ruined spas for me, and it's really the first and only time we've ever been to one."

"We couldn't afford this before, not even a single manicure. Not with the taxes we had to pay." I snort through my nose. "We've probably been spending all the money we gave Cal in the first place."

"True," she cocks her head. "We all know Seraphinus have all the money in the world. You know, with that cuff, we could afford anything we've ever wanted. We should go shopping."

I roll to face her with a screwed-up face. "That would mean leaving, which is against the rules."

"We're banished."

Kicking at the floor, I sigh. "Mass said to stay, and we aren't cut off. We just can't go home."

"Banished."

"This place isn't even relaxing anymore. It's like we've been locked up, and Cal threw away the key. It's just monotonous motions I'm going through."

Sitting back on her heels, Ness runs her fingers through her hair, collecting it up and securing it in a ponytail. "Let's get out of here. We can go to a bar, get drunk, dance with hot guys."

"Tracker," I say, lifting the cuff.

Rolling her eyes, Ness scoffs. "He doesn't care where you are so long as you aren't in front of him."

I ignore the way that makes my stomach churn and the icy stab of betrayal in my lungs. I don't understand what happened, and I miss Cal. I thought he was my home, but he's not. "I don't need to get us in even more trouble."

The door opens, and Massimo strolls in. "Trouble?"

Ness winks at me and turns to Massimo. "Yeah, for going to that sex party last night."

His eyes grow wide, his features lighting with fury. "You did what?"

Smirking, Ness rolls her eyes. "You aren't here to yell at us because you saw it on the tracker?"

"You are not serious." Massimo turns to me. "If you went to some weird human sex thing—"

"If?" Ness asks and bats her eyelashes.

He snaps and points a finger at her. "Woman, I will kill you."

"That's hot." She laughs. "Tell me more. It's the most action I've had since this season last year."

I burst into laughter for the first time in days. "Mother, Ness, stop. He looks ready to actually murder you."

Ness rolls her eyes, beaming at Massimo. "It's cool if you do. Just make sure you cop a feel first, at least," she says, wagging a finger in a circle over her chest. "Bonus points if it's during so I get a rush before I go to the afters."

He gazes at her in disbelief. "There's something broken in your head."

Grimacing, I hug myself. Ness has it bad, and I'm not sure why. It might be because Massimo is the only man who has never looked twice at her.

I jerk my chin in a nod at him. "We're fine. There's no need for you to keep coming by here every few days." My tone is nastier than I intended, but I won't apologize for that or defend myself. My denial that I've lost whatever I had with Cal is dwindling to anger.

"Speak for yourself." Ness giggles. "I like the extra pop of eye candy. I'm getting sick of Roger and Todd."

Massimo scowls. "What?"

"I'm referring to the eye candy that works here. I got it on in the closet with Roger earlier, and I swear, I'm this close," she says, holding up pinched fingers, "to getting Todd to give me a happy ending on the next massage."

I step to the bed and sink into it next to Ness, joking back. "No, you're not. He's been in the closet with me."

Massimo drags his hand down his face. "I strongly advise that you two are lying to me."

Ness snickers. "Nope. Caught Tallie two days ago with Todd on his knees. My girl here was screaming."

Struggling to keep my composure, I roll my eyes. "I was not screaming."

Massimo sighs, hanging his head. "For your sake, you had better be lying. If Cal ever found out—"

I crack up that he's believing our jokes. "Dude, we're banished! Cal doesn't give two fucks about us or what we're doing."

He kicks at the floor, drops his arms, and sits on the bed, then leans forward with his head in his hands. "You belong to Cal, and if you're telling the truth, he's going to fucking snap."

I roll my eyes with a derivative scoff, but Ness rubs his back. "Hey, I'm expendable, and Tallie's banished. Cal's not going to give a shit about a couple O's."

Mass picks his head up, turning to Ness over his shoulder so I can't see his face. "O's?"

Ness beams. "Orgasms."

He keeps his face to her, and she dissolves into giggles, slapping at her knee. "Stop. Talking." Massimo's voice is deep and terse.

"Just because you don't want to touch my boobs doesn't mean other–smarter–men don't, and I like fun noodles–the reptile and penis kinds alike."

"What the fuck," Massimo says, facing forward and shaking his head.

I grin at Ness, not sure if we've broken Massimo with our humor. I slip off the bed, and Massimo turns a desolate face to me.

I shrug. "Speaking of Todd and the closet, I have a date."

As I move toward the door, Massimo makes an attempt to grab my arm. I dodge his grip, glaring, "Dude."

He stands, eyes hard. "You belong to Cal."

"I'm banished, and there's nothing in my contract against fornicating with anyone, *and*," I add, taking a couple of steps closer to the door while eyeing Massimo, "I'm making the most of, you know, Cal's coin paying for services, so, see ya."

I hurry out of the room as Massimo makes another grab for me, his Dark racing to ensnare me. "Tallie, stop."

My heart races as I scamper along the hallway, not sure if he'll chase me or even where I'm going. It's the best move I can make for Ness, though, giving her a couple fractions alone with Massimo. If I could have even a single fraction of a rune with Cal, I'd take it.

Chewing on my lip, I slip down to the ground floor, jogging through the stairwell and into the cool evening air. I walk the stone paths in the garden until I find a secluded bench. Dropping to it, I lay on my back, staring at the dusk sky of pink fading to a deep green, then navy blue. A few brave stars glisten in the developing night sky.

"Little Star," I breathe.

The idea that Cal would care if I was screwing Todd–if there even was a Todd–gives me squirming eels in my stomach. It would be nice if he did care, but the reality is he doesn't even want to see me, much less care what I'm doing.

Weird sensations creep through me, cold seeping into the middle of my chest and spreading out further with each pump of my heart. The little hairs on my skin stand up, and my arms are covered in prickling bumps. I close my eyes, refusing to see the stars twinkling above me and breathe, trying to understand this ache.

The night bugs are coming out. They buzz in the air, and a few land on me. I brush them away, then get up to make my way back to the room. I keep my eyes on the path lit by flood lights, taking my time as I follow the twisting paths at a sluggish pace, returning to my room.

I knock on the door, having left without grabbing a key chip.

Massimo opens the door. I blink, and then my adrenaline kicks in. "You did not fucking kill her."

He frowns. "No."

"I'm here, babe," Ness yells. "Totally alive, still useless and expendable, but I was giving him the info from the book. How was Todd? Must have been hot. You've been gone over a rune."

I force a smile onto my closed lips and stare Massimo in the eye. "Can I come in, or am I banished from this room, too?"

He leans in close, eyes blazing. "I'm telling you to stop. My orders are as good as Cal's, so whatever just happened in the closet was the last time, and Cal never knows."

I stare back without care. "Whatever. Are you going to let me in?"

He steps back and aside. I slump past and crawl onto the bed, lying face down. Cuddling a pillow, I yawn and stretch out. "Did you ever order dinner?"

"I got distracted. Want me to call now?"

"I'm just going to pass out, but I can stay awake long enough to swipe if you need." I hold my cuffed wrist up.

Massimo says in a terse voice, "Under no circumstances are you to be involving yourselves with others. As of now, you are celibate, and that's an order."

Ness giggles. "Question. Does that exclude self-pleasuring? Or what if Tallie and I do each other?"

He grumbles and then says, "That's two questions."

"Fine. *Questions*," Ness stresses.

"No one touches you. You don't touch each other. You don't touch yourself–just no touching."

"Clarification," Ness asks with laughter. "You're referring to sexual touching, right? Cause, like, I'd like to shower, and that requires touching myself, plus we're at a spa. The whole point of this place is paying people to touch you for various reasons."

"You are the reason I'm going to drink tonight."

"I'd rather be the reason you touch yourself tonight," Ness purrs.

Massimo sighs. "I'm leaving now. Give me the notebook."

"If you take it, I have nothing left to translate onto."

"Fine. I'll be back tomorrow at Sun's rune. I'll bring a new one and take that one, and under no circumstances am I going to hear about touching."

"You are going to be so disappointed."

Massimo's footsteps get further away, and the door clicks. I roll over and stare at Ness. She lifts her eyebrows back. "Todd was that good?"

I crack up, whacking at her with the pillow. "I think he bought it a little too much."

"I'm not going to stop masturbating, and I'm going to tell him I do it while thinking of him." Ness tosses her long dark hair over her shoulder, glancing at the door.

"Babe," I sit, shaking my head. "He's about to snap."

"Good. Maybe he'll fuck me into submission."

Giggling, I roll off the bed. "I'm going to shower. This mango crap is giving me a headache."

"Detachable shower head," Ness yells as I shut myself in the bathroom. "We can name it Todd!"

CHAPTER 10

CALLAHAN

After a late-night workout, I go searching for bourbon and find Massimo in the lounge with an open bottle. The cap is discarded on the table, and he has no glass.

I stop on the threshold, lifting my eyebrows. My friend is slumped forward, head in his hands. "Mass?"

He lifts his head and blinks, rubbing a hand down his face. "You're going to kill me."

I glance at the contract on the back of my hand. It is normal. There's no irritation or signs of raised lettering to indicate Massimo broke it.

'You answer to me. We respect the contract. We protect each other. We act in our best interest. We protect Natalia.'

I'd added the fifth line after Natalia had proven herself useful in Ilbuio. That's when I decided I wanted her to be my queen. Sighing, I scratch at the stubble on my jaw, moving further into the room. "Why?"

Chuckling, he picks up the bottle and takes a long drink. "Trust me, you're going to kill me."

I do a quick mental scan of Massimo. He's involved in

everything, in charge of my finances because that gives me a headache in five fractions of a rune, but his duties span my empire and our friendship alike. "Bad investment? How much did I lose?"

"Your finances are fine, one billion, seventy-one million if you care to know. Mine are a paltry twenty-three million, but Islandal is still exceptionally profitable."

I bob my head. Islandal lies in the north near the Avgora Mountains and where Massimo grew up. He negotiated to ensure it remained owned by the Verta lineage when he signed my contract because he wanted something for his eventual lineage seed to inherit.

I retrieve a glass from the cabinet before settling on the couch next to Massimo. Pouring myself a drink, I lift the bottle of decade-old scotch, eyeing the mouthful remaining. "Mass."

"I needed a drink, a good drink, and you can afford a new one."

"Apparently, several." I hand him the bottle. "What's going on?"

Massimo drains the bottle, then sets it aside and slumps forward, head between his legs. "Something you don't need to know about that I am taking care of."

I lift an eyebrow and smirk. "Where is she?"

He scoffs, shaking his head. "I'm not that drunk."

"Where?"

"Pierre's daughter."

"I know. Where is she?"

Massimo lifts his eyes to mine. "You're not going to kill her? No dismemberment? Use her to fuck with Pierre?"

Smiling, I take another drink. "I don't have to inflict pain on her to use her against Pierre. That bastard will hate that she serves the Dark, and I'll keep her serving long after he dies. Having her contracted is a good enough annoyance, and he'll have a conniption when she's the Dark Queen. I want my star back."

He waves at the door. "They're at the spa. Go fetch."

I freeze, the glass halfway to my mouth. I could have collected her at any point. "You're right. I should kill you."

"Last place you'd look is the one place you think I moved them from."

I groan. "I fucking hate you sometimes."

He flops back, arms limp between his legs. "Nessy is about finished with the codex. She only a couple more pages."

"Nessy?"

"Woman is gorgeous and twice as fucking nuts, but from what I saw, the translations make sense. We should have them tomorrow."

"Good." I take a drink as an explosion detonates in the front of the house. The bottle rattles and falls, rolling to the floor. We lurch to our feet, and another explosion rocks the house, the ground rumbling.

Drunk and unstable, Massimo topples, falling into me. We land, my head smacking into the corner of the table.

On top of me, Massimo catches himself, puckering his lips and making kissing noises. "Wanna make out?"

With my temple throbbing, warm blood rolling along my scalp, I shove him off as the world rocks again. "You're not pretty enough."

The ceiling cracks, and I get my feet under me, putting a hand on the wound to apply pressure. A head rush spins the world, and I wobble, staggering forward. Someone is going to die as soon as I find them.

Pulling my hand back, I glare at the blood and then move my gaze to my forearm. Natalia's name glitters at me, brilliant and beautiful. She'll be in contempt, unable to comply so far from me. Gritting my teeth, I warn my Dark. It hisses, a protective desire racing through me.

It understands.

I hope that's enough to spare her as another boom detonates. She's too far for me to alter her side of the contract.

The world quakes, and then silence rings. Looking to Mass, I bare my teeth and head to determine what the commotion is. I don't get far before the world rattles and shakes again.

I stumble into the side of the hall, and Massimo grabs hold of me, ripping me backward as plaster falls from above.

Growling, I shove him away. "Get off me. Someone's destroying my home. I'm going to find them, and when I do, they are going to die."

I start to move forward again, set on locating the cause of this mess and dealing retribution to the imbecile who dared to attack me in my own home. At the end of the hall, I check left and then right.

Thomas runs toward me, bleeding from his nose and temple, covered in dust and grime.

"Cal!" He launches himself into me, taking me to the floor, and we crash into Massimo.

Another explosion tears through the air, this one closer, and the world screeches, coming apart around us. Thomas gets up, brushing off plaster, grabbing me by the shoulders and shaking hard. He's yelling, but all I hear is ringing in my ears as I watch his mouth move.

"Magia," Thomas shouts. "The red hoods."

I brush him aside, glaring from where Thomas came. A figure steps into sight wearing a red cloak, face obscured by the hood. It lifts something, pulling back and releasing it into the air. I try to make out what it is as it comes toward me—a glass jar with water inside.

"Oh fuck," Massimo yells, and black tendrils rush to it, grabbing it before it hits the floor.

I blink, scouring for the Magia, but it's gone.

Thomas grabs me, shaking me. "I tried to warn everyone not to use magic, but," he pants, "I didn't stick around to see if they would listen."

The world spins. I press the heel of my palm harder against my temple. Rational thought is difficult when my head is the size of a watermelon and throbbing with searing heat.

Massimo grips the jar in one hand, inspecting it. The world trembles. "What is this?"

"That's what's doing this, but fuck if I know what it is, and they've got lots."

"Ki-cha," Massimo says, shouldering past. "Has to be what Ness threw at the fuckhead, like Tallie's blood."

"That's blood?" Thomas gapes in horror.

I drop my hand, the world now quiet and still. I step forward, but Thomas grabs my arm, digging his heels in even as I drag him forward. "I heard they're setting charges. This is just a distraction. You have to get out of here."

Dragging his fingers away from my arm, I yell, "This is my home! My city! I'm not running from a fight."

A familiar male voice yells back further up the hall. "Where is she? Where's Nat?"

"Mass, go. Take Thomas to safety. I'll deal with this." I stalk toward Tony as he throws back his hood.

He sneers, pointing a finger at me. "Answer me, you Darkling fuck. Where's Nat?"

I punch at the air, sending my Dark at him. "I don't answer to you." I drag him closer with my magic, even as I feel it being sucked away by his Ki.

Tony hits back, but I evade. He's close enough for me to take a swing, but Tony holds out a hand, and I fly backward, propelled by an invisible force. I land on one shoulder, sliding across the hardwood flooring. I shove up, getting to my feet to meet Tony sprinting at me.

One of my wings rips free, catching Tony and slamming him into the wall. I dial back, my fist snapping his head to the side. The force of my hit knocks him sideways, putting him on the floor. Tony scrambles to get upright, but I kick him in the chest and slam my foot onto his sternum to keep him on his back.

Coughing, Tony spits blood at me. "Tell me where she is, and I might just be able to save her."

I crouch low, grabbing a fistful of his shirt. "She's not even here, but even if she was, I'd be the one saving her." I throw all the burning fury in my veins behind another punch.

Bones crunch under the force of my fist, but the world shatters around me in a roar. The air screams with the house as it collapses around us in deafening cracks. A shock wave force rips through me in a piercing sound as everything comes apart.

Orange flames race around me, heat searing my flesh as I let my magic free. My limbs snap and my skin shreds as everything crashes down onto me.

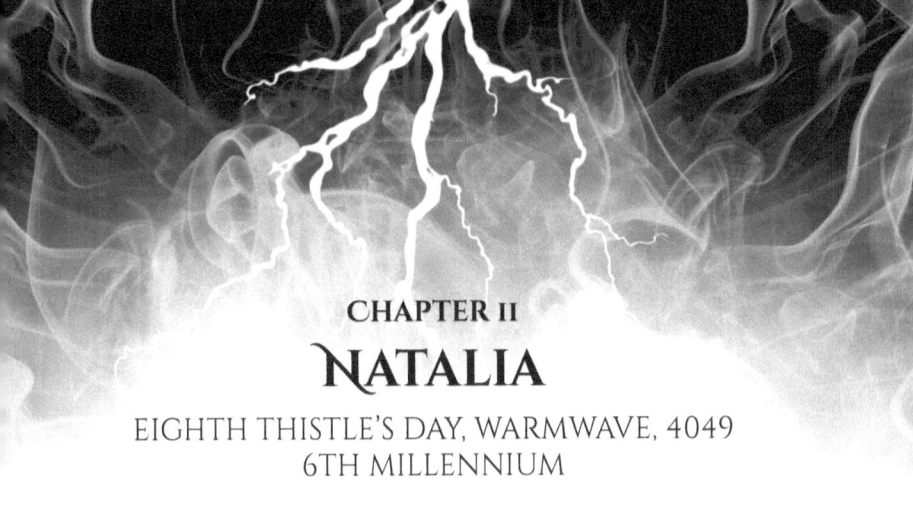

CHAPTER II

NATALIA

EIGHTH THISTLE'S DAY, WARMWAVE, 4049
6TH MILLENNIUM

I wake up in the middle of the night, my arm burning like I'm in contempt of the contract. I scratch at it, but the searing itch increases. Groggy, I shift, my clothes sticking and pulling like I'm soaked in sweat. Shivering, I throw the covers off and rub sleep from my eyes.

I peer at the damn thing in my skin, the words raised and swollen, edged in red. I wrap my hand around them for relief of cool skin. It doesn't last, and I stumble into the bathroom. I get the sink on, the knob for cold wrenched to full blast, before sticking my arm under it.

The stinging eases but persists. I scowl at it, flipping the light on. "Hey, you stupid thing, I don't know what your problem is, but I'm banished. I'm not able to do whatever it is you think I'm supposed to be doing."

"Babe," Ness's sleep-soaked voice calls from the doorway.

Without looking up, I say, "Go back to bed."

"What's wrong?"

"I don't know. Something, but I don't know what, and I

don't know what to do about it. This stupid thing is pissed off, though." I gesture at my arm under the flow of frigid water.

Ness scowls, cuddling a pillow, but steps into the room. "Should we go?"

"Go where?" I snap. "Where do we go? Showing up at Cal's place is going to get us killed. If he sees us, we're dead, remember?"

"What are you doing?"

"Cold helps."

Bobbing her head, Ness turns away. "I'll go get ice."

I stay standing in the bathroom until she returns, and then Ness helps me wrap my arm up in ice. I curl up in bed, staring out the window, unable to find comfort long past Ness returning to snoring. I toss and turn, struggling to delve back into sleep. Anxiety coils around my chest, squeezing to the point of suffocation.

Ness rolls over and murmurs in her sleep. I flip to my back with a sigh to stare at the shadows on the ceiling. Cal is in trouble. I ache to do something about it, but I can't.

The contract isn't trying to kill me like last time, so maybe it understands. Tears fill my eyes, hopelessness settling over me like a death shroud. My heart wrenches with each pulse it makes. Cal is in trouble, and I'm lying here, unable to do anything to protect him.

AT SOME POINT, I fell asleep and waking up brings relief. The contract is quiet, which sends a fresh wave of fear through me. I unwrap my arm and sit up. Cal's magic has settled the contract in its normal state.

I breathe out a sigh of relief. Massimo can explain when he comes by this morning. Then I can relax.

Ness is missing. The clock on the wall shows it's three-quarters through Sun's rune. Mass might have stopped by. They might be elsewhere together.

The door bangs open, and I jump, twisting toward it with my hands lifted for a fight.

Ness races into the room. "Babe, don't panic."

I lower my shaking hands. "You fucked Massimo yesterday, and you're finally telling me?"

"I wish." She grabs the remote and turns the entertainment screen on. The translucent glass pane flickers to life, turning opaque with images. "It's bad."

Ness shuffles backward and sits on the bed, trembling and wide-eyed. I frown at the way she's shaking, my heart starting to race as Ness pushes buttons on the remote. She cranks the volume and then tosses the controller to the side.

I turn to the media report, the whirring of a helicopter filling the room. I blink, and my heart skips a beat, sending a twinge of agony through my chest. Cal's home is in smoldering ruins. The screen goes blurry as I fumble over to Ness on the bed.

Horror threatens to turn me into a quivering mess of tears and hysteria, so I grit my teeth and force myself to my feet. I draw upright and center, taking a deep breath and collecting my Ki, wrapping myself in it like armor. The panic and terror fade to a dull roar within me, and I open my eyes.

The image splits, the banner at the bottom reading "Dark Seraphinus City Owner Callahan Reported Dead Early This Morning.'" The second half of the screen shows a Magia figurehead covered in a deep, blood-red fabric hood obscuring the face. The voice is distorted as the news plays the footage.

"This is a warning to all Seraphinus. You are no longer

lawless. You are no longer walking the world as the most power-ful, and you will no longer do as you please. We are the Magia, and we are many. We are watching, and you will answer to us."

Ness sniffles. "Guess they're tired of being ants." She turns to me. "What happens to your contract when he dies?"

"I—I don't actually know. Cal said it defaults when he dies to release me, so I didn't transfer to someone if they killed him."

Ness grabs my arm, eyes locked on it. "Doesn't look any different."

I shake my head.

"That's good, right?"

I stare at her, lost. "You think I fucking know? We don't know how their magic works."

She gapes. "It's his magic, right? If he dies, wouldn't it go away?"

"It's a piece of his magic," I whisper, cradling my arm to my chest, the only thing left of Cal. "Only a piece of it. Maybe... Maybe because it's in me, it's still alive even if he's..." I can't say the words.

"Mother," she whimpers. "What are we going to do? Oh, Mother, Mass?" She lets go of me, turning back to the televi-sion to wring her hands. "He said he'd be here at Sun's rune. He didn't show."

We stare, stupid and numb.

The news rolls, the word "Live" blinking on the screen next to footage over and over of the desolated estate, emergency services trying to put out fires, flashing lights everywhere. Winged men and women start to drop into the footage, pushing back on the rescue teams. They're yelling to turn the cameras off, to get off private property, waving their hands and then start throwing bodies and the footage cuts.

"...experiencing technical difficulties," the perky news woman says with a laugh as she shuffles pages on a desk. "We'll keep you up to date as the situation evolves, but the Seraphinus Callahan..." A picture of him in sunglasses flashes on the screen. "...is reportedly dead."

Goosebumps cover me as cold rushes over me as if I'm submerged in an ice bath. Waves of frozen shards pulsate from my heart as it stalls and stutters. "Cal."

The woman on the screen clears her throat. "Let's roll the feed of the entity calling themselves the Magia again. We'll get the news out there that the humans have an ally. The Magia are already being celebrated in the streets, people heralding them as heroes."

Ness squeezes my hand hard. "You know how I said don't panic. Well, I am. I'm freaking out, babe."

I nod but can't find my voice as pictures of me and Ness are put up on the screen.

The female broadcaster says, "While we work to get the feed of the wreckage, let's remind everyone these two are wanted by the Magia. Any news related to their whereabouts is being asked for. You can call the number on the screen. It has been set up as an anonymous tip-line. Any lead that results in their capture is worth a crisp million."

Ness flinches. "Can they do that? They can't do that, can they?"

The female's voice plays over their pictures, the phone number listed below them. "These two women are working with the deceased Seraphinus, known as Callahan Barraco, wanted for crimes against humanity. They are to be considered dangerous and combative and are not to be approached. Please call the number if you have any information, and stay safe, folks."

"What?" Ness yelps. "We're not–They can't do that! That's fucking outrageous."

I lick my lower lip, suck it into my mouth and take a deep breath. "Babe," I whisper. "We're going to count to three, then we're going to move. Got it?"

"Where the fuck are we moving to?" She leans her head on my shoulder and sobs. "We're so screwed."

"We've been here for weeks. Everyone knows us. Someone is going to call for that million. We need to move." I give her hand one last squeeze and then detangle.

The news keeps playing in the background as I get dressed in leggings and a sports bra, then throw on a loose white shirt that hangs off one shoulder.

I stand and grasp Ness by the shoulders. "Ness, move now."

Ness twitches to life. "I never got to sit on Mass's face. I never played with his fun noodle, licked his muscles..."

My eyes well up. "Yeah, well, take it from me, be happy you don't know what you're missing."

I pace, running my hands through my hair and fidgeting as Ness gets shoes on.

She pulls upright. Her warm brown skin is tinged green, her big, brown eyes wide. She's staring at me with her lips parted and vacancy in her expression. I register she's in shock, knowing that means I can't break apart. "Ready?"

She nods, lacing her fingers in mine.

"Come on. We're going to move."

Ness squeezes my fingers, and I yank her toward the door, out into the hall and through the stairwell in silence. At the bottom of the stairs, I hesitate. Cal taught me to move, that staying put or trying to hide is a good way to end up cornered and dead, but I have no clue where to go.

Our faces are plastered on the media reports. Cal is dead. Mass didn't show as promised, probably because he's deceased too. The Magia are coming. This is where being a better person and having friends would come in handy, but I already have my only friend in hand.

I wrack my brain as I head down the hall. There is only one place I can think of that would be safe, that I could exist long-term, that the Magia wouldn't be able to reach us. "History and geography-related question. Ready?"

Ness nods. "Maybe."

"Where is Izul? Please tell me it's on this continent."

"Um..." Ness scrunches her eyes shut. "Yes."

The first good news of the day. "Then we don't have to deal with the bridges. Pierre Bordeaux offered me a home in Izul while I was in Ilbuio. I turned him down then, but it's supposed to be outstanding. Ready to switch sides?"

"There's a joke about both ways there, but I can't find one," Ness whispers.

I pull her with me. "Tell me how to get there. That's where we're going."

We slip out the door, and I pull her away from the building. We need to get away from here, and I'm heading straight for the front gate across the pristine lawn, ignoring the winding paths and the signs that are posted to remain off the grass.

Ness whispers, "We need to go south, way south, like we need a ride, and it'll take a couple days to drive."

I eye the black cars pulling through the gate and tense. "Let's get out of here, then we figure it out."

"Magia are everywhere on this continent and the next. We can't run from them. They're in every city."

The cars come to a halt, three of them, and red-cloaked figures spill out. Ness curses. "Shit, fuck. Think they saw us?"

"Standing in the open lawn hand in hand? No. I think they're blind," I answer in a drawl. The figures start toward us, and I shake my hand from Ness's. "Run, babe, you know they're coming for me."

Ness laughs in hysterics. "I have a strict no-running policy, and I'm not leaving you."

I lift my hands, leaning back on one foot as the dozen figures approach in a slow gait. I center, collecting Ki and threads of silver Light dance and swirl over my hands and arms as my heart pounds with adrenaline.

The one in the lead stops. "Natalia Swan, you are guilty of betraying the Magia."

"Sorry 'bout that," I say, lifting my chin.

"The Darkling that coerced your servitude is now dead. We are not ignorant of your plight. If you come quietly, leniency will be granted."

Rage sparks in my chest, the Light over my skin sparkling brighter. They killed Cal. "I'm not going anywhere with you, and Cal didn't force me to do anything. Take your leniency and shove it up your ass."

"Restrain her," the hooded man says, motioning with his head, pulling a syringe from the inner pocket of the cloak and lifting it. "I will apply the Ki blocker."

"Ah, shit." Ness sighs, swinging her backpack in front of her, zipper ripping through the air as two advance on us. Pulling out the codex, she brandishes it and yells, "Stay back, fuckers."

"Vanessa, you are of little consequence. Fight, and we will kill you."

"You know," she says, lifting her voice, "I've heard that a lot, and I'm getting real sick of it."

I roll my eyes and step in front of her, the two hooded figures moving to flank us. "Is there a clause in your no-running policy, babe?"

"No."

I block an attack from one side with my forearm and duck the other. From one knee, I throw my hand out and Light blasts through one figure, knocking it prone. The other kicks at me, and I redirect the force, flipping the attacker over. The hood falls back as he groans up at me, and I frown at Henry.

I know these people. They know me. Hesitation creeps into me, but Ness crouches and whacks him with the book. "Asshole. You are a crappy driver, and your girlfriend is way too hot for you."

The book hisses and releases a black smog.

Laughing, I'm upright, fending off another pair as Henry screams. I break an arm, my strength resolving. They killed Cal. I'll never see him again. Fury rips through me, and I scream, withdrawing the Ki I wrapped myself in, letting my rage blossom.

Firelight crawls over my skin, and the air charges around me. I hold tight to the burning pulse in my ribs that comes with the knowledge that I'll never be beneath Cal again, never taste his power or hear his laugh. I take down two more, and Light flashes as I blast Ki at a third.

My ears fill with little zaps of electricity. I reach to the sky and rip the air down, all my fury ripping from my core. I want them to hurt. I want them dead like Cal. I scream, the Light burning through my body with more force than I've ever known. The sacred geometry down my spine ignites, the lines searing like open wounds sliced clean into my back with dull razor blades.

The Light answers me, a bolt of magic streaking toward the ground, branching to strike all the figures surrounding me. The world screams with me, and I stumble, ears ringing from the boom emitted from the smite.

Phosphenes of bright colors dance in my vision, and a hand grabs my arm. I twist, throwing a punch.

Ness rocks sideways and hits the ground. She scrambles, picks up the codex and then shoves me, yelling, "What the fuck, bitch?"

"Sorry, you—"

"We're moving." She pushes me forward while tucking the codex into her pack. She latches onto my hand, and I blink around us in a daze, my knees wobbling and threatening to collapse.

Ness half drags me onward. "We need to go."

"Babe," I manage as Ness pulls me out through the gated area of the resort and onto the road.

"You punched me. That hurt. You better be preparing an incredible apology."

I rip my hand free and stop walking. "No, I..." I falter as Ness turns back with a frown. "Cal's dead," I sob, covering my mouth.

Ness nods. "Yeah, I know, and you loved him."

Twisting my face away, I squeeze my eyes shut. "No, I–I don't know, but... But I think I could have. I could have loved him."

Hands land on my shoulders, giving a gentle squeeze. "I know, babe, but we need to go now."

I cover my face with both hands and sniffle, trying to get a good draught of air. There are far more Magia coming, and I'm not sure I have the strength to fight them right now. I'm woozy, straining to stay upright with my legs shaking. My chest burns with a numbness, my heart clopping along with sharp stabs of pain.

I breathe out. "Okay." I bob my head, dropping my hands as I blink away the tears. Gripping my fists, I collect Ki, wrapping myself up again to keep the pieces together like taping up a broken glass. "Okay. We're moving."

CHAPTER 12

NATALIA

The suns have set as we trudge down roads, steering clear from prime sources of population. My body aches, every step I take on tender soles that throb with swollen heat. As much as I was sick of the spa, I miss it after walking for runes.

Ness is drooping, her hands clutching the straps of her backpack. "I need another break."

Izul is south on the border of the Shining Sea coast, according to Ness, so we need to find a vehicle. I stop and eye a parking lot next to a dilapidated bar advertising a two-for-one special. "You need a break, and we need a car."

Ness comes to a stop and sighs. "We have no identification. We have no coin cards or phones connected to accounts. We have literally nothing. Cal took all of it when he took us. We were on contract and together, so it didn't seem to matter much, but now?"

"We have boobs."

"Yeah, great. Are we cutting them off and selling them?"

I roll my eyes and lift my wrist. "I have Cal's bracelet, so we have coin, and the boobs stay attached. It should still work for a while until his death officially hits his accounts, and even then, I don't know how this works. If it transfers to someone else, they might not notice with the chaos, but let's focus. Men like boobs. We have boobs. You remember how we scored free drinks when we were broke?"

"Dumb blonde routine?"

"Exactly." I lift my chin at the bar but step back off the shoulder of the road into the cover of trees.

Ness bobs her head to the side, following. "Steal a car. Sure, why not? We're already fucked. Might as well tick things off our 'to do before we die' list. Wasn't exactly on my list until now, though."

I scoff and check that we're obscured by the foliage. "Chin up, babe. I need you with me on this. You said we could figure it out, so let's figure it out."

"One step, one next thing, fight until you make it." Ness sighs, reciting lyrics but not singing. "Come burning afters, come Ancients, come what may."

I nudge her with a shoulder. "We can sing every Dark Marrow song we know while we drive to Izul."

"Great. Just don't punch me again," she says, rubbing her blue and swollen cheek. "It freaking hurts."

"Will you heal yourself already and quit complaining? Getting punched is supposed to hurt." I give her a dirty look. "Just don't grab me like that in a fight again, and I won't punch you."

"Well, you weren't answering after the light show, and by the way, I forgot to mention, the book didn't like that. It chattered at me like an angry chipmunk, and this black dome surrounded us." She closes her eyes, and the bruise recedes.

"Us? Babe, it's a fucking book."

"That thing is alive. I'm telling you, I don't know how or, like, what the fuck, but it's alive and it freaks me out."

I glare at her. "Then why do we still have it?"

"It was useful to bash Henry over the head, and it smoked him. He didn't get back up. I think I killed him, or the book did, so it's to whack people with if we get into a fight."

I check the traffic on the winding two-lane road. "We should avoid fighting. We don't need the extra attention. You want to be the dumb one or me?"

Ness inspects herself, then eyes me. "You're in a white shirt. How about we do the 'wet t-shirt contest'?"

Glancing down, I sigh, then yank my shirt off and pin it between my knees before peeling my sports bra off and flinging it at Ness. "Put that in your bag."

Ness takes it, and I get my shirt back on. "Well?" I hold my arms out to display my chest.

"Brilliant. I can already sort of see nip."

We head for the bar, and I open the door, waving Ness inside. Stepping in, the air conditioning blasts me in the face. I stand up a bit straighter, shocked into awareness. My girls stand up, too, nipples shrinking to hard peaks that could cut metal. Giving into a full-body shudder, I follow Ness to the bar.

There's a group of rowdy guys playing darts in the far corner and an old man in a stupor hunkered down on his stool nursing a stout. A few other tables are occupied, a couple eating, a pair of older women who look like they've chain-smoked their whole life while partying hard, and a group of guys sipping beers.

I plaster a vacant giggle on my face, staring to see the end of my nose and stand at the bar.

"Two martinis and two shots of vodka," Ness says to the lady on the other side.

"Do you want to start a tab?"

Ness nods. "Sure do."

"Card," the woman says.

With a forced giggle, I extend my wrist. The bartender grabs the scanner, holding it against the metal cuff. It beeps an acceptance, the little light turning green, and together, Ness and I breathe out in relief. The woman gives us an odd look, checking the scanner, but sets it aside to begin making the drinks.

I catch Ness's gaze and cut my sight to the guys playing darts as they roar with excitement. Ness bobs her head to the crappy speakers blaring pop music with vigor and static. "Yup."

The drinks are offered up, and Ness grabs both shots, offering me one. We clink the tiny glasses, tap them on the bar, and throw back the shots. It's enough alcohol that I'll get a buzz for all of two fractions of a rune, thanks to my Magia metabolism.

I take a deep breath as I set the shot glass aside and then force my eyes wider. Grabbing Ness's wrist, I yell, "They look like they're having fun. I want to have fun."

Ness turns to follow my line of sight to the men playing darts. "We can see if they'll let us play."

Squealing as if I'm excited, I head toward the men, dragging Ness at my back. I stop with a little hop near the men to make my boobs jiggle. They do a slight bounce at best, but I'm working with a small handful, so that's the best I can do.

Beaming, I lift my voice, "Hey there. Can we play?"

The men stop, a few dropping their eyes to my chest. I hike my grin higher and wait. One takes a drink from his beer, another grinning and waving me closer. "Fuck yeah, come on. You play darts?"

Shaking my head back and forth, I say, "No, never, but gosh, it looks like fun. What do I do?"

One of them, stumpy and frowning, pulls the darts from the board and walks over, handing them to me. I hold my hand out to accept them but twitch and allow them to hit the floor. "Oops. Haha. Oh no!" I bend at the waist, legs straight and my butt in the air to pick them up, taking my time before I stand.

"Here," Ness shoves a martini at me. "You forgot this at the bar."

The martini sloshes over the edge of my glass as I take it with a giggle, licking at the spilled fluid as I make direct eye contact with the man next to me. I wink. "Can't waste any."

The guy nods. "Yeah, sure. It's alcohol abuse."

My stomach churns. He's cute, with a boyish charm to his features and brown hair, but he's not Cal. I face the dart board. "So, I just throw them at the thingy over there?"

"Yup, hit the bullseye. It's the red center. That's how you win."

Taking a long drink, I inhale as much of the alcohol as I can in a single gulp. I need it. Batting my lashes, I extend the drink and ask, "Could you, like, hold this for me?"

He takes it, and I approach the board, standing with my legs apart in a stance. Closing one eye and sticking my tongue between my lips, I move the dart back and forth like I'm trying to aim really hard. I throw, leaning forward and flicking the dart toward the board.

I step forward, kicking the back of my opposite heel and waving my arms, half pretending to trip and force a gaudy laugh. The dart hits the board and bounces off as I gape at it. "Oh, no. Wasn't that right?" I glance over my shoulder.

One guy is at the table staring at my butt. The one holding my drink laughs. "Fuck no. But come on, try again." He sets my drink down. "Mind if I help you?"

I shake my head with a giggle. "Nope."

The guy gets close, taking my hand and positioning a dart in my grasp. "That's how you hold it."

"Oh, that makes more sense. Okay, now what?"

"So now," he wraps his fingers around my shoulders. His hands are gentle and warm as he guides my body into place.

A pang twinges through my gut at hands other than Cal's touching me. It feels wrong. It is wrong. He said I was his.

I try to shove it down, to ignore the misery and hurt.

"Yeah, like that." He chuckles. "And here." His hands tighten a bit, pulling my torso back. "Now lean back on one foot."

I allow him to move me, accepting his manipulations so I can take advantage of him later. "Yeah, and now I throw?"

"Throw." He steps off to the side, bobbing his head.

This time, the dart hits the board, the needle sticking into the cork, and I stay upright. "Yay!" I scream with faux excitement, jumping in place and clapping my hands. "That's so fun."

"You get more." He holds up an array with a smirk. "Maybe I can help you hit the bullseye?"

I nod and let him touch me again. Every brush of his soft hands against my wrist as he shows me how to throw, the other resting with casual ease on my hip, sends a fresh wave of heartache through me with deep pulses of an angry wound.

Feigning enthrallment is wearing on me. All I want to do is curl up and break apart, to mourn what I've lost. Blinking burning eyes, I grin wide at the guy and then glance around for Ness. I wave her over, yelling, "So much fun, Messy, you've got to try this."

Ness shrugs. "Sure."

She brings me another martini, but the liquid shimmers like straight vodka without a single olive. Smiling at the man who has been helping me, I say, "I'm Estelle, but you can call me Telly." I giggle, waving a hand at Ness. "And this is Melissa, but everyone just calls her Messy. Can I buy you guys drinks?"

They all give consent, and I drain the martini glass before

taking down orders then skipping to the bar. The bartender gives me a long look but takes the drink order with a sigh. Returning to the table with a bucket of beers, I begin handing them out with a big grin.

I do a quick scan of the table and see plenty of phones sitting out in plain view, along with peeling paper coasters with wet rings but no keys. I'm going to have to get creative.

Latching onto the guy who was teaching me to throw darts, I hang on him, swaying like I'm drunk and flirting with him. Ness is laughing with a second male who's playing darts. She sways her hips, bumping into the male. The drunk, dumb act is becoming annoying even as I giggle and run my fingers through the first guy's hair, but the way he's grinning tells me he's having a good time.

We all do a few rounds of shots, the guys getting rowdy and loud. Ness clings to one, grinding against him, so I swipe the darts from her hands. I pull my chosen target with me to play another round of darts, giving my Magia metabolism time to process all the alcohol. As much as I would love to be drunk, now isn't the time.

I hit the bull's eye. Throwing my hands in the air, I whoop with excitement. "I am awesome!"

The guys all cheer, and then I turn, purposefully twisting my feet into each other and doing nothing to stop myself from falling. I crack up on the floor, reaching my hands toward the guy. "I think I need help."

He takes my hands in his, tugging with a laugh. "I've got you, sweetheart."

I push with my legs to help him get me off the floor. Cal could have yanked me with his pinky and done a better job, but I flop into the guy like he pulled me with super strength. "Oh, oh, I'm so sorry."

He chuckles, one of his arms wrapping around me to hold me against his chest and steady us. "No worries."

"Maybe we can sit down for a fraction?" I smile. "I think I've had too much fun. Head rush from the excitement. I needed this, though. This is awesome."

"Yeah, it's fun. How come you needed it?" He sits down.

I slip onto his lap, twisting my arm around his neck and pressing against him. Wiggling my butt in his lap, I detect hard objects digging in. "Oh, you know..." I sigh, but a real tinge of bitterness slips into my façade. "My boyfriend broke up with me."

He winces. "Hang on, sweetheart, you're digging my keys into me."

"What? Oh." I cling tight to him, shoving my breasts into his face and lifting myself up.

He laughs while fishing the keys out of his pocket. He tosses them on the table. "All right. So, you're just out here looking for fun?"

"Yup." I plop down, grinning for real and pick up my martini glass, but there's not much left, so I drain the vodka and twist around, attempting to locate Ness. "Mess! Messy!" I lift my empty glass.

Ness turns away from the guy she's talking up and blinks at me. "What?"

"I need another one. No, make it two, and I'm going to drink them both at the same time." Pointedly, I hold her gaze and then drop my eyes to the table.

The guy I'm sitting on shifts me a bit. "Maybe you should slow down; just get one right now."

I don't bother telling him the drinks aren't going to wind up in me. There's a waft of guilt through me. He seems like a nice guy. He hasn't gotten grabby or inappropriate despite me throwing myself at him.

I stick my tongue between my teeth and wrinkle my nose. "After these two, I will if you promise to call me tomorrow."

He grins, face flushing. "How about I make you breakfast?"

I laugh for real. It was a great line. "Deal."

Ness comes back with two martinis and hands them over. She leans against the table, hands gripping the ledge. "This I've got to watch."

Everyone is watching as I lift the drinks side by side, the rims of the glasses touching. I move them closer to my mouth and dump them straight down my chest. Cold alcohol soaks my shirt, and I giggle, flailing and falling out of the guy's lap.

I cackle on the floor, staring at the ceiling, keeping my arms away from my torso to make sure my breasts are on full display. The guy lurches to his feet, one of the others coming to help as well. Together, they pull me to my feet, the second moving away, but my guy keeps his hands on me.

Ness steps closer, pulling me away from the guy. "That was so stupid," she says, then whispers in my ear. "Go."

I giggle, pushing her away and try to wring out my shirt with a pout. "I'm all wet."

A random guy yells, "That's what she said!"

They all crack up, but Ness tucks me under her arm. "All right, babe, it's time to go."

The guy I was sitting on cuts us off as Ness turns us to the door. "Wait, hang on. You should stay."

Ness shakes her head and sighs. "She's drunk. I should get her home."

"We're having fun, right? She wants to stay." He stares at me.

I roll my eyes, pretending to push away from her. "Yeah. It's fun. I'm fine."

"Girl code," Ness says with flare, grabbing her backpack. "No, I'm taking you home."

"Aw, come on," I lean into her, giggling. "A little longer?"

"Nope. Now. You just tried to drink two martinis at once and fell out of his lap. You're drunk." Ness slings the bag on one shoulder and grabs my hand. "We're leaving."

Ness's grip tightens to the point of pain, a slight growl to her words. I'm trying to make this look good, but maybe I'm taking it too far.

The guy follows a few steps. "Hey, wait up."

Ness rounds and puts a hand on his chest. "She's drunk, buddy."

He has the nerve to look ashamed. "No, no, I know. I realize that, but I was just going to ask..." He glances at me. "Can I get your number? I'd still love to take you to breakfast."

"Oh." I blink, caught off guard. "Yeah."

The guy pulls his phone out, and the screen lights up. He taps on it a few times and then looks at me.

"977 16955 10725," I say, giving him my real number. It won't matter. The phone was taken when I signed Cal's contract, and it was either thrown out or blown up in the explosion that also killed Cal. My eyes burn, and I inhale through my nose, faking a wide grin. "Call me tomorrow, yeah?"

He nods. "I'm Nate, by the way."

"Nice to meet you, Nate," I say and almost mean it.

Ness shoves me toward the door. "See ya later, Nate," she calls back at him, forcing me out the front door.

In the cool air of dusk, I drop the act, my face falling. Ness lifts the keys, holding the small rod by the end and waving it at the parking lot. Lights flash on a silver sedan parked nearby, and we hurry toward it.

Ness climbs behind the wheel and throws the backpack at me as I settle in the front passenger seat.

She peels out in a hurry before I can even get my seatbelt

buckled. On the road, I take a deep breath, the connector snapping, and I adjust the strap across my chest for breathing room.

"Jeez." Ness cuts her eyes at me. "You made me work for it back there."

"What? I dumped two drinks on myself, hit the floor, and gave them a show." I wave my hand down my front.

Scoffing, Ness shakes her head. "I cannot believe they fell for that."

I shrug, looking out the window at the passing blur of forest in the glow of the headlights. "Like they really thought we were there to steal a car?"

"What's with giving the guy your number?"

"I had to give him something."

"You could have given him a fake one," she says. "They're going to call officers, and they'll figure out it was us."

Leaning forward, I fiddle with the stereo nobs to turn something on. The silence is haunting. I need to keep my mind focused, or I'm going to break. "Babe, our faces are all over the news. Flash a picture of us, and those guys are going to identify us in a heartbeat."

"Fair point."

I find a station, breathing out a puff of air. "How much fuel do we have?"

"Half a tank. This thing says three hundred and ten miles to go, so plenty of time for you to get some sleep. I'll get us going in the right direction, and then when we refill, you can take over, and it's my turn to catch up on beauty sleep."

I nod, slumping low in the seat and crossing my arms over my stomach. There's no possible way I'm going to be able to sleep, but I close my eyes anyway. I've got a sinking sense in my core, a sense that I shouldn't be doing this, but I brush it off.

As much as I long to have Ness turn around, there's nothing to go back to.

CHAPTER 13

NATALIA

EIGHTH THORN'S DAY, WARMWAVE, 4049
SEVENTH MILLENNIUM, A.I.

I stir, shoving away from the door panel and stretching my neck. Rubbing my eyes, I stare around, groggy and unsure of where I am. Blinking sticky eyelids, I glare in the early morning light, one sun low in the distance hovering over the horizon.

Covering my yawn, I fight through it to ask, "Where are we?"

"Just outside Niche, heading straight south on P-92, but we're down to twenty miles, so I'm trying to pick a place to stop."

I shake my head. Niche is roughly four-hundred-and-fifty miles from Narwal. Ness's ability to drive like an old person at night with cataracts usually makes for great fuel economy with ammonia energy and vehicle regeneration technology.

"Normally, I'd be ecstatic, but babe, we're *on the run,* and you still can't go over the speed limit?"

"Are you kidding me?" She glowers with mean side eyes. "That's all the more reason to drive safely and responsibly. I'm already breaking the rules by driving without my license, which I am not okay with, and you want us to up the chances of getting pulled over? Besides, I got great range, further than I thought, so I've chipped away at that distance *and* gave you more time to sleep. Sadly, that means I pulled over and peed on the side of the road. Very unladylike, I know, but a girl's gotta do what a girl's gotta do."

I sigh, leaning forward over my knees and shoving my fingers into my loose hair. "Great job, but pretty sure I killed the Magia, most of them, that is. You offed Henry with a book, we stole a car, and you're worrying about missing your license?"

"The rules of the road are not up for debate. We had to do those other things, but speeding is a choice, one we can choose not to do."

I roll my eyes and point. "Here, this exit. We can grab something to drink, food and shit while we fill up, and then I'll take over, and you can get some sleep."

Taking the exit, she pulls off the parkway and into the fueling station. I hold the cuff to the payment scanner and sigh with relief as it beeps with a green light illuminating. "At least we have a bit of luck left."

Ness gives me a squeeze from behind. "It's going to be okay, babe. Really, we've got this, and hopefully, Pierre hasn't changed his mind, and we'll get into Izul. Just the next thing, one more thing," she whispers.

"I know. I'm a trashy whore for using my tits to steal a car, the smell of alcohol is all over me, the Magia—our freaking family, friends, the people we grew up with..." I shake my head. "I just feel gross."

Ness lets go. "We keep moving," she says. "I'm hungry."

My stomach gurgles at the thought of food, so I nod. "Yeah, me too."

We remain silent while grabbing snacks. Together, we load up on water, moving through the convenience aisles. The attendant eyes us with curiosity. "Where are you two heading?"

Ness cocks her hip. "Girl's trip to the Glinting Mirage."

The attendant checks his phone, inspecting us. "Where are you coming from?"

I lift my eyebrows.

Ness lifts her voice. "Islandal."

Tapping the cuff, I say, "Have a great day."

I head back to the car with Ness, shoving the door open and letting her go first. I linger, catching the attendant speaking low, "I have a tip on..."

I let the door close and walk faster. "Ness, move it. That guy is calling us in."

She laughs as we get into the vehicle. "At least we told him the wrong destination."

I speed onto the parkway, using my teeth to tear open a granola bar wrapper. "Not exceptionally helpful as they share similar routes."

Ness stares out the window, opening a bag of crisps. "You know," she says, "I still don't think this is the worst breakfast I've ever had. That's got to be with Josh, the morning after our graduation when he took me to that crappy dinner on Fifth. I paid because he forgot coin, and the food was burnt. Pretty sure the grits were someone's throw-up." She shudders. "And the sex was super awkward and disappointing, so that didn't make up for it."

I make a lane change to avoid an exit-only lane and sigh. "Mine was at Tony's place. His parents were there, and the food wasn't bad, but Mother, it was an awful morning. I had to sit through his mom telling me about having children, what to expect, the process of it and how to ensure I got pregnant." I bite into the granola, fruit and nut mixture.

"Oh." Ness nods. "I remember you telling me about that. I think I pulled something laughing."

We nod in silence, neither of us laughing now. I finish the bar and throw the wrapper over my shoulder into the backseat. "Simpler times."

"Who would have thought?"

The radio cuts in and out, and I poke at buttons to find a new station. It doesn't matter what station, but I need music. I'll settle for anything with Niche on the horizon. We've got so many miles to go, and the car is saying seven-hundred-and-forty-three miles to a refuel, but I'll see if I can stretch that.

Ness finishes a few bags of chips and then leans against the door panel. She stares out the window and says, "I don't regret it, you know. Getting the contract, following you to Cal."

"What?"

"I don't want you to think I'm upset about this thing–the Magia hunting us, leaving home."

Tightening my grip on the wheel with both hands, my knuckles go white. "All this shit we're facing is my fault."

"You saved someone's life. That's a good act, and sure, it was like a bomb went off in our lives, but at least my life isn't boring anymore."

I laugh. "No, our lives are going to be anything but boring for a while."

"I met Mass. I've never met a man like him before. Mother, he was handsome, even with that scar, and a gentleman, even though he seemed to hate me."

I hum. I don't want to hear about Massimo. That will make me think about Cal.

"So, positives." Ness hunkers down lower. "Focus on good things. We do the next thing, and we figure it out, but don't for one second blame yourself for me being in this with you, 'cause, babe," she grins, "I want a girl like you."

"I am sorry you're in this mess, but I'm so glad you are because I don't think I could still be going if I was on my own."

Ness snorts. "Load of shit, that is. You'll be taking steps out of sheer stupid stubbornness even after you're dead."

A twinge in my chest sends my eyes to the remnants of my contract. With all that strength and power, it's hard to believe Cal's gone.

He'd been Dark by every definition, but he had been able to handle me, push back, take my shit, and still come out on top. I needed that. A man who was strong enough to handle me, not cave to me. It's weird, but I almost wanted to be put in my place. I wanted someone who could stand toe to toe with me and not let me feel like I was the stronger one. He had been someone I could trust, someone able to take care of what I couldn't.

Taking a deep breath, my chest crackles like it's filled with broken glass. I'm not going to cry. This isn't the time, but someday, after the next thing and the next, maybe when there's no more after that next thing, I'll give into my grief. I'll allow myself time to mourn what I've lost, but not yet. Right now, I'm going to survive.

CHAPTER 14
NATALIA

Too much time in a car has deteriorated my nerves. I pull off the highway, going straight across the overpass and stopping on the shoulder of the on-ramp, then shift into Park. Ness frowns, glancing up for the first time in runes from translating the creepy, weird book.

"I need out of here."

Ness's big brown eyes grow wider, and she glances around. "Out of where? Where are we?"

"Bravoit. Well, just outside of it...north." I check traffic entering the highway over my shoulder. "We still have a hundred miles in range, but I need to move, stretch, something."

Ness nods, checking our surroundings and snapping the book closed. It hisses, the scales clicking. "Sounds good. Ten fractions of a rune, though. I don't like sitting here in the open. Someone may stop to help or check on us, and that attendant reported us. The last thing we need is anyone stopping by."

I nod. "Agreed."

We get out of the vehicle, and I move to the passenger side

to join Ness. At least there's little traffic through this part of the continent. This is a stretch of the Arid Plains, not much populace. There's little reason to be in this area.

Stretching and twisting, I try to get blood to flow to my extremities. Ness leans on the car, arms crossed. "You know, the Arid tribes are still living out here? Yeah, and trying to shut down this stretch of road. They claim it was illegally built over sacred grounds."

I frown. The fountain of random facts Ness has been spitting out is becoming a kaleidoscope of mashed-up nonsense in my brain. "Arid tribes?"

Ness shrugs. "Yeah, they're like the Magia. A failed experiment of the Seraphinus according to written history, although they claim direct descent from the Ancients themselves in the oral traditions of their tribes."

"I don't remember that from school." I spread my legs and bend over at the waist, reaching my ankles.

Ness stands and paces. "They were the first attempt at making the Magia. Supposedly." She holds her hands up and forms quotation marks with her fingers. "Texts are limited and or vague at best. But come on, we know some Seraphinus now. They aren't the infallible gods they want us to believe they are. You think they didn't fail at making us what we are at least once?"

I lean into a half-split, lifting my eyebrows. "You read way too much."

"Reading is one of the best things in life, following only after sex, pizza, tacos, and warm blankets. Scratch blankets, that's a necessary part of reading, so redundant to list."

Tipping my head back, I force a smile at the suns beating down on us. I close my eyes, inhaling the warm air, soaking in the rays of light. It lifts my spirits. "All right," I say with a sigh.

"Let's move before this Arid tribe gets pissy about us being here or someone comes by."

Ness moves to the car. "I only have two more pages, and then the codex is translated, so I can..." She stops, staring at me across the car. "Fuck."

"What?" I blink at her, squinting with confusion.

"I mean, they're dead. Cal and Mass. I can't give them the translations." We stare at each other. Ness drops her gaze. "I think that just...finally, like, really, truly registered." Her shoulders slump, and she opens the car door and gets in.

Following suit, I slide behind the wheel and grip it tightly, my knuckles going white.

Time ticks by, heat pooling in the car until sweat beads up along my spine. Together, we sit in the car, staring out the windshield, not moving or speaking.

Cal and Massimo are dead. For a brief shining moment, I have clarity of piercing pain through my heart, and then it hazes over again, the ache settling to a throb.

The mechanics whir to life as I start the vehicle. "How far until Izul?"

Ness sighs and runs her fingers over the book. "Maybe tonight, if I remember my maps? Should be today. We're driving from the edge of the plains to the coast of the Shining Sea, and Izul sits on the coast. Its neighboring city is Castler. Can we stop there for a real dinner? I miss food."

I bob my head. "Yeah, sure, babe. Whatever you want."

"Yeah, so we're on the right track. We'll be there tonight, thank fucking Mother for that. I'm ready for a bed. Cal's place had the best beds."

My head keeps bobbing lifelessly and mechanically from momentum alone. "Cal was the best for anything bed-related."

"At least you finally got to sit on a face, and it had been a great face to sit on."

"So good." My body does an involuntary little shiver at the memory. "You know what I'm sad about?"

"Everything?"

I burst into laughter. "Well, yes, actually."

Ness snickers. "What are you sad about?"

"I don't even have a picture."

"Of?"

"Of anything. Nothing about him." I set the auto-drive regulator and rest back in my seat. "I have zero anything of Cal."

Ness flicks my forearm with Cal's contract. "You've got that, and I've got this little note–" She lifts her notebook. "–in Mass's handwriting from one of the times he stopped by about a word I couldn't figure out. So, we've each got something to at least know they were real."

"Oh, good, we have evidence they existed. We didn't dream them up." I roll my eyes. "I was super worried about that."

"You know what, I'm trying to stay positive here."

"What's with you and Mass anyway?"

"Now? Nothing. He's dead."

I snicker. "Let the irreverence begin. I guess that's the end of the mourning period. But, really, you and him?"

"Yes, an intelligent smart ass with jokes, muscles that could cut through marble—might have been actually cut in marble–badass of a man, with skin I wanted to lick, and the best laugh I've ever heard. Yes, no idea where any of this is coming from," Ness says, flipping her hair and turning to face out the window. "Makes more sense than you and Cal did, Miss Don't Tell Me What To Do all goo-goo eyes for Mister You Will Obey Me."

Grimacing, I admit, "You have a point. He was big on the orders, wasn't he?"

"*Mhm.*"

I smile, but my eyes burn. "Every time I put my hand in his, I felt like I'd found home."

Ness shifts and leans over the center console, putting her head on my shoulder. "Yeah, and Mass gave me the taste of sugar." She's silent for a minute. "This shit blows. Where's the music?"

Reaching out, I crank the dial up to drown out the sadness.

CHAPTER 15

NATALIA

Izul is a shining beacon, a bubble of clear brilliance shimmering around it, the city itself glowing, gold buildings glittering.

Night stretches as dense, rolling green across the sky as I lean against the hood, staring at the city in the distance. Arms and legs crossed, I frown at it from the parking lot, staring with mistrust.

There's a tug in my chest, like an invisible thread is pulling me through the center of my torso toward the city. I drop my head on her shoulder. "What do you think, babe? Ready to go yet?"

"Give me another fraction. I can't shake this feeling that once we do this, we can't go back, and it isn't like when I knew it with Cal's contract. I knew there was no coming back from that, but I was ecstatic. I don't like it this time."

I snort through my nose. "Not quite how signing my contract went, but I know what you mean. I've got mixed feelings going on over here, too, but what else do you want to do?"

"Don't know." Ness lifts and drops her free shoulder. "Just, something's not right here. I can't explain it, but now that we're here, I don't want to go in."

Sitting up, I sigh. "It's just dragging feet. We don't want this because it's final. It means they're dead, and this makes that real."

"I don't want it to be real."

Pushing my hair out of my face, I puff up my cheeks. "I don't either, but we don't have a choice. We don't get to decide that they're alive and pretend like this isn't happening because it is."

Ness curls her lip and turns her head to the side toward the ocean in the distance. "Can't we just..." She closes her eyes and tips her head back. "Let's take a beat to breathe. We took off like crazy and haven't stopped to think this through, and I have this awful feeling I can't shake."

"Is that why you didn't eat much?" I shake my head. "If this isn't what you want to do, give me something else. I'll go with you, but we can't just stay here, and we can't go back. They're– There's nothing there for us other than Magia ready to kill us."

"You," Ness snaps. "They're going to kill you, not me. I'm expendable, inconsequential, useless. No one gives a shit about me."

I laugh. "A, I love you. B, you're not useless. You got me here. You did this," I say, pointing to the ground between my feet. "This was all you. All I did was show my tits as a distraction. You grabbed the keys, and you know I would have gotten lost."

She shrugs. "We, you and me, working together, both of us did something." Ness stands. "Let's sleep in the car, and if we still both agree this isn't right in the morning, we drive until we find somewhere we both feel is right. Deal?"

I face Izul, frowning at it. The pull draws through me,

getting stronger. It's a weird sense. I don't want to go, but I need to. "Deal."

Ness moves to get in the car, opening the passenger front door. "You can have the backseat." She slides in and closes the door.

I flip my middle finger at the City of Light and move to the car. I sit on the hood, staring it down. "I see you." I lift a brow. It looks like a capsulated city, almost like I'm holding a snow globe against the skyline.

After a while, I give up and get into the back of the vehicle. I shut the door, frowning at Ness. She's got that creepy book cracked open–the window down to help with the putrid smell. "That's becoming an obsession."

Ness bobs her head. "It might be. There's this word I can't figure out. Mass didn't know it either. It pops up only twice, and it's driving me nuts."

I lean between the front seats. "What's the word?"

"Sub-tork-shin? Tork-shun? Tork-jhun? Could be Sube in front. The root of it is tork, I got that, but like, super weird."

"What does tork mean?"

Ness spells it out. "T-o-r-c-q-u-e, which is Dark and not like a lack of light. It's, you know, how Mass and Cal are Dark." She flings a hand at the book. "Now torcue without the q is dark, like just lacking a light source, and torque without the c, I have no idea, and it's only like that twice when it's written as 'subtorque'."

"Maybe it's dark, but if removing the q is without a light source is without the c, maybe with a little bit of light? Think shadows?"

Ness screws up her face, cocking her head to the side and staring at the book. "Could be. Context use of the word isn't helpful. Leave it to the Seraphinus to come up with some bull-shit like that."

"And sube? Sub?"

"Eh." Ness winces. "And that's where this gets shitty drunk. Sub is a bastardized version of Sube. Sube is bad. It's all bad, and it's all through this codex. Cal didn't want me talking to you about this stuff, and I get that after working my way through this thing. This thing is like pure evil. It's alive, which is scary enough, but it's not alive in a good way either."

"Oh, good."

Ness laughs, turning to look at me. "I can finally tell you, it was part of my contract. He told me to not discuss any of this with you ever. To be fair, I requested the amendment that allowed me to be able to lie to you about this because I knew you'd ask," she shrugs, scowling at the book. "I wanted that contract."

"I'm aware. Cal and I discussed it." The memory of sitting beneath the hysterium with him smacks me in the face, and I try to force my mind elsewhere. "So, Sube?"

"Sube is— You know how we say pure evil? It's like pure evil meets psychopath with a dash of wicked afters thrown in for fun. It's the worst evil imaginable, and it's what makes the Dark, the torcque with the q, run scared."

I lift my eyebrows and shy away from the book with concern. "Sounds lovely."

Shrugging, Ness closes the codex, running her fingers over it. The scales seem to shudder at her touch, but not in a bad way. I cringe, but Ness just keeps stroking it. "I think the Sube is what was broken to make the codexes."

"So, the Sube isn't a description; it's a thing?"

Ness shifts, still running her fingertip over and around the scales. "From what I can pick up on in the translations, yes, the Sube is a thing. Depending on context, it's a noun or adjective, but it might also be the origins of the Dark. According to Cal, there's seven of these things, so I'm missing a lot."

"Oh, lovely. We're only carrying around a piece of the psychopathic pure evil thingy." I roll my eyes and set my chin on the top of the driver's seat, staring out the windshield.

"Whoa," Ness breathes. "Look at that."

"I see it."

There are three figures flying through the air toward us with wings of Light beating in long strokes. The book in Ness's lap starts clacking, like teeth chattering in the cold, a strange rapid click. We both turn to it.

Ness frowns. "What's wrong with you, you stupid thing?" She wraps her arms around it and lifts it, peering at it, then turns to me. "This is what it did when you put on that light show."

I glance at the Light Seraphinus looming closer. "It doesn't like the Light, babe. Light burns out Dark until it doesn't exist. If that thing is really alive and part of this Sube thing, it probably hates the Light, maybe even afraid of it."

"Right, right. Mass said that a lot." She shakes the book. "Shut up. It's fine. They'll fly over us and go away soon enough. I won't let them hurt you, m'kay?" She hugs it close.

I give her a revolted side-eye. "You've got the weirdest relationship with that book."

"It's like a pet." She flashes teeth without humor. "It's that confusing, smelly, old cat that hates everyone, and I adore it. It's been so much fun translating it."

The Seraphinus fly low overhead, and the book screeches. Black tendrils twist out of it, testing the air. I lean back. "Is it supposed to be doing that?"

Ness frowns. "How should I know?"

"It's your pet."

Ness holds it close, curling around it. "They're not going to hurt you, you stupid thing. It's fine."

The Seraphinus swoop back overhead toward Izul, but they

pull up and bank, one leading the two. "Uh…" I slip my torso between the seats, craning to see out the windshield. "I think they're coming right at us."

"Oh, yeah? What the…?" Ness's voice stops as she screams, her eyes rolling in the back of her head to pure white, but they fill with black darkness. The book shudders, chattering in high-pitched squealing.

I grab her shoulder, Light racing over my skin as the tendrils of black rush into Ness's chest. She convulses and moans, slipping lower and tipping into the door.

I reach for the book, wanting to fling it away from Ness. Black twists around my hand, strands twinging up my wrist. They pull back as I yank on the book in another futile attempt to get it away from Ness. The black strands pierce into my forearm, and the chatter exceeds the decibels I can hear, my ears ringing.

Pain lances through my arm like razor blades slicing through my skin as another couple of tendrils slip beneath my flesh, writhing like veins risen to the surface. I recoil from the book, gaping at the Dark wiggling and twisting around my forearm, bleeding up through my pores as ink through paper, solidifying as a double set of figure eights, a pair of twin lines that intersect and cross around my forearm.

The book slips to the floorboard with a rustle of pages, ash filling the air. Ness groans, slumping into the door with a heavy thump. My arm stings, but the lace of my Light is gone, along with the Dark tendrils. My panic ebbs as Ness's breath fogs up a patch of the window.

I wrap my hand around my burning arm as the Seraphinus land in front of the vehicle. "Ness?" My stomach knots, that sense in my chest building to extreme pressure, threatening to crush my ability to draw air. I hiss, "Ness!"

The Seraphinus wings disappear, all three of them

standing tall. I reach out to shake Ness. "Babe?" I crane forward, staring at the book. It's still and quiet, the scales curled like dead spiders. "What the fuck did you do?"

The Seraphinus peer through the windshield, the front runner turning to speak to the two at his back.

"Ness," I yell.

She stirs and moans.

"Oh, thank the Mother. Ness, talk to me."

"Ow." She shudders, blinking and sitting up. "Fuck."

One of the Seraphinus leans over, hands on the hood, checking inside, but the other two are missing. The door next to me opens, a hand reaching in. I lean over to the passenger side, kicking at it.

Both passenger side doors open, and I spill backward out of the vehicle. I go with momentum, doing a back roll and popping to my feet.

Ness spills to the concrete in a heap, muttering. One of the Seraphinus reaches for her.

Centering, I step into an open palm strike, Light flashing. "Fuck off."

The Seraphinus sprawls sideways, letting go of Ness.

The one across the car yells, "Natalia, stop!"

I hesitate in shock at hearing my name. Pivoting, I glare at the head floating over the roof of the car. He's male with pale skin and golden hair. His hair is pulled back from his square face, his chin pointed, and his lips thin.

I gape at Pierre Bordeaux. "What the fuck are you doing here?"

He closes the car door and walks around the back of the vehicle toward me, taller than average with broad shoulders in a cream shirt. "Natalia." He lifts his hands in a defensive position, stopping a few paces from me. "Please, do not. Do not run. Do not fight. There is no cause for you to panic. I am not here to hurt you. Quite the opposite."

I flick my gaze to Ness as she pulls herself to her feet using the open car door. "And the other two?"

He drops his hands onto his hips. "They are my vassals and will do nothing without my permission. Natalia." He stops. "My apologies. You prefer Tallie, yes?"

"Whatever."

He scans the horizon toward Izul. "Let us bring you to Izul, where we will be safe. I will explain everything to you."

I turn to Ness, who's staring into the distance, eyes out of focus and glazed over, features lax. "Ness?"

Ness starts and blinks, turning to me. Rubbing the center of her chest between her breasts, she asks, "Yeah?" She drops her hand and grimaces.

"Izul was the plan, but we had a deal."

"It's not like we have a better option with Mass and Cal dead and the Magia hunting us."

Pierre takes a step closer but stops as I glare at him. I lift my hand, letting my wrist go limp as I flick my fingers at him. "Back the fuck up again, asshole. I came here to seek refuge, but I'm not about to blindly trust you."

He frowns, then shakes his head at the ground, smiling. "He didn't tell you."

"Who didn't tell me what?"

"Callahan." Pierre lifts his blank white eyes to mine. "You are my offspring, the result of a relationship I shared with your mother years ago."

I stare with horror. "What did you just say to me?"

"I am your father. You are my daughter. You are a continuation of my heritage. You are a seed of my Light." He gives me a tight-lipped smile. "I am not sure how many other ways I can say it."

I tip my head back as laughter boils out of my chest. I clutch my stomach with one hand and lean forward, hysterical. "No, you aren't." I dissolve into further giggles. "That's the most ridiculous thing I've ever heard."

Pierre watches me with irritation. "As amusing as you seem to find this, it is true. Your mother had an affair with me."

"No." I shake my head, still chortling. "No way. Mom would *never*."

Pierre gives me a half smile. "She most certainly did. Although I would like to think my charms had something to do with compelling her to the act."

I cock my jaw. "Bullshit. There's no way. No fucking way."

He lifts his eyebrows, but his eyes are dancing with humor. "You seem to be struggling to accept this. I understand. I was shocked as well, but the fact remains your mother did have an affair with me, and you are a result of our actions."

Throwing my hands up, I shake my head. "No. Just no. There's no way I believe you. My mother is a follow-the-rules-to-the-letter kind of person. She doesn't allow shortcuts or bending of the rules, and definitely not straight up breaking rules, like cheating."

"She's opinionated and strong-headed, too." Pierre chuckles. "Very independent, loves rice wine, sugar-coated grapes, and never dare give her an answer to a word puzzle she's working on if you value your life."

That sounds like my mother. I glance at Ness, who's drooping against the car door, eyes closed. That book did something to her, to both of us, although Ness got the worst of whatever it was. It's uncharacteristic for her to be silent, especially about something like an affair and development in my parentage.

Pierre takes a step forward. "I felt your magic, my own in you, calling out, bringing me to you," he says, taking another step closer. "It's how I found you here. It's how I know you are my offspring. Come to Izul. Let me teach you. I can help you understand the Light and show you where you belong in the world."

"You said 'calling out.' Is that like a pull?"

Pierre lifts his eyebrows again. "You can feel it?" He tilts his head. "Yes, that's the call of like. We refer to it as *similis*."

"Am I not supposed to?"

He shrugs. "You're a Seraphim, not Seraphinus, because of your mother's bloodline. I knew you were strong, stronger than any other Seraphim I've encountered with the way you withstood my smite, but that surprises me."

"You're a fucking asshole for that. That could have hurt Cal."

Pierre chuckles. "That was the intention. I wanted to free you from him to bring you home." He waves a hand at Izul. "I had every right to do so under the authority of the Council."

Home. I almost laugh at the use of his word. I am so far from my home. Cal was ragged and sharp. He'd make me bleed, but he was honest and safe.

"You don't get to hurt him. I told you no. I told you I was fine where I was." I throw my hands up, scowling at the sky. "Moot point now."

"And now?" Pierre asks with an open face. "Will you come to Izul, where you belong?"

I suck in a deep breath as I fixate on Cal's contract. My home is gone, and no matter where I am or where I go, it will never be home. I see no other option. My best chances will be in Izul, and Izul can act as a shield against the Magia for me and Ness.

Gripping my hands into fists, I exhale, deflating. "Yes, on one condition." I point at Ness. "She comes to, and I still don't like you or trust you, got it?"

Pierre smiles. "That is two, but I will accept both for the current moment at hand. We do not know each other, but I would like to get acquainted. You are my child, after all." He motions the others forward. "Owen, please carry the other. Zan, you will take my daughter. I will follow. If there are any attacks, I will deal with them."

I scoff. "Magia don't have wings. Once we're off the ground, there's zero worry."

The Seraphinus stepping toward me chuckles. "The Magia aren't the concern."

"Callahan is dead," Pierre says, holding a hand up. "While there is little concern from the Magia, I am not one to take chances."

"Yes, sir," the man responds. "Tallie, if you'll take my hand?"

Warily, I turn to face him. "Sure." I drag the word out and then lift my gaze to his lean, slender torso, reaching higher to his face, having to lift my chin to meet his eyes.

Recognition flares within me at the man's long face with a prominent brow and straight, flared nose. He grins, his full lips pulling back. "Hi, Tallie."

I splutter, squeaking out his name. "Zan?" I open my mouth in shock. "*Zander?*"

His grin grows wider as he reaches up to run his finger around his ear, pushing a stray piece of his blond hair from the braided crown behind it. "Hi, Tallie."

Pierre asks, "Do you two know each other?"

Zander chuckles, his fair skin staining pink over his cheekbones. "Yes, we have met once before. Your hand, please, love." He extends his to me.

I gape at him, having never expected to see him again after the wild moment we shared. I'd been caught by a riptide, pulled out to sea and struggling to keep my head above water.

125

I'd flailed, believing that it would be the last moments of my life until Zander pulled me from the ocean.

Pierre asks, "How do you know each other?"

Winking at me, Zander speaks to Pierre. "She was getting dragged away from the shore by a tide, and I couldn't help myself. A beautiful woman like her needed to live."

He doesn't mention the activities that followed, which suits me. I don't care to share Zander flying me to a nearby island off the coast and that I'd used him sexually in a moment of reckless abandon. I hadn't cared that he was a Seraphinus. He was handsome and fit, and I didn't want to waste an opportunity to be rid of my virginity.

I nod. "Yup, he saved me from drowning."

Pierre gives us a hard look, then shakes his head. "I sincerely appreciate your efforts, Zan. I'll have to find a way to reward you for saving her."

There's a groan and a thump. I twist around to find Ness on the ground.

Owen kneels, scooping her into his arms. "You're okay, little one. We'll get you somewhere safe."

I lean into the car. "I'll grab our things."

I collect the book while trying to hide it from sight as I shove it into the backpack. An instinct warns me that the Light shouldn't see the codex, or maybe it's because it was Cal's wish.

Slinging the pack over one shoulder, I face Zander at Pierre's side. "Okay, I'm ready."

"Very good." Pierre nods, checking our surroundings again. "I would like to return home before any incidents occur."

Zander steps over and scoops me into his arms. His wings spread, golden illumination brightening the world as he lifts off the ground. I cradle the backpack against my stomach, turning my face against his shoulder to avoid the rush of wind.

He glides through the air. "Are you okay?"

"It's fine. I can handle the wind."

He chuckles. "I know you can handle this. We've done it before. I'm asking you, are you okay?"

"Oh," I frown.

"The Dark is brutal. Callahan binding you in contract and forcing you into servitude is unfathomable. I heard you were at their contender games. Call me old-fashioned, but we've been intimate, and I want to make sure you're all right."

"That's..." I snort through my nose. "Why do you call them games? Games are fun. Those aren't fun, and they're deadly."

Zander laughs. "You'll have to tell me about them. I've only heard rumors."

When he asked, I thought he was asking about the loss of Callahan. I thought he cared about how I'm coping, about how I'm feeling. Dejection settles in my stomach like acid.

He dips side to side, rocking me. "How have you been? I haven't seen you in a while."

"While? Like..." I roll my eyes to the top of my head. "What, eight years?"

He shifts me in his grip. "At least you're dry this time."

"Still needing to be saved, apparently." I sigh. "Like a twat."

"Love, you're not– I'm not even repeating that word. You're fine, and considering what you're up against, it makes sense you could use some help."

"I'm running from the Magia." I sigh. "To be fair, it's more that there are so many of them and only one of me."

He snickers. "I saw the news. You'll love Izul."

The city looms closer, and I chew on my lip. I had loved Cal's house. It was sleek and beautiful. It's where Cal stretched me out, broke down the wall in my head, and where I gave up all of myself to him.

I clear my throat. There is no going back. I'd have to rebuild the wall and move on. "It looks great."

CHAPTER 16
NATALIA

We land on a small balcony attached to a shimmering gold tower. As Zander sets me on my feet, I crane to see the ground below. Vertigo sets in as I move away from the banister and further onto solid ground. "Where are we?"

"Home," he answers, opening the glass door by pushing it inward. "If you please?" He ushers me through and into an illuminated white hallway. Light leaks from the seams of the walls, where they connect to the floor and ceiling in a brilliant, golden glow.

I walk at Zander's side, Owen carrying Ness at his other. He strides down a hall, gesturing to the left at a crossway. "This way, please."

Bobbing my head, I glance at a small statue on a pedal stool. "What is this place?"

Reaching forward, he turns the gold knob with a fancy framework, opening the door for me. "In here, love." He gestures inside. "This can be your room for the evening. Pierre will make alternative arrangements in the morning."

I glance at the interior, rub my eyes, and inspect it again, but it hasn't changed. I sigh at the white, gold, and gilded wood color palate. Everything is bright, the room illuminated from around the seam of the ceiling and walls.

Squeezing one hand into a fist, I press it against my other to crack my knuckles. "Any chance you have a room that's dark blue or shades of gray, maybe just not so white?"

A smile plays on his lips, his eyebrows pushing together above his flared nose. "You've been without illumination far too long."

"So, is that a no on the less...?" I gesture inside the room.

"There is nothing in Izul like you describe. It's not befitting nor beneficial for the Light within us. You should get some rest. You'll feel better in the morning." He turns to Owen. "We'll set her in here with you for the evening."

"I'm good sharing a room with her."

"This entire floor is property of the Bordeaux heritage. There are enough rooms that you do not have to share."

"Don't care."

"You'll want your own space after you get a good night's rest."

"I don't know what I want, and I'm not trusting you."

Zander rocks back on his heels and crosses his arms, frowning at the floor. "Tallie, while you may not know or trust Pierre, I have given you every reason to trust me to this point. I saved your life without knowing you. I didn't search for you as you requested, although I did want to, and I didn't hurt you. I'd like to think I even gave you pleasure. If no one else, trust me."

Shifting my weight, I talk to the ceiling. "I appreciate that, all of that. But I– My world has just imploded. My head's spinning, and Ness is my rock."

"I understand." He lifts a hand, motioning with two fingers at Owen to come.

He shoulders between Zander and me, moving to lay Ness

on the bed. He turns, nods at Zander, and leaves. I blink at him, receding down the hall and turn back to Zander.

He inclines his head. "Sleep well."

As he turns, I say, "Zander?"

Facing me, he lifts his eyebrows. "Yes, Tallie?"

I wince. "Did you... I mean... You... Is this a coincidence?"

He laughs. "A happy one, I hope, but yes. When I met you, I had no knowledge of your heritage."

"Oh." My brain goes numb from overload.

"Is there anything you need?"

I laugh, but it rings hollow. "Can you bring Cal back?"

He tenses, inhaling through his nose. "Even if I could snap my fingers and bring Callahan to life before your eyes, I wouldn't." His lips pull tight in a grimace. "I cannot begin to fathom the extent of damages wrought on you for you to even wish such a thing, but you're all right now. The Dark and the Magia will not be able to reach you here, and Pierre will do anything to protect you. Trust in that. Trust in me, and the rest will come."

Bobbing my head, I kick at the floor and cross my arms. "Sure."

He bobs his head, the tense posture relaxing. "Tomorrow, I shall fetch you in the morning. If Pierre allows it, I'll show you around, and perhaps you will allow me to take you to dinner now?"

"I will need to eat, and I guess there are no rules about that anymore. Well, not Magia's rules anyway." I glance at myself, "I'm going to need clothes."

"Pierre can help with that. Anything else?"

"Not right now."

Zander gives me a nudge into the room. "Then in you go. Rest. Be at ease. But Tallie?" I meet his gaze. "Please don't leave this room until I come to fetch you. You'll get lost, and it is a very big city. I could spend days trying to find you again." He shuts the door with a soft click.

I frown at the door and then trudge to the bed, dragging my sneakers across the marble in fatigue.

Ness cracks one eye at me and then opens the other as she sits upright. "Are they gone?"

I nod, sit on the edge of the bed and pull the backpack off my shoulder to toss it to her. "I grabbed your smelly cat even though it bit us."

"Oh, good," Ness says, tossing the pack to the floor. "What the fuck did that thing do to me?"

I stick my arm toward her. "You mean, what did that fucked thing do to *us*?"

She grasps my wrist, her brown skin stark against my pale skin as her fingers close around me. "The fuck is that?"

We both stare at the thin black lines twisting around my forearm. "Yeah." I drag the word out and pull free of her grip. "Did that book say something about this is how to let the terrible evil out?"

Ness grimaces and checks her arms. "No."

"It really should have come with a warning label." I curl into a ball, hugging my knees to my chest. "Well, we're in Izul."

"Yeah, and it's fucking bright. I kept my eyes closed this whole time 'cause it's so cursedly bright, like squinting at the sun." She gets off the bed. "I need a shower. I feel gross."

"You go." I shrug. "I'll go after."

Ness heads into the bathroom and closes the door. A fraction later, she shrieks. I'm on my feet as the door bursts open, Ness in the doorway with an angry glare and no shirt, her finger pointing at her chest. "What the fuck is this?"

I blink and then jut my head forward, my lip curling in disgust. "What is that?"

132

"I don't know. That's what I'm asking you. My dad said he'd kill me if I ever got a tattoo that wasn't my marks."

Sliding off the bed, I move to her for a closer look. There are small runes in black from mid-chest running down to the top of her abs. Lines swirl out along her ribs in elongated, mirroring, thin, swirling lines.

I glance at my forearm and then back to Ness. "Uh...? Any idea what that says? Looks like the writing in the book."

"No freaking clue," Ness says, shoving her fingers into her long black hair, pushing the strands back. "Oh fucking Mother! What did we just do? Did we set the Sube free?"

"*We?*" I move my finger between us with hard eyes and pursed lips. "We didn't do anything. That stupid smelly cat did this all on its own."

"Yeah, but, like, babe," she whines, "we brought it to Izul."

"No, it didn't even make it to Izul. It freaked out near Izul and the Lighters."

Ness throws her hands up. "Nope. I am going to say no to all of this, whatever it is." She slashes at the air in front of her, crossing her arms. "Just no. I'm going to shower, and I'm going to sleep, and tomorrow..."

We stare at each other in silence. My ears ring as she turns around, using her foot to close the door, leaving me to wonder about what we do tomorrow.

CHAPTER 17
NATALIA
EIGHTH NIGHT'S DAY, WARMWAVE 4049 6TH MILLENNIUM

Knocking rouses me from nothingness, a steady pulse of knuckles against wood beckoning me to answer. With a groan, I throw the sheets away from me, detangling my legs to walk toward the summons as I rub one side of my face. Answering the door, I leer at Zander.

His golden hair is pulled back, one half of his crown in a braid, loose wisps hanging in front of his ear on the other side. I yawn, considering his plain white shirt, the front hem tucked into his fitted khaki pants.

"Why the fuck are you all so pretty and perfect?" I lean against the door for support, unsure of the day, the time, or where I am. A cocoon spins tighter around me as I try to recall small details.

Zander's smile widens, crinkling the corners of his eyes though his lips remain closed. He leans against the doorframe. "You think I'm beautiful?"

"Pretty. I said pretty, didn't I?"

Looking to the floor, his lips part as he grins, a pink haze touching his cheeks. Clearing his throat, he meets my gaze. His

134

eyes are full white, narrow set against his nose. My heart sinks as I stare back, longing for black instead, for shadows and tan skin. Instead, all I have is Zander, his pale skin stretching over high cheekbones and an angular jaw.

"Cal is dead. I'm in Izul."

"Yes," he says in a quiet voice, leaning toward me further into the doorway with his shoulder pressed against the jamb. Golden wood and white walls are perfect consonance to the man before me. "You're in Izul, the heart of the Light, where you belong."

Everything in me wants to scream I belong in Narwal, in Cal's bed, wrapped up in his Dark. All I can manage is a defeated whispered, "Debatable."

"I know it's early, but I'm required to bring you to Pierre's office."

"I need clothes."

Zander scrunches his nose. "Pierre is going to address those concerns along with all the others." Pulling upright, he says, "I am to escort you and her." He sticks his head through the doorway, looking toward the bed.

"Ness."

"Ness," he repeats, inclining his head. "Don't fret about appearances. Pierre is aware of your situation and will not hold your dishevelment in regards given those circumstances."

Yawning, I narrow my eyes and cover my mouth with a hand. Shaking myself away, I turn toward the bed, stepping closer to wake Ness. "Babe?" I shake her by the shoulder.

She twists to her back, slapping me away and mumbling. "Too early."

I yank the covers back, exposing her to the cool air. "Wakey, wakey, Nessy."

With a groan, her big brown eyes open, and she lifts a hand over them. "Fuck this bright crap. Turn the lights off and let me wake up like a human." She sits, glaring at me, her long black hair matted to her scalp. "Gross."

I motion to Zander. "We've been summoned."

"We need food."

Zander steps into the room, to my side. "All of your concerns will be answered once I take you to Pierre."

I glance at him. "Does he have food?"

"Please, ladies." He fades toward the door with a faux grin plastered to his face. "Pierre will see to everything, but first, I need to get you to him." He uses both hands to motion out.

I look to Ness. She glares at me. Slapping the mattress, she plants a hand and hoists herself over the edge and to her feet. "Lead on, you weirdly tall, beautiful thing."

Zander lowers his gaze. "Ladies, you will need shoes. We do not walk around barefoot."

ZANDER LEADS US DOWN HALLWAYS, straight passages with perpendicular corridors intersecting white-marbled walls with golden veins and dust. Everything is bright and harsh glares no matter where I divert my eyes in search of relief.

Zander stops in front of a door, tapping his knuckles against the surface three times. In the silence, I glance at Ness. She shrugs, looking around us. I'm assuming she's more intrigued by the artifacts and paintings on the walls than what lies on the other side of the door.

A voice wafts through the door. "You may enter."

Zander presses down on the latch release above the sloping curve and pushes. The door swings inward.

He turns to me with a bow. "Tallie, you'll enter first. I will follow, then Ness...darling... Ness?"

She whips her head toward him. "That's my name."

"Yes, pay attention. To do otherwise causes another to use more breath to speak, repeating themselves and steals time from the one you are ignoring. It is selfish and disrespectful."

I let my head fall to the side, glaring from the tops of my eyes. "Calm down, she's not being disrespectful. She's fascinated by the stuff you have sitting around here."

Ness cocks a hip and crosses her arms. "True, but I don't need you to speak for me either."

Pierre stands in the doorway, clearing his throat.

We all turn toward him, but Zander ducks his head. "My apologies, sir."

"The fault lies not with you." Pierre inhales, torso lifting as he runs a hand down his center, following the buttons of his shirt to his belt. He motions me forward with two fingers. "Welcome and be welcomed."

He steps aside for me to move into the room. I keep my eyes low as I enter, lifting my head once he's behind me to inspect the area. There's a door in the far-left corner, a desk offset in the center of the room yet closer to the back wall, and the only notable items are on the walls. A gold sword is showcased so that it's above whoever sits behind the desk. Several other smaller daggers are positioned in a pattern of decoration on the right wall.

The door closes with a soft snap. Ness steps to my side, head turned away from me to the right wall where a massive fan is splayed open on display and tacked to the wall.

Pierre moves toward the desk, lowering to the floor to sit on the other side, lifting his chin to meet my eyes as he motions with an open hand, palm up to indicate the space before him. "Please sit."

I nudge Ness, then move, cross my legs, and drop to the floor in front of him on an available white cushion. I expected stiff and scratchy, but if I ever could sit on a cloud, this would be the feeling. Ness drops next to me on the left. Pierre's lips twitch and drop at the corners, then Zander kneels, bows his head at Pierre, and sits back on his heels.

I look between the men. Zander is stiff, straight-backed, and his shoulders squared, his hands resting on his thighs.

Pierre's eyes widen and relax. He nods to Zander, then smiles at me. "Tallie, welcome and be welcomed. This is my personal productive room where I meet for the intentions of conducting formal business and attending to matters of duty."

"You can just say office."

His thin lips twitch. "I realize our ways and conducts will seem strange to you, altogether foreign and unknown for a while. However, that will be remedied."

"Sure."

His ears pull back, his face tightening. "Daughter mine, you are the Light, but you were not raised in our society, falling prey to the Dark. You have forgone mannerisms of our character, even acquiring revolting habits of disrespect and impropriety."

I roll my eyes.

"You have much to learn about who you are and our ways. For you to have a home here, you will need to adhere to our customs and show respect when it is due. I expect you will embrace your true nature in time as you accept what you truly are."

"What's that?"

"The Light, honey." He tries to smile, but it's a pained expression. "You are the Light. You carry within you a seed of the Bordeaux heritage. We are a prestigious heritage, and we strive to bring honor to our heritage in every way, paying respect to those who came before us and those who will follow us."

Cutting my eyes to Ness, I try not to laugh. "Right."

Pierre looks upward to the ceiling, tipping back his head. His blond hair is pinned back from his face, the bottom strands still loose about his shoulders, impossibly straight aside from several thin braids adorned with cylindrical gold beads. They glint as he lowers his chin, meeting my eyes.

He's preparing to speak again when Ness asks, "What is that?" She's pointing at the fan.

Pierre shakes his head. "My daughter and I are having a conversation. Do not interrupt. Tallie, I understand that from the moment you were born, you had begun a journey far from your proper home. I was unaware of your existence, and the fault is mine that you were raised outside of our customs. I will not pretend as if I can erase the damage wrought by this fact, but I will request your willingness to *try*. Please, honey, try to learn our ways, beginning with respectful mind, actions, and attitudes."

"Dude—"

Zander chokes, lowering his face toward the floor and clearing his throat of a chuckle. His lips are turned up on the sides, I can see, and his features are struggling to maintain composure.

Pierre says, "'*Dude*' is an unacceptable address of your elders, young lady. I do not require 'sir' from you as you are my heritage, but perhaps you can try the use of 'father.'"

"Yeah, that's not going to happen, but fine. Look, uh... Pierre, I'm not sure what you're going for by calling me damaged goods, but it's not the best start."

"Our ways are linked to the very thing that we are. For you to disregard basic respect is to spit upon your heritage."

"I'm not being disrespectful. You and I just have different definitions of the word." I shrug. "Is there food anywhere?"

"You have captured my point with precision. For you to have been left outside of the Light with the Magia and then coerced into the Dark—"

"Not coerced at all."

He frowns. "Please allow another to finish speaking prior to beginning your remarks. Interruption is rude." He flexes his hands and rests them against the desk. "As I was saying, our definitions are unaligned due to your upbringing. You were not raised as the Light but as something else and then subjected to the vulgar ways of the Dark that have instilled in you an ideology that is incompatible with the very thing we are–the Light. You are going to have to unlearn in order to progress."

I stare at him. "Fine."

He inclines his head. "Very good." He leans away and slides out a drawer under the center of the desk. He places two phones on the glittering, pale wood surface. "I understand you shared a room with Vanessa last evening when you arrived in Izul, but you are to have your own rooms. Vanessa will be across the hall. I have made all the arrangements. You are mature women who will need your own spaces." He picks up one phone, offering it to me in both hands. "These will be for you to communicate at your convenience. They will send written communications at your leisure."

I pick it up, tapping the center button at the bottom to bring the screen on, realizing it's only a touch past Dawn's rune. A wish to know Cal's number forms in my chest, but even if I called him, he wouldn't answer. There's no way to talk to those in the afters. I push the button, turning the screen off as Pierre extends the second to Vanessa.

He says, "Vanessa, as any vassal, you will be given a stipend. Your device is linked to the account your stipend will be transferred into, and you can view the balance at your discretion. I've deposited your first payment already."

"Ness isn't a vassal. She's my friend."

"She may not be beholden to a contract, but for her existence within this city, she will hold the position and stature of a vassal. She is no heritage of mine, so she will either accept her role, or she will have no place in Izul."

"That's bullshit."

"That is generous," he snaps, his voice hardening, "considering she is not even the Light. She is human, and humans are not often allowed within this city."

Ness leans into me. "It's fine, babe. I was a vassal for Cal, and at least this time, I'm your vassal," she looks to Pierre as she shifts upright. "Right? I'm *her* vassal?"

Pierre inclines his head. "I will allow you to be my daughter's vassal as long as you adhere to your station. Should you decide to act above your position or with disrespect, you will no longer be qualified to be in her employment, and I will have you removed from Izul."

Bristling, I grip the phone in my hand and say, "If you throw Ness out, I go with her."

"No. I will not allow that, given the risk to your life. You are my daughter, my heritage, and I will act to protect you in any manner I see fit, up to and including protecting you from your own stupidity."

I stare at him, opening my mouth in shock. Closing it, I glare at the ceiling. "Are you even allowed to call someone stupid? Isn't that disrespectful?"

"Acknowledging truth is difficult at times but does not negate my right to state facts," he says. "Tallie, your device is linked to my accounts directly. As my heritage, you have full access to my accounts for your use. Neither of your devices possesses access to the connection lines. This is to prevent contact with the outside world intentionally, and continuing on the topic of your safety, you'll notice your devices also have a tracking application installed should I need to locate you. I will not tolerate any attempts to circumvent either of these precautions I have set in place, nor contact with anyone outside of this city."

I gape, a pit of rage developing in my stomach.

"Furthermore, until I decide, you will not be at leisure to roam Izul on your own. You both will require a chaperone to leave the Bordeaux level of this tower at any point for any reason. Should you attempt to leave this city, I will interfere, and you will be confined within this tower until I decide you are permitted to leave once more. Do you understand me?"

"Oh," I drawl, rage mounting. "I understand. We're prisoners."

He holds my gaze, blinks, and looks away. "Daughter mine," he says under his breath and shakes his head. When he meets my eyes once more, he's smiling. "Your very life is in danger from those beyond the walls of this city. I will not accept contact with the outside world for fear of risking exposing you to that threat in any capacity. For now, you are here in Izul, leaving the Magia none the wiser of your location. For me to incite their attempts to attack this city, regardless of their capabilities–a nuisance they will be–I will be held accountable to the Light for bringing them here."

I can almost hear Cal telling me that hiding is an act of cowardice against the Dark's honor code. Dropping my chin to my chest, I stare at the phone. "Anything else?"

"Your seed is at risk, so young and still developing. It will require being near the heart of Light to grow into its full capacity. For you to leave this city will bring ruin to it, so any attempts to leave will be considered an attack against yourself and against this heritage, and I will respond in accordance." He sighs. "Tallie, honey, I'm acting in your best interests. Please don't fight me."

I want to. I want to scream as loud as I can for as long as I can until my lungs bleed. I want to punch and kick and break something a thousand times over until my body is too weak to comply. I want to run and run–straight into Cal's arms and be wrapped up in his Dark and his strength.

Blinking stinging eyes, I swallow the lump in my throat, clearing it away as I bob my head in compliance. What I want and what I need to do are two separate things. I need to be smart. I need to do what's safe, and I need to ensure Ness is safe as well. I can't fight a war against the Magia on my own.

Shifting, I tell him, "Best I can say is I'll try. I won't make you any promises."

"A very good first step, honey." He smiles, then adjusts his focus to Zander, motioning at him with his hand. "I'm aware you two have met, but it pleases me to introduce you properly. Tallie, honey, this is Zander Fairly."

Zander picks his head up and winks at me. "Hello, Tallie. It's a pleasure to formally meet you."

I look from him to Pierre, back to him, then tell Pierre, "Yeah, this charade is so not necessary. We know each other."

Pierre sighs. "Zander was my ward for a long time and has transitioned into one of my best and most favored vassals. He comes from a good heritage, one that is strong and highly regarded within the Light. I approve of him. Therefore, I will grant him the task of being your chaperone and guide to learning our ways." He lifts his voice. "Owen?"

A muffled response comes from behind the door. "Yes, sir."

"You may enter."

I turn my chin over my shoulder to eye the man entering. He bows at the waist, his black hair cut shorter and glinting in the ever-constant and weirdly without a source illumination around us, then straightens and closes the door.

Pierre says, "This young lady is my daughter, Natalia, but she prefers to go by Tallie. Tallie, this is Owen, a vassal of mine who is rather brilliant and resourceful."

Owen bows again. "It's a pleasure to make your acquaintance, Miss Tallie."

I lick my lips. "Um, thanks."

"The other is Vanessa. Vanessa, this is Owen. I have decided he will be best suited to being your chaperone and introducing you to the ways of the Light. Owen, please meet Vanessa."

Ness twists, waving at him. "Hi. It's Ness. The only one who calls me Vanessa is my mom, and she only does that when I've irritated her. Well, really, that's like all the time, though."

I bite my tongue against remarking that Cal called her Vanessa. I need to let go of him and the memories. Holding on to them–to him–trying to keep him alive in my mind is only going to hurt worse.

Owen inclines his head. "It's a pleasure to make your acquaintance, Ness."

"Zan, please take my daughter to get clothes and food. I expect you to ensure she is presentable and prepared as much as possible before Evergreen."

Offering his hands to me, Zander twists toward me. "Tallie, love."

I stare at them.

His fingers wiggle, a smile to his voice. "I won't hurt you."

"That was never my concern." I glance at Cal's contract in my arm.

'Take my hand when I offer it.'

It took fractions for me to break that rule after I'd signed the new contract. I'd give anything for it to be warning me of contempt for delaying the obvious gesture Zander is making.

With a sigh, I smack my palms to Zander's and his fingers close. He rises, drawing me to my feet. I tip my head back, blinking up at him. "I seriously forgot how damn tall you are." I drop his hands.

He chuckles. "I'm shorter than my father was." He jerks his head at the door. "Shall we?"

I look at Ness. She lifts and drops one shoulder.

Pierre says, "Go with Zan, Tallie. He will see to your needs. I'll speak with Owen and Ness regarding expectations and precedent."

Zander says, "She'll be fine. She's in excellent company." He opens the door, waving me through.

I step into the hallway, giving Ness one last glance before I turn my back on her. Holding the phone up, I wiggle it over my shoulder. "If you need me, babe."

Zander yanks the door shut and heads down the hall. I frown at his back. The image of a man in black slacks and a dark gray shirt materializes before me, overlaying Zander. He's shorter by half a head with broader shoulders and a hint of grumpy to his stride.

I breathe out slowly, following Zander into the hallway. Letting go of Cal is going to be difficult, and now he's appearing to me as a ghost. I can't blame him. If I had been the one to die, I would have found a way out of the afters to haunt him.

CHAPTER 18
NATALIA

Zander stops and waits for me to catch up, then puts his hand on my lower back to guide me along. He slows his pace as we approach a row of gilded double doors. "There's a lot I need to cover, so I'm going to go quick. If you have questions, please ask immediately." Zander draws us in front of a set of double doors. "This is the flight shaft. There are stairs through that door at the end." He extends two fingers in its direction.

I frown at the intricately decorated metal doors. "I don't have wings."

"No, love." He chuckles, smacking the button next to a set of doors. The doors slide open to reveal emptiness. "I do, though."

He shrugs and turns, stepping into the shoot, where wings of Light spread from his shoulders to keep him hovering in midair. He winks, extending his hand. He seems to glow, his wings vibrant against shadows inside the empty air.

I gape, leaning into the empty square shaft, my fingers curling around the edge of the open door as I close my eyes and inhale. The air is cool and damp, a breath of life against my face. The cool, crisp air brushes against my face, and for one brief fraction of a rune, I'm in Cal's company, his Dark brushing against my cheeks in a calming caress.

The moment breaks when fingers wrap around my wrist. "Come on, love. We've got a lot to go over and do before Evergreen."

He scoops me into his arms, hoisting me in his grasp. I slide my arm around his neck, meeting his eyes. Pure white, a barely discernible silver ring in the middle, the opposite of Cal's full black eyes.

Zander smiles. "Are you all right, love?"

"Yup. What happens at Evergreen?"

"Very good. Pierre has arranged to present you to our queen. Hit that button, please."

I reach out and slap the protruding gilded button. The doors close, plunging us into darkness, the only source of illumination from Zander's wings. I tip my head back against his shoulder and close my eyes.

"Found the dark," I whisper with a smile.

He sighs. "Yes, maintenance is working to fix the block of light. It happens from time to time. Something falls or breaks, and it blocks the heart of Light from seeping into the area. While they are searching for the cause, it is full of shadows in here." He shivers. "It's every shaft for some reason, and they haven't been able to figure out the block. I'm anxious for them to get it fixed soon."

"I like it."

The air rushes around us as he chuckles. "You've spent too much time away from the Light. Button, please."

With regret, I slap the button, two doors sliding open and brightness chasing shadows away from me, filling the world around us once more. Zander steps into a hall and sets me on the floor. He reaches behind him to close the doors, waving with his other hand. "Welcome to the entrance hall."

I start walking through the massive white room, intricately carved columns lining the length. I move to one, brushing against the relief carvings in awe. "What is this?"

"This is the *Corarum* Tower. Mostly, we call it the Gold Tower, but *Corarum* means the heart of gold in the Seraphin language. These columns–" He presses his palm to it, brushing over sculptures. "–are the tales of the clans and our history as the Light. They are known as *narratio de aurarius*, but that just means golden history." He smiles down at me.

I crane around him, staring at the rows of columns as far as I can see. "There are so many."

"There are many stories." His hand falls from the artwork, resting on my lower back.

My muscles twitch at his contact, his hand warm and large, seeping through my shirt. "Ness is going to love these."

Zander guides me forward. "You're going to notice three columns are made of gold instead of gilded marble. Those are the three great clans of Light that came together to form the first council. There is one for the Lamonts, which is the royal family, the Hallows, who are extinct, and the third..." he smiles down at me, "is your heritage's history. The Bordeaux clan."

I inhale until I can't draw in anymore, then let it trickle out. "What happened to the Hallows?"

"The Dark." His chin drops toward his chest. "The last of them–three brothers–died protecting the Light Queen at the time from an attack. There's a Hallows Festival each year on the anniversary of their sacrifice where we honor them."

I bob my head, focusing on the columns as we pass by each, gliding across glistening marble beneath our feet. "Oh."

"The loss of the Hallows heritage was devastating, but

with them gone, that shifted the Bordeaux heritage's position in the Light. Your heritage is second only to the royal family now."

As we approach a wall of glass, an older man stands from a stool, making his way toward the position of the handles in the center. He smiles as we approach, and Zander asks, "Good dawn, Luke. Have you met Tallie yet?"

"No, sir," he gives a slight bow, "Good dawning, young lady."

Zander turns to grin at me. "Tallie is Pierre's daughter."

Luke gapes but recovers quickly with a wide smile. "The pleasure of your acquaintance is mine. My name is Luke, and I am the concierge here at Gold Tower." He bows, his torso level with the floor and a fist to his chest over his heart.

I stare, lips apart, one eyebrow up. "Did you just fucking bow?"

Zander gives me an exasperated glance. "Please, Tallie, suitable language. Yes, he bowed as a sign of respect, which is to be common for those below you in rank. You will need to have a much more appropriate response in the future and may want to bow your head in a sign of acknowledged respect."

"Dude." I blink a few times. "What?"

Luke smiles, but his eyes flick toward Zander, his face full of concern. "If there is ever anything you need, please let me know, Miss Tallie."

Lifting and dropping a shoulder, I say, "Sure."

Zander nudges me with his body. "The appropriate response is to thank the gentleman for the offer of his time and resources."

Sighing, I bob my head. "Thank you, Luke."

Luke straightens. "Of course, Miss Bordeaux, always a pleasure." He opens the door, and Zander guides me through it. Outside is somehow even brighter, a garish glare and illumination hitting me like I've run face-first into a wall.

I glance back at Luke as we pass through the door. "What is with the bowing?"

"You're Pierre's daughter. It will command respect among the Light."

"Why?"

"Pierre's heritage." He halts and gives me a wide grin. "It's your heritage too. It is one of the most respected heritages for their history and not only their ability but the sheer strength of the Light they manifest with. The only more respected and powerful heritage belongs to the royal family."

"The current royal family?"

He shakes his head. "They've always been the royals. We aren't like the Dark, fighting for power. The Light doesn't even work in the same way. With the Light, power is maintained through heritage. The animal—" He stops and clears his throat. "The Dark doesn't work that way. Just because the parent's magic is strong doesn't guarantee that the child's is."

"So...I..."

"As Pierre's seed, you are going to be powerful because the Bordeaux heritage is powerful. That is why our heritage determines everything and why Pierre's indiscretion is so bothersome to some. He's tainted his heritage with mortal blood."

"Seraphinus aren't immortal. And did you just call me a taint?"

My glib receives a sharp glare. "You are correct. Only the Ancients were said to be immortal, but we live much longer than humans.

Zander continues speaking as I blink and squint, pushing me forward with his hand. "The Bordeaux heritage holds a very important role. Don't worry about duties yet. Some will come in time, though for now, Pierre is head of your heritage and carries all responsibilities. Still, you are a representation of him and your great heritage, so you need to act accordingly."

"Great." The Magia wanted me to be a baby machine. Tony wanted me to be Sasha. Cal wanted me to be his weapon. Pierre will be no different, trying to make me into something that suits him. I shiver, still struggling with the brightness of the world.

"Are you cold, love?"

"No." I stop walking and rub my eyes. "The whole constant and ridiculously bright shit is hurting my eyes. When does this turn off?"

"Never." Zander's voice falls solemn. "The Dark has no place here. The Light burns it out so that it does not exist. Izul is the beating heart of the Light, all that stretches out across the world, the root of all Light Seraphinus' magic, and it will never go out."

"Great." I drag the word out, rubbing my eyes even more.

"Pierre made arrangements with the owner of Versalliusm to open early to provide you with a wardrobe. We are headed there first, and you'll have the store to yourself while you shop."

"What about Ness?"

"Don't be concerned about her. Pierre will ensure she has what she needs. Versalliusm provides tailored clothing of high quality. Ness could expend several months of her stipend trying to buy a mere outfit. It's not compatible with her budget, so he'll see to it she is offered a more suitable selection."

I glare from the tops of my eyes at the brilliant yellow glow above me. Just as in Ilbuio, there is no trace of clear skies or even sight of the suns. "So, she's getting cheap?"

"Mmm." Zander holds his other hand up, level with the ground, before tipping it side to side. "Suitable for her station. However, there is nothing inexpensive in this city, if I am honest." He chuckles, rubbing the back of his neck as he studies the cobblestones beneath our feet.

Licking my teeth, then clicking my tongue against them, I cock my jaw and look away. "Whatever."

"The Light is very staunch about our hierarchy, love. You are going to have respect for being a Bordeaux that she will only dream of as a vassal, and she's going to be sneered at for being human. Pierre is making exceptions as well as accommodating your adoration of her, though. Be grateful and give him a show of appreciation for that."

"Sure. Thanks for treating my friend like shit."

Rubbing a hand down his face, Zander sighs. "Love, she is being treated far better than some vassals I know. We're going to turn up here, and we'll get you clothes for everyday wear, but your priority should be a dress to present to the queen. May I suggest you begin by selecting a dress so that they have time to tailor it while you search for other clothes?"

"When am I going to eat?"

"Clothes, then I'll take you to your room to clean up. When you are presentable, I will take you to get food."

Biting down on nothing, I lock my jaw closed. Cal always got me food as soon as I asked unless we were in the middle of a game in Ilbuio, in which case he ensured I ate as soon as possible.

'I need to behave.'

That thought sends fissures through my heart. I can't afford to act out. While Pierre won't throw me out of Izul, he made it clear he's willing to toss Ness in the dust. She won't survive outside of Izul without me, and I don't know if I'm capable of escaping.

I don't feel capable of much right now. Cal banished me. I served no use, no purpose for him anymore. Shoving the thoughts from my mind, I rub the burn from my eyes, pretending the brightness is causing them to prickle and well up.

CHAPTER 19
VANESSA

Watching Tallie waltz away with dreamy number one, I chew my lower lip and glance at dreamy number two. It's uncanny how gorgeous they all are and unfair.

He's about my height with black hair and deep golden skin. He almost looks like a human who has spent time in the suns if not for his white eyes and ethereal beauty.

Pierre clears his throat. "Vanessa."

"Ness."

"You are here because of my daughter's adoration, and at her behest, I have acquiesced to your presence. I am accepting you into our home as a great act of charity, but my considerations and patience have limitations."

I frown at him, then rub the space between my eyebrows. "I'm really tired, so if you can just speak slowly and clearly...?"

"You will not be contracted to Tallie. You will not be a vassal in an official capacity. However, I will support your meaningless and very short life to ensure Tallie's cooperation."

"Cooperation with what?"

"Taking her place in society, acting as a Bordeaux, continuing my heritage as is her right and duty, and overall, being what she always should have been–the Light. I will see to it that she is protected and has what she needs to come into the Light."

"What am I doing?" I stare at my hands, fitting my fingers together. My palms have started to clam up, nerves tingling in my scalp.

"Encourage Tallie's cooperation and do not interfere with her transition into the Light." He doesn't even feign a tight-lipped smile. "Do those two things, and I will keep you here within Izul, where you will be safe. I will provide you with comforts, and I will–within reason–provide you with your wants. Do we have an agreement?"

I flex my fingers backward, stretching my hands as I consider. Cal offered me a contract with the condition that I keep Tallie useable for his whims. I was less fearful for her then, even if she was referred to as a thing to be used instead of a woman. Pierre isn't inferring his use, but I can't shake the sense that this is worse for Tallie.

I'm sitting in a Lighter's office, quivering under his stern gaze because the Magia are hunting us. We both agreed to come to this city because we had nowhere else to run to. We've been marked as traitors to the Magia, and they exist in every city across both continents.

I have no identification. I have no job. I have no coin, not even a cuff like Tallie. I have nothing and no one beyond Tallie. I have no option but to bite my tongue and nod. "Agreed."

"Very good. You are both excused."

Owen inclines his head, ushering me through the door. "Ness, if you please?"

"Sure thing." I step forward, moving in the same direction Tallie went, chasing after her like I always do. "Can we get food? I'm starving."

"That is good news. I am under orders to introduce you to the city and our customs, and we can begin with breakfast. I will need to teach you meal etiquette."

"Open mouth, insert food."

Owen sighs, staring straight ahead with indifference.

When we reach the flight shafts, Owen hits the button and offers me his hand. "May I carry you? This will be quicker than the stairs."

Slapping my hand in his, I say, "I'll take being carried in your arms over stairs anytime."

"That is fortunate," he grunts as he swings me into his arms, "as you are not allowed to leave this tower without me for the foreseeable future, and we are on the fifty-seventh floor."

"Why do I require constant supervision?"

"Your safety and the presence of others. You need to be versed in our ways to prevent being a burden or discomfort to everyone else." Wings of golden Light sprout, the tendrils waving aimlessly, and then he steps into the shoot. He twists toward the open doors. "Please hit the button."

I smack it, the doors shut, and shadows close around us. The air is damp, full of secrets and promise. Tipping my head back, I inhale with my eyes closed, reveling in the darkness.

Owen shudders. "Are you Dark?"

"Magia."

We descend, and he's out of the flight shaft, setting me on my feet and pulling away from me in a hurry, doing a full-body shudder. He rubs at himself like he's trying to be rid of shadows, and then he glares at me down his nose as he smacks the button to close the doors.

Leaning closer, he peers at me with mistrust sprinkled with disgust in the way he wrinkles his nose and turns away. "This

156

way, please." He turns, sauntering between two rows of massive columns of marble.

I gape, stepping toward one. "Wow."

"They are carved with the history of the Light. Please keep up."

I scamper after him, doing my best to scan each column, buzzing with a need to stop and inspect. "Can I leave the fifty-seventh floor to come down here anytime I want?"

"No." He opens the door, pushing through, and I follow at his heels out into the world. Turning around, I stare up at the building, a gaudy gold structure. It's impressive engineering but nothing fancy.

Turning, I realize Owen is waiting, watching me from twenty paces away. I walk in long strides to catch up, jerking my thumb at the building. "What is that place?"

"The Gold Tower, home to the most respected prestigious heritages of the Light, including the royals." He cuts his gaze to me. "The higher the floor, the higher the rank held by the heritage. Never go above Pierre's designated floors, or you will be trespassing on the royal's property. It is a crime punishable by death."

"Noted."

"Floor fifty-seven is the only floor you are to be on without an escort. This way." He steps off the curb, across a brown and red cobblestone street to the other side.

"I haven't seen a single car."

"You won't in this area of town. All vehicles are stored in the structure next to the gates."

"Then why are there roads?"

"The streets are from the old world."

"From the time of the clans?"

He stops, showing interest for the first time. "Yes." He resumes moving. "Down here," he says, gesturing to an alley.

"Uh..." I stop, holding my hands up. "I have rules against alleyways and strange men for my own safety."

He lifts his eyebrows, cocking his head. After deliberating, he bobs his head. "You are safe with me. I find you repugnant."

That zings through me. Lowering my gaze, my tongue tries to slide down my throat, my skin wanting to delve inside my body where it's protected. "Oh...kay...then..."

He shrugs and turns away. "You're human."

Head down, I trail behind him down the narrow alley to the other side and across another street to a red door. He opens it, moving through before me. Inside are glossy white and golden-brown accents.

A few clusters of Lighters glance at us from around the open ground floor, but Owen moves to the middle of the large square room and glances up. Looking at me, he offers his hand again. "There is no choice this time. There are no stairs in this building."

I move closer, uncomfortable in his arms, as he lifts me. Slipping an arm around his shoulders to hold tight, I look up. The center of the building is vacant space to the glass top, built in rigid square levels.

His wings come out, and I focus on them. They make no rational sense, random threads of Light that lift us higher and higher.

I lose count of the floors, too mesmerized by the inaccurate physics of his wings. He sets me on my feet and moves toward a Lighter standing behind a golden wood podium.

He gives a curt, halfway bow. "Welcome and be welcomed."

"We are welcomed and welcoming," Owen says in return. "The two of us request seating and food."

The man picks up two small rectangular wood slabs and

moves further into the open space, leading us to a low wood table.

Owen gestures to one side. "Please sit there."

I drop onto the cushion, and he descends with more grace than I have in my whole body to the opposite side of the table. He accepts the tablets with both hands, and the Lighter handing them off asks, "Would you like time to determine your choices?"

Owen turns to me. "If you are agreeable, I will order for both of us at this time."

"Sure." I shrug. "I'm not picky."

He inclines his head and then focuses on the Lighter. "Two traditional style *jejinn,* please."

He hands the tablets back with both hands. The Lighter takes them with a full bow and two hands, then recedes.

I stare after the Lighter, asking, "What is *jejinn*? I'm not familiar with the word in Seraphin."

"You are familiar with our language? How very strange." He studies me with his head shied back, eyeing me down his upturned nose. "The word is not found in the Dark. It belongs to the Light. It's a term derived from Beenin's love of an early meal."

Tucking the information in my head, I study the table, built of thin strips of wood. Running my fingers over it, I ask, "What is this?"

"We are in a *vescor*. The word is a combination of food and enjoyment, and they serve traditional foods only for the first and second meals of the day."

"Oh." I glance around. "So, a café?"

Owen shrugs.

"But I was asking about the table. It's…" I check the table out. "Whoa, this thing is really thin, but…" I press my fingertips to it, applying force. There's no inflection.

"*Gramen* is the old-world word," he says. "In the modern tongue, it's referred to as poaceae."

"Heard of the stuff but never seen it." I sigh, tracing my fingers over the visible but intangible seams. It's a beautiful golden brown with a glittery and impossibly silky surface. "It's gorgeous."

"It's found mainly on the other continent."

"Grows in the Mikkanos Rainforest and Glinting Mirage both. I've seen pictures, but they don't do it justice. It's too expensive for most humans."

He hums. "Opal marble, gilded marble, gold, and *gramen* are our main building materials. We ensure they are readily available for our use, which excludes the ability for mortals to obtain the material without worthwhile compensation for the annoyance."

"Yeah, we're just a bunch of ants to you." I roll my eyes.

"Ants?"

"God." I fling my hand at him and then point at my breasts. "Ant. You step on us and crush us for being in the way."

Shrugging, he says, "Humans pollute the world and clutter space. They easily procreate to replace any we remove from the world." His lips turn up at the corners. "Ants. I like the turn of phrase."

"No one should have to ask for the right to live."

"Do you kill ants? Perhaps other pests that invade your space?"

I frown.

"Do they not share that same right by your logic?"

I've killed spiders for Tallie too many times to count because she's terrified of them. We've had to set out poison to be rid of rodents living in the house because they got too bold, crawling on me in the middle of the night, and crushed cock-roaches galore because they're gross.

"Mmm." He flexes his eyebrows upward and asks, "How are you familiar with our language?"

"School."

"Interesting. How versed are you?"

"Very. I like studying history and language and cultures. I've never been able to afford to travel much, so I do that through books."

"You can read it and speak it?"

Rolling my eyes, I say, "Does anyone really speak it?"

"Your attitude is unappreciated," he says in a curt but frosty drawl.

"Eh." I duck my head, feeling like I'm walking a very thin line, and if I cross it, I'm dead. It's an odd sense. I haven't been threatened with death per se, but I'm scared of being killed all the same. "Read it? Yes. Speak it? My pronunciations are terrible, according to Mass."

"Who is Mass?"

I lick my lower lip, sucking it into my mouth to press my top teeth into it. "Massimo. He was Cal's contracted." I wince at the use of past tense, my heart still raw.

"An animal, but one that would be able to determine your abuse of our language."

Lifting my eyes to Owen, I glare.

He shrugs. "The Dark are volatile and violent animals. We have a library."

My heart lifts, excitement racing in my veins. "Really?"

"I presume you'd be interested in knowing its location?"

"Can– Can I?"

"I will discuss with Pierre if you can have access to it. He will no doubt need to provide an exceptionable allowance to grant you use of our books." Owen leans forward, eyeing me. "You are certain you are not the Dark?"

I hold my hands up. "See any magic? It would be warding you off if I had any, right?"

"Mmm, yes." His tone tells me he doesn't believe me. "After we eat, I will escort you to a shop nearby for attire. I will then deliver you unto your permanent lodgings."

"Not the room I was in last night?"

"That was a spare room Zander selected. It was his choice to provide a simple accommodation for the evening until Pierre made his decisions." Owen presses his lips and looks away, his tone sour. "He is above me."

"I left some belongings in that room."

"I will take you there to collect what is yours before delivering you to your new rooms."

A tray is delivered, a glass teapot full of yellow water, a gold insert bobbing in it. Owen inclines his head, and the delivering Lighter retreats.

He sets a glass before me, rounded, wide, and low, and places a second before himself. He picks up the pot, pouring a splash into a small shimmering white dish. Picking up a paintbrush, he dips it into the liquid on the plate and brushes the rim of my glass and then his before he fills the glasses halfway, mine then his. He repeats the process a second time to fill the glass fully.

When he sets the teapot back, he says, "That is the proper way to serve tea. As your elder, our customs would be that you serve me in the future. The youngest always serve the elders, and you always serve the other or others before yourself. You will be required to adhere to these customs, or you will not be welcome in our home."

I'm being made into a servant. Taking a deep breath, I try to stay polite, but it's difficult to bite my tongue. "Understood."

There are no jokes to be made about being thrown out, no honesty about the possibility as there was with Mass, merely a thinly veiled threat. I'm more terrified than I was as Cal's contracted. Tallie and I are out of options if we are thrown out of Izul.

My heart thumps like a hammer just drove a screw through it: sheer, blunt force ramming the threaded shaft through soft tissue without requiring spherical pressure. It would be a death sentence. There's nowhere to hide from the Magia on either continent, and we can't run and fight forever.

A small voice reminds me that Tallie wouldn't be ejected with me. I would be expelled on my own. The Magia would use me, vying for Tallie. It's a personal death sentence if I get tossed on my ass on the other side of the gates.

Tallie would fight to come with me, but then we'd both be dead. Sooner or later, our luck would run dry. She would be defending us both without much help from me. Never before have I believed I'm useless baggage. The realization leaves me hollow and frail.

Owen lifts his cup, one hand on the bottom as support, the other wrapped around the side. "This is the proper form to lift and drink. Do not slurp."

I lift my glass, staring at it. I've never enjoyed any kind of tea, and I expect this will be no exception.

After gagging down two cups of tea, the second being served by me for Owen to inspect my ability to repeat his process, another tray is delivered with a dozen smaller bowls and two long and narrow dishes.

He gestures. "Serving the meal is the same. You would serve me, but I am going to show you the proper order, and I will explain each dish."

My mouth is watering. I don't care if I'm served, and I don't want to waste time serving. I want to eat. My stomach is clenching and gurgling at the delicious scent wafting in the air.

By the time he's done explaining the thinly slice, marinated pork, the leaves it's wrapped in, the ginger-garlic cucumbers, the fermented radish, sweet bread, rice, and egg loaf, I'm drooling.

It takes him twice as long to serve me and show me proper etiquette, and I'm about in tears. I'm already picking up pork to slap into a large, pale green leaf when he clears his throat. "The eldest prepares theirs and takes the first bite. You must wait."

I hate this stupid city.

CHAPTER 20
NATALIA

My stomach squirms and demands food in squelches and gurgles that draw a smile from Zander as he walks us up to the glass doors of the tallest tower. "Once I show you to your permanent rooms and you are cleaned up, I will take you for breakfast."

Tipping my head back, I crane to stare up the length of the shimmering tower of gold and amber glass windows. He stops, waiting for the doorman to grant us entrance. "Thank you, Luke," he says, guiding me through and down the hall of columns.

At the flight shaft, Zander slips my numerous bags over his arm to hang from his elbow and swings me into his arms with a wide smile. "I've got you, lovely."

I meet his eyes, tipping my head back. He said those words when he yanked me out of the water. I'd been so relieved and grateful, a rush of adrenaline overcoming me. Without thought of what I was doing, I had grabbed his face and kissed him.

"No?" He shies his head. "Don't remember?"

Forcing myself to smile, I say, "I remember."

"Any chance you're going to respond in the same manner?" He wiggles his eyebrows, grinning at me.

I almost laugh, pushing air out of my nose. "I've been in these same clothes for days. I reek of alcohol and sweat. I feel gross. I *am* gross, really, and I need a toothbrush before I stick my tongue in anyone's mouth."

"Ah." He chuckles. "That is an excellent point. In that case, love, please push the button." He twists me closer to the wall.

I embrace the shadows that close in around us as he ascends. All too soon, he's asking me to push the button, bringing us back into that awful, ever-present glow. He sets me on my feet, and we walk through the hallways. This time, he leads me to a dead end, turning to the right.

"If you turn the other way," he says, "there you'll find Ness's chambers. Yours are here at the other end." He nods toward the door we are approaching.

He opens the door for me, nudging me into the room. It's massive. Everything is white, the seams in the corners and along the ceiling glowing with golden illumination that fills the room. One whole wall is a massive glass panel overlooking Izul.

"Do you like it?"

I face him. "Can I paint it all black?"

"No." He gives me a tight, forced smile, then steps to one of two doors. "This," he opens it, peaking inside, "yes, this is the bathroom. The other will be your closet," he says with a wave toward the door next to the bed on the opposite wall.

"I get clean, and then I get food, right?"

"Yes." He chuckles. "Shower, clean up, get out of those nasty clothes, and I will take you for breakfast at my favorite place."

Taking the bags from him, I head into the bathroom and kick the door shut. I'd turn the light on if it weren't already on.

I'm starting to get a steady and permanent throb behind my eyes.

I shower, fighting my urge for food to enjoy an extra couple of fractions in the hot water. There are already the basic necessities available, which I try to ignore. Cal had everything ready for me in Narwal when I signed his contract, including clothes. It was creepy, considering I had turned down his offer for a contract, signing in a spur-of-the-moment, split-fraction decision.

He knew I'd sign his contract before I realized the inevitable. I couldn't stay with the Magia, and he was offering me an escape.

I lean against the wall of the shower, closing my eyes and whispering to the steam. "Could really use another escape, babe."

My eyes sting. My throat clogs. Magia can kill Seraphinus, and they'd killed Cal.

Smacking the wall, I pull upright and wrench on the controls to shut the water off. I killed him by running. I put him in their sights by contracting myself to him. He was raw power and strength wrapped in gorgeous features. My Darkling had been wicked beauty and honesty, everything I ever craved for, and he's now gone from this world because of me. In the end, I hadn't even served a purpose for him, yet I still cost him his life.

Digging through the bags for an outfit, I rip tags off articles and get dressed. I fuss over the sink, brushing my teeth and running fingers through my damp hair. It's gotten longer, the tips resting against my collarbone as they hang straight.

With a sigh, I exit the bathroom to face Zander and hold my arms out from my sides. "Why aren't there normal clothes here?"

"I'm afraid I don't understand your question," he says, offering his hand. "Ready?"

I cross my arms and glance at myself. "Everything is white, gold, tan, beige..." I throw my hands down at my legs in exasperation. "I'm wearing tan pants."

"You look beautiful."

"I want black."

Zander moves to the door. "There is none here, love."

"I'll settle for dark blue."

"You won't find anything remotely close. We abhor it." He shakes his head, grinning, and his fingers press between mine as he takes my hand. I frown, but he pulls me through the door and into the hallway, stepping backward with a smile. "You're all mine until Evergreen."

"Mmm." I press my lips. "It works better when you growl in my ear before you say, 'You're mine.'"

"Don't be absurd. I do not growl." He laughs. With a squeeze of my hand, he says, "You are not something to be owned, love. Possessed if you are willing to be, perhaps, but you are never property."

I hum again, turning my head away from him and walking down the hallway, hand in hand. I can't think of a valid reason to pull away other than the image of Cal's furious scowl. He owned me, and I had wanted that—to belong to him.

At the flight shafts, Zander pushes the button and lifts me into his arms, cradling me. "I've got you, lovely."

"I see that."

"About my kiss?"

"Not happening, dude."

He grins and steps into the shadows. "Alas, I will have to try again then."

I LOWER TO the cushion across the low table of gold and glass from Zander and glance around. He kneels, bows his head, and then sits cross-legged. He accepts the menus with both hands from a blonde Lighter, who bows deeply.

She stands straight-backed and straight-faced. "Would you appreciate time to look over our options?"

"Yes, please grant us time to make our selections."

The Lighter bows her head and walks away.

I glance around again. "What is this place?"

"A traditional *vescor*. An eatery. They are most popular in the mornings and afternoons. Most *vescors* do not even operate past Thorn's Rune. Would you like me to order for you?"

"Guessing vodka isn't an option?"

"No. Tea is the customary beverage for breakfast, often the first choice for midday meals and after dinner. Alcohol is only available during evening runes and dinners."

I stare at him, recalling the first meal I shared with Cal. I started with a glass of vodka and explained the marks of the Magia inked down my spine. It was the first time I glowed. There's no trace of silver webbing on my skin this morning, and alcohol isn't available anywhere in Izul.

I want to punch something.

Ducking my head, I rub behind my ear, telling myself, "This is not somewhere I belong."

"Of course, you belong," Zander says. "You are the Light, and this is your home."

"Yeah, sure." I try to laugh but wheeze out, "I don't fit in here."

Zander sets the menus aside, smiling at me, but it's forced. "You were not raised in the Light, and worse, you've been subjected to the Dark. Our customs might seem strange now, but in time, you will adopt them as your own."

I didn't know what to expect of Izul, but it's solidifying as a dreary and miserable hovel rather than the glinting, gilded, shimmering promise I thought it was. If I could think of anywhere else in this world that I could take Ness and run to that would be safe, I'd try to leave, Pierre's warnings about my Light be damned. I rack my brain, no helpful ideas formulating in the percolation of misery accrued there.

Zander smiles. "Have you been swimming lately?"

I slump lower. "Most recently, I went swimming in the maze."

"Maze?" Zander lifts his eyebrows. "What is that?"

Squirming, I look down at the table, not sure if I should be sharing this. I can't shake this image of Cal sneering at me and saying this isn't for the Light.

Bobbing his head, Zander sighs. "In Ilbuio?" I nod, and he asks, "What is this maze?"

"Made with the venom of nightmares. It...whatever. There was a hallway with a pool that Cal and I had to swim across." I sit up, leaving out the near drowning and seeing Cal shift for the first time.

"That must have been awful. Nightmare venom is potent and an excruciating experience."

"You've been infected?"

He grimaces. "A few times. None of them were pleasant, so let us discuss something that is. What do you enjoy?"

"Vodka. Music. Yoga. Ness. Cal." I stop, wincing. "Um, what do you like?"

"Combat training and painting. Music as well. What kinds of music do you enjoy?"

"Dark Marrow is hands down my favorite band." Zander pulls a face of disgust, but I shrug. "Yeah, I know, they're Dark Seraphinus, but even before," I wave my hand, "everything, when I was just a Magia before I even earned my marks, I fell in love with their stuff. Trust me, my parents weren't thrilled that I'd buy their music, but it's so good. Ever listened to it?"

"No." He chuckles. "Absolutely not. I'd never tolerate anything from the Dark."

I roll my eyes. "My whole life, I was told to just kill your kind—Light or Dark. I didn't care about it being frowned on then, and I won't start now."

Checking around us, Zander leans close. "Love." He presses a finger to his lips. "Shh. That's not something you should be declaring loudly or publicly."

Leaning back, I cross my arms and my legs. "Dude, you know what I am."

"Extensively, both your heritage and your upbringing, and I'm aware of the laws of the Magia." His lips curl, gleeful and gloating. "Thank you for breaking those laws with me."

I bite back a retort as the Lighter returns to take our order. Zander ducks his head, rubbing the back of his neck as he smirks at the table. Clearing his throat, he lifts his head composed, albeit blushing and places the order.

When the server withdraws, he turns to me. His eyes are crinkled at the corners, the flush of embarrassment heightening, his cheeks pink. "I enjoyed myself."

I shake my head and look away. "What kind of music do you like?"

He laughs, a bright sound of humor. "All right, we'll move on, but I would like a chance to say I respected your wishes to not search for you nor contact you with great resolve to honor your request and not because I did not wish to do so. Now that you are here, and I have full rights to contact you anytime I want, might you allow me to—"

"Moving on, dude."

Some of the mirth dies from his face, his tone stiff. "I believed you enjoyed our time as well."

I cock my jaw, turning my face away. All I can think is Cal was better. "As long as I don't think too hard about the age gap," I joke. "How old are you?"

"Ah." He looks up. "Three-hundred-and-twenty-seven."

Staring at him, I realize I never knew how old Cal was.

Zander smiles. "I may be old for you, but in my world, I am still very young."

"Old? No, you're downright ancient to me."

He laughs. "I am glad you found your way here to Izul and back to me." He reaches across the table, laying his hand out.

I stare at it, the implication there for me to take his hand. His skin is pale, with no trace of scars visible, his fingers long, and his palm large. It's bigger than Cal's hand, but then, Zander is taller than Cal. Shoving the comparisons of the two from my mind, I rest my hand on his, Zander closing his fingers around me.

I swallow my emotions, not mirroring the sentiment he shared. If I had a choice, I'd still be with Cal. Blinking my prickling eyes, I force a smile. "So, music?"

A tea tray is delivered on shimmering gold wood. I reach for a glass, but Zander holds a hand up. "Please, I am to serve your heritage. Therefore, I will serve you."

"I can pour myself tea."

"I have no doubts of your ability, but it is our customs, and Pierre will not take kindly should someone report to him my failure to serve."

I get through breakfast, annoyed at being served like the spoiled Magia heiress everyone I grew up with thought I was. I

172

grind my teeth, trying to ignore it as I shove thoughts of Cal into the back of my mind.

Zander discusses painting and life in Izul. I discuss my love for music and Ness. Conversation is choppy and awkward several times, but things grow smoother as the meal comes to an end.

When the server returns to collect payment, I use Cal's cuff. It's an automatic reaction, something neither Zander nor I are thrilled with. I just bought a Lighter a meal on Cal's coin, which makes the food in my stomach turn sour.

Zander scowls. "What is that thing? If you wanted to pay, you should have used Pierre's accounts."

"Um..." I look down and away, wincing. "It's, uh, connected to my previous account."

"You don't need that anymore. Pierre will provide for you."

"Yeah, um, it won't last long, so..." I shrug, fiddling with the silver band.

Zander frowns, his eyebrows drawing together. "It's from Callahan, isn't it?"

"Yes." I drop my hands below the table to hide it from sight, sending a silent apology to him in the afters. He wouldn't be thrilled, but he'd understand my inability to rely on Pierre, the incessant need to be self-sufficient that's rooted in my core. Not that using Cal's coin is being self-sufficient, but it feels less dependent oddly.

"You shouldn't use that thing. In fact, you need to remove it."

"No." I shrug and stand. "What's next?"

He sighs as he stands. "Love..." He drags it out. "Give me your hand. Pierre will not approve of that device, and neither do I."

"Don't care. I'm keeping it." I wrap my hand around it, needing to shield it from Zander's view.

Rubbing his forehead, then dragging his hand down his face, Zander bobs his head. "I'll show you around the city, then we'll return to Versallisum to pick up your dress before we return to the tower to prepare for your presenting. I will review a few laws and general etiquette."

"Your laws," I say. "I'm Magia."

Chuckling, Zander stops in front of a set of double doors. I frown at the intricately decorated metal doors. "You have your head in the clouds, love."

"All I need to know is the best restaurants."

He rests his hand on the small of my back, guiding me out. "We need to ensure you stay out of imprisonment. However, that is not the only plausible punishment nor the worst of them. In extreme cases, an individual's magic can be bound. This can be decreed in both heritage and legal matters."

"Bound?"

"Yes. Every head of a heritage and the royal family can bind the magic of an individual. That is why the royals are the leading family. All Light comes from them, the originals."

"Okay."

"Pierre is the eldest of your heritage, and so he is also capable of binding your magic."

"What exactly does that mean, though?"

"Your heritage is his, so your magic is a piece of his. As you are his child, your magic is the seed of his."

"Makes sense." I scratch behind my ear, checking around.

"Most believe magic-craft to be fantasy, but it was real once. The Ancients were said to be proficient." He waves a hand, dismissing his words. "I don't know about all that, but there are very old texts containing spoken words that trigger certain effects from the Light."

"What happens if your magic is bound?"

"If someone binds your magic, be it the head of your heritage or a royal, they will control your magic, essentially robbing you of the ability to call your magic or use it. You wouldn't even be able to do something as simple as form wings–well, bad example for you, as Seraphim have no wings, but you wouldn't be able to fight. It wouldn't protect you against the Dark or any other threat," he adds quickly. "You would essentially be human."

I force a laugh. "So, imprisonment over having my magic bound."

"Best to avoid both, love." Zander takes my hand, pressing the back to his lips. "While you are still new to Izul, you'll require an escort should you choose to leave the tower, so I will be with you when you are in the city, there to help keep you safe."

I bristle, cutting my eyes to him with a sharp glare. "I'm starting to feel like a prisoner again."

"You are not, but you are unfamiliar with our laws, with the city, with interacting with the Light, and as I mentioned, there are those who are displeased with Pierre's indiscretion. It's for your benefit that Pierre insists you not be alone."

Rolling my eyes, I say, "I can take care of myself."

"Were you permitted to wander Ilbuio on your own?" He glances at me with amusement.

"No," I shove through gritted teeth. I hadn't been allowed to stray from Cal, rarely from within an arm's reach.

"For those very same reasons, you are not to be roaming Izul on your own."

I squeeze my fingers into fists and release them, flexing my hands open and dropping the topic. I never felt like a prisoner with Cal, but I have an unshakable sense that despite Zander's claims, I'm very much being locked up. "What happens if I leave the tower without you?"

"Pierre will be displeased, and I will be anxiously looking for you."

"What if it's just for food? I get hungry a lot."

He smiles down at me. "My number is in your phone. Send me notice of anything you want at any time, and I will comply." He slips his arm around my shoulders, pulling me closer as his face lowers, his mouth closer to my ear to whisper, "I do mean *anything* you may want."

The offer slides through my ear, down my throat, into my chest, and settles in my lower stomach. I widen my eyes and clear my throat. "Will Ness get the same response from Owen?"

"He will provide food, but I doubt he's offering the full extent of options I am."

"Food. I was talking about food."

He grins with a sly expression. "I wasn't."

"What rune did Versallisum say my dress would be ready?"

He chuckles. "Blooming. We have time to get reacquainted."

CHAPTER 21

NATALIA

Before Cal, I had never worn dresses much. They were my sister's favorite attire, but I'd always felt awkward without pants. With Cal, I'd gotten used to them more. Coming to the conclusion that I was capable of fighting in them was helpful, but the gown Zander convinced me was the best choice has brought back my revulsion in full swing.

The fabric is thick and heavy, a shimmering gold material embroidered with white. The dress has a high neckline that will encase the back of my neck, opening to a v-shape between my collarbones, and short, puffy sleeves that make my shoulders look massive. The skirt is cumbersome as I shuffle out of the bathroom, kicking at the hem to move it as I glare at Zander.

He smiles. "You do not appear pleased."

"I didn't pick this thing."

"Do you require assistance?"

"Zipper." I thumb over my shoulder toward my back.

He stands from where he was perched on the foot of my bed, moving around me. His fingers brush along my spine.

"These marks are new, aren't they? Or was I so mesmerized by you I overlooked them?"

I lick along my top teeth. "New."

"Do they mean something?" His fingertip skims down my spine.

"Yeah, when someone sees them, it means that I need them to *zip up my dress*."

The whir of the zipper intermingling with his soft chuckle fills the air, the fabric tightening around my midsection, chest, and shoulders. Using both of his hands, he gathers my hair, drawing the strands from the collar of the dress to hang loose.

Zander returns to stand in front of me, meeting my eyes. As he stares at me, his lips curl and part until he's grinning ear to ear. "Love, you are adorable when you are displeased."

"You think I'm cute when I'm angry?" I snap, my teeth clacking as I bite the air. "I'm capable of killing you."

Sliding his hands around my waist, he shuffles closer, dropping his chin and lifting his eyebrows. "Love, remember your manners. Respect is paramount when addressing the queen. We don't want your magic bound or for her to refute your rightful place in the Light because you're throwing a tantrum."

"I'll show you a tantrum."

"No," he says and taps my nose, scanning my body. "No one enjoys formal attire, but wearing it is a show of respect, and wearing it in spite of that fact is even more respectful."

I stab my finger into his stomach. "Says the one not wearing stupid, uncomfortable clothes."

"I am not going to be before our Light Queen." He puts his hand over mine, pressing it forward so my palm rests against his abdomen. "I am to see to your needs before my own, and, believe me when I say, I will enjoy doing so in every service I may perform for you."

"Maybe you should have tried that the first time?"

He lifts his hand as a loose fist, sliding his thumb along my jawbone. "What do you mean?"

Pulling my hand back, I gather the massive skirt of the dress to avoid tripping on it as I step back. "You didn't exactly get on your knees for me."

He cocks his head, then recognition fills his face. Laughing, he says, "Love, I'd just pulled you from the ocean, and I hadn't been in charge of much."

Zander had scooped me out of the ocean and carried me to a nearby island. When he landed on the beach after saving me, I'd jumped on him like he was a bought and paid-for prostitute. I hadn't stopped to let myself think or even consider what I was doing.

I had been nineteen at the time and had never had sex. When the riptide tore me away from the others, I'd tried everything to keep my head above water without much avail. All I could think about were all the things I had never done and would never get to do. Sex had been near the top of that list, and Zander was there, a handsome savior.

"It's a good thing my life philosophy is not to look down on someone unless they're giving you head, or I might still think less of you, even if that's a fair point." I fluff my skirt. "This thing weighs as much as I do."

He offers me his arm. "More to the point, I had been in a bit of shock that a human would be so bold as to tear my clothes off. I hadn't realized what was really happening until I was on my back, and you were—"

"What made you save a human?" I accept his arm.

Leading me toward the door, he hums. "I don't know. I was flying up the coast to Aveoaiheva to carry out an order from Pierre, and when I saw you. I almost kept going. Something in me told me to turn back. Perhaps I was caught in the webs of fates, or it was *similis*."

My skirt swishes, the fabric heavy and rubbing against itself as we move through the hallway. "So, the Light Queen...?"

"Yes, a few things to remember beyond basic respect, which include: no use of foul language, bow when you meet her, no pointing, do not raise your voice, thank her for her time, and do not call your magic in her presence."

"Got it."

"You'll be presented by Pierre, and you can expect Ashley to be there as well. Pierre will introduce you."

"Ashley?"

"Pierre's daughter—other daughter."

I blink a few times, processing the realization that Pierre has other children. It never occurred to me. It was a mindless disregard of common sense. "Oh."

"I did not intend to disregard your heritage link. It's merely an adjustment I need to make to my habitual words."

"No, it's fine. I'm not sure about this idea that I'm his daughter." I flick my wrist, backhanding the air before me.

"He is adamant that you are, and I believe him."

Pierre strides toward us from the other end of the corridor. "Zan?"

"Sir." Zander inclines his head, bringing us to a stop before Pierre.

"I'll take charge of my daughter from here. After her presentation, I intend to take her to dine with me, and I will not require a vassal for the evening."

"Yes, sir." Zander nods, dropping my arm and turning to me. "I'll see you in the morning then for breakfast."

I look at the ceiling. "Let me think if I have plans... Oh, no, I don't," I say, lowering my sight to his face, "because I can't do anything without you anyway."

He gives me a tight-lipped expression stuck between a grimace and a smile. "Keep the quips to yourself when you speak to the queen, please, love. I don't want you to end up imprisoned and an actual prisoner."

Rolling my eyes, I look away. "I'll try. No promises."

"May the fates hold a pleasant evening for you."

"Sure, thanks," I mutter. "Can't wait."

Pierre says, "Thank you, Zan. You have the rest of the day for your leisure. Tallie, please follow me and be quick so we may avoid delaying our arrival and be prompt." He steps by me, and I meet Zander's gaze. It's difficult to do with the Seraphinus as there's no pupil visible unless my face is close enough to feel their breath.

"Respectful speech, love," he says, giving me a tight smile. "You'll be fine. Pierre will see to it."

With a sigh, I spin on my high heels and take off after Pierre. This is going to be worse than any terrible, awful decision I've made drunk on two dozen bottles of vodka. I couldn't even behave for Cal when I wanted to.

At the flight shaft, Pierre pushes the button and spreads his wings. The entire palace of Ilbuio would hold less awkwardness than this situation as he scoops me in his arms. It's not charming or cute like when Zander holds me, and I stay limp in his hold until we reach the ground floor.

My feet hurt by the time Pierre leads me up the wide, white marble steps of a building. It's a rectangular, four-storied, plain white marble structure. Of all the buildings with fancy architecture and gilded fascias in this city, I would never have presumed this to be where I would find a throne.

I traipse up the polished steps, carrying my ridiculous skirt in my hands in my best attempt to avoid falling on my face. At the top, I drop the fabric and stumble forward between a row of columns with a curse.

Pierre glances back as he passes between the columns. They have simple inset groves from top to bottom, unlike the details of those on the bottom floor of the tower.

"This place," I huff, fumbling with my gown and catching up to Pierre. "Seems like a shit hole compared to everywhere else I've seen."

"Hold your tongue," Pierre says, cutting his eyes to me. "Show respect. Beenin lived simply, believing in the beauty of minimalism, that true elegance was found when not lost under an abundance of details. This building was founded on her ideology and is in honor of her and of her creation of the Light for justice and righteous protection against the beasts of the Dark."

The double set of golden glass doors is opened for us when we approach within several paces. Pierre neither slows nor acknowledges the act, and he continues to the far end, where a grand, spiraling staircase leads us to the next floor. He doesn't continue further, which I send a silent thanks to the Mother for as my swollen, pulsing feet are demanding a respite.

He stops in front of a chaise. "Please have a seat."

With a sigh of relief and a *whump*, I drop onto the over-stuffed velvet cushion, squirming and fidgeting with my skirt. Pierre pushes his eyebrows together. "I will need to see to arranging etiquette lessons for you."

Nothing witty comes to mind in response, so I tip my head back, staring at the ceiling, waiting to present to a queen I don't care about in a ridiculous gown that cost more than ten years of living taxes, staring down a future I never wanted, where I'm made into something I'm not.

I hate this dress, tailored so tight I can't even take a full breath, the bone-corseted top threatening to snap my ribs at every attempt I make to catch my breath. I want to go home, but I don't even have a home to run to.

Heels clack against the hard floor, setting me on edge. Tensing, I look toward the source, a tall, glamorous woman striding forward in a gown like liquid gold on the arm of a man about a hand shorter than her. The woman leans in closer, whispering something in his ear while her eyes remain pinned on me.

His bronze skin has a golden shimmer reflecting the illumination of the world as he smiles in response.

I cock my jaw and drop my chin to my chest, watching from the corner of my eye. Pierre says, "Tallie, I would like to introduce you to my elder daughter and your sister."

I look at the woman.

Pierre sighs. "Stand, Tallie, as a sign of respect."

Getting to my feet, I step on the train and stumble. "Fucking fuck," I snap, grabbing at the fabric and tripping forward. I get the skirt sorted out from beneath my feet and fluff it into a proper place. Smoothing it with my hands, I look up, all three of them gaping at me.

Pierre shakes his head, his eyes closed as he lowers his chin and rubs the back of his neck. The distinct sense he is repeating my words in his mind lingers in the air, and then he opens his eyes and returns to composure. "Tallie, this is Ashley, my elder daughter and your sister."

She unwinds her arm from the man, clasping her hands before her. Her eyes lower down to my feet and then flick up to meet my gaze again. Even in heels, I have to look up to meet her eyes. "Hi."

Her eyebrows raise, her gold-coated lashes flaring as her eyes widen. "Hello, Tallie. It is a pleasure to see you in Izul, where you can find welcome amongst your kin." She licks her bright red lips, patting the perfect chignon her honey blonde hair is pinned into behind her ear. She motions to the man at her side. "This is Akash, my future mate."

He's lean, average height, with dark hair. He's attractive with round features.

I shrug, hugging myself. "Sure, yeah. Izul is great. There's nowhere without constant bright illumination, and every time I say the word fuck, someone stares at me like I've insulted their mother."

Pierre drops his hand to his face, but Ashley steps closer to me, floating across the floor as only a glamorous, self-assertive and confident woman can. "Using a foul word does not make you cute. Might I suggest instead concise language with precise meaning to convey your thoughts? This will provide a more appropriate response than barbaric verbiage."

I stare at her, narrowing one eye in confusion. "Fuck is the most versatile word in the world. I don't know how I get more concise."

She hums and presses her red lips, both eyebrows flexing upward in a quick motion as she diverts her gaze. "Right." She gives the male a quick look, rolling her eyes, before focusing on me again. "My father advised me you were here. I felt pity for you, but now I see my familial empathy was a waste."

Pierre's voice is tight. "Ash, she is your sister. She was not raised amongst us, and it is far from her own doing. The fault lies not with her, and I am asking you for patience."

"Of course, Father." She runs her hand over her chignon again. How she has managed the perfect hair style, lipstick, and skin, I have no idea. I could spend hours in a bathroom attempting to appear as flawless as she does–have several times when presenting as arm candy for Callahan during Gathering Shadows–and never achieve that level of perfection. "I'm certain she will find Izul to her liking. After all, like mother like daughter, they say, and we've all heard the way she threw herself at Zander like a whore, but then what should we expect?"

"Ashley." Pierre drops his hands on his hips, her name a clipped warning.

I tense, rolling my shoulders back. Akash stares with disinterest, but Ashley smiles coyly, having the nerve to bat her lashes at me.

Narrowing my eyes, I ask, "Excuse me?"

"Oh, dear." Ashley feigns mock hurt and puts a hand to her chest at the base of her throat. "I'm sorry, was that too complex for you to understand? Let me clarify–that is, simplify–for you my proper use of language. You and your mother..."

"Ash!" Pierre interjects.

"...are nothing but a pair of whores."

Gripping my fists, I take a step toward her. "Call me a whore again. I dare you."

"You must think highly of yourself if you are challenging me, but as far as any here are concerned, you're nothing but a weak fool who was forced to serve the Dark," she says, shrugging.

I smile, slow and full of malice. "I wasn't forced. I signed that contract because I wanted to."

Ashely's eyes widen, and then she tips her head back and shrieks with laughter. "Blasphemy." She angles toward Pierre. "Father, you cannot still sincerely consider giving her a place in the Light, in our home, in our heritage, upon learning of that fact."

"Tallie is my daughter. She is your sibling seed. She was

not educated or raised to understand her place. I will not abandon her when the fault lies not with her but in circumstances beyond her control." He pauses, his head swelling. "Now, I know you are upset with me, but Tallie is unaware of how we do things, and she's been subjected to the Dark. She's bound to have lingering issues, but we will deal with them."

I roll my eyes. "Seriously? Give it a rest. I can and have taken care of myself without all the righteous bullshit you spit out."

Ashley steps forward, speaking to her father. "She doesn't belong here. Her, or her human pet."

I bristle, gripping my skirt. "Ness isn't a pet. She's a woman."

Pierre holds a hand up, glaring with a hard gaze. "Stop. Now. Both of you." He glances at me, then returns his attention to Ashley. He softens. "Honey, she needs to be given her place so she can learn who she is, including proper etiquette and honor. Now, I know this will take some time, but I expect you to overlook her ignorance in accepting her upbringing as Magia and for signing a contract to Callahan Barraco and help her find her way into the Light."

Ashley's eyes flash, a flush of pink tinting her cheekbones. "Callahan Barraco?" She turns to me with a putrid sneer. She steps toe to toe with me, staring down her nose in a highly effective manner, given our height difference. "He held your contract?"

I square my shoulders without remorse, a whiff of pride in my soul. "Yes."

Ashley clicks her tongue, wrinkling her nose. "You willingly submitted to the whims of that pathetic, mangy mutt?"

A door opens to the side of us. "The Light Queen..."

I ram the heel of my palm upward into Ashely's face. She rocks back with a sharp shriek.

"...welcomes you and requests your welcome in audience."

Pierre shouts, "Natalia!"

Golden ropes wrap around my arm, wrenching me off balance. I topple to the side, gripping on my dress and hitting the floor. I shove up, scrambling and kicking at my skirt, screaming at the top of my lungs and from deep in my chest at Ashley being steadied by Akash. "If you ever fucking insult Cal again, I'll kill you."

Akash glares back at me, but a hand on my shoulder twists me to stare into Pierre's rancid face. "That is unacceptable behavior."

I scoff. "She insulted–"

"I do not care," Pierre snaps. "That kind of behavior may have been acceptable in Ilbuio, but here we have rules. You will not harm nor threaten anyone of our kind. We have laws, and attacking another is against those laws. We are not savages like the Dark. We do not act like beasts without civility. We are the Light, and we act with dignity and respect." He gives my shoulder a slight shove and rounds on Ashley, "Ash, honey, are you all right?"

Trembling, Ashley is on her feet, supported by Akash, a hand to her face. She pulls it back, blood leaking from her nose and glistening on the skin of her palm.

Pierre swells up, Light glimmering out of him from his pores. His eyes look ready to burst from his face. He glares, lips pressing hard enough to disappear.

Common sense should tell me to cower or show remorse. I can't. All I can see is Cal laughing with his head tipped back.

A female voice wafts in the air, musical and airy, as a woman says, "Excuse the interruption on my part, but as you are here to see me, and I have been waiting, please, someone tell me *what* is being carried on."

I look to the open doorway, a short Lighter standing with

his hands on both doors, frozen in the act of opening them with his jaw hanging low. At his elbow, a woman with the whitest skin and hair I've ever seen stares at me with raised eyebrows.

A crown of clear jewels twinkles on her head as she shifts her gaze to me before passing to Pierre. "Pierre?"

Pierre smooths his tie, settling it into place and turns to her. "Marisa, my sincere apologies."

She feigns a smile, a mask doing nothing to hide the venom in her eyes. "Of course. Apologies have been offered, and I shall accept with grace."

He gives a curt bow, and she gives a weak nod in return. "Perhaps we might attend to business– Oh dear, is that blood? How revolting." She stares at Ashley with full airs of shock, a hand to the base of her throat.

I shrug and cross my arms. "She deserved it."

Marisa's attention snaps to me, her gaze intense with radiating ire. "Deserved?" The word is soft, dripping with rage.

"Tallie," Pierre says, my name cutting through the air, leaving the world reverberating. "Be silent. You have done and said more than enough."

"Oh, I do believe quite the contrary," Marisa says. "Please... come in."

Given her tone, I'd rather irritate the Dark King again and be infected by nightmare. I square my shoulders and lift my chin, taking a step toward the Lighter, still gawking in the doorway.

"Larles," she says, flicking her wrist, "move out of the way, and Ash, darling, you really ought to clean yourself up now."

Ashley mumbles, "Yes, Majesty. I will."

Larles shoves one door, shuffling closer to the other and dragging it with him to give me a wide berth for entrance. He ducks his head and shies away from me with a sneer of disgusted awe as if staring at a man on fire, succumbing to the flames with writhing and twisted screams.

I step into the room, a square, recessed pool of still water in the middle, a gold throne situated before it on a dais.

Marisa stands to the right near a low table set for tea with gold cushions. She lifts two fingers and bends them toward herself twice in a quick fashion, beckoning me.

Pierre steps next to me, gripping my upper arm. "You are to wait for your elder to enter before you, and you wait for the queen to sit first, then your elder." He drags me forward toward the table, his hand clamped tight to the point of pain. Bowing to the queen, he says, "Marisa, we apologize for the disruption to your schedule and the disgusting altercation that caused the delay."

She nods with a smile. "Your apologies are not upon deaf ears, but the amends are not yours to make."

"As she is an extension of my heritage, I hold myself accountable, and her trespasses reflect and fall upon me." He turns to me. "This is Natalia, my second daughter. Tallie, this is the Queen of Light, Marisa Lamont. You will address her formally and with respect as 'Your Majesty.'"

Clicking her tongue, she gestures at the table. He hesitates. Her lips curl, the smile not reaching her eyes. "As your heritage has decided to disregard decency already, I believe we may forgo any further attempts of formal etiquette for this presentation in turn. I insist, Pierre. Sit."

Releasing me, he kneels and sits back on his heels on one of the cushions. His composure is flawless, even if rage is radiating from him.

Marisa fixes her gaze upon me. Clasping her hands, she takes a step toward me, sizing me up. "Now, I would like to take a look at you, young lady."

Zander had taken the time to explain how a presentation

goes. Pierre would enter the throne room with me. Pierre was to perform a proper introduction. I was to bow, keep my eyes low, and exclaim it was an absolute honor and my sheer delight to make the acquaintance. Beyond that statement, I was to speak only when spoken to and present myself in a demure, meek fashion with the utmost respect.

He didn't bother to provide instructions for this scenario. I don't think he expected me to break Ashley's nose.

Marisa stalks forward, shying her head to the side, eyeing me at an angle. "She is certainly beautiful enough to be made of Light."

Pierre says, "Yes, but I believe she takes after her mother still."

Marisa smiles wide. "I dare declare she would pale in comparison if they were to stand side-by-side. We of Light are fashioned after Beenin's likeness, and she was the fairest and most beautiful of all her kind. No mere human could ever outshine, for we burn bright with the Light itself."

I shrug. "You should have seen my sister."

Turning away, Marisa moves to the opposite side of the table, lowering to the floor and adjusting to her comfort. She gestures across the table toward the vacant spot next to Pierre.

Stepping forward, I drop on the cushion next to him in a heap of fabric and limbs. He sighs.

Larles hurries forward, bowing and beginning a ceremony of washing the teacups with tea and then filling them. Marisa ignores him, focusing on me instead. "Pierre has without hesitation proclaimed you as his seed, a continuation of the Bordeaux heritage, and yet, he was unaware of your very existence. It was not until it was made known to me by the Dark that one of ours was being held within their clutches, and I dispatched him to correct the revolting matter. Why is that?"

"You'd have to ask him."

"Pierre, please enlighten us."

He inclines his head. "I will speak directly to my daughter if you'll allow. She is as unaware as you."

"Of course."

Pierre takes a long draw of air. "Ashley's mother, my mate, was murdered nearly three centuries ago. I never formed another attachment on that level, although your mother came close. However, Annika ended our relationship abruptly. At the time, though I mourned her loss, I thought I was honoring her wishes by staying away. When I spoke to her recently to confirm your origins, she made it clear that the Magia had rules against her involvement with me in any fashion other than my death and had been forced to cease contact. When they learned of her relationship with me, they threatened her elder daughter, Natasha, so she dissolved our relationship. Upon learning of this, I immediately began trying to rectify the wrong laid at your feet. My failure to take charge of you and teach you as you should have been taught."

I frown. "Then you returned to Ilbuio. That's why you were there? To tell me?"

"I did my best to make arrangements to wrest you from Callahan's control so I might bring you here, to give you your rightful place and to help you come into the Light as you always should have been." He almost smiles, a flicker in one side of his mouth. "Your inability to allow one to finish a simple statement prevented my plans."

I snort through my nose. "You could have told me."

"I realized you would not leave willingly, and I had my reasons to withhold the information. I sought other measures to free you instead, which failed abysmally. But in the end, our *similis* won. You did come willingly to my doorstep, and I will see to your education so you may take your proper place."

"Not so much willingly, but whatever." I roll my eyes.

He faces Marisa, and she raises an eyebrow. "You whole-heartedly trust in the spoken words of her mother? That this is, without a doubt, part of your seed?"

"*Similis* exists between us. I need not trust nor words of another to know what she is. It is so strong even Natalia can feel the pull. She informed me without even knowing what it was that she experienced."

"Then a Bordeaux she shall be known as," Marisa says as she lifts her cup. She takes a drink, bowing her head.

Pierre picks up his cup. "I will immediately begin her training, ensuring she can survive her growing Light."

Marisa lifts her hand, silencing him. "I will grant the right to acknowledge kinship and heritage, yes. However, there remains the concern of granting standing to one so volatile. Indeed, one may grow bold enough to claim you tarnish your heritage by associating your name with such a savage." She clicks her tongue.

Pierre's response is guarded, slow to come and spoken with care. "Natalia was exposed to the brainwashing of the cultists known as the Magia, then contracted by an animal in the Dark, subjected to violence and cruelty beyond our recognition. I will admit she is unbalanced, capricious even, in ways foreign to us because of her upbringing. This reflects directly upon my failures as her eldest in heritage and her father to bring her into the Light as she ought to have been. I will take responsibility for her in every measure."

"She served the Dark willingly. That alone is blasphemy, but she also attacked your elder daughter. It spilled your seed's blood not but moments ago."

Pierre tenses. "I'm aware. She has bad habits developed from environmental influences that will be rectified. I intend to see to her lessons of etiquette and of our customs promptly to eradicate her dismal conduct."

The queen grins wide as she continues. "Dismal. Deserving. How very ghastly a declaration both statements are."

Contemplative, Pierre leans back. "What that dog put her through—"

"Cal," I snap. "His name is Callahan, and he's not a dog. He's damn well-earned respect, and you don't get to talk to me about him like that."

The queen smirks, ducking her head to hide the expression behind her teacup. Pierre scowls at me. "Tallie, we do not interrupt, and we do not defend the Dark."

"No," I sneer, fluttering my eyes and rolling them with disgust. "Just kill them."

The queen sets her cup down against the table with a sharp rap. "Yes, child, we do. We are the Light, and we snuff out the Dark until it no longer can exist." She flicks her hand toward Pierre. "He removed an entire contender's list, five of the strongest enemies of the Light subdued. It's a pedestal of pride on which I've placed him, providing him with platitudes and honor for the accomplishment."

Widening my eyes, I open my mouth, preparing to shriek until my lungs bleed.

Pierre lifts his voice. "Tallie, you will not disrespect our queen."

I twist toward him, redirecting my rage. "That was Cal's fucking father."

He holds up a hand, his eyebrows pushing together with concern. "It's going to take some time, but this is where you belong. These ideals you disregard or disagree with are the foundation of who you are at your core, no matter what despicable charades they've been made into by that ignorant cult or the barbaric animals that have twisted you. You will learn respect and our ways. The Light does not save the Dark. We burn it out until it no longer exists." He twists his head, speaking to the queen, though his gaze remains locked with mine. "She does not know any better, and she's been tainted by the Dark. As I said, this will take time. You are combative. I understand why. That animal—"

"I told you—"

"Putting you through those dark games—"

"You don't get to talk about him like that."

"The contract, his abuse of you, and whatever he did to hurt you because of me—"

"Cal didn't hurt me."

Pierre lifts his chin, pressing his lips. "Natalia. I am warning you for the last time—"

I scream, "And for the last time, you don't have the right to insult him. Ever. Not for his name. Not for what you think of him. Not for what you think he did to me, not a single fucking word or derogatory remark about him or his name ever again, or I will show you a savage."

The queen hums. "I do believe that will be quite enough." She looks to Pierre. "I have heard everything I need to decide she's hardly deserving of a place among us. Her words are caustic, her attitude foul, her behavior disrespectful, and her beauty is overshadowed by her lack of true Light."

"She is my daughter, Marisa."

"Yes, and I granted recognition. However, to give her the stature of a Bordeaux, even standing in our court, is impossible in her current state. Beyond the aforementioned reasons, she served the Dark of her own volition and attacked one within our city right in front of you–your daughter, in fact."

"I am aware, and I brought her before you in good faith, now, before I could correct her behavior, in acknowledgment of your stature. However, I am requesting time." He pauses. "I need time with her to eradicate the bad habits she has been ingrained with."

The queen shakes her head, taking a sip of her tea. Coddling the cup in her hands, she turns to me. "Child, are you aware of the punishment for attacking another within this city?"

I lift my chin. "No."

Pierre rubs his forehead, staring into his lap. "She is beyond ignorant."

"You may claim her as your seed, and I will grant mercy upon such a wretched creature, left to the devices of others and abandoned by the Light for so long, but it will do to teach her consequences." She takes a drink, frowning into her cup. "Fifty days instead of fifty years."

"You are far too generous, Marisa," he responds in a dry tone that conveys his impression of the opposite.

"Yes, but a pathetic child should not suffer retribution for the faults of its elders without an extension of redemption." She smiles, batting her white eyelashes. "I will grant leniency while she is incarcerated for her benefit, but she will remain imprisoned for the entirety of her sentence for the benefit of all others."

"You do have others to consider."

"A lesson she will do well to learn as well." The queen drains her cup, setting it aside. "While she is considering her uncivilized actions, you will be responsible for undoing the damages wrought. We shall see how she reforms in fifty days. If she is agreeable at the end of her sentence, then we will continue to an extension of this discussion."

The queen stands, and Pierre is quick to follow. I look up and then away, struggling to my feet and fussing with my skirt, finding solid footing by clearing the hem from beneath my feet.

She tilts her head in my direction. "Do use these fifty days to your advantage. Think long and think hard about your actions. Consider wisely how you will present yourself and conduct your business in the future. If you cannot be civilized, I will be forced to abide by our laws. A reckless abandon will not be suffered. Your Light will be destroyed."

I gape. "Wait. What?"

She turns away. "Larles."

"Your Majesty?"

"Fetch two avengers to have them escort this child to our dungeons."

"Yes, Your Majesty." He scampers to comply, slipping away.

With wide eyes, I turn to Pierre. "Dungeons?"

He stares back with indifference. "Yes, Tallie and you are going to accept with gracious appreciation."

"Like fucking curses I am going to thank someone for locking me up."

The queen laughs as Larles returns in a hurry, two men at his back approaching with grim expressions. "Dear child, curb that tongue, or it will be the death of you."

CHAPTER 22

NATALIA

I half-consider trying to run, but I'm not able to breathe in this dress, and even if I lose my heels, I don't know if I can find my way out of the city before I'm caught. It's not like I have anywhere else to go. Even if I get free of Izul, I may never be able to stop running ever again, and right now, I'd abandon Ness if I did escape.

I barely have the mental fortitude to postulate the scenario. The idea of actually doing it, living that nightmare, drains all the resistance from my soul. I'm a wrung out husk of myself, brittle from the internal carnage Cal has wrought.

The queen steps toward me once more, tilting her head. "Accept your consequences with grace, child, or I will retract my leniency, and you will be bound and imprisoned for fifty years for your infraction as the laws state. You will be without hope of redemption when next we meet."

Pinching my lips, I twitch the end of my nose to the side in a show of annoyance, but I keep my mouth shut. I won't take an easy way out, but there's a limit to my stupidity.

"Good girl," she says, gesturing behind me. "They will see

to it you find your way to your quarters, where you will wait out your sentence."

Spinning on my heel, I turn my back on her without complaint and face the avengers. They scowl, and Pierre says, "Marisa, you are without a doubt remaining as effervescent and tactful as always."

"My appreciation, Pierre, for bringing this matter to me to deal with." She steps next to me, keeping her eyes forward. "My dear child, I will see you again upon your release. Use this time wisely."

"Sure," I say, stepping toward the men eyeing me with disgust. "Where am I going?"

One lifts his chin. "Please allow us to lead you."

I follow the avengers out of the throne room with Pierre. We head for the spiral staircase, leading down across the empty front room to the other corner of the back wall and down again.

There's a long corridor with doors spaced along one side, and the avengers step to the first. One opens the door while the other moves behind me, saying, "Please enter your assigned lodging to begin your incarceration."

I glance at Pierre. He inclines his head. "Please step inside, Tallie."

"Is this really happening right now?"

"Yes, daughter mine," he says and sighs. "You attacked another within the city limits, which is against the law. You made Ashley, my elder daughter, and your sibling bleed. You did so well within view of our queen, and it is her decision. She is being kind in offering a chance for indemnification."

Scoffing, I step across the threshold, turning around to say, "This is fucking bullshit."

The door closes and disappears. I reach out, feeling around for a handle, a pressure sensor, anything that will allow me to leave. There is none. I throw my hands in the air and twist on my high heels to inspect the room.

Four white walls and a big, white bed with white bedding pushed to one side. There's a standing, white, trifold screen positioned near the back wall. A white armoire in the corner of the far wall between the screen and the bed.

I kick at my skirt, grabbing it up to stalk toward the bed. Halfway there, I kick off my heels and pad barefoot against the cold, white marble floor before falling face-first into it with a groan. It's like falling into a warm cloud offering free hugs.

Pushing up on my elbows, I frown at it, glancing around the room once more. Other than white, Light glowing in the seams of the corners, ceiling, and floor, there's nothing bleak about my surroundings.

Cal locked me in a room at his house in Narwal.

I'm never going to see him again. The only thing left is the ruins of his once gorgeous estate and probably a mutilated corpse.

With that grotesque sight in mind, I get up, needing to occupy my mind. Checking behind the screen, I find a grand, four-legged bathtub and toilet. Reaching for the zipper on my dress, I turn the tap on.

I strain and yank and grunt, grappling with the zipper, trying to get out of this stupid gown. The zipper slips to about my shoulders, but I can't get a good angle to drag it the rest of the way. Giving up, I grip the two sides and tear them apart, stitches ripping, the zipper making an awful growl, but I wriggle free of the heavy fabric, kicking it toward the corner.

Waiting for the tub to fill, checking the water temperature, and dancing in place, I try to find something, anything, to hold my attention in the room. I can hear the Light intensifying, laughing at me from every right angle it enters the room from. I cover my ears and glare at the tub.

I remove my underwear and slip into the water, letting the warmth wash over me, positioning myself so I'm submerged everywhere but my face, floating in the heat.

Cold still radiates from my chest, pressing further through my limbs with every pulse of my heart. Cal had been warm. There was a fire kindled beneath his skin, flames that burned down my walls of protection and seared him into my core. He had a candescence even in the shadows that wrapped around him. I want to feel that aura of heat and strength as cool shadows caress my skin one more time.

Closing my eyes, I take a breath and slip all the way into nothingness, blocking out everything, hoping to drown my thoughts until the need for air drags me to the surface once more. Cal remains in my mind, permeating every inch of me.

Curling into a ball, I hug my knees, holding tight for strength as I sob into them. I'm never going to see him again. He'll never offer me his hand again. I've lost my home and my heart.

I cry for both until the tears won't come and the water is cold, chills puckering my skin. Reaching for the towel hanging on the wall, I climb out of the tub and pull the drain, letting my misery and the water flitter to unknown pipes carried to depths far away from me.

I return to the bed, slipping naked between the sheets, pulling them over my head as a cocoon, curling around one pillow while using the other to shield me from the ever-imprudent Light filling the room as I dream of my Darkling, of home, and of words I'll never say.

EIGHTH MOON'S DAY, WARMWAVE, 4049 SEVENTH
MILLENIUM A.I.

SOMETHING WAKES ME, my senses prickling. For a suspended moment in time, I'm numb to everything. I'm almost okay, cuddled and swathed up nicely, but the impending footsteps cease near my head, invading my cocoon.

"Love?" The pillow lifts from over my head.

I crack one eye open, glaring up at him as he laughs. Making a grab for the pillow, I sit up, the sheets falling and cold air claiming me. Grabbing the sheets, I press them against my bare chest, narrowing my eyes at Zander.

His hair is braided back in a complicated style today. He asks, "What were you doing?"

"Sleeping."

"With a pillow on your head?"

I point away from me. "This constant damn brightness isn't conducive for sleeping."

He sighs, setting the pillow on its end, gripping it hard as he gives me a long look. "Well, I hope you are pleased with yourself. You are officially a prisoner of Izul."

"I'm aware." I glance over my shoulder. "There's literally not a door to get out. It's kind of hard to miss the point."

His shoulders sag. "You need to take this seriously. Any member of the Light that does not conform, that goes against our pillars, is unwelcome in society. However, for the sake of all unity within the Light, if there is a Light that develops wrong..." He hesitates. "If the Light isn't cohesive with our ways, not merely non-conforming, but actively pursues against our beliefs, the Light is to be destroyed."

"Like take my magic somehow? Not just bind me?"

His eyebrows push together above his nose. "To have your Light destroyed would kill you."

I drop my jaw. "If I don't act the way you like, you kill me?"

Zander tosses the pillow aside. "It is uncommon, but there have been a few instances notated in the history of a seed of Light being rogue, of being too wild to be controlled, which results in disaster. The host becomes violent, they challenge our way of life, they disrupt the system, and they—in the past—have even tried to take control of the Light."

I cock my jaw and turn away. He won't say what he means, but I understand enough. Any Light that dares act out, perhaps even to mirror the Dark in conduct, is considered a rogue Light.

"You're going to be fine, love. I give you my word that Pierre and I will do everything we can to teach you, to help you come into the Light so you can take your place and have a long and hopefully happy life."

"Don't know how happy I'll be faking pleasantries and adding superfluous dialogue to my life," I say. "I think I might prefer being destroyed."

"Please don't say that." He puts two fingers under my chin, lifting to force me to meet his eyes. "I am fortunate enough to have you return to my life. I prefer your continued existence over the alternative."

"Dead?"

"Not in my life," he says, his face dropping toward mine.

"You know we don't really know each other."

He smiles, his eyes half-closed and lowered toward my mouth. "I know I enjoy you."

Leaning away, I pull back. "I use fuck like a comma, and you cringe every time."

He laughs. "I have clothes for you." He motions toward the door—or where the door ought to be.

"Did you bring me food?"

Checking his watch, he says, "Breakfast will be delivered in a quarter of a rune. You'll be given three meals a day." He gives me a wry smile. "There will be no alcohol."

"Fucking Mother," I groan, rocking back to glare at the ceiling.

Chuckling, he sits on the edge of the bed. "It's only fifty days, and then you will be offered another chance to try presenting again. You'll know everything you need to by then."

I adjust the sheet tighter around me, blinking prickles from my eyes. He reaches toward me again as I sniff, so I smack his hand away. "Don't," I snap.

Sighing, Zander drops his hand. "You are not without hope. We just need to polish you up a bit. Teach you a few manners. I'll spend every fraction of the next fifty days locked in here with you if I must."

"Can I see Ness? Where is she?"

Zander shakes his head. "Her Majesty's leniency extends to family only."

"She's family."

"No, love."

"More than you."

He frowns at me like I've insulted his best joke. "I'm contracted to the Bordeaux heritage, and Pierre raised me like a son. I have ties to your heritage, some deeper than even yours, though I carry the seed of Fairly."

"Pierre raised you?"

He ducks his chin to his chest. "A point of strain in my heritage's history. My parents–well, my heritage–serves the trinity. They are the great heritages that keep order and harmony. The royals, Lamont, the Hallows, Beenin watch over them in the afters and the Bordeauxs." He nods toward me.

"Why?"

"When the clans came together, the strongest of all the

203

Light, my heritage, bowed in respect to the others, accepting the duty to act as protectors so that the other great heritages would rule in safety."

"Why wouldn't they rule? If your heritage is the strongest, wouldn't that make more sense?"

"No. The Dark acts that way, seeing strength as a way of demanding respect. The Light sees strength as a call for duty. Those who are strong enough shall protect those who are not."

"That sounds like an alpha."

"We do not use such crude methods or displays of aggression." He slides further onto the bed and continues. "My heritage bows to the trinity, and only them, as a show of respect to our strength, but we have always been avengers. I would be as well, but I am forbidden because I and my brother are the last of the Fairly heritage. Until we create others, and many, we are to be protected to avoid a repeat of losing an entire heritage, like the Hallow's heritage."

I force my lower lip to bend into an exaggerated frown. I'd always hated being viewed as someone who could only ever serve the purpose of creating a life to replace mine. "You're a baby machine?"

He runs his fingers through his loose, long, golden hair, flipping it to the other side. "I have a responsibility to continue my heritage, no matter the personal sacrifice, as it will serve all. I am serving the Light and my kin. It's an honor I accepted with mixed feelings, but I cannot think of only myself." He tries to smile. "My parents were both killed in altercations with the Dark. Those responsible were executed by the Council, but the damage was wrought. My brother and I were still in our first century. I was about your age. Pierre took me in. Her majesty took in my elder brother, Larles."

"The guy with the queen?"

Giving me another tight-lipped smile, Zander says, "He's

mortified by my affection for you after the scene you made yesterday."

I try to recall Larles in my mind to compare them. "He was shorter."

"A point of contention and best not mentioned. Both of our parents were tall, and he's bitter about his lack of inherited height."

Zander stands. "I'll excuse myself over here while you get dressed. Breakfast will be served soon, and you'll want proper attire to receive it in."

He heads for the wall with the invisible way in and out of this room, retrieving a large, taupe canvas bag from the floor. Depositing it on the foot of the bed, he inclines his head, then about faces, walking to the wall and studying it closely.

Rolling my eyes, I grab the handles and slip from the bed, seeking refuge near the tub, using the screen as designed for coverage as I get dressed.

"All right," I say, stepping from behind the screen to hold my arms out and spin in a circle. "Clothed."

He turns, hands in his front pockets. "Very beautiful, love. Please clean up your area in preparation for our meal, and in the future, keep things neat. If you use something, put it in its proper place when done. The Light maintains order in all things."

I glance at the discarded towel. Instead of rolling my eyes, I kick the towel up, nabbing it from the air without a retort. I'm a grown woman. I can clean up after myself. That's not a ridiculous request on his part.

"When the meal is served, we can chat, and then Pierre has arranged an etiquette tutor for you."

I hang the towel on the hook. "Etiquette...tutor?"

His grin blends into a grimace. "Everyone goes through

lessons, perhaps not at your age, but all the same, it's customary, and you are in desperate need of a few lessons."

I curl my lip, unable to conjure a response, too disgusted by
the idea that I need to be polished and changed.

"Love," he says with a chuckle, "you got yourself imprisoned. You need a few adjustments."

"Maybe the Light needs an adjustment," I mutter under my
breath.

Zander lifts an eyebrow, giving me a look of humor, but I'm
saved by a knock. He calls out, "You may enter."

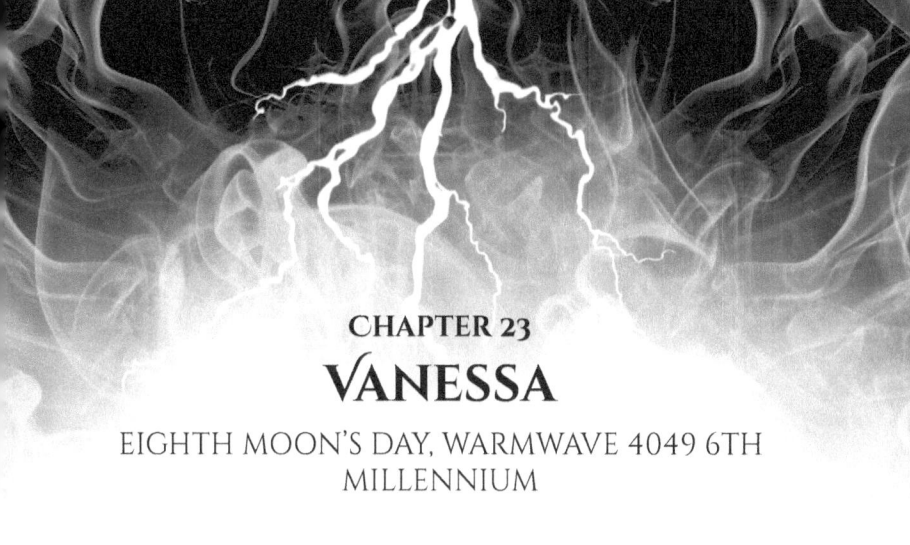

CHAPTER 23
VANESSA

EIGHTH MOON'S DAY, WARMWAVE 4049 6TH MILLENNIUM

The sound of knuckles rapping is worse than any alarm clock I've ever owned. Groaning and kicking at nothing, I drag myself out of bed and into a bra and other appropriate attire, all to be escorted to get something to eat and then be dumped back in this room.

I'll have to serve Owen his disgusting tea and *jejinn* like a servant, waiting for his permission to scarf down what little I can get. The meals I was provided yesterday were never enough, and if I stay here long enough, I'll be as thin as Tallie. I'm not sure how I feel about that.

It took me years to be comfortable and confident in my body. Sure, I'm long-legged like a model, but that makes me tall like one, too, which men don't want. I'm curvy with boobs and butt, thick thighs that rub together when I walk and the matching love handles. It's an appeal men are divided on.

Taking a deep breath, I go through my affirmations. I am not in this world to please men with my body. A scale doesn't measure my worth, just my relation to gravity. My body is for living, not showcasing. Beauty is in the eye of the beholder and I will look at myself as a gorgeous woman.

I swipe gold liner on my lids and glare at the mirror. There's no black makeup in this entire city, not even mascara for my dark eyelashes.

Properly secured in boob jail with pants and a t-shirt, I open my door, but I find two men waiting for me on the other side instead of one. I blink at Owen, who motions to the man next to him.

"This is Kazez. Kazez, please meet Vanessa."

Kazez frowns, his round face wrinkling. Unlike every other Seraphinus I've met, Light or Dark, Kazez is short and stocky, with wide, rounded features. I'm tempted to make a joke that I thought it was a requirement to be tall, fit, and gorgeous to be a Seraphinus, but Lighters tend not to have a sense of humor. Plus, it's mean.

"Hello, Miss Vanessa."

"Um..." I glance at Owen and back to Kazez. He's not ugly, but he's not as dreamy as Owen. "Hi?"

Owen forces a smile. "Kazez is one of Pierre's contracted with duties in the library."

"Oh?" I perk up, eyebrows raised, my mouth sticking in the small O-shape as I freeze with excitement.

"Yes, Vanessa, Pierre has been able to secure a special allowance to grant you entry and use of our library."

"Eee!" I squeal and jump in place, clapping my hands.

Smirking, Owen says, "Kazez will be responsible for collecting you, providing your breakfast meal, and then escorting you to the library. Once inside, you must wait until I collect you for dinner, and then I will return you here to your room. You still require constant supervision, and if you are not willing to cooperate—"

"I am! I so am! Whatever you want if I— I mean, it's not a

look, but don't touch situation, right? I get to read whatever I want?"

With a hand, Owen motions to Kazez. "The library is his domain and expertise, not mine. He will have more details and will explain the necessary information. I was merely here to introduce you two, but I will collect you at Thorn's Rune from the library. Enjoy your day." He turns and disappears down the hall.

I fixate on Kazez, my new favorite Lighter in existence. He steps further into the hallway, "If you please, Miss Vanessa?"

THE LIBRARY IS on the northern edge of town, furthest away from the sea, in the most exquisite building I've seen in the city. The exterior is exclusively made of snow and opal marble, a grandeur with columns and spiraling architecture, and my new favorite place in all of existence.

Inside are gilded and decorative spiral staircases and twinkling crystal chandeliers. It takes my breath away as I enter every new room, every turn we take as we twist through the aisles and shelves, each floor, each room grander than the last. There's too much to see, and I'm not ready to leave when Kazez escorts me back to the front doors.

"Please, Miss Vanessa." He ushers me through the inner cloister toward the main entrance. "It is half past Thorn's rune, and Owen will be waiting to collect you."

I glance over my shoulder, trying to take in more of the intricate gold and painted glass mosaics surrounding me as I keep up with his quick gait. "Can't he wait a little longer?"

"You will return tomorrow."

He waves me through the marble archway and into the small foyer where Owen waits.

Checking his watch, he drops his hands to his hips and frowns. "You are late."

"My apologies." Kazez bows to Owen. "Please, the thing is curious and delayed me."

I glare. "Thing?"

Owen motions with two fingers and a stern expression for me to follow, then pushes open one-half of the massive doors. Outside, he stops on the steps and cocks his jaw as I step to him, the door banging shut behind us.

"I stated I would retrieve you at Thorn's rune, and you did not heed my notice. You have every day of the rest of your incredibly short life to spend in our library. I expect punctuality. It is a sign of respect to me not to waste my time."

"I'm sorry," I say, almost whining as I go on. "I don't think I got to see even half of the building, and I didn't get to so much as touch a book today."

"I do not care about your pitiful concerns. When you delay me, you take time from my allotted personal time of the day. I care more for my life than yours." He turns and heads down the steps.

He sets a brisk pace for returning to the Gold Tower, and I'm dizzy from the flight up the shaft, Owen rocketing to the fifty-seventh floor in mere fractions of a rune.

"Hot date?" I ask when he sets me on my feet.

"My affairs are not your concern."

I sigh and glance around at the old and rare antiques lining the hall as we run to my room. Crossing my fingers, I hope I am correct in my summations. Perhaps his mood would be improved for tomorrow if he gets off tonight.

He rips my door open and gestures me inside.

I shake my head, slumping past him. "Didn't mean to make you late. I apologize."

"As you should. It has forced me to be late, which is unacceptable. I have notified Pierre of the occurrence and that he will need to make alternative arrangements for you to be fed. You've now inconvenienced four with your actions. Kazez will collect you in the morning at Dawn's rune, and I will be escorting you for dinner. Please be punctual."

"Thorn's rune." I bob my head, keeping my eyes on the floor. "Got it."

Owen storms off, and I wait until he's out of sight to slip across the hall to Tallie's room. There's no answer when I knock, so I grant myself entry. She won't mind.

It's empty. I stare around the room, searching for something, not sure what I'm looking for. Her phone is on the bed, discarded or left behind. Willing her into existence isn't going to work, so I return to my room to wait for someone to escort me to dinner while I flip through my translations of the codex.

It's an odd mix of magic and entries like a journal. I stop on an entry, re-reading the passage:

THE DAYS GROW LONGER *in the cage of my prison. Fate is my only companion. How long will I endure? There is no heart in me left to carry on, nothing but bitterness to sustain me. I seek warmth, finding none. There are but shadows and echoes, the world dark, and my blood runs black. I curse at beauty, sneer at affection, no solace to my condemnation. Califum felixia deporum.*

THOSE FINAL WORDS have no translation I could find, and Mass didn't know those either, claiming them nonsense. To be fair, the author of the codex did seem to be descending into madness, incoherencies suffered by the writer breathing through the pages.

A knock on my door drags my attention away. I shove the translations under my sheets before getting up. I answer, staring down Pierre.

His lips press, a frown of disdain. "Good evening, Vanessa."

"Hi."

He steps aside, perpendicular to my door. "If you please?" He waves in front of him. "I will escort you for a meal."

I step into the hallway, closing my door. "Thanks. I'm starving. I haven't eaten since this morning. Where's Tallie? I checked her room, but she wasn't there."

"Tallie has broken our laws and has been imprisoned for her grievances."

I gape, frozen. "Wh–what?"

He rubs his forehead, staring at his feet with his other hand on his hip. "She is willfully stubborn beyond measure, lashing out with violence and unbecoming vernacular. It's obvious that animal corrupted her, and it is going to be difficult to undo the damages." He sighs, dropping his hand from his face to his hip. "She will be given another chance to present after her sentence. Pray to Adontis that she adjusts her behavior."

I stare at him with an open mouth. "What does that mean?"

"For the next fifty days, she will be held in confinement, and after her sentence is concluded, she will need to make amends while exhibiting proof she is capable of adhering to our customs, or she will be put to death."

"What the fuck?" I yell.

He glares. "Volume. Tone. Language." He ticks the words off on his fingers. "You delayed one of my vassals, in turn delaying a second, and have brought down on me an inconvenience during a personally trying time for me. The results of your actions have inconvenienced four in total. Your careless disregard for punctuality and respect will be overlooked this once. In the future, you will endure consequences instead of allowances. I encourage you to take in the lessons Kazez and Owen teach you and conform to our customs, or you will be removed from Izul. We won't bother expending the energy to kill you as Tallie would be, but I believe that is a death sentence for you all the same, is it not?"

Closing my mouth, I look to the floor, dread gripping my stomach hard enough to hurt, my hunger strangled from me. "Yes...uh, sir."

"Very good. Please follow me. I will take you to a *velkeno*."

"Eat quick?"

"You will be able to find prepared meals for you to select one to take with you. You'll eat in your room this evening."

CHAPTER 24
NATALIA

NINTH NIGHT'S DAY, WARMWAVE, 4049 6TH MILLENNIUM

What I've seen on the entertainment screen about prison led me to expect overcrowding of humans clogging a system with pushing and shoving. Fights are bound to happen, pent-up frustrations exploding into physical altercations. The food would be bland, mushy, and served with a single spoon.

This is not that.

I have no cellmates. I have a massive, comfortable bed to myself. It's quiet, almost too quiet: the silence rings when I'm alone, but it's not often. My tutor is a near constant intruder, educating me in how to walk, always in heels and dresses. My posture is critiqued, elegance and grace required in my movements.

I have learned how to serve tea and proper responses to questions and comments. Every day I talk until my throat is raw, garnering sharp glares and sighs at every failure.

There is absolutely, without question, no fighting and no cursing allowed.

My tutor looks at me, lingering by the open doorway after a

grueling experience. "Remember, dear, words are more dangerous when honed than any fist."

"Ashley's nose would beg to differ."

The tutor's eyes flare.

I duck my head, wincing at the floor. "Uh, have a good evening."

"Good evening, Miss Bordeaux. May you have a pleasant time, and might I suggest reflecting upon your less-than-correct response. We shall see what you discover during tomorrow's lesson." Her response is tart, her face tight with contained ire.

When the wall seals shut, I let out a deep sigh, staring after her. I screw up my face, rocking my head back and forth. "Less-than-correct response," I mock. Releasing my expression, I flip the door off. "I didn't say her *fucking* nose would disagree."

Turning, I shuffle to my bed and fall face forward into it with a groan. "Fuck, I fucking miss saying fuck." I relax, letting myself sink into the mattress and take a few deep breaths.

Knocking carries through the room. I pick my head up, craning toward the wall. "You may enter."

The door opens, and Pierre enters, his golden hair cut short, not the longer locks he wore. I scowl at him, dragging myself upright until I notice the case hanging in his grasp by a handle.

My heart skips a beat, spiking with an excited pulse. It's black. It's shaped like a guitar.

I stand and straighten, shoulders back and chin up, even if my eyes remain trained on the instrument case. "Hi. Welcome and be welcomed. What's that?"

Pierre steps to my bed, setting the case down. "I am welcomed and welcoming. Welia has said you've made great improvements over the last several days. She has high hopes that you will continue the trajectory and be ready by the end of the next forty-three days."

I blink, a bit dazed. "It's only been seven days?"

"This is your sixth day in confinement."

"Shit."

He presses his lips. "Yes, well then," he says, "small steps."

I stare at him with nothing to say. Flicking my gaze to the case and back to him, I lick my lips, daring not to breathe for fear I do it wrong.

With a genuine smile, he waves toward the case. "I know you're getting settled right now, and things will take time, but I'd like to have a relationship with you."

Staring at the instrument, I chew on my lower lip.

"I understand I cannot force you to do anything, but are you willing to try?"

"Sure." I eye the case with fervor, torn between my dislike of him and my desire for the instrument.

"I see I'll get naught from you until I've satisfied your interest in my gift to you. Go ahead."

I lurch to it, fingers sweating as I pop the brass latches. When I flip it open, my heart stalls. The surface of the instrument is polished, but the edges are worn. The card in the strings on the neck sends a message in a scrawl of black ink.

"*Tallie, thanks for being a fan. Take care of my girl. Shawn Gittemeier*"

"Oh, my Mother," I scream, picking up the guitar. I gape at it, and then I spin, sitting on the foot of the bed, pulling the card free and setting it in the case. "How did you know?"

He smiles. "Call it a father's intuition."

I snort through my nose, staring at the instrument. "Zander told you."

He laughs. "Perhaps. Does it make you happy?"

I run my fingers over the strings, resting the guitar on its back, tracing the letters etched into the surface. "You're not home."

I can't tear my eyes from the line. A lump forms in my throat as I rest my fingers over the lyrics. My chest aches, threatening to crush under the force of longing. My breath catches as I try to pull in air like I forgot how to breathe.

I am not home. I'm far, far from home. I'm away from Cal, and all I want is to take his hand and feel at home again, but it's impossible.

"Tallie?"

Facing Pierre, I blink and clear my throat, adjusting the guitar in my lap and holding it as if I'm about to play. "Yes?"

"Does that mean something?" He's tense. "Those words?"

Pulling my eyebrows together, I frown. "Yeah. Shawn Gettmeire is the lead singer for Dark Marrow and the sole writer of their song 'I'll Stay.' They're lyrics from that song. How did you get this?" I drink in the sight of the guitar, running my thumb down the strings. "This is incredible. I can't believe I'm holding a Dragola–*Shawn's* Dragola."

He gives me a closed-lip smile that seems more of a grimace. "When you're alive as long as I have been, you're bound to make connections."

"Right, but I know this guitar. He played it on tour all the time." I draw a finger over the lyrics again. "At least, I think this is the same one. I don't remember the words being engraved, but it's not like I've seen it up close."

"He was happy to give it to a fan."

I cut my eyes to Pierre in disbelief. "Right, and for a ton of coin, I'm sure."

"I have coin. That's never to be a concern for you. The Bordeaux heritage is vast and wealthy."

Narrowing my eyes, I say, "Dark Marrow is *Dark*. You're

Light. Zander outright refuses to even listen to this band because of that. How did you manage this?"

Pierre breathes out long and slow, pulling up and running a hand down the buttons of his shirt. "You are a very special case, and as I said, they were happy to provide this for a fan and, yes, coin."

"He's Dark. You're Light," I repeat with venom. "There's no way he would have sold it–no matter the price–to someone like you. Your kind despises each other, and I mean like putrid, acidic, burning with the intensity of a thousand suns kind of hatred. D.M. has several songs about what they think of the Light, and it's not indicative of a willingness to sell a prized possession. This is a Dragola, for fuck's sake. There are only a dozen in the world. He wouldn't have just handed this over, and certainly not to the likes of you."

"Tallie," Pierre warns.

I snap back, "How did you get this?"

Pierre shrugs. "I paid coin."

I narrow my eyes. "Dark Marrow is massively popular, selling out shows across both continents, and the cheapest tickets cost almost as much as the living taxes I paid every year. Coin wouldn't be enough."

"It was."

"No. No, I don't believe you. Shawn is particular about his guitars. He's said so in interviews. There's no way. You would have had to pry this from his dead fingers." I glare and scream, "Did you fucking kill Shawn Gettemeir?"

"Lower your voice."

I take a deep breath through my nose.

The Lighter, who calls himself my father, watches me, then says, "I have influence across much of this world. Regardless of Light or Dark, I have reaches further than you know. There are ways of Light and Dark communicating without bloodshed, and I used my resources, not violence."

"Then you have a way to contact him? I'd like to speak to him, maybe say thank you personally."

"No," Pierre snaps, quick and harsh. He takes a deep breath and sits next to me. "I'm sorry, but no. This was arranged through a third party. As you said, they are the Dark, and we are the Light. I made a very special exception for this, but seeing or speaking to a Dark isn't considered acceptable."

I bob my head, disappointment drowning me. "Right."

"They received compensation for this property, that is more thanks than the Dark deserves, but I hope you like it."

Hugging the guitar, I try to put into words how much I love it, but all I can manage is "Yes."

"The words on it, you said they are a song? That seems to have some kind of importance."

I adjust my fingers on the frets and find the right cord, strumming a few notes. "Something like that."

"I didn't realize you played the instrument."

I glance at him in confusion. "Then why did you buy me a guitar?"

"You're a fan of the band. I thought you would like something of theirs, and," he smiles, "I thought you might be interested in learning as a way to occupy yourself between lessons and meals when Zander is unavailable to keep you company."

Shrugging, I strum a chord, then let my hand fall away, gripping the neck in the other. "I stretch to occupy myself, but this is going to be a lot more entertaining. You said a third party. So, theoretically, I could send a response the same way? I really want to thank him."

"Who?"

"Shawn." I frown. "Seems like a shirt would have been easier than this if you just wanted to get me something."

"Perhaps," he says. "Rather less entertaining for you, though."

I perk up. "It would be black. Is that an option, too?"

Pierre shakes his head with a forlorn expression. "You should have been brought here upon your birth. I should have brought your mother here before your birth. You should have been born in the Light where you belong, nurtured and raised in our traditions in the sanctity of our ways to flourish as a seed of Light." He props his elbow on his thigh, dropping his face into his hand. "You need to be taught so much. I suppose this is a good place to begin. Wearing dark colors can be restrictive to your Light."

"Clothes?" I screw my face up with disbelief. "Are you serious? I've always worn black. It never hurt me."

"If you have always worn black or darker colors, then you do not know the effects it will have. You'll find differently after your time in the Light, and appropriate tones adorning you will change your mind. It will dampen you when next you try a muted palette. Do you accept my gift?"

"Yes," I pluck at the strings, focusing on the guitar.

"Good," he stands. "The Light has an etiquette. When you receive a gift, you repay in kind, of something in equal or greater value."

Cradling the instrument, I laugh. "I'm going to accept this trick because I love this thing more than you'll ever know. So, what do you want?"

"Have dinner with me. I want your time. I will consider the gift repaid."

Setting the guitar back in the case, I shrug. "I can always eat."

"Very good. It will give you a chance to practice serving your elders, and you can tell me about this song." He knocks on the wall. "We are ready to eat."

220

I smirk at the guitar as faceless vassals bring in a low table and cushions, others carrying dishes and tea. There is no way I will discuss "I'll Stay" with Pierre.

Pierre says, "Tallie."

I glance from the instrument to him. He's kneeling on the other side of the table, watching me. "You seem to genuinely cherish that item."

With a sigh of regret, I leave the guitar to join him, kneeling across from him. "You have no idea."

"The song? 'You're not home?'"

"Those are the words. The title is 'I'll Stay.'"

"It seemed to bring a tear to your eye. Is it your favorite?"

"No." I swallow, inspecting the table and trying to recall what to do first. "I hate that song, now more than ever."

"Why?"

"Why does Ashley hate me? Other than the obvious answer that she's your real daughter."

He shakes his head as I start pouring tea. "You and Ashley are both my *real* daughter, but she is having as difficult a time accepting it as you are. I know her reasons, but not yours. Why are you having a hard time accepting this? I am not trying to replace the man who raised you if that is your concern."

"No." I laugh at the ceiling. "And Dad, my dad, that guy, won't even talk to me. He stopped years ago, just pretends like I'm not there."

"Why did the relationship you share with the man who raised you change?"

I lift my hand, rubbing the side and the back of my neck, frowning at the floor. "Nicky, my brother died."

"You have my deepest and most sincere condolences."

I give him a baffled glare. "Fuck you. In the nicest way, I mean," I add in a hurry, trying to recover myself. "You didn't know him, and you don't actually care."

Pierre gives a long look. "Please mind your manners and language. I did not know your sibling, but I may conjecture to your pain and empthaize."

"You don't know a damn thing."

"About you," he says tersely. "I do not. That is why I am making inquiries. I lost my brother. He was slaughtered by the Dark."

I tuck my lips inward and bite down on them.

Smoothing his shirt down his chest, his chest swells and his shoulders raise, then he slumps with a harsh exhale. "Now, you have promised me your time in return for my gift. I expect you to uphold your gift to me."

I bob my head. "Nick was my younger brother. He didn't pass initiation. It's a Magia thing. They test you to see if you have Ki and if you can control it."

Pierre nods, picking up his teacup. "How do they test you?"

"You drink poison."

He stops, his head snapping up, his eyes locking to mine with shock. The lines on his face deepen as he repeats, "They make you drink poison?"

Leaning back, I cross my arms. "You think the Dark is bad? The things the Magia did to me are worse."

He shakes his head and sets his cup down, staring into it with a pathetic expression. "I am so sorry, daughter mine. I knew naught of your existence, or I would have collected you, brought you home much sooner, spared you the pain..." His eyes close, and he sighs. "Tallie, I failed you. I should have been able to prevent all of this–the Magia, the subjection to the Dark, even the events that led to you being imprisoned."

I shrug. "Nick wasn't strong enough to survive. It happens." I say the words I heard so many times from others, using them as a shield. I wave a hand in a circle to encompass his whole being. "Whatever bullshit or guilt or whatever you're feeling, it's fine. It's not your problem."

"You are my daughter. Of course, this is my concern."

I stretch my eyes open, blink a few times, and then laugh. "You're a sperm donor."

"Unbecoming in the vernacular, but we will get there. Your brother, Nick, would you care to speak of him?"

"No."

"The man who raised you?"

"Doesn't talk to me anymore, disowned me, told me I'm not his dau–daughter." My brain catches on fire. It's like a smite just detonated in my skull, and the world goes out of focus. "Fucking Mother."

"Honey?"

Pierre tilts before me as I grip the table for grounding. "He knew," I whisper, unable to pull my surroundings into focus. "He knew about you...me...that I'm...he knows. He said it. He told me I'm not his daughter."

"Tony mentioned you always differed from the rest of the Magia."

"No. No, it— Everything changed after Nicky. Something happened. Wait, you know Tony? How?"

He presses his lips. "I met him in my quest to determine your heritage."

"Oh. Why?"

"He was present during Callahan's coercion of you into a contract."

"Cal didn't force me to do anything."

"We were speaking of your father?"

I shove away from the table, get to my feet and begin pacing, running my hands through my hair at every turn to double back. "It doesn't make sense. It's never made sense. Sasha should have made it, and she didn't. Nicky—Mom said that the poison was in the shot they offered him to calm his nerves, which is why he couldn't back out. It was too late. He'd already drunk it, but they didn't offer me a shot. They changed it for Nicky."

Pierre frowns. "Tallie, calm down. Take a deep breath. Anything that has happened is in the past. There is nothing either of us can do to alter those actions."

The fabric of reality rips apart from the inside out, destroying everything I know. I want to punch something but lean against the wall for support. The cool of the marble helps to center me, and I breathe through my nose.

I want to run straight to Cal and wrap myself in his strength. I need to hear his voice.

"Fuck," I mutter, rubbing at my face and standing upright. He's not here. The Magia took him, too. Something burns white-hot from within the depths of my soul, silver racing over my skin.

Pierre says, "Calling your Light outside of the arena is against the law."

I swallow the taste of hatred and shove it down, burying it again. "Yeah, sure, because it's not its own thing living inside of me with a will of its own."

"The Light is its own entity, yes, but you must conquer it, become its master, control it. Have you not learned to do so yet?"

I curl my lip at him. "I can get it to do things, but it still does what it wants."

"Callahan." Pierre sighs, shaking his head and tipping it back, staring up. "He attempted to train you, didn't he?"

"Yes."

Pierre motions for me to sit. "That is a treacherous tragedy. He maintains no knowledge of how our magic works and you have not received the proper guidance you deserve. Worse, you've learned habits of the Dark. It might have done irreparable damage."

I move in a mechanical fashion, going through the motions of serving the meal in silence, dying inside with every sickening squelch of my heart echoing between my ears. I fumble with thick, numb fingers. My dad knows I'm not his Magia bloodline, but something else, a mix of Seraphinus and Magia.

I can't shake that what I am has a bearing on Nicky's fate, but I can't fit those pieces together in my mind. It's like trying to force a square-shaped object through a circular opening. It looks like it could fit, but trying to mash the object through the hole is impossible.

Pierre's voice draws my mind from the puzzle. "When did you start to play the instrument?"

"School days. I used to want to be a singer. Mom bought me my first guitar for my fifteenth birthday," I answer with indifference, lost to the maelstrom in my mind. The information is irrelevant to me, easily dispatched.

"Do you sing as well?"

I nod. "Yes."

"After our meal, will you honor me by playing a song on your guitar and singing? I would enjoy it."

"Sure." I shrug. "I like singing, and I'm dying to play that guitar."

He smiles. "I'm glad it is a worthy gift in exchange for the chance to know you." He studies me. "As soon as I brought you here, I assigned someone to fetch your mother. I am waiting for her arrival, and I will let you know when she is here."

I flick at imaginary dust on the table. I'm not sure how I feel about my mother. On one hand, I could not care less about where my mother is. On the other hand, having my mother here in Izul with Pierre is pretty much the last thing I want. I don't need to see them together. I also know my mother has a way of making things in my life worse for me than seems necessary.

Pierre reaches across the table, his hand resting over Cal's lingering contract. "I can burn this out of you."

"No." I recoil, resting my arms against my stomach to hide Cal's contract from him. "He's dead. It doesn't matter anymore."

"I cannot help but wonder why you would wish to wear his name on your skin."

I lift and drop one shoulder, staring down at my arms, a protective greed overcoming me. "It's my arm."

"You are my heritage, a representation of the seed of Light within us both. It's a disgusting brand that looks ill upon us both."

"It has nothing to do with you."

"I can grant you release from him once and for all."

"I can burn it out whenever I want, but I don't, so I won't, and neither will you."

He sighs and pulls back. "When you are ready."

"Never," I snarl with chilled fury. The black script in my arm might not be a contract anymore, but it is a piece of Cal's magic, the last piece in existence. Massimo might have another if he survived. Either way, I'll protect it as long as I live, keep it safe in my skin, a part of him that belongs to me.

Pierre bobs his head. "In time, when the scars of what the Dark did to you begin to fade, you will change your mind."

"Did anyone survive the Magia from Cal's house?"

"None that I'm aware of. It seems the Magia are apt at killing our kind. How is that?"

"Magic. Really? No one?" I add force to the question, eyeing him with mistrust. The Magia would have targeted Cal for contracting me. Others might have been disregarded. If Massimo survived, I have another option.

"The Magia have killed dozens now. They are becoming intolerable in cities. It's something I've spent time discussing with our queen." Pierre presses his lips. "Why do you wish to wear his name? What made you serve him with loyalty? He spoke of why you took the contract with him during the Council hearing, but there seems to be more to the matter than he allowed me to believe."

I rub my hands together beneath the surface of the table. "Look, sperm donor, I'm not talking to you about Cal."

"Tallie."

"He's mine!" I slap an open hand down on the table. "You don't get to have anything to do with him or that."

Pierre jerks back, the lines around his mouth pulled tight. "You say he was yours, but you were the one contracted to serve. If anything, you were owned. The Dark is not one for softness or kindness, and love is not in their repertoire."

I look away.

"You were held captive, under contracted servitude, forced to endure horrors of sick contests and the gods only know what else, yet you want to wear his name. Why?"

"All Cal did was offer me a contract. When I accepted it, it gave me an escape from the Magia, and he bought me anything I wanted. A guitar, pretty dresses, this amazing sugar scrub, and all the vodka I could drink, which is a lot of vodka. He took me to dinner and kept Tony away from me." I take a deep breath, my eyes burning, "He protected my life in Ilbuio and the games. Even Mass said he treated me differently than a contract. He didn't need me for anything but the Light. The worst thing he ever did was force me to tell him—" I stop short, straying too close to the secrets of my soul.

Pierre sits back. "Tell him?"

I shake my head. "Things that he only got out of me

because of a contract, which you don't have. He tried to help me train the Light and sex. It was great, massive—"

"Okay." Pierre shifts and runs a hand down the buttons of his shirt. He clears his throat, looking around. "I do not need to hear about that filth defiling my daughter."

Smirking, I point at Pierre. "It was Zander who *defiled* me in the first place. Literally, the first to do it."

Pierre appears a bit whiter. "He confessed you two had an intimate moment, but he neglected the severity of it."

"Cal's is bigger."

Pierre rubs his forehead. "I would be happy to know about your other interests, perhaps about this Ki, you mentioned earlier. Is that the magic Magia wield?"

"Didn't my mother tell you about that? At least Cal was a gentleman and got on his knees for me," I say with a wide grin. "That's more than Zander did."

"Is this topic of conversation necessary?"

"Necessary is a strong word, but it is fun." I laugh. "I can keep going, or you can tell me why Ashley hates me so much."

Pierre puts one hand on the table, strumming his fingers. "Ash is distraught that she is no longer the sole heir to my heritage. She is upset that I so carelessly created another, and she believes I have tarnished our heritage by procreating with one not of our own kind."

I raise my eyebrows. "Why does it matter if I have your heritage too?"

His face softens to gentle contemplation. "There is only ever one child of a heritage or lineage active in society. Any other is contracted and removed to isolation. It's a practice that started in times of clans to ensure there would be another to carry on the heritage or lineage should the first be killed."

"Back before your Council and accords?"

"Yes. Death rates were higher with constant fighting

between Light and Dark. The strongest sibling remained in society. Any other was hidden away. This ensured the strongest would protect the clan and their land, and also that there would be one of their heritage to produce another generation."

"So, it's a contest between Ashley and me to see who stays?"

"Ash is concerned about this practice, yes. It is known as Ritual. The Ritual fight is combat between two siblings, a fight to submission or even death." Pierre gives me a smile, like I'm an invalid simpleton. "The two of you will have no reason to fight. However, she is disgusted by the idea of Ritual. If you were to win somehow, it would replace her in society and remove her from her home—the life she's known. You are not Seraphinus, therefore not capable of carrying on the heritage or taking her place in society. Ergo, Ritual shall not apply."

"Cal mentioned Seraphim aren't favorable in society. Ha." I grin, "look at that. The Dark and Light have something in common." I raise my glass at Pierre and then drain the contents.

"You are not wholly my heritage. I cannot deny that, and there are those who believe that as a Seraphim, you aren't entitled to be here. Fret not, though. I'm not fond of politics, and as my daughter, given my standing along with the position our heritage holds, I will see you given the proper stature." He rests back, lifting his glass. "Were you this ornery for..." He flicks two fingers toward me.

"Cal?" I scoff. "Do you have any worn contracts?"

"Yes."

"So, you're aware of what happens to your contracted when they disobey as a worn contract?"

"Yes." His eyes glint like the edge of a blade.

"Yeah, me too." I smirk. "It almost killed me one night."

229

Pierre drags a hand down his face. "I've never been horrified and proud at the same time before, but you are certainly giving me new experiences. I'm glad you fought the Dark's control over you."

"Yeah, it was a confusing time in my life." I spin my glass on the white tablecloth. "Fucking a Darkling and taking his orders."

"I understand why you would be contrary to the Dark, but why you seem to abhor me is confusing. We share the same heritage."

Snorting through my nose, I take a drink.

"This, this exact moment, is what I am referring to. How can we have a relationship if you are unwilling to have an honest conversation?"

Cocking my jaw at the wall, I say, "Probably because the use of sarcasm and jokes isn't allowed." Resting my chin on my propped elbow, I say, "We are having an honest conversation. I hate lying more than anything else."

Pierre almost seems to squirm, his expression pained. "Honesty is a valuable trait one can possess."

I lift my eyebrow, eyeing him with my head rocking to the side and my chin in my palm. "Is Ness okay?"

"She is conforming only slightly better than you but less difficult on the whole. I obtained permission for her to have access to the library. She spends her days there."

I breathe out in relief. "Oh, she must love that. Thank you for that and for taking care of her."

CHAPTER 25

NATALIA

NINTH MOON'S DAY, WARMWAVE, 4049 6TH
MILLENNIUM

Zander lingers after an early meal is cleared away, fidgeting and smiling at me. "Weila has been notified that her services aren't required for today."

My heart lifts. "I get a day off?"

He shakes his head, one side of his hair loose and the other braided back. "No, today, instead of etiquette and manners, I am going to teach you to connect to your Light." He rests his hands on my hips, guiding me to the middle of the room. "After you are in control of it, I will teach you combat skills."

I retch. "Please don't. I can handle myself."

"I'm sure you've got moves already, but once you learn to control your Light, I'll work on basic combat skills with you to ensure your training is fully complete."

"Yeah." I drag the word out and then push hair from my face. "If you hadn't saved my life, you'd have seen my moves already."

He wiggles his eyebrows at me with a glib twist to his lips. "I saw a few different moves."

"Just be glad I decided to be nice."

Smiling down at me, he tucks a piece of hair behind my ear, trailing his fingers along my jaw. "I am very, very glad you decided to be nice."

Dropping my chin toward my chest, I smirk at our feet. "All right," I say, meeting his crinkled eyes. "What am I doing?"

Zander lifts a hand, Light glimmering beneath his skin. "I want to see if you can call the Light at will. In Ilbuio, your magic would have naturally protected you, come to the surface and warned the Dark away, the same as being anywhere near the Dark. I want to start with seeing if you are capable of calling it for your use."

I lean away from him for room to breathe. "I am. You know, this whole mess started because I killed a Lighter?" I wave a hand at his chest, watching him stiffen with a nasty expression. "It was trying to kill Cal. I thought he was human, so I intervened and killed it."

Zander stares at me, eyes pinching. "Never say that again. I'll say this once then we shall never speak of it again, is an impressive statement. If they were after Callahan, then it must have been an avenger, and avengers are our best warriors. However, what you have confessed to is a punishable offense by death. It is unholy that you committed the murder of one of our own as well as saving the life of a Dark."

I shrug. "A, not one of my kind, I'm Magia, and B, I didn't intentionally save Dark or Light. Had I known he wasn't human, I would have let him die. The Magia are supposed to protect humans from your kind. I thought that's what I was doing."

"Our," he grinds out low. "You carry Pierre's heritage. You hold the Light within you. Regardless of what you claim to be, you are one of us."

"Sure, fine, but Magia law or Light law, either way, what I did was illegal. I thought I was defending a human, which is what Magia law requires. I wouldn't have done it had I known, although it's not like that's the first time I broke Magia law either."

Zander smirks, tilting his head and taking my face between both his hands. "No, it's not, is it?"

I roll my eyes. "I'm a rule breaker."

His fingers tighten, curling around my jaw and tipping my head back. For one ugly moment, I expect he's going to try to kiss me, but he steps back. "All right, love, call the Light."

"Right," I say, fighting the urge to vomit. I scratch behind my ear, looking down and away.

I lift my hands, searching my palms. Frowning, I think about all the times the silver webbing threaded over my skin when I was around the Dark. The Light flickers in pinpricks, and I focus on trying to force it to the surface the way Cal did by simply being near me. My chest aches, and the Light goes out.

Zander puts his hands over mine. "It's okay, we'll start there. Did he try to teach you about magic? Light and Dark share very few similarities, but they both unite in the fact that magic is a living entity. It is alive within you, a part of you as much as blood, bone, and tissue."

I nod. "He mentioned that and said if I didn't learn to control it, it would strangle my life."

"Good. He's smart. That's true. If the host isn't strong enough to contain the magic or if the host doesn't form a bond with it, the magic will destroy the host."

I smile at our hands. "He was smart."

Zander's fingers wrap around me with care. "The Light, you need to connect to it."

"Cal said that, too."

His fingers tighten. "We've established that he is intelligent. You can talk to me about him. About anything." Zander's hands shift, his palms to the back of my hands. "He's a serious player on the board for the Dark. I would expect him to have significant skill and understanding. I expect that he explained the foundations of magic, but due to the detriment of your training's effect on your life, you'll have to excuse me if I repeat him."

"It will kill me if I can't connect to it. Cal told me to feel it."

"Yes, and you will in time. It will be a voice in your head like a conscience. Your Light will become a comfort, a helping hand, and yes, it will talk to you, but connecting to it comes first. You need to join with it first. Everything else follows."

"How?"

"Everyone has their own way of connecting. It's personal, a deep, soulful connection to their magic. Every strain of magic, even those that share the same heredity, is highly unique." He smiles. "For example, Callahan and his sister—"

"What?" I yelp, my hands twisting over to grab hold of Zander's. "Cal has a sister?"

His smile widens. "Yes. The Light has made it a point to track the most powerful Dark lineages. But back to the topic at hand, they both share the same type of magic, but how they connect to it, use it, would be different."

My heart hammers in my chest. "Why wouldn't he tell me about her?" The words trickle from my thoughts to my lips without intent in a whispered breath.

"Whatever you think you were to Callahan, he viewed you as nothing more than another contract."

I bob my head, swallowing the heartbreak, my fingers digging into Zander for stability. There were dozens of times I had told myself that very fact, but he also said he wanted me to be his queen. I want to ask if that was using me, but I won't reveal Cal's secrets. "I know I was a contract."

"The Light, to connect to it," Zander whispers, shuffling

closer, standing between my arms and pulling our hands to his side. His mouth finds my ear, and he breathes low, "Will you trust me?"

My eyes slip closed as I inhale the scent of him. It's sharp and tangy, like warm pomegranates and cloves. "I don't know."

"Honesty is good." His lips curve against my cheek. "The Light, your magic, you can't lie to it, and lying to yourself will erode the connection."

"How do I connect?"

"Patience." He snickers. "Find your center, take a few deep breaths, and relax. Listen to your heartbeat and answer it."

"That's the stupidest thing I've ever heard."

He sets my hands on his waist and wraps his own on either side of my neck, tilting my head back to meet his gaze. "Listen to your heartbeat. What is it telling you?"

My heartbeat. I hate the sound of it. It's always been the most annoying sound in the world, but I focus on it, listening. "Pump, squelch, thud."

Zander laughs. "Yes, very good description, but I meant less literal and more figurative. The sound of your heart, your heart's desire, the passion of your soul—there are a few ways it's been described. It's always abstractly described, but it's the seed of your soul, the fortitude within, the illumination of desire."

"What is it for you?"

"Highly personal."

Squeezing my eyes shut, I try to listen. For so long, I've drowned out the noise with the words of others, volume set to eleven to avoid the bitter sound of my heart. The coursing blood is a soft stream deep between my ears. Everything else fades as I hold tight to Zander, rubatosis settling in.

Zander's voice is far away, whispering like smoke dancing

on the edge of my senses. "Find the answer in your heart. It is there; it has always been there long before you knew the question."

A scintilla bursts behind my eyes, a sliver of silver ribbon forming and dancing. It swirls, and Callahan's face forms in its wake. It's out of focus, blurry, the details gone, a rudimentary form that only takes shape by sheer desire, but I know it's him, even if I've forgotten what he looks like.

His mouth pulls back to one side, my own voice echoing in my mind, *"It's not your undoing. Just let go of the idea that this will ruin you. To accept your strength won't erase the battles you've fought and won."*

My heart cries for Callahan. It cries for his belief in me. It cries for home, but that isn't the answer. I trusted him far greater than I ever realized.

I let go, my fingers unfurling from Zander, and my hands fall to my sides even as my consciousness falls through the darkness. It rushes around me and then bursts with stars dancing behind my closed eyes. They gather together, turning inky blackness to deep blues punctuated with glistening silver stars.

Taking a deep breath, I open my eyes. Warmth blossoms in my chest, Light racing over my skin in a pretty swirling lace, darker than it has ever been before, less white, more blue. Lifting my hands between Zander and myself.

Cal had tried to pry my grip away and told me to let go. He is gone, but I can trust the Light within me.

The Light glows brighter, and Zander inhales with a faint gasp. "I've never seen Light like yours."

His hand comes up, taking mine to lift it closer to inspect the Light drawing patterns over my skin. I trace the lines sparkling like starlight on a moonless night. He presses his palm to mine, his Light answering with a glinting gold glow.

Zander presses his fingers between mine. "So beautiful, love."

I'm a bit breathless, terrified of where I go from here. "It is."

"It is you. You're beautiful."

I stare into his colorless eyes, aching for dark ones instead. Swallowing, I drop my gaze and nod, breathing out through my nose.

He squeezes my hand, still holding on even as he takes a step back. "You found your answer then?"

"Yes."

"Very good. That is the start of your connection, but you will need to nurture it and deepen the connection before you can control your Light."

CHAPTER 26
NATALIA
TENTH STAR'S DAY, WARMWAVE, 4049 6TH MILLENNIUM

Weila stands behind me as I sit in front of a mirror. "Makeup is an essential part of preparations for a lady. We want to appear as beautiful as we can at all times under scrutiny of others."

"Pretty much a basic feeling of life," I answer, inspecting all the little tubes and containers in front of me. My nails glisten, cleaned and filed round to match the contour of my fingertips.

That was the first half of this lesson. Nails are very important. The small details show true appreciation.

My strength of will is growing, flexing and strengthening with every clamp of my jaw, withheld remark, and swallowed groan. Weila is synonymous with torture. I'd rather be subjected to the games in Ilbuio than endure another etiquette lesson.

The only thing sustaining me is Cal. He made me promise to survive, and I hold tight to that memory every time Weila seems to skewer me with her presence. There had been no time limitations on his request or my promise. If I must pretend to be one of them to save myself, I will. It's an abhorrent test of my patience, though.

I stare at myself in the mirror. A thin face with a pointed chin stares back, blinking wide-set, upturned eyes of liquid silver on either side of my nose. My mind turns to consider what Cal saw when he looked at me. If my full lips were too big, if my eyes were too far from my nose, if my cheekbones weren't high enough, or if he ever realized my nose is the same as Pierre's.

Cal told me I was gorgeous. His hand took up one side of my face when he kissed me. He always kissed me with fire and hunger alike, as if I could be devoured to satisfy his need.

Weila clears her throat. I flick my gaze to her over my shoulder, meeting her frown in the mirror. Displeasure is evident in her lips puckered with ire. "Tallie, you are not paying attention, forcing me to repeat myself in a blatant disregard for my time."

"My apologies." I duck my chin, focusing on the beauty supplies. "My mind wandered away with itself."

"Your apology is appreciated as a reflection of acknowledging your failure, so I will accept. Shall we begin with your hair?"

Her eyes shift, and I look at myself in the mirror, the white strands hanging straight, surpassing my collarbones. I can't recall the last time it was this long or colorless. Long ago, in another life, I'd taken advantage of the lack of color in my hair to dye it all the different colors I could imagine. I almost miss being controlled by the Magia as Weila forces me to braid my hair, shake it out, and repeat.

In frustration at the hundredth attempt, I grumble, "My fingers were not made for this."

"Practice will increase their aptitude." She picks up the scissors from the table. Snipping the air a couple of times, she says, "The best hairstyles are those that suit your face, and you've done naught but allow yours to grow. Length is acceptable if maintained with clean ends, but I do believe another style will suit you better."

I fight with every ounce of willpower I have not to bite at her hand as she begins cutting. Tensing my abs, I struggle to keep a straight face, to not say a word or roll my eyes.

When she sets the scissors aside, I have shorter pieces around my face. I have the equivalent of long bangs and the urge to say, "Thanks, I hate it," but press my lips, fake a smile, and bob my head. "Lovely," I drawl, doing my best to keep the word neutral.

"You are very beautiful, and the purpose of these curtain bangs is to highlight your features. We want to present the best and brightest we have to offer to the world for the pleasure of others."

Ness would call that toxic behavior, but I smile wider. "I understand."

By the time she's through with the lesson and leaving, I'm at the end of my rope, clinging to adherence through sheer stubbornness. I have gold-coated eyelashes and gold across my eyelids, my skin moisturized and features highlighted with gold dust, and my hair in a fancy, pain-in-the-ass braid that is so complicated there is no reason it should be used.

I smile and bid her fair well, determined to take a bath and undo her work as soon as she steps out the door. My hopes are dashed as she exits the threshold, and Pierre meets her under the watch of avengers guarding me.

The door closes, and I take the opportunity to open and close my jaw, wiggling it side-to-side to release tension as I wait for Pierre.

There's not enough time for me to relax before the knock comes. I call out in a sickly, sweet voice. "You may come in."

Pierre enters, carrying a box.

I hitch a smile, though my cheeks twinge at the overuse. "Welcome and be welcomed."

"I am welcomed and welcoming," he says. "I believe, daughter mine, that there is reason to hope you will execute your presentation with perfection. Weila is speaking highly of your continued improvements."

"Splendid news."

He offers me the box. "Another gift for you."

I consider the glossy black ribbon and blood-red sheen of the box. "That did not come from Izul."

"An obvious note, yes, but you'll understand why it must be that way."

Narrowing one eye, I take the box in both hands, asking, "Is this you give me something, so I have to give you something?"

He smiles. "Yes, honey. That is our custom."

We stand there, both holding our own side as I debate, taking it from his grip. Given the packaging and its originating source beyond Izul, I'm certain I want what's inside. Until I know what it is, I can still walk away without having to pay up. The moment I fall in love with the contents, I'm going to have to acquiesce to his whims.

I pull the box closer and turn to the bed to sit, balancing the box on my knees as I tug the ribbon aside and flip the top to the floor.

It's black. It's fabric.

I snatch the thing, lifting it and standing so the bottom of the box falls to the floor. I stare, fingers curling tighter as greed rustles in my soul.

Pierre clears his throat as my jaw drops. "I thought perhaps you may find comfort in it while—"

I squeal, hugging the one-piece suit, complete with a hood that has giant, floppy rabbit ears attached. Rushing to the screen, my high heels slip against the slick floor. It doesn't stop me. I scramble to stay upright, waving one arm for balance and refusing to drop the rabbit suit.

Behind the screen, I fling my heels off, kicking them away and wiggling out of my dress to ram my feet into the legs of the one-piece, shimming it up and zipping it closed. Flipping the hood over my head causes one long, floppy ear to fall before my face.

I step in view, spreading my arms and beaming at him. "I'm a fucking rabbit."

His lips twitch as he struggles against a smile. Even he can't pretend to glare, considering how cute I know I am.

Jumping in place, I clap my hands and laugh, my skin sparkling as my spirit soars. I point to myself, "Hey, it's black, and I'm fine, see?" I spin in a circle laughing, stopping to jump in place as I clap my hands, the hood slipping off my head. "Oops." I giggle and pull it back up.

There's something sad about the expression adorning his regal features as he watches me, his forehead wrinkling.

"What do you want? I'll give you anything."

His face relaxes into contemplation, tinged with melancholy. "Time," he says. "Are you hungry?"

"Wait, I get this," I point to myself, "and food?" I laugh, dancing in place.

"That is to be worn only when you are alone, in the privacy of your quarters."

"Fine." I do a little dance, grinning ear to ear. "It's a shame, though, 'cause I make a cute bunny."

I wrinkle my nose, but my ecstasy comes crashing down around me like a bucket of ice water dumped over me. I'd said the same thing to Cal in Ilbuio as we wandered the palace handcuffed together, running from players hunting us. He didn't want me to wear the rabbit ears, marking me as a target even if they made me adorable because he had wanted to protect me.

He had always wanted to protect me. I guess, in a way, when he banished me, it was his last act of shielding me. If he hadn't, I would have been in his home when it exploded. I'm not certain if I would have preferred to be wrapped up in him and sent to the afters. The memories plaguing me have no cure.

Pierre tilts his head. "Tallie, honey, are you all right?"

I sniff, pulling the long sleeve over my hand, using the heel of my palm to swipe at my nose. "I'm fine," I lie, looking away. "I'll change. You won't want me wearing this while we eat."

He takes a step toward me. "Did something change? Do you no longer like your gift?"

Smiling at the floor, looking down at the cozy, soft black material encasing my body, I pretend like it's Cal's Dark covering me. "I love it, actually." Lifting my eyes to Pierre, I ask, "Why, though? After all the talk about me not being allowed to wear dark colors..."

"I decided to give you a bit of leeway on the matter." He drops his chin, staring from the tops of his eyes. "Never outside of your personal quarters, honey. In fact, I'd prefer no one ever knows of its existence. However, I hoped it would help make you more comfortable while you wait out the rest of your days in confinement."

I hug myself, bobbing my head, the rabbit ears flopping up and down before my eyes. "It will."

"Then I will accept it as attire while we eat." Widening my eyes, I grin even as he holds his hand up, chuckling. "One time only, as it is the gift you are giving me your time to repay, and then I shall never see that wretched thing again."

CHAPTER 27
VANESSA

FIRST SUN'S DAY, HARVEST, 4049 6TH MILLENNIUM

Standing and stretching, I move my stiff body, having sat in the unforgiving chair bent over the text for far too long. It's an issue I have: getting lost in ink on parchment. My mother used to threaten to lock up every book in the house if she caught me reading past my bedtime one more time.

She never carried out the threat and I got better at hiding it. She hated my love of reading, like learning wasn't something I should be concerned with. Albeit I'm aware enough to be conscious that my love of reading qualifies closer to obsession, but my mother wanted me to be like Tallie. She wanted me to achieve pinnacle rather than merely reading to understand what qualifies for pinnacle.

Kazez leaves me on my own ever since he completed the tour of the library. I have an explanation of every section of the library, although I had to write down everything to remember which floor, which wing, and which section is what.

I glance around and lift my arms over my head, fingers interlocked to bend backward as I elongate my spine and force muscles to lengthen. They burn and twitch, fighting movement after the extended period of stagnation. With a sigh, I drop my arms, walking aisles to get my circulation flowing.

Turning down an aisle, I brush my fingers along cracked leather spines and gold-plated ones alike, their presence comforting. Something catches my attention, and I stop, redirecting my gaze to the man standing a few paces ahead.

He's on the other side of the aisle, a book resting open in his hands. I cock my head at him, studying his face. I expect a Lighter, but his hair is golden-red, the strands long and hanging loose over his shoulders. Several beads adorn braided and clustered groups of his hair. I've never seen anyone with that color of hair before, human or Seraphinus.

He lifts his head, peering at me. My heart thumps harder in my chest, excitement racing through my veins at his human eyes. This isn't another Lighter that will avoid me.

I smile. "Hi." I cover my mouth, embarrassed by the volume of my outburst. Lowering my hand and my voice, I say, "Sorry, that was loud. I just can't believe there is another human here. I thought I was the only one."

His head cocks, his hair shifting with the weight of the beads.

Taking a few steps closer, I wave. "I'm Vanessa, but you can call me Ness."

"Aydian." He closes the book, tucks it under his arm and extends a hand to me.

I take it, expecting a handshake, but he yanks. I stumble closer as he lifts the back of my hand to his lips. His mouth grazes my skin, and he pauses, dipping his nose to my wrist and inhaling.

Aydan's gaze flickers to mine, eyes half closed as he studies me down his thin nose. I stare, not sure what to do, caught in the hard glint of his jade eyes. "What are you doing in Izul?"

"Asks one human to another." I laugh. "I'll tell you if you tell me?"

One thick eyebrow lifts as his lips twist to the side. "Very well."

"I'm with Tallie."

He blinks.

"Er, Pierre Bordeaux's Seraphim daughter? Yeah, me and her are besties, so when she came here, I came with her."

The cold jade of his irises warms with humor. "You are a servant of a Light?"

"No." I yank my hand from him. "I'm a woman, a friend, not a fucking servant." He shrugs, standing taller, and I have to lift my eyes to still meet his gaze. "Why are you in Izul?"

"I seek knowledge." Glancing around, he inhales deep, his chest swelling. "This is the largest source in the world, and if the secrets I seek are to be found, they will be here, sealed away to be forgotten as is convenient."

"The Lighters just let you in here?"

"Let me?" His whisper is silk in the air but red as blood and rage. "No." He grins, his lips stretching back to expose two front teeth set between three wicked canine fangs.

Shock widens my eyes as I stare at his teeth, the top-pointed fangs descending in length. Those are not human teeth. The urge to scream grips me, crushing my lungs so that when my mouth opens, no sound comes.

He takes a step back, sliding the book he pilfered from the shelf between two others. "Tell me," he says, meeting my eyes once more. "What are you? For certainly you are not human."

"Magia. A mix of Light and Dark in human bodies. What the fuck are you?"

His head tips back as he laughs. "This has been a pleasure in an otherwise dreary day, Ness. Perhaps I will see you around as I search for that which I seek."

"Uh, dude, you're freaking me out. Am I in danger here?"

"There is no need for you to fear me, but you are without doubt in danger, surrounded in this city by enemies."

"You're not a Lighter."

"No, nor friend of one."

"Then how did you get in here?"

"In exchange for that answer, I have a simple request to ensure your safety. Do not speak a word of me to another living creature. My presence is not welcome here."

"So don't tell anyone you're poking around and reading books?"

"Yes."

Cocking my jaw, I consider. I can hear my mother telling me books are a waste of time. Someone willing to risk their life, human or not, to read books tugs on my heart. "All right."

"Aggika." He bows, then returns upright. He smirks, lifting a hand to the level of his eyes, and snaps. Aydian disappears.

"What the shit?" I whisper, glancing around to confirm he's gone. I rub my eyes and check again.

I'M WAITING on the front steps as Owen jogs up them. I watch him, hugging my knees to my chest. He stops a few steps below me, panting a bit. I frown, almost sorry for him the way he's flushed and his hair is a mess.

"Ness, you have my sincere apologies for being delayed." He checks his watch.

Shrugging, I stand, brushing non-existent dirt from my butt. "Don't worry about it. It's not like I have a hot date to get to or anywhere else to go."

He gives me a curious glance, head shied to the side.

I throw my hands up. "Don't worry about it, dude. It's not a big deal. I'm not an asshole like you. Cool? Great. M'kay, honey? Glad we sorted out that I'm a better person than you. Can we go now?"

"You've got an attitude tonight."

"In think that might be the first time you smiled at me." I start moving down the wide steps, ignoring the quip.

He follows, matching my pace. "I don't recall."

"Mmm," I hum, flexing my eyebrows. "Whatever."

"Did Kazez annoy you?"

"No."

"I was under the impression that the library put you in a good mood." He makes a turn, cutting my steps off to herd me along the walkway with him.

"It does."

He chuckles, directing me down another path. "Then why are you full of firelight this evening?"

"Maybe I've just decided to be who I am and screw the rules?"

"Ah," he chuckles. "I will accept foul language this evening in return for being late if we can agree both things will be concealed from Pierre."

"Sure, but mostly because I don't fucking care. Being late happens, and it's not disrupting my day enough for me to be a complete jerk about it."

"Very good. This way."

He leads me to a restaurant, one with air that sings with pastries and savory meat. My tongue prickles, hunger settling in.

A Lighter shows us to a table. I wait for Owen to take his seat, then follow the action. I scan around me, noting everyone else seated are couples leaning close, holding hands, and various acts of obvious intimacy. I shift, trying to get comfortable. He'd made it clear that I am not his preference.

He smiles at me, propping his chin on an elbow resting on the table. "Your mood has improved with the walk."

"Um..." I glance around. It's beautiful, the gilded and white decorations like a visual aphrodisiac. Most days, we eat in what I assume is the equivalent of a quick, lost-cost style eatery, half a step above the take-and-go options. "I guess. This place looks expensive, even for Izul."

"I have had a long, frustrating day and wanted something better than our regular choices. It's my treat to us both in hopes my day improves." He sits upright, the corners of his lips turned up. "Have you managed to see the whole library yet? You've had time to do so several times over, but Kazez says you read."

I nod. "Yeah, I walked the whole thing once on my own after Kazez showed me everything. It's incredible. Have you spent much time there?"

"Not since my lesson days. I'm afraid they ruined the place for me. Too many assignments and forced time within those walls to spark enjoyment."

"Guess that would do it." I roll my shoulders back in a weak shrug. "Not for me, though. I enjoy learning."

"What do humans learn?"

"I assume the same things you do. Language, history, math, and science. I studied several languages and history for my secondary education."

"I doubt we learn the same things. My history differs significantly from yours."

"You mean like Beenin?"

"Mmm, yes." He leans closer. "Kazez said you were inquiring about literature on the Sube."

I widen my eyes. "I wasn't aware I was being monitored."

Owen smiles, his white eyes crinkling at the corners. "Of course you are. You're human, and you were loyal to the Dark. Those two things do not relay trust."

Frowning, I chew on the inside of my cheek. "I won't deny that I was contracted to Cal or say a bad word about him or Mass."

"Did they treat you so well?" He lifts his eyebrows, his expression open, lending an air of earnestness to the inquiry.

I grip the skirt of my dress, adjusting in my seat. "Tallie got contracted. The Magia were going to kill me if she didn't return as punishment, so Cal signed me to a contract to save my life. So yeah, I was loyal because I like living."

Owen chuckles. "It is only natural."

"My quality of life went way up, belonging to a Seraphinus. Most humans don't get the same luxuries."

"Ah." Owen tips his head back, laughing. When he meets my eyes again, his features are soft. "Ants."

"Yeah." I set both elbows on the table, resting my chin in my hands. "Ants, and it sucks."

"You enjoy learning. I'm sure he was able to teach you much. Did he teach you about the Sube and the Sune?"

"I've been searching for information about the Sube. I don't know the word Sune."

"They are linked. Where did you discover the word Sube?"

My mind flickers to the dark codex stashed in my room. Cal warned it wasn't for the Light, and I say, "Don't remember why, but Cal said it once."

A female Lighter delivers a tray with two glasses, serving Owen and then me something fizzy and clear. Rice wine isn't carbonated, and after Owen takes a sip, I lift my glass, sniffing the liquid. It's fruity and sweet.

I wet my lips to test the substance and widen my eyes in

shock. What it is remains a mystery, but it's delicious. I take a long drink.

"Rizvor," Owen says. "Do you like it?"

"Yes, it's delicious."

"Good. It's expensive due to the length of time required to make it. You should read up on that instead. It is far more worthy than whatever that animal said."

I take another drink to avoid lashing out in defense of Cal. It would get reported to Pierre, and I would be in for another stern lecture or worse. "It's bothering me like a puzzle I can't finish."

"Your curiosity knows no bounds. Ah, let me see if I recall my lessons." He wrinkles his nose. "I have forgotten so much in my old age."

"You look halfway through your twenties."

"Far, far from. Those days were so long ago, centuries in fact." He tops off my glass. "The Sune and the Sube are the origins of the Seraphinus."

I'd already guessed as much, but that confirms my suspicions. "Then the Seraphinus aren't made of Light and Dark like the Ancients?"

"The Seraphinus are made of either or, not both. Sune and Sube are nothing more than archaic terms for Light and Dark."

I study the table. That's information I surmised on my own. If my research is being monitored, I won't directly ask about the *subtorque*. It would be impossible for me to inquire after unless I bring up the codex. If I mention the codex, Owen will report it to Pierre, and my translations and the codex would be at risk.

Owen's hand slides toward me into my view of the table. "You seem disappointed."

"I don't recall Sube or Sune being words in the Seraphin dictionary."

"Right again," he says, and I lift my eyes to his. "They are the tongue of the Ancients. As for why he used such odd language, well, he's dead, so only the gods will know."

I chew my lower lip, a pang in my chest at remembering Mass is dead. Most days, I try to forget, to focus on the gorgeous architecture and words on a page that tell me fascinating things. Both help to distract, but Mass is impossible to forget.

"No need to look so miserable over the mystery." I try to smile, and he lifts an eyebrow. Cruelty claims his features as he lowers his voice to a whisper, "Or are those tears I see for the animal?"

"I'll never know the reason he used the words."

Owen cracks, his face brightening as he laughs. "You are far more intelligent than I would have ever given you credit for and more curious than I knew a human could be."

Lifting one shoulder, I ask, "Why would the Ancients use different terms than Light and Dark?"

"Bastardizing the Seraphinus." He drains his glass, glancing around. "It was a way of degrading what we are because they hated our kind for being different—an insult to the fact that we were not created of both Light and Dark."

"I guess that makes sense. History does say Beenin and Mallafic were both punished for creating your kind." I sip my drink and then take a longer draught. "Shit, this stuff is good."

He snickers, refilling my glass.

I lift it, warning him, "If you're trying to get me drunk, give up. Magia metabolize too fast. It would take at least a dozen bottles." I shrug and drain the glass again. "We're a blend of Seraphinus in human bodies."

"Gods, what a miserable side effect."

I giggle. "The cost to get drunk is a definite downside."

He shakes his head and sits back as food is delivered.

When the Lighter withdraws, I serve Owen and then myself. It smells amazing, but I wait for him to take the first bite.

He does with a wink. "You can eat now."

I dig in with glee. "Is the myth true that they ripped apart Mallafic and imbued him in books?"

Owen laughs. "Utter nonsense. Mallafic was killed by Beenin in retribution for his attempts on her life. The Dark buried him somewhere. I believe it was the Avgora Mountains where he hid to create them originally. Beenin was condemned by her fellow Ancients. They put her to death for her role in creating chaos in the world. She accepted with grace and bravery as she did with all things." He takes a drink, eyeing me. "What else are you curious about?"

I need to know what was in the codex, but I'll have to find that answer on my own. I won't trust Pierre with knowing whatever was in the book is now in me. The library should have answers.

"Are there other humans in Izul?" I ask, thinking of my red-headed friend. "I wouldn't mind meeting them, maybe making friends."

"Several, used as servants, though rare and unlike you, restricted to personal lodgings. Introductions will be impossible."

Aydian must be one of them. I agreed to keep his secret, though, so I switch topics before Owen grows wary. "Magia have different magic from the Seraphinus. Are there other magics?"

"Not since the time of the Ancients. They had their own magic, different than Light and Dark, a spoken word carried effect, symbols and materials used at times."

I shrug and add that to my list of things to investigate. Aydian said if there were secrets to find, they would be buried in Izul's library. The answers to the Sune and Sube and how Aydian disappeared with a snap of his fingers are stowed somewhere. I'll find them on my own.

"Do you know how Tallie is?"

Owen pauses, meeting my gaze. "I do not. I would suggest you inquire with Zander or Pierre."

I shift. "Zander?"

"Pierre's favorite vassal, very much like his own son. He is training Tallie to connect with her Light and, I believe, keeping her company more so than not."

"Isn't she in prison?"

"She is imprisoned, but it's under special circumstances, given her heritage. Pierre's sway is powerful in the Light, almost more so than the Light Queen's. It's a dissension within our society and something treated with great care to prevent upsetting the balance." He scratches behind his ear. "Forgive me, that is beyond your scope. The Rizvor has stolen my wits."

I press my lips, puckering them before twisting them off to the side in a show of annoyance. "Anyway, he's hanging out with Tallie? Zander is?"

"Yes. If you require more news of Tallie, that information is beyond my scope." He curls his lip and takes a drink.

"I get the feeling you don't like Zander."

"What is not to like? He's tall, beautiful, perfectly worded, polished to perfection, adored by the Bordeaux heritage, and carries the seed of Fairly." Owen mutters barely above the sound of his breath, "Bloody fucking perfect bastard no one can compete with."

I burst with a laugh, covering my mouth quickly as Owen gapes at me.

"Ness, you have my utmost apologies for—"

I wave a hand between us, trying to hold in my humor and not make a scene. "No apologies," I wheeze, swallowing my mirth and choking. "That was great. I think that's the first time you've acted like a real person."

He hangs his head, wagging it back and forth. "I beg of you, never speak of this moment, ever, to anyone."

"Don't worry, dude, your secret is safe with me," I say, smiling at my food.

Now I have two secrets.

CHAPTER 28
NATALIA
THIRD BLOOM'S DAY, HARVEST, 4049 6TH MILLENNIUM

For the first time in what seems to be years, neither Pierre nor Zander trade places with Weila after my lesson. I'm giddy and quick to change into my rabbit outfit and play my guitar.

I roll through songs, singing as loud as I want, channeling Ki into my fingers to force them to take the abuse. I break only for my evening meal, wincing at being caught in my rabbit costume when it's delivered, then too full and lazy to care when the table and remains are cleared away.

I return to my guitar, singing until my throat hurts. The urge to play "I'll Stay" grips me, so I play the notes, letting them wash over me, but no words pass across my lips. I don't know if I'll ever sing of home again, and it's too painful to say the true lyrics, the wound Cal left still pulsing with frigid agony deep in my core.

Knocking interrupts me before I can finish the tune, so I abandon it, blinking and staring at the ceiling to compose myself. Sniffling, I open and close my eyes a few more times, cursing the makeup I didn't bother washing away before getting into the one-piece. "Come in."

The rectangular outline appears, then the door opens. Zander steps inside, "Hello, lovely."

I lean over my guitar, hugging it close. "Hey."

He comes to the bed, holding something up. "The humor of humans will never cease to amaze me." He wiggles a stuffed seowolf at me. "I had an errand to run, and I saw this. I thought you might like it."

Reaching for it, I take it, bringing it closer for inspection. "It's cute."

Sitting on the edge of the bed, he says, "Those things are notoriously dangerous."

I smile at the seowolf, pinching one of the velvet green wings between my fingers and dragging my fingers across the surface, the material shifting to a deeper green. "They are massive."

"You've been near one?"

"Once," I sigh, shaking my head and setting the plush toy on the bed before me. "Cal and I drew a straw to kill one during the games. After, I found its pup. It was just a baby, an adorable, little boy. I picked him up—was going to keep him as a pet with Cal." I stop, my heart breaking all over again.

Zander reaches toward me. "This does not seem to be a happy tale."

"They made Cal kill it." I shake my head, eyes stinging. "It was just a baby. It let me pick him up and carry him, and he just seemed so happy to go for a ride without a care in the world, and Cal was going to let me keep him." I can barely whisper, my throat shrinking. "They served it to me as dinner that evening."

Zander is silent, so I lift my gaze to him. His face is stuck in a mask of horror.

Jiggling one shoulder, I hum. "Welcome to the games that aren't games at all but terrorizing death traps."

257

"I had no idea I'd incur misery by bringing this to you." He reaches for the seowolf, but I snag it, holding it in both hands and frowning at it.

"I mean, it's a shit memory, but I guess I finally got my seowolf pup. I don't have to worry about how big he'll get or what to feed him." I look at Zander with a straight face. "This one isn't going to do a damn thing to protect me though, so, you know, downsides too."

"I'm so sorry, love. I did not intend to distress you. The opposite, in fact."

"You didn't." I plop the toy down in front of me. "Now I'll have an audience when I play."

Zander tries to smile, but it's strained. "The Dark is violent and cruel. They don't even deny it, almost seeming to take pride in that fact. You never should have been exposed to them."

I shrug. "Anyway, thanks." I tap the tiny snout. "What do you want in return?"

"Will you play me a song?"

"I can do that." I find the frets I want.

"This song," he taps against the body of the guitar over the lyrics engraved into the surface.

"Nope."

He chuckles. "A very decisive answer. All right, then, something else perhaps." Rubbing his chin with two fingers, he takes on the aura of grand deliberation before saying, "Will you watch a movie with me?"

I lean toward him over the guitar, faking a whisper. "I don't have an entertainment screen." I bite my words off to catch myself before I call him an idiot.

He leans toward me, bringing his face close to mine, with a quirk to his lips and humor belied in his feigned whisper. "We can watch on my phone."

"That's a small screen."

"Hmm." He wiggles his eyebrows. "You might have a point." A strand of Light extends from his shoulder, wafting in the air through my peripheral vision, moving over my shoulder.

I narrow my eyes.

The hood of my one-piece is yanked over my head, covering my eyes. Zander laughs. "I guess we'll have to cuddle," he says, pulling the guitar from my lap as I adjust the hood out of my line of sight.

"Be careful with that."

He stands, tucking the instrument with care into its case and closing the lid, securing it with a snap of the latches. "Safe and taken care of, love."

Returning to the bed, he moves to the side, slipping his shoes off, then adjusting pillows against the wall to lean against, his legs outstretched before him.

He holds his arm out closer to me and reaches into his pocket with the other, pulling out his phone. "You're going to need to get closer."

I stare at him. "Let me get this straight. You give me a stuffed toy, so now I have to cuddle with you?"

"No." He sits up, his posture stiff. "I would never manipulate such an agreement. I want to spend time with you, but I will not force you to endure contact you do not want."

"Just so I'm clear about what's mandatory." I shrug, snagging the sewolf pup and cuddling it close as I shift to mirror his position and press my shoulder to his. "Although, if anyone had the right to force me, it would be you. I'm pretty sure I raped you on that beach."

He laughs. "Love..." He shakes his head, staring at the ceiling. "I could have stopped you at any time. I didn't. I cannot say with full honesty when I landed on the beach that I wanted to end up underneath you, but when the option was presented, I was more than delighted to enjoy myself."

"Yeah." I draw the word out, tipping my head to rest on his shoulder. "I was a bit over-eager."

"Adrenaline does strange things to the mind."

"Let's go with that." I wiggle, nestling in. "I am sorry, sort of. It wasn't like I planned what happened."

He tucks me closer with his arm around me. "I don't need an apology. I don't want one. We were both consenting. I have no regrets for saving you from the water, carrying you to the beach, or allowing you to have your way with me. Until you returned to my life, it was a memory I visited often in my mind for joy."

I almost make a joke about masturbating.

"My regrets come from what I didn't do. I would have liked to take you to dinner, to spend more time speaking with you after our intimacy, and I regret not realizing who you were—a Light alone in the world that needed to be brought home. If an apology is owed, it is from me to you for my lapse, for not being a gentleman and overlooking your true self."

"It's fine. I don't want or need an apology either."

"Shall I decide the movie?"

"Sure."

He hits play, and then two strands of his Light take hold of the phone, holding it aloft as the movie plays. The premise is set, and I'm warm. The hero makes a stupid choice, and I yawn. It's not my choice of action, more drama than I care for, and it's not holding my attention. My eyelids are heavy, so I close my eyes.

Zander is warm and solid, chuckling at something. I drift away into sleep, too exhausted to care about even trying to witness the conclusion of the motion picture.

TWELFTH EVERGREEN'S DAY, 4049 6TH MILLENNIUM

A THROAT CLEARING startles me to consciousness. I pick my head up to leer at Pierre standing at the foot of my bed.

Groggy, I push myself off Zander's chest, rubbing at my eyes. "Hi."

Zander jolts into a sitting position. "What time is it?"

"Halfway through Blooming's rune." Pierre's voice is as harsh as his expression.

Zander tenses with a sharp intake of air.

"I pondered where you were, what could possibly have prompted your tardiness, and when you didn't arrive at all, I began to contemplate what in Beenin's good graces could have possibly impeded you from your duties."

I look from Pierre's furious face to Zander wincing.

He ducks his head with shame. "I have no valid excuse for my failure."

Pierre rubs a hand over his mouth then rests both on his hips. "This is exceptionally unlike you, Zander."

I roll my eyes. "Oh, come on."

Zander shakes his head, speaking low. "Don't love, the fault is mine, and I accept I made an error." Louder, he says, "Sir, I apologize for my disrespectful actions and accept full responsibility for them. I have no reason to—"

Holding a palm toward us, Pierre smiles. "A mistake now and then is bound to happen. I won't take grievance with a misstep, given your excellent history. There is, however, the matter of you sleeping with my daughter."

Zander turns pink, tucking his chin to his chest under Pierre's glare.

I laugh. "We were sleeping. That's all."

"Acts of intimacy between couples not in a proper relationship are not to be excused. It is unbecoming, and I will not stand for my daughter to be tarnished."

Zander clears his throat. "I was hasty, but I will offer my defense as such: I did not intend to fall asleep nor remain here for the entire evening. I obviously had duties to attend to and would never wish to degrade Tallie in any manner."

Pierre smiles, trying to rub it away. "I believe we have something to discuss."

"Yes, please. I enjoy your daughter's company."

"I am in a very unusual situation."

"I recognize the imposition."

I shift my eyes back and forth between them. Opening my mouth, I reconsider, close my mouth and arrange the words in my head. To ask what the fuck is going on is improper. "Might I inquire as to what is happening?"

With a chagrin laugh, Zander says, "A relationship must be approved by the head of the heritage. As I am still his ward until I age out of my fifth century, he will be the deciding factor for any relationship I might choose to pursue."

I fold my lips between my teeth and hold my breath to avoid expletives and yelling. "*Mhm,*" I manage in a whimper.

"He is also the eldest of your heritage and, therefore, the decider for any relationship you may wish to enter into."

"*Mhm.*" I grip the baggy fabric of my one-piece rabbit suit, squeezing as hard as I can to prevent exploding.

"As we both must seek his approval for each other, it is

uncommon. In any regular scenario, you would need to seek permission from my eldest."

"That's incredibly..." I don't have *eloquent* words to respond further.

Eyeing me, Pierre says, "You may not like it, daughter mine, but that is our custom. We must consider the evolution of heritages to ensure we take proper care of the Light we further. It would not do to have a Bordeaux mix with a Trilo, for instance. The Trilo heritage would approve, but a Bordeaux cannot. While Trilo would find it an advantageous union, it would be diluting the Bordeaux heritage."

"Uh-huh. Fascinating."

Zander rests a hand on my shoulder. "It may do to clarify." He glances at Pierre. "If I might?"

Pierre holds an open hand, palm up at me in response.

"The Light is not like the Dark. Our strength passes down through the heritage, unlike the Dark, which does not possess that same level of quality. For example, the Dark King, by their ways, was strong enough to take the throne. However, his seed may be too weak to even survive in their world. This is not the case for the Light. As a Fairly, I inherit my strength of magic."

Smiling, Pierre says, "Avery good lesson to teach her." He crosses his arms, bending one up to stroke his chin. "As a Bordeaux, I have no concerns with the Fairly heritage. If anything, it would strengthen that of my heritage. However, Tallie is not wholly of the Light or even Seraphinus. I cannot in good conscience agree to the Fairly heritage entering a union with a Seraphim, doubly so as Zan has a clear duty to multiply his heritage."

Zander sighs. "That is a valid concern. One my heart chose to ignore the logic in."

I'm not sure what his heart has to do with anything.

He goes on, saving me from myself before I lose control and

say something. "However, Tallie is not a mere Seraphim either, and a Bordeaux Seraphim ought to be stronger than that of lesser heritages of our kind."

I'm grinding my teeth at being weighed as an object for validity. The question of if I want to be in a relationship with Zander hasn't been offered, a conundrum I possess no answer to even if it were asked.

"I agree," Pierre says. "A quandary, if ever I were posed with a valid one. Yet, she is born of Seraphinus and Magia."

"To my point." Zander chuckles. "She is beyond anything a mere Seraphim ever has been. If I may, perhaps no official decision can be made to renounce our right to have a relationship until we know the extent of Tallie's capabilities. After all, she did survive the Dark, even their barbaric ritual of—what do you call them, love? Games?"

Scoffing, I say, "They're games like poking yourself in the eye hard enough to blind yourself is fun."

"Yes." His words come faster, excitement bolstering them. "Even untrained and barely matured, she was strong enough to face their strongest and live. That alone is enough logic for me to disregard her Seraphim nature as a potential mate. There should be no question that the Fairly seed and her seed would result in anything short of spectacular."

I bite the tip of my tongue between my front teeth, forcing myself to count to ten in an attempt to subdue my need to shriek. The only one who hasn't treated me as a stallion to be bred is Cal. That sends my rage from a boil to a simmer, a pang between my ribs clearing the red haze in my mind.

With a forced frown, Pierre looks to the ceiling. "I will raise the possibility with our queen. We shall see her opinions on the matter."

Zander gets up, bowing to Pierre. "My gratitude for your

consideration of me knows no bounds. It would be beyond an honor to accept Tallie as a potential mate."

"An honor in turn that you should unionize with my heritage." Pierre claps Zander on the shoulder with a wide grin. "We shall see what our queen believes before I disallow the pursuit of my daughter, but know this: if I must decline you as a suitor, it will not be for fault found in you. I see you as nothing short of a worthy option for my daughter."

Zander puts his shoes on with a wide grin. "Without a doubt in my mind, I see no reason the queen might impose an injunction." He stands and turns to me. "I'll see to everything, love."

With a bounce in his step, he exits the room.

Pierre nods to me. "I shall return him when we have finished our responsibilities. Please clean yourself up for Weila. She shall be along shortly. Enjoy your day."

He walks out, the door shutting and the wall sealing.

I stare at the wall, snarling, "If anyone even cares what I think, my answer is fuck off and let me live my life however I want. M'kay?"

Pierre and Weila stare at me as I spin in a dress for their inspection. Weila turns to Pierre. "Your thoughts, sir?"

"I see no faults."

"Neither do I. Your daughter has progressed very well, given the odious behavior ingrained from her upbringing that led to my necessary labor."

"You deserve platitudes beyond measure."

I swallow my retort that I want to vomit, listening to them and force a smile. I am about to present to the Light Queen for a second time, under scrutiny, to determine if I can exist within the Light. I will spew their pointless drivel with fake grins and feign delight in order to survive.

I'd promised Cal. I'd promised my beautiful, wicked Darkling, and I won't let him down. I won't break my promise, but this is tedious. Painful. I'm going to break out in hives soon from swallowing all my sarcasm and curses.

Checking his watch, Pierre says, "I'll speak with my daughter a moment, but I cannot express my gratitude for your services with any efficiency to make you understand how deep that appreciation goes."

"Please do share my abilities so I may continue to serve the Light." She bows to him before turning to me. "Tallie, your beauty knows no bounds. It has been an absolute pleasure to watch you grow into the Light. I have the utmost respect for your apparent ability to reform. Please mind your manners, and should you wish to ever seek improvements again, I will be honored to be available to you at your leisure."

I stretch my face to widen my smile as if I'm enjoying any part of this. "That is very gracious of you, Weila, and I appreciate your offer."

Bowing to me, then to Pierre again, she says, "May your webs of fates be fortunate."

"Thank you, Weila. Beyond what those simple words can begin to convey, thank you." She walks out of the room, and Pierre turns to the waiting avengers. "Please close the door until I am ready. I want a private fraction with my daughter."

One of the avengers bows his head, complying with the demand. When the wall seals shut, Pierre faces me. "Daughter mine, you look very beautiful, but you will need to mind your manners and that sharp, forked tongue of yours yet. If you displease our queen, she will not hesitate to destroy your Light in service of our kin." His gaze lowers as he rubs his forehead. "Please be perfect, make amends for your actions through a show of repentance, and for the love of Beenin, please show respect."

I don't bother faking a smile. "I'm trying."

"I'm aware." He gives me a half-hearted curve of his lips. "When you are given standing, I have a gift prepared for you already in turn for your gift to me."

I lift an eyebrow. He provides the best gifts.

"Yes," he says, giving me a rare genuine smile, "I am attempting to bribe your best behavior."

"At least you're honest about it, but I'm certain the need to survive is instinctual, and I will do everything in my power to ensure my Light is not destroyed."

"Very good." He checks behind him toward the door, then offers me his arm. "Shall we be early?"

"It is a show of respect for the time of others," I respond, repeating the nonsense that's been crammed into me by Weila. There were days I rehearsed appropriate responses that could be used when I knew not what to say that was basic and polite until I hated the sound of my own voice.

Pierre steps to my side and knocks on the door. "We are ready."

It opens, the avengers a pace behind and flanking us as we walk to the staircase, following the spiraling steps to the top, across the entrance hall to the other side, and up to the second floor. The dress is as heavy as the first, extravagant with jewels and embroidery abound, but Weila's training pays off as I move without stumbling on the fabric or having to fumble with picking up the skirt to maneuver. It irks me.

I've changed. I've allowed them to cut and trim and reshape me to their desire.

Who am I now?

Pierre draws me to the same chaise I plopped down on before, nodding to me. "Rest while we wait, Tallie. I have never envied the shoes women chose to wear."

Lowering to the cushion, I sit at an angle, my legs to one side, adjusting the skirt of my dress in a pleasing manner to avoid wrinkles and present a pretty picture for any to see. There's a remark to be made about an actual choice in my footwear, but I neglect it, not wanting to create conflict.

Instead, I run a hand over my hair, checking for any flyaway strands or loose locks from its styling.

The avengers stand on either side of the doorway, one aimless in his staring, the other watching me. Any other time, I might have poked at him for my amusement. It's a thought wafting through me, so I turn my head, looking down the hall to ignore his judgments.

Staring down the hall, I let my mind go numb and try to focus on determining what shade of white the marble is. Weila had been firm in her education on the differences between cream, eggshell, and ivory. Never before had I known white was so diverse.

The door opens across the way, Larles standing on the threshold. I look at him, his face thin, his nose a mirroring example of Zander's. They share plenty of similarities, but not height.

Both doors are fully opened, folded out of the way and Larles bows in the threshold. "Pierre Bordeaux and Miss Tallie Bordeaux, please be welcoming and find welcome with our Light Queen."

Pierre gives a curt, half bow. "Thank you, Larles. We are welcomed and welcoming." Holding his hand out, palm up, Pierre turns to me.

I put my hand in his, allowing him to help me rise to my feet with a grace Weila would be proud of and smile. "We appreciate your welcome, Larles, and will be sure to be welcoming."

Larles' left eyebrow twitches up ever so slightly, his lips pulling to one side. He fades into the room, gesturing to the side.

Pierre leads me, entering first and escorting me toward the Light Queen kneeling at the low table. She's pure white and gold, her painted lips of gilded yellow lifting at the corners. She lifts without ever seeming to move somehow, maintaining perfect posture during the transition.

Her massive tulle skirt swishes as she glides around the table to greet us.

Pierre bows. "Marisa, you are glowing."

Her eyes move to me, and I lower my head, bowing from my hips to be parallel with the floor. I exhale, count to three, and then pull upright.

"Tallie, you are positively ethereal, darling."

"Thank you, Your Majesty, but I am naught in comparison to your radiance." I incline my head. "If you will allow, I would like to express my remorse for our previous encounter. I was incorrigible at best, failing to act with any amount of tact."

She clasps her hands, shoulders flexing back as she lifts her chin. "An absolute picture of horror, you were, but now..." She steps closer, her fingers forcing my chin up for her to inspect my face. "You have come into the Light quite nicely. It does shine through you fully now and, I believe, in quite an unusual color, if I am not mistaken." She looks to Pierre.

"Yes," he says, "her Light is an odd coloring, silver instead of golden."

"How very strange, child. Can you account for this?"

I open my mouth, scrambling for anything to say other than I don't fucking know. "No, Your Majesty. I have no knowledge of the cause."

Humming, she turns away, returning to the table to kneel, adjusting her skirt. "Please, won't you join me?"

Pierre steps, kneels, and then I follow into place, being sure to lower with care rather than falling to the ground in a clumsy heap.

The Queen smiles. "She has come a long way. You declared her your daughter, and I was concerned the Bordeaux heritage would forever be tainted with your actions and such a beastly addition, but you were right, as always." Her grin seems to be more a baring of teeth in ferocious warning than sweetness. "You claimed all you needed was time, and it seems to have worked exceptionally well."

"Your recommendation of Weila was most welcome. She is a treasure we should cherish."

"Indeed." The queen nods, turning her head to the side. Her profile displays her straight nose protruding like a triangle, her lips indiscernible from her chin. "Larles, the tea, please."

He steps forward, kneeling at the end and begins the preparations to serve tea.

"Now, then, child." She fixates on me. "You've had time to become accustomed to being in the Light. How do you feel about your time in the Dark?"

I grip my skirt, begging Cal to forgive my next words. "I was enamored by the offered escape the Dark presented, failing to know my true self and proper place. The Magia presented a tribulation that was exploitable by one who used me for their gain. I'm abhorred at my gullibility and ashamed of my acceptance of a contract. The Light should never bow to the creatures of the Dark, and I can defend myself no further for the embarrassment I made of the Light and the mockery I made of myself."

I might vomit all over the table or cry. I'm not sure which impulse is gripping my throat. What the fuck did I just say?

Larles sets a cup of tea in front of the queen. She grins like a predator. "A lesson well learned. You were a vulgar display of your heritage, to be sure, a time you'll want to forget, no doubt."

With full honesty, I smile with closed lips and nod. "Yes, I very much would like to forget."

Pierre's cup is placed before him, and the queen bats her

eyelashes. "I have come to understand you wish to enter a relationship with Zander Fairly."

Larles halts for a single heartbeat on his way to deliver my cup of tea, then the cup slips from his fingers, falling to the table and tipping over. I lurch at the liquid splashing.

Larles gapes at me. "Miss Tallie, my deepest apologies."

I laugh, waving him off. "Do not think of it. I am no worse for it."

He clears his throat, gathers up the cup and starts to stand.

The queen drawls, "Larles, a moment."

He settles, going still.

"Is this true?"

Pierre clears his throat. "It is, Marisa. They became acquainted prior to Tallie coming to Izul, unaware that they were already wound in webs of the fates to reconnect here."

She places a hand on the table close to Larles. "Zander is your sibling seed, your younger heritage. Has he expressed genuine interest in such a relationship?"

"He has, Your Majesty."

She clicks her tongue. "What are your thoughts?"

He looks toward me, his eyebrows shifting as he frowns. "I'm aware Zander has affection for Miss Tallie. He speaks highly of her transition to the Light, and he finds her entertaining, enjoying her wits." Larles pauses, his nostrils flaring. "Her first impressions have left a bitter taste, in my opinion. She was near rapid upon her introduction and far from anything I would want to be associated with and even further from anything I would accept defiling my heritage. However..."

His shoulders drop. "Zan has spent significant time with her, so much that I have no right to overrule his choices. I know my brother to be an exceptional demonstration of what we are, capable of reason, and above all else, he is dutiful and diligent in all things. If he sees her as worthy of the Fairly heritage, I can look beyond what was to what is, even to what can be. If she is his choice, so be it."

Pierre says, "Well said, Larles, and I appreciate your candor. I recognize the intricate situation I am in with deciding if the union is beneficial and will remain as impartial as a father is able. I am fond of Zan. He is as dear to me as my own daughters, and I take very seriously the responsibility of ensuring the continuation of the Fairly heritage. Tallie and Zan are both aware of his duty and of the seriousness of that duty, and no formal decision is being made on the validity of a relationship until we know further the strength of Tallie's seed."

Larles bows his head. "You have my deepest gratitude for caring for my brother as well as seeing to the benefit of my heritage."

I dig my thumb into my index finger, the nail pushing into my skin. I press hard enough for my fingertip to throb. No one has yet to inquire if I even want a relationship with Zander. More and more, that fact seems disregarded as irrelevant. It's not like being forced into an engagement with Tony. That was repulsive and reprehensible at best. While I have no objections to Zander, attractive and sweet, there's not a stitch of my heart that's interested.

"Very well," the Light Queen says, flicking her hand. "Pierre, the decision shall be yours to determine. If she is strong enough to either maintain or bolster the strength of Fairly, I will not interject any objections."

He gives her a wry smile. "I appreciate your trust in my ability to decide what is best for them."

"But of course." She laughs, an airy waft of music filling the air. "There are two more matters on which I must hear from your daughter."

"As you desire." He motions to me.

I lift my eyebrows, giving her my full attention and keeping my face blank. She taps her index finger against the rim of her cup. "You were raised by the Magia."

"I was."

"They are attacking Seraphinus across both continents."

"Dreadful."

She narrows her eyes, but I flinch on the inside like a winner. "Yes, very. They seem capable of killing our kind." She gestures toward Larles. "How are they capable of killing our kind? Just last week, two were killed in Capali outside a museum that had invited humans within its walls at no charge, an honorable offer from their patron, Reghan."

I wet my lips, my heart racing. "The Magia have magic of their own, Your Majesty. It differs from Dark or Light."

"They were once powerful, but we cast them aside for the inability to exist within our world in peace. Did you know they've tried to take power from us before?"

"I was made aware of that fact, Your Majesty."

"Mmm." Her lips press. "How do they kill the Light? Are you capable of doing so as well?"

"I believe so, Your Majesty. Though not all Magia are capable of performing the magic."

She eyes me, her head shied to one side. "What is the magic?"

"Ki, Your Majesty." I hesitate. I am going to have to give her something to end this inquiry. "Those who are fully trained are capable of intaking the Dark or the Light in order to wield it for their own. That is what Ki does."

"Very well. It is as if we battle our own in that case." She lifts her teacup, taking a drink. "Larles, you may return to your duties. Please clean up your mess and finish serving Tallie her libation."

Setting her cup aside, she watches Larles abandon the

table and stride away. When he is further out of earshot, she faces Pierre. "The last matter is that of Ritual."

Pierre tenses. "Ritual does not apply between my daughters. Tallie is a Seraphim, not wholly my heritage."

"You cannot claim her as your seed, give her a place in society, and ignore the customs for sibling seeds."

"Ignore is a harsh description. I have considered the act of Ritual, but the Ritual fight takes place between two sibling seeds of Seraphinus. Our laws are clear on that distinction."

She flicks her wrist. "If she is strong enough to deserve a union with a Fairly, then she is strong enough to be deserving of her place. Regardless of her origins, that qualifies her to be a worthy successor and subjected to Ritual."

Pierre wraps his hands around his teacup and stares into it.

"At a loss for words? My, how very unusual for you, darling." Her words carry a humor masking malice. "Did you think I would accept you having two daughters in society, both active in standing, while one enters a union with a Fairly? *Tsk*."

"You mistake my protection of my heritage for combat, Marisa." He lifts his teacup, chugging the contents. Setting it down with a sharp rap, he says, "The laws of Ritual are yours to twist as you see fit to serve our kin. If you deem to force the Ritual fight upon a Seraphim, you have the ability to do so, but I will not disguise the abuse of your position."

Larles returns, using a white towel to sop up the spilled tea. He keeps his head low and focuses on his work.

The queen smiles with venom. "As always, Pierre, you overstep. Ritual will apply."

I glance at Pierre.

His mouth is pulled tight, his eyes narrowed. His ears pull back as his face relaxes. "The decision is yours to make."

She grins. "Made it has been." Turning her eyes on me, she says, "My dear child, you are without question beautiful. I applaud your acceptance of the Light and reformation. Do see that you do not disappoint me in my decision to give you standing and refrain from winding up imprisoned once more. It would be such a shame to deny your looks to the world. I look forward to your future, understanding the scope of your true abilities and the results of Ritual."

I incline my head, but Pierre drawls, "It will be a long time before she is prepared for Ritual."

"Perhaps." The queen nods. "Perhaps not as long as you would like. Dear me, I do believe Ashley will be highly motivated to win."

CHAPTER 30
NATALIA

When the queen dismisses us, Pierre walks me out of the throne room and down the spiral staircase in silence. We descend to my imprisonment chambers, and I squirm.

"Relax, honey. I presume you'd like to change into something more comfortable and less formal."

"Oh, considerate of you. Yes, please."

He pushes the door open. "I will wait. Please knock when you're ready. Leave everything inside when you've finished. Your things will be delivered to your quarters in the tower this evening."

"My sincere thanks."

I change into a simple white dress with mesh sleeves and shoulders that stretch across my collarbone, the rest of the fabric fitted. Keeping the same glittering, gold heels on that I've been wearing, I knock to be released.

Pierre leans his head to the side toward the steps, turning to walk before me as we return to the main floor.

Focusing on Pierre, I cock my head, asking without words why we are standing here. He gives me a tight smile in response. "We concluded early. Zander should be along momentarily. I presumed you would enjoy a celebration dinner for your accomplishment of a suitable presentation to our queen and would welcome Zan's attendance."

I press my lips, drawing my features together in a frown. "May I ask if I have any say in my relationship with Zander?"

"I doubt there will be any reason for me to deny your union, but for the sake of the Fairly heritage, I cannot give my consent until I am certain you will do it justice. I have others to consider beyond myself and my heritage. No matter how much I may value my daughters, the position I hold comes with responsibilities, and that of securing the Fairly heritage is a dire service to all of the Light."

We pivot toward Zander, walking across the hall. He stops before us, nodding at Pierre. "Sir."

"Be at ease. Tallie did splendidly, passing inspection and acting with grace. She has received her acceptance into not only the Bordeaux heritage but into society as well."

Zander grins. "That is excellent news." He laughs, slipping his hands around my waist and lifting me up to spin us in circles.

"Zan!"

He sets me down, pulling me close and resting his chin on my head. "You are without doubt a brilliant Light, love. I am delighted beyond ecstasy with your accomplishment."

I want to roll my eyes but lean back with a smile, pressing my palms to his chest. "I am happy you are pleased."

Pierre clears his throat. "Zan, I'll remind you I am standing here, and as you are in public, anyone might stumble upon this scene."

Zander takes a step back, winking at me. "I'm sure she's far more interested in dinner anyway." He offers me a bent arm. "Shall we?"

Taking his arm, I say, "I am most assuredly excited by the prospect of food. Can Ness come? I would love to see her." I look to Pierre.

He shakes his head, and my heart drops into my stomach. "She is in the library still, honey, and will not be available until Thorn's rune. You'll be able to see her after."

I bob my head, and Zander puts his hand over mine in the crook of his arm. "Have no concerns. You'll see her soon enough. In the meantime, we have time to honor your accomplishment. We'll be dining at Lor Loch, and they have rizvor."

Pierre starts walking, and Zander pulls me in step while I ask, "What the–what's rizvor?"

They either don't notice or, more likely, choose to overlook the slip in my words.

Pierre says, "Rizvor is a delicacy even for us. It takes decades to create and is a favorite of the Light for its airy, simple tastes."

Zander chuckles as he opens the door for Pierre to pass through first before he pulls me with him to the outside. "You'll love it. It's a delicious liquor."

I snap my head to the side, not even taking a moment to savor the fresh air and being out of the palace for the first time in eternity. My heart races with excitement. "Alcohol?"

"Yes, love, alcohol."

"Please walk faster."

ZANDER GUIDES me back to my room, Pierre having excused himself for a meeting he was required to attend.

When we reach the flight shaft, Zander says, "They still haven't repaired the block."

I perk up. "It's still not illuminated?"

"No." He presses the button. "I wanted to warn you."

I stare into the shaft, the swirling shadows seeming to hiss at the disturbance, twisting out of their domain to spread out. The coolness wafts across my senses, calming me. I close my eyes, inhaling the dank, hollow promise they offer.

"Love?" Swinging me in his arms, he steps into the shaft, wings sprouting through his shirt. "Are you all right? I know being this close to lack of brightness must be difficult for you since being placed into the Light, but I will fly swiftly and get you back to the Light quickly. You have my word."

Ignoring his stupid words, I picture Cal as I stare over Zander's shoulder to his wings of Light. They move in thick ropes, flexing as he lifts us higher from solid ground.

I want to ask why Cal always has holes in his shirts after his wings have sprouted when no one else seems to. The words stick in my mind.

Zander gets us out of the flight shaft quicker than I'd have preferred, but I keep those words to myself as well. He keeps me in his arms, walking through the halls, and I relax into him, still clinging to the lingering effects of the liquor from dinner.

The rizvor was as delicious as promised, and I had drunk more than enough to horrify both Pierre and Zander. I had ignored their mortification, laughing about Magia metabolisms. I'd managed to get drunk before I was cut off, and though the alcohol is nearly out of my system, I'm drowsy from the effects.

Zander stops, whispering, "Are you asleep, love?"

"Mmm." I open my eyes as a golden rope twists the handle of a door, pushing it open before withdrawing back into Zander.

He shoulders the door open further, moving into the room straight to the bed. "You're all right, love."

I pick my head off his shoulder, pointing and gaping at the shelf unit pushed against my window wall. It's lined with bottles of vodka, every bottle emblazoned with the blaring green stamp on the glass of my favorite brand: "Grassel."

Zander chuckles. "Pierre's gift to you for your behavior. A bottle for every day you were in confinement. It is your preferred brand, yes?" Ropes of Light twist in the air, pulling back the comforter and sheets. Zander deposits me in the bed, quick to remove my shoes, then tucks me in as I yawn.

"Wait." I sit up, blinking sticky eyes. "Ness."

"It's three-quarters through Night's rune, love. She'll be asleep, and in the morning, I'll be here to fetch you at Sun's rune for breakfast. Tomorrow, I'll be working on training your Light with you. You'll want your rest." He kisses my forehead. "Good night, Tal. May Beenin grace you with sweet dreams."

I lay back and wait several fractions after he's exited the room before I slip from beneath the covers and out of my room, walking on the balls of my feet in a sleek stalk through the hallway, glancing down the corridor connecting to it before scurrying across to avoid anyone noticing. At her door, I reach for the knob, opening it a crack to peek inside.

"*Psst*," I hiss, sliding in and closing the door. "Ness," I whisper.

She picks her head up from her hand, eyes lifting from the book in her lap. Her big brown eyes widen as far as they can, taking up her whole face. She opens her mouth, but I put a finger to mine to indicate quiet.

I grin, running to the bed and hopping onto it, landing on my knees. She meets me there, wrapping her arms around me and squeaking in my ear.

"Oh, babe." I wince, giggling. "I think you might have cracked a rib. Less force, please."

She lets go, leaning back and grabbing my upper arms before scanning down my torso, then back up to meet my gaze. "Did you just say please? To me? What the fuck happened to you?"

I sit back on my heels, resting my palms on my thighs. "I was supposed to present to the queen, but I met Ashley right before. She called me and my mom Magia whores, then she insulted Cal." I hang my head. "She called him a pathetic mutt. I snapped, so I, you know, snapped her nose."

"Good for you, babe."

Shaking my head, I stare at the bedspread between us. "They have so many rules."

"And they're big on respect and serving and being on time and have no sense of humor and—"

"D, all of the above." I take her hands in mine.

"This place is insane in the worst kind of ways."

"It's... I'm sorry. I didn't have a choice. I had to stay in that room for fifty days for what I did. How are you?"

She shrugs. "Wasn't your fault. Not really, anyway. You were defending Cal." With a sigh, she shrugs again. "I'm okay. They let me in the library."

"I heard. I'm sure you're loving that. Any update on the marks on you?"

"No. The Sube is the origin of the Dark, and the Sune is the origin of the Light. Sube and Sune are words of the Ancients, not the Seraphinus, though. I learned that much."

"That's new."

She bobs her head. "Yeah, and the Ancients used the words because they wanted to insult the Seraphinus, more confirmation that the Ancients despised the Seraphinus." She flicks her wrist. "The word *subtorque* isn't something I've found anything on, and um..."

Lifting my eyebrows, I wait.

"And, um, nothing else to share. What about you?"

Taking a deep breath, I tell her about being imprisoned, the etiquette lessons and my guitar and rabbit suit. I do my best to explain what I've learned, why I'll do what they want so my Light isn't destroyed, and how I'm being pushed into a relationship with Zander.

When I finish, she blinks in rapid succession. "What the absolute shit show is this place?"

"It's not Cal's home or Ilbuio, that's for certain." We stare at each other in the silence. My heart rolls over, like its struggling against death, but it keeps beating, refusing to quit. "I don't know why I feel sick, but I do."

Ness lets go of my hand, rolling to sit, hugging her knees to her chest. "Have you cried for him yet?"

"A few times." I crane my head, trying to see Ness's face, but she has her forehead to her knees.

"I've cried for Mass," she says in a low, thick voice. "For what I lost. A few times now, and it's not getting better. It was barely even a thing, if one at all."

I shift to press against her, putting my arm around her. "I'm sorry, babe."

Ness shrugs. "It is what it is, but still, surrounded by all this freaking eye candy, because seriously, is every Seraphinus gorgeous? All I can think is what if?" She tips her head back and sighs. "What if I'd gotten more time? What if I'd worn him down and gotten a ride? What if I'd just fucking made a move that last night at the spa?"

"You should have. I went to find Todd so you would have the room."

Ness does a back roll, grabs a pillow, and whacks me with

it. "I'm so mad about that! He died thinking I was screwing Roger."

I rip the pillow out of her grip, cuddling it close. "Mass wasn't giving you the signals he was interested."

Ness crosses her ankles and forms a ball again. "No. I really was looking forward to telling him I was getting off to the idea of him." She drops her forehead to her knees. Ness sobs, mewling in a broken voice. "I don't know why I'm so heartbroken about this. I feel like I lost the love of my life, and I keep crying, but I bare—barely knew the guy."

I squeeze the pillow harder. I can't explain the hole ripped out of me from losing Cal, but the idea that he was supposed to be that great love of my life, the one the Mother created me for, is too close for comfort.

"Whatever you're feeling is acceptable."

She sniffles. "I feel like I'm being crazy."

"No." I lift up and walk on my knees to her, cuddling against her. "You aren't crazy. Sometimes there's just a click, and something connects."

Ness shudders, sucking in a breath. "I don't even know his last name, and I can't stop crying over him. You were screwing Cal, but you aren't a wreck. You're dating Zander."

"Low blow, babe," I whisper. "I haven't even said I wanted to be in a relationship, but I'm not being given much of a choice. He's not bad, but I'm not interested in having a relationship with anyone."

Ness goes through another body-wracking sob. "I hate it here. Everyone stares at me like I'm a freak, and no one wants to talk to me. They just glare if I ask for a book at the library, and the constant brightness gives me headaches."

Leaning my head on her shoulder, I rub her back. "I'll talk to you."

"Oh, shut up." Ness picks her head up, dropping her legs to

sit crossed legged and wipes at her face. "Mother, I'm sorry, babe. I didn't mean that."

I tip my head back. "Yeah, you did, and it's okay. I get it." Picking my head up, I meet her wide, dark eyes. "Do you want to leave?"

She lifts her eyebrows, blinking. "Is that an option? We have to get permission to leave our rooms without supervision. I'm asking for you," she says, rolling her eyes. "No one gives a fuck what I do."

"I have no idea." I pick at lint on the bedspread, sitting cross-legged, propping my chin on my hand. "This place is pretty awful, though, so if you want to take our chances out there somewhere else...?"

"I don't know," she says in a defeated whisper, hanging her head. "Do you want to leave?"

We stare at each other.

She shakes her head, turning her face away. "It's safe here, and the library..." Her eyes roll into the back of her head as she lets out a groan.

I bob my head. "You love that place, don't you?"

"Yeah." She laughs. "I really do. You have to promise to come see it, though." Her lower lip protrudes, pouting.

"I'll see what I can do, but I won't make a promise I can't keep. I have no idea what I'm going to be allowed to do, and I know I can't tomorrow because Zander says I'll be training my Light." I pause, staring at the bedspread. "If we leave–the Magia are killing Seraphinus–and I'm not sure they've given up on hunting me just yet. I don't want to live always looking over my shoulder."

Ness bobs her head. "I'm useless."

"No, you're not."

She tilts her head, features pulled downward. "Babe, thanks for pretending, and no, I'm not useless in everything, but I couldn't help fight if they found us. You'd be alone and have to take care of both of us. I don't know how long we'd last."

"If I thought we had somewhere to go," I shake my head. "If I thought maybe Hiro and Thames would take us in and where they were? If Mass survived?"

Ness cleans under her eyes with shaky fingers. "If they survived, they would have kicked down the door and gotten us by now." She flings a hand at me. "You're wearing a fucking tracker. They'd know where we are."

"Then we stay here for now, I guess."

"At least I'm here. That instantly makes this city a thousand times better."

Forcing a smile, I say, "Absolutely. And in case you need something to get by, I have a whole shelf of vodka in my room that we can share."

"Grassel?"

"Grassel."

"And you didn't bring a bottle for me because?"

"How about I go get a couple, and you can tell me about the library?"

"Why are you still sitting here, babe? Go!"

CHAPTER 31

NATALIA

FIFTH STAR'S DAY, HARVEST, 4049 6TH
MILLENNIUM

My head barely hit my pillow when Zander woke me up. He'd been quiet through the morning meal while I keep gaping at the intricate war-like braid his gold hair is finessed into today. It's awe-inspiring.

After we finish eating, he guides me further up the street with a hand at the small of my back, leading me through the city.

"May I know where we're going?"

"The arena. Pierre has instructed me to begin your training, and that must be done within the confines of the arena." He stretches his head to the side. "It's the only place within Izul where physical and magical abilities may be engaged in combat. It is the only place you can—and I will stress *consensually and respectfully*—engage in a fight."

"I could legally punch Ashley in the face in the arena?"

Zander chuckles. "If she agrees to a fight, then you can enter combat under the rules of engagement. I believe the Dark shares those rules with us, a common ground. Are you familiar with them?"

I flex my shoulder blades together. "Yes and no. Cal mentioned the rules of engagement once or twice, but I never got a list." I take a deep breath, the pang between my ribs along my left side sharp. "He wasn't big on details."

"You were naught but a tool for him to use. He wouldn't have seen it necessary to explain anything, believing you to exist merely to satisfy his orders. You would have been expected to comply without asking questions."

I grind my teeth but can't deny that Cal never explained things. The closest he came was when he shoved a box of books at me.

"The basic rules are simple. Conduct yourself in all means of self-preservation. If both sides agree to be peaceful, to attack is breaking the rules. A fight two parties have agreed to enter is not to be interfered with by another. You fight until one side is neutralized or yields. If death occurs in a fight, it is not punishable by law, and there will be no attempts of retaliation either."

"Seems straight forward."

He stops us in front of grand double doors. I tip my head back, inspecting the tower. It's sleek and glossy, like a high-end office or living space.

"This is the arena. It is used for training of all kinds. Strengthening equipment is provided, and there are designated areas for specific training. I'll explain it all before we begin." He opens the door, "After you, love."

I step inside and gape. "Holy fuck, this place is massive."

Zander chuckles, the door swinging closed behind us with a heavy thump. "This entire building is used for training. Have no concerns. I will show you around before we begin." He offers me his hand, "You need to remember to mind your language."

'Take my hand when I offer it.' It's not Zander's hand I should

be holding, but resigned, I take his hand, his fingers fitting between mine.

"This main floor is where most of the combat happens. It is where the strongest of us will engage under the rules of combat to further our abilities."

"Do you train?"

"I haven't for many days now, my duties preoccupying my time, but before your arrival, I spent every other morning here, honing skills and improving myself." He gives me a smug grin. "There aren't many who will engage with me. It's an embarrassment for them to even try."

I lick along my upper teeth. The respect Cal had amongst the players during the games was evident from the quips and comments of others. He didn't need to brag about his prowess.

"I see my words are not sufficient to convince you of my strength. I'll have to achieve your approval in another way." He leads me forward a couple of steps. "The upper floors are designed for learning certain skills, rooms designed to withstand smites, electrical attacks, even firelight. There are floors for cardio training, and there is weight training as well. Here are the stairs for you to reach any level you choose. The arena is open to anyone of all ages, and so there will be plenty using the arena without wings."

I'm dizzy and panting from walking too many steps, but Zander brings me back to the second floor, leading me to an open area.

"Today, I want to see how well you've connected to your Light. We'll try a few exercises to see how much control you have, testing the basic use of your Light."

"All right."

Light unwinds from him, moving toward the wall off to the side, picking up two small, round weights with handles. They are deposited a few paces from us, and Zander motions to them. "The most basic skill is using your Light as limbs. Your Light is akin to any other muscle in your body. It will need to be stretched to increase its reach, and you'll need to perform weight training to strengthen it so it can lift heavier objects."

"Okay."

"Like a muscle, your body will pose limitations as your Light's vessel. My Light has more room to grow in me, more space, so it will be bigger than your Light could ever be. That's not to say your Light can't be strong, but as my Light is larger like my bicep is larger, so will my Light be stronger than yours. The bigger your Light, the stronger your Light, the more powerful it becomes, and the more energy it can channel into other attacks, like smites."

I frown at the weights. "You'll always be stronger?"

"Yes, but do not let that be of major concern to you. Your strength and right to be my mate will not be judged negatively for that fact. It is merely a fact of the Light for you to remember." He grimaces. "It's why Larles is so disappointed in his lack of height and physical stature."

I look away. "Zan, about this relationship we're in?"

"We'll take things slow. I'm not going to rush anything, and I recognize your struggles with coming into the Light. You have more pressing and present things to attend to, so I will be patient. Now, to begin, I want to see if you can pick up those weights. We'll adjust how we proceed from there."

I resist rolling my eyes, focusing on the weight. "How do I make my Light do something?"

"As you have a connection, all you have to do is ask it."

"Like think to do it?" Several strands of my Light unwind, and it picks up one of the weights.

"Very good, love. Now, move it forward a bit. See if your Light can stretch under weight."

"This is stupid."

I pull my ears back, widening my eyes at Cal's snarl in my head. I glance around, my heart shattering, when I can't locate him.

"I'm not doing this. Tell the pretty boy to get fucked."

The weight sails across the room. Several Lighters gape and glare. I stare with an open mouth as Zander offers apologies.

His hand rests on my shoulder. "Love?"

"Um..." I blink at the weight embedded in the wall at the far end of the gym.

"We'll work on finesse, I think."

Several stands of my Light unwind to pick up the remaining weight and drop it at Zander's feet. *"Tell it no. I'm bored and won't be doing any more of this."*

The strands sink into me again, and I clear my throat, wincing as I rub behind one ear. "Um, Zan? We need to do something else. Something less boring."

He draws his eyebrows together over his nose, the ends pushing upward. "This is a necessary step. I understand this is not an exciting exercise, but a solid foundation– Curses!" He jumps, one knee bending his foot into the air.

My Light withdraws from the weight it dropped on Zander's foot. I stare. "Uh..."

Zander glares. "Are you controlling your Light?"

"That would be a very firm no."

He cocks his jaw. "You need to learn to control it. It will be wild, testing the world around it, but to allow it..."

"It talks too much."

"...to freely act is dangerous. It will overrun your life. It will kill you."

"Pretty Boy is stupid."

I grumble, "Can we just maybe try to do this for a fraction or two?"

Zander asks, "Try what?"

I point to my ear. "Does your magic...talk?"

"Eventually, it will be a voice in your head. Yours is far too young to possess that capability."

Lifting my eyebrows, I tell him, "I am one hundred percent certain my Light is talking."

His features collecting in the center of his lean face. "You shouldn't be able to speak with it yet, but if it is speaking, you can answer it with your thoughts."

"All right."

"With as strong as it is, you are going to have a struggle, but you must become its master. You need to possess the Light in you, forcing it to abide by your commands in strict obedience."

"I won't be doing that."

I scowl, speaking to myself. *"Maybe reconsider? You know, with the whole 'if we don't conform, we die' law? Specifically, the law that my Light is destroyed?"*

There's a growl in my head. *"I don't like this place. Leave."*

"I would if I could," I think, chewing on my lower lip and shaking my head.

"I'm going back to sleep."

I laugh. Zander cocks his head, and I cover my mouth, stifling my humor. "It's really not interested in doing your exercises."

"You need to get it under control." Zander squares up to me, crossing his arms. "It's strong, but strength is useless without use. Once you can make it compliant, we'll go through the basics. After you're capable of demonstrating the simplest commands of your Light, we'll progress to other acts and skills. Take a moment to see if you can manage to get your Light under control while I go retrieve the weight you threw and determine how to undo the damage you wrought."

He walks away. I watch him yank on the weight, but it

doesn't budge. As he struggles to get the weight free, I ask my Light, *"Any chance you'll do the boring things so we can get to the less boring?"*

"You do the boring things yourself. I'll wait until it's interesting."

I drag a hand down my face. *"We've done boring to get to fun before."*

Indignation bristles along my spine. *"Moving toys is a waste of time. Manipulating the soul was just tedious."*

Zander lurches back as the weight pops free. He scowls in my direction over his shoulder before turning and carrying it back to me.

Dropping it on the floor, he says, "I seem to have severely underestimated the strength of your Light."

Cal's laugh fills my mind. *"Idiot."*

I scratch behind my ear and wince. "Can you please consider I have training from the Magia and Cal?"

Zander crosses his arms. "This is far too important to be disregarded in a careless fashion. If you're not in control of your Light, if you cannot use it, and if it is too independent, it will grow beyond what you can maintain as a host, and it will kill you." He glares, narrowing his eyes. "Do you understand me, Light? You'll strangle your host."

"Why would I do that? I like it in here."

I force a smile at Zander, telling my Light, *"We do the boring stuff to get to the fun things."*

Silver vines of my Light streak to the wall of weights, picking up two enormous balls with handles on either side and dropping them with thuds next to Zander. *"Then we use these."*

Zander stares at me with a mixture of terror and awe.

I shrug, holding my hands at my sides, palms up. "It wants those."

He puts his hand to his face. "Love, it doesn't matter what it wants."

"If you want stupid games, you'll get stupid prizes. I spent years training with the Magia, working with Cal, and I went through the games. Asking my Light to lift teacups isn't going to work." I gesture to the weights. "Is there any chance we can compromise?"

Zander shakes his head, dropping his arms. "You shouldn't be this strong, though. I have grave concerns about your Light's possibility to kill you."

"I have grave concerns Pretty Boy is going to bore me straight into the afters," my Light drawls in disdain.

My Light moves the weights at the whims of Zander, every task as boring as the last until Zander decides we've concluded the day's task.

His Light returns the weights to their proper place as he says, "I'll return you to your room and report to Pierre. He'll have guidance on how best to proceed with your training."

WHEN ZANDER DELIVERS me to my room, he assures me he'll return at Thorn's rune to take me for dinner, requesting I clean up and be ready to leave at that time.

I close the door, leaning against it and eye the Grassel vodka. Leaning over, hands on my knees, I close my eyes, searching my mind. *"Are you there?"*

"I'm always here."

"You sound like Cal."

"I must sound like something." Dejection swirls in my gut.

Upright, I sniffle, heading for the bathroom as I wipe under my eyes with my fingertips. I get in the shower and lean against the wall. Sinking to the floor, I curl in a ball, hugging my knees tight.

I trace Cal's contract in my forearm, and my Light wraps in thin strands around my arm, one end stroking over the remnants of Cal's magic. "*I liked the other one. Pretty Boy is boring, and I miss my friend.*"

"*I miss him, too.*"

"*My friend was shadows and coldness.*"

"*You mean his Dark?*"

"*Hollow emptiness that echoed at my touch. It was pissy all the time. Great fun to play with.*"

I smile, my eyes welling up. "*His Dark. You liked his Dark? You know it would feed on you, right?*"

"*Yes. It was my friend. I let it.*"

I struggle to pull in a breath, fending off a sob and tip my head back.

My Light says, "*I hurt too, babe.*"

Coming undone, I squeeze my eyes shut and give in to the grief swallowing me. My Light stays silent, Cal's voice disappearing from my mind, and no matter how hard I try, I can't recall the sound of his voice.

CHAPTER 32
NATALIA
THIRD THISTLE'S DAY, DECAY, 4049 6TH MILLENNIUM

This golden tower-turned-prison is cold and aloof, worse than Cal's glare when I'd irked him. Maybe I should grab Ness and leave. I'm not sure if Pierre would allow it or if the Magia have quit hunting for me yet. Dodging Pierre and the Magia seems like a losing game. I have no idea where Ness and I could go to hide or how we'd survive.

Cal's accounts will have closed or transferred by now. The bracelet around my wrist has been reduced to a useless trinket, a memento of what I once had. Pierre won't fund me running from him. Ness and I would be destitute, lacking resources and friends.

Exhausted from training all day, I wash up and head to Ness's room, knocking on her door to occupy my time before dinner with Zander.

We go days without seeing each other, sending the occasional message. I'm not sure if she's sitting around, waiting on me today, and I can't blame her if she's not.

Pierre has granted her the right to return to the library at her leisure. Some days, she remains in her room, reading in comfort when she has enough material.

When we do talk, she speaks about Owen being somewhat of a friend, and he will often take her back to the library after her evening meals, but on the rare occasion, he'll extend their dinners to an establishment for drinks and conversation.

There's rustling from within, and then the door opens. Ness blinks at me and steps back to let me in. "You okay, babe?" She closes the door, moving to clear away the books on the bed. She stacks them, setting them on the nightstand as I sit on the edge of the bed.

I flop to my back, staring at the ceiling. "This bright light all the time thing is still creeping me out. I can't stand it."

"Flight shaft?"

"Flight shaft."

I SIT NEXT to an open flight shoot, my face turned to the dark. It pours into me with each deep breath, expanding my ribs to their full extension. The taste is fresh, lingering on my tongue like a sweet drop of water when parched. It's a cool relief that soothes my eyes and soul.

Ness sits on the other side, a closed book in her lap, head turned into the dark, too. "So much better."

Laughing, I strum my guitar, moving through a couple of notes. I hum along with the cords, piecing together another string of lyrics. I scribble them on an open notebook, finding the right prose.

I try it a few times, then cross out the line and change it.

Ness is watching with a frown. "Are you songwriting? You haven't done that in ages."

I shrug. "Working on something."

"Yeah?" Ness sits up, snatching up the notebook. "You aren't 'working on.' This looks finished."

Pointing at the notebook, I say, "That's how I'm coping."

"Not listening." Ness holds a finger up, face down, eyes flickering as she reads. Lowering her hand, she looks up. "What are you going to call it?"

"Callahan."

Smiling with eyes welling up, Ness nods, turning to face the dark again. "I love it. Finish it." She tosses the pad back over to me. "When it's done, we should sing it and do something for Mass and Cal, like putting them to rest."

I resituate the notebook and find the right rift. Strumming, I say, "That would be nice. I'll play, you sing, we can light a candle, maybe toast with a bottle of Grassel."

Ness bobs her head. "Sounds good to me. When can I expect this magical moment?"

"Soon," I scrunch the side of my with disgust. "I should be done now, but I'm nitpicking. I can't seem to be done, finished."

Ness settles back, closing her eyes. "Play it."

I clear my throat before I start to strum but stop. Clicking footsteps approach, and I turn to Ashley and Akash walking toward us. Dread fills me. We haven't seen each other since I broke her nose.

I make eye contact with Ness, whispering, "Move. I don't want to be in front of an open drop some fifty stories up."

Ness scrambles, getting to her feet and pressing her back against the wall. I shove my notebook out of the way and stand, coming face-to-face with Ashely, the shoot at my back. My stomach knots.

We stare at each other, and then Ashely turns to Akash, "Darling, you know, I think I left my purse. Can you fetch it for me?"

Akash inclines his head and turns, walking away.

Ashley turns to Ness. "Would you be so kind as to give me a moment with my sister?"

Ness cuts her eyes to me.

I shrug. "It's fine. Can you just make sure you grab my notebook?"

"Yeah." Ness bends over and plucks it up. "Got it, babe. I'll just," she points, "be over there."

Ashley stares at me, and I stare right back. This close, I can see the thin silver rings in the middle of her eyes, and they flicker, dropping to the guitar. "I saw you in the arena today."

I bob my head, holding tight to the guitar by the neck. "Pierre is having Zan train me." I try to step away from the open shoot.

Ashley sidesteps, blocking me in. "I wonder why."

"Because if I can't control my magic, it'll kill me."

"Hmm." Ashley's face never moves. "That's true for Seraphinus, but you aren't Seraphinus. Seraphim don't have magic strong enough to tear themselves apart."

I lift my eyebrows, offering in a sugar-sweet tone, "There's no reason to risk it?"

Smirking, Ashley steps in closer. "I know our queen decreed Ritual will apply. I hardly dare presume to guess why she would do such a thing. You're a Seraphim, unworthy to face me in combat."

Lifting my chin, I say, "She did, but that's not my fault, and Zan is training me to control my Light so it doesn't strangle me."

"It's an absolute disgrace that a Bordeaux is so weak, and it's salt in the wound that I would even have to face something like you. You aren't an equal. You don't even have wings." She hums, turning her face to the side.

I tighten my grip on the guitar with sweating fingers. "Ash, I'm sorry about your nose, and I'm sorry about Ritual. Only one of those things is my fault. I didn't choose Ritual."

She eyes me, looking me down and up. "It would be a much kinder act to you to prevent that altogether. Wouldn't you agree?"

A flash of golden light erupts from her chest. The pulse thrusts me back, and I step off the edge. My heart stops, my eyes growing wide as I hang in the nothingness for a single heartbeat as I meet Ashely's eyes, her triumphant smirk twisting her painted red lips.

It feels like an eternity that I hang there, fear coursing through me as Ashley gloats.

Then I plummet.

I scream, the shrill sound echoing in the black around me. Air whistles past my ears, my blood and organs rushing into my skull. I grip tighter what my fingers are clutching, and I realize I'm still holding Shawn Gettemeir's guitar.

A burst of panic rips through me as I realize the guitar is going to be demolished on impact. Bones I can mend, but not Shawn Gettemier's personal guitar. I can't ever fix it or replace it.

I pull it in close, trying to curl around it as if that would somehow protect it. My eyes burn, and I sob that I'm never going to play Cal's song on this instrument.

Light races behind my unshed tears, and the skin on my back burns as if sliced open with a knife. Pain sears through my shoulder blades, the shaft filling with brilliant, silvery-blue light.

Muscles flex on instinct, and I jerk, halting in midair, my

heart racing, every pore of my skin exuding sweat as I curl tighter around my guitar. I squeeze my eyes shut, waiting to hit the ground, but fractions of a rune tick by, and I pant, opening my eyes.

"Tallie!" Ness screams down through the shaft toward me.

Stunned, I hug the guitar and check left and right as far as my eyes can see, not daring to turn my head, too afraid to move. "Ness," I yell back.

"Tal? Oh, fucking Mother. Tal, are you all right?"

Trembling, I find enough courage to tip my head back. I can make out a face sticking into the shaft high above me. "Find Zander."

I take shallow breaths, squeezing my guitar with dread, too afraid to breathe deep and lose my grip. I hold onto it for dear life, not daring to relax. My heart hammers in my ears, and my hands sweat, threatening to dissolve the grip I have on my instrument.

Light winds around the guitar and my torso, binding it to my body. I still can't ease my grip, my arms burning and twitching with fatigue, and still I tighten around the Dragola.

Runes seem to pass as tears roll down my face. All I can think about is Cal's song and the need to play it on Shawn's personal, favorite guitar.

Golden light brightens the shaft further, a deep chuckle coming from above me, and then Zander descends into view. "You all right, love?"

"No," I say, unable to so much as shake my head.

He reaches out. "Give me your hand."

"I don't want to drop it."

His fingers close around the neck. "Will you trust me with it?"

"Okay."

"You can let go, love." He snickers. "I've got it."

I pry my arms away, but my heart skips a beat as it falls to Zander's side. A soft whimper escapes me, but it hangs safe in his grasp.

"I've got it," he says in a soft voice, several ropes of Light winding around his wrist and the neck of my guitar, tethering the instrument to him. "Now, give me your hand."

I swallow, lifting a stiff, shaking arm to put my hand in his.

His hand closes around mine. "Good job. Now, dig your head out of your shoulders and relax. Your wings—"

"Wings?" I squeak.

Zander laughs. "Yes, wings. Your body and your magic are working on instinct, which is why you're hovering in the air."

"I have wings?"

"Yes." He bobs his head, grinning wide.

"Oh, fucking Mother." I close my eyes and try not to panic.

"You're okay, love. Push your shoulders down."

I do and lift in the air. My eyes pop open in shock, and I lift my shoulders in fear. I squeal in terror, dropping lower.

Zander grabs me by the forearm with a chuckle, shaking his head. "You're okay. I've got you."

"The guitar. Not me. I can heal."

"Love, it's just an instrument. It's not as important—"

"Yes, it is," I yell. His eyes widen, his amusement fading. "I can't fix it if it breaks. I can heal me, but not that." I lower my eyes to the guitar. "Please."

He nods. "It's safe. As are you. I can handle both of you, but if one of you is getting dropped, I'm letting this thing go before I let you hit the ground. This far?" He glances down. "You'd break bones."

"No." My eyes burn, my heart stammering and picking up speed. A ball of emotion clogs my throat, strangling my voice.

"No, please, I can heal. I can use Ki. It would take only a fraction. Don't drop it. No matter what, don't drop it. Promise me."

He stares at me, eyebrows pushing together. Concern washes across his handsome face, the shadows darkening the expression. "This thing really means that much to you?"

"Yes, please, please don't drop it," I beg. "Me, I can fall. I can heal myself. Promise me, if it's me or Shawn's guitar, that you save the guitar."

He shakes his head and then grins with a low chortle. "You have my word. I will make sure this instrument remains in one piece, okay?" He bobs his head. "But in exchange, let's get you on solid ground again. Then I want answers about Ki."

I nod.

"Push your shoulders down hard, and then pull back quick and repeat. Can you do that for me? Or do you want me to fly you up?"

"No." I close my eyes, searching for the Light within me. "Are wings just my Light?"

"Yes, they are a manifestation of your magic."

I draw in a full breath through my nose. My Light has been quiet since the first day of training. I think with force, "*I trust you.*"

Stars gather behind my eyes. A phantom expression ripples in my mind like Cal laughing. It's more of a response than normal.

Tension melts down my neck and spine, my shoulders stretching. "I'm ready," I whisper, opening my eyes.

"Okay, love. Hard down, quick up, and don't worry about fluidity. That comes with practice."

I push my shoulder down, rising in the air. Over and over, I make quick little motions of flexing my shoulders, rising higher and higher. Zander keeps his grip on me, and I keep my eyes on the guitar all the way back to the open doors of the flight shaft.

"Okay, now, just flex," Zander says. "You'll hover, and I need my hand back now."

I let go of him, my wings moving of their own accord. Zander grabs the edge of the door, angling himself past me and out of the shaft. I watch over my shoulder as he carries the guitar aloft, setting it down with care before turning back to me.

Pierre is waiting, his hands on his hips, face tight with fury. I'll worry about that after I get on solid ground. Accepting Zander's hand, I allow him to pull me to safety.

Standing on my own two feet, I let go of Zander, craning my head to see silvery blue tendrils wafting in the air behind me, creating a ghostly pair of wings protruding from my back. "Holy fuck."

Something collides with me, "Tallie!"

I jerk backward, reaching for something before we tumble down the shaft. My fingers find the edge of the door, and Zander's long fingers lock my arm, jerking me to a halt.

"Oh, Mother, I thought for sure you were dead," Ness squeals, her arms wrapping around me.

"I'm okay," I say, pulling myself upright with Zander's help.

He chuckles. "Let's get away from the fifty-seven-floor drop, please, ladies."

Ness lets go, backing up, and I move a safe distance away from the open doors. Zander smacks the button, lingering in front of the doors as they close.

I glance at Ness and then Pierre. His lips press and pull down at the corners. "Tallie, honey, are you all right?"

"I have wings."

He smiles. "Yes, I see that."

I gape, pointing a thumb over my shoulder. "I have fucking wings."

Zander laughs. "Say it a few more times, love. It'll sink in."

I glance between the two. "How the fuck do I have wings?"

Pierre studies me with concern. After a moment of consideration, he runs a hand down the front of his button-up shirt and then slips his hands into the front pockets of his slacks. "That is an excellent question, but for now, let us be thankful that you do."

Ness steps to my side, sliding an arm around my waist and leaning against me. "I'm thankful as fuck, babe."

I sigh, bobbing my head. "Yeah, that would have hurt."

"It would have killed you."

I twist toward her with confusion. "No, it wouldn't."

Ness laughs. "Babe, I don't care how fucking good you are. You would have smacked that pretty little head on the ground and been out, done, dead. You wouldn't have been conscious to heal."

The reality hadn't occurred to me. "Yeah, you're right." I go lax, widening my eyes. "I almost died."

"Yeah."

"No, for real, I..." I stare at her. I've always trusted in my ability to heal, relying on it as a failsafe, but Ness is accurate. I wouldn't have been conscious and waking up would have taken too long. "Thanks for getting Zander," I say, turning my head toward him. "And thanks for coming."

He chuckles. "You would have figured out how to fly without me."

Pierre takes a step closer, crossing his arms. "What happened?"

Moving my gaze to Ashely, who's standing several paces behind her father, I scowl. Her face is a mixture of hatred and shock, like her features can't decide what to do.

I straighten my spine, lifting my chin and forcing my eyes back to Pierre. "I don't know."

"Vanessa has accused Ash of pushing you."

I jerk my elbow into Ness's side. "Ash stepped toward me. I took a step back. It was a stupid mistake." Pierre narrows his eyes, and I shake my head. "I'm sure from where Ness stood, it probably looked like she did."

Ness tenses, picking her head up and giving me a frustrated glower.

I shoot daggers with my eyes. Whatever laws there are don't matter. This is war, and I'm going to put Ash down on an equal playing field the same way I dealt with Telra. And when I put her down, I want her to know it was because I'm better than her, not because I took a cheap shot.

Pierre holds my gaze. Everything about him screams his disbelief of the story, but it passes as he relaxes and turns to Ashely. Akash has his arm around her, coddling her against his chest.

"Akash," Pierre says.

He picks his head up and blinks, "Yes, sir?"

"Any plans you and my daughter had for the evening are canceled. You are excused, as are you," Pierre says, turning to Ness.

Akash kisses Ashley on the forehead and then bows to Pierre before walking away. Ness grits her teeth but stomps forward, grabbing her book and my notebook before heading up the hallway.

Pierre fixates on Zander. "Zan."

"Sir?"

"Take Ash to my office and wait with her there." Zander bows and he and Ashely walk away, her heels echoing in sharp clicks up the hallway. Pierre takes a step closer to me. "Push your shoulders together."

I do what he says, rolling my shoulders back and trying to force my shoulder blades together. The muscles sting and the glimmer of my magic fades. I glance behind myself to find the wings gone. "Neat."

Pierre rubs a hand over his mouth, staring at me. Time ticks by, and then he drops his arm, hands on his hips. "Tell me the truth. What happened?"

"I thought only Seraphinus had wings."

His eyes harden. "What happened?"

I cross my arms. "What happens if I tell you she pushed me down that shoot?"

His mouth becomes a hard line. He breathes deep, his chest swelling, and then he exhales, and his face relaxes. "Are you all right?"

"I don't fucking know right now. Ask me again tomorrow."

"Language, honey, please." He gives me a weak smile.

"Sorry. I don't fucking care about the words coming out of my mouth because I just fell a few dozen floors, and my guitar almost got shattered, and, oh yeah, I have flipping, freaking, fucking wings."

Pierre takes the last step forward and rests his hands on my shoulders. "For your own safety, I am going to ask one last time. Did Ash push you?"

I cock my jaw and then roll my eyes. "Ashley never touched me. How do I have wings?"

His lips press. "I was concerned about this. The Magia are Seraphinus bloodlines of Light and Dark. While unorthodox, because of the Seraphinus blood from your Magia heritage and the Seraphinus in my heritage, you may be a very unconventional creation of Seraphinus."

My shoulders drop. "Well, fuck. What the curses am I?"

He smiles with real humor. "I do not know for sure. What I do know is you are certainly unique." He moves to my side, putting his arm around my shoulders. "I will return you to your room. When I am finished with Zan, I will send him to check on you again. The boy has an affection for you, and he was an absolute wreck upon hearing you went down the flight shaft. I've never seen him run so fast."

CHAPTER 33
VANESSA
SECOND THISTLE'S DAY, SNOWDROP, 4050
6TH MILLENNIUM

I move through shelves to return my most recent conquest, a hefty law book. My brain is a quivering mess, too many laws and subsections of law mashed into my neurological receptors. I've written notes and basic outlines, reading over Light, Dark, and Council laws for weeks after giving up on the Sune and Sube. I've come across nothing of use in that direction, even stooping to the children's section of bedtime stories and basic history tales.

In exchange, I've started delving into the society of the Seraphinus, searching to find a way for Tallie and me to escape Izul in legal terms. Pierre won't allow it, but ever since Ashley pushed Tallie into the flight shaft, I've been riddled with anxiety. She isn't safe here in Izul.

Slipping the book back into its home, I chew on my lower lip, staring at the spines on either side, the exposed wood of the shelf cleared of dust from where I'd slid the book free and replaced it. At least the collection of powdered age helps me return books to their proper place.

With a sigh, I turn and then gawk. "Aydian?"

He smiles. "Hello, Ness."

I grin with joy. "I'm so happy to see you, I could kiss you."

With a wry smile, he turns his face to the floor, the beads in his hair glinting as they swing forward several braids and lock with the shift of his weight. Clearing his throat, he takes a few steps closer.

Toe to toe with me, he lifts his head, fighting a grin, his jade eyes dancing with mirth. "Is that an offer? I haven't kissed a woman in a very long time."

Reaching out, I curl my fingers around his narrow face and yank it to mine, pressing a closed mouth to his. "Muah!" I let go, taking a step back as I laugh. "I can't believe I just did that." I cover my mouth, embarrassment flushing across my cheeks.

His eyes sparkle, his lips curling with smugness. "I can no longer claim it has been a long time."

"Not unless fractions count as a long time." I giggle behind my hand. "Did you find your secrets?"

"I am pleased to say I have uncovered several." He lifts an eyebrow and his chin. "Have you?"

Shaking my head, I sigh. "No. In fact, I've given up."

Aydian's features sour. "Disappointing. I presumed you were more than that."

I turn to the shelves, running my fingers down a nearby spine. "It's fine. I'm used to being a disappointment."

He hums a low note carrying disdain. "To settle is unforgivable."

Turning back to him, I say, "Honestly, I hit a dead end. I haven't actually given up per se, but I'm out of ideas."

"What secrets do you seek? Perhaps I may offer insights to your inquest."

"The Sune and the Sube."

His eyes flash, his face tensing. "Why would you seek such forgotten things?"

I lick my lips, glancing down at myself. "I found the word only once in another book, and I can't resist my own curiosity."

He lets a puff of air through his nose as he smirks. "Inquisitive minds are not often found at rest, for curiosity is a powerful magic if only one gives into the pull of it." He shrugs. "Alas, most do not, willingly breeding ignorance."

"Wait." I hold a finger up, "I know that. That's a quote. A really old quote from..." I roll my eyes toward the ceiling. "Damn, it's right on the tip of my tongue. It was a poet. Starts with an M."

"Melmar."

"Ah, yeah. Thanks." I grin.

"Melmar was a great poet." He sighs, eyes unfocusing. "Days past, in a time before this world."

I lean against the shelf. "His stuff gets wordy for me at times, but you'll come across a few real gems."

"You have read Melmar's works?"

"When I was, like, seventeen." I roll my eyes. "So, a long time ago, but yeah. It was a copy I picked up from a second-hand bookstore. I didn't know what it was, but it was old and just... The way it looked called to me."

I meet his eyes and then turn my head, looking away with a wince. My mouth and passion run amuck too often. My mother always warned me about oversharing my adoration of books. She told me I would frighten people away.

I clear my throat. "Sorry. That was a stupid thing to say."

"Not at all. *Delalappel.*"

Perking up, I ask, "What's that?"

"The call." He holds a hand up, fingers straight and pinching together, dragging through the air. "*Similis* is a form of *delalappel.*"

"The call of like."

"Is *similis*." He inclines his head. "There are many varia-tions of *delalappel*. What you describe is normal."

"Maybe, but my mom always said it made me 'too much,' a bit weird. She said they are just books, and no one cares." I suck my lower lip into my mouth, biting it between my teeth.

"To experience *delalappel* is to mean you have a soul. How very rare and beautiful a thing that is."

Letting out a whoosh of air, I relax. "Everyone has a soul, but I guess it's rare 'cause you only get one."

Aydian lifts an eyebrow, lips twisting to the side with amusement. "Mmm."

"Is there a word specifically for a call of books?"

"With great sorrow, I regret to inform you there is not. Perhaps I shall create one. We can establish a word for you, inspired by your heart's desire to read and learn."

"Ha. That would be amazing. A word for me?" I lift my hand, smiling behind it. "You know, I taught myself how to translate Seraphin using that book–Melmar's poetry."

Aydian tenses. "Seraphin?"

"*Delalappel*? *Similis*? That language." I turn to the shelves, touching spines in euphoria, closing my eyes, and inhaling the scent of the parchment and binding glue. "I always loved books, even as a child, but when I read Melmar's collection, it was in common. After I read it, I went on this deep dive into history, learning who he was. It started my love of history and language alike." I face him, grinning wide. "Still think I'm not weird?"

He unhinges his jaw but keeps his lips closed, rocking his lower jaw forward. When he speaks, his tone is tight. "The winners write history, twisting facts to suit their tales. The Sune and the Sube are aberrations of Light and Dark. When Mallafic was entered by Nehil, the god became twisted by Mallafic's bitter soul, and so it is no longer true nothingness but something else. The Seraphinus that claim they are Dark are made of this distortion. They are not darkness. They are the Sube."

"Then the Ancients didn't use the word to bastardize them. They are bastardized."

"Ancients?" Aydian's features twist with acrimony, the word a taut release of rage. "The Seraphinus are desecration."

I stretch my head to the side, running fingers along the muscles that connect my neck and shoulder. "What is *subtorque?*"

Aydian's eyes blaze as his fingers curl into fists at his sides. "Where did you get that word?"

"A book?" I try to grin, but it wobbles, my facial muscles uncooperative. "Am I not supposed to know it?"

He stares at me, lips pinched tight enough they begin to lose color. "What kind of book?"

"A normal book? What do you mean 'kind of book?'" I pretend to open and close a phantom book in my hands. "Cover, pages, back cover?"

His fury evaporates, and he lifts an eyebrow. "Did you speak of me to another?"

"No," I shake my head. "Not even Tallie." I wince. "Mostly because she's always so busy, but your secret is safe with me. I wouldn't ever throw someone under a bus for reading."

"Throw someone under a bus?" His eyebrows push together, but amusement tinges his words. "What am I to accept that to mean?"

"Screw them over. Put them in a bad spot."

"Betrayal." His eyes lower, one side of his mouth tugging back in a flicker of a grimace.

"Yeah."

"An interesting statement coming from you." He slides his

hands in his front pockets, rolling his shoulders back. "Mallafic was betrayed."

My insides squirm. "What does Mallafic have to do with me?"

One side of his mouth curls, a devious mask claiming his face. "You're inquiry of the Sube and the Sune, of *subtorque*. That which you seek begins with Mallafic."

"Ah, yeah, that makes sense. Can I ask, how do you do that snap-and-disappear thing?"

He laughs. "It is *agikka*."

I frown. "I don't know that word."

Aydian stares as one side of his mouth curls at the end. "I wouldn't expect you to. It is not your tongue nor Serpahin." He spits the last word with distaste.

"Hey, you know all kinds of languages. Maybe you can tell me what *'califum felixia deporum'* means?"

"Mockery before truth," he says, a twinkle coming to his eye. "Where did you find the phrase? Another book, perhaps?"

I laugh. "I may have an obsession with reading."

He inclines his head, the beads in his locks glinting. "Alas, I came to say until *diead*."

"What is *diead*?" I cock my head. "This all seems to be some other language I'm not aware of."

"It does not translate well. I wish you fortunes in your web of fates, Ness." He steps in close, brushing my cheek with the back of his fingers. Leaning in, he whispers in my ear, "Please leave this city soon."

"Wait," I say as he goes to snap his fingers. He lowers his hand, tilting his head as I ask, "Could you– Your snap thingy, can you do that and, like, take others?"

"Yes," he answers, eyeing me with mistrust.

"Could you, maybe, do that for me and Tallie?"

"For you." He strokes my jaw with his thumb. "I would take

you anywhere you desired. I do not know Tallie nor have any reason to do such for her."

"Oh."

"Is there somewhere you wish to go?"

"Not without Tallie."

"Then until *diead*." With a kiss on my cheek and a snap of his fingers, he disappears in a blink again, leaving me alone in the aisle of books.

CHAPTER 34
NATALIA
THIRD HOPE'S DAY, SNOWDROP, 4050 6TH MILLENNIUM

Every morning, I trace Cal's name on my arm, memorizing the curves of his magic. Once, I swear a tendril lifted and wrapped around my finger, but it must have been a dream. The only relief I have is when I wake and confirm that the contract remains intact, his magic still surviving. I'm terrified one morning, it will be gone.

After caressing Cal's Dark in my skin, my days begin when Zander collects me for breakfast, and then we head to the arena for training. The only thing that differs is the skill Zander teaches me, constantly giving me plaudits for how quickly I am progressing.

Learning how to use my wings is weird and awkward, but I can go up and down the flight shafts, even carrying Ness with me, which saves us time when we go out.

I see her rarely. On most occasions, it's one of many celebrations the Lighters have. The library is closed during the days when the Lighters rejoice. Ness and I have gotten to see a tea festival in the Harvest season, the honoring of the Hallow heritage, and a festival for the year-end.

It's starting to become a rhythm, but there's a lingering hitch to it, a random note wrong in a song that I just can't place. The Light comes easier each day, and once a week, Pierre gives me some gift or another to buy my time. It's an unfair game because somehow, he comes up with the best gifts, and I can't refuse, caving to spending time with him.

After another day of training, Zander sees me to the tower but lingers at the front door. Luke has it pulled open to let us inside, but Zander takes my hand, pulling me to a halt. I turn to him.

He jerks his chin over my shoulder. "There's something I must attend to. May I take you to dinner later?"

I bite my lower lip, chewing at the chapped skin as I stare into his eyes. "That's the fourth night in a row. I haven't seen Ness in days."

He grins with all his charm. "I'm working toward spending every night with you, and Ness will be just fine. She's an adult who can take care of herself. Besides, it is your birthday. I want to celebrate with you."

I stare at him, my lips peeling apart from each other. The urge to scream 'no' builds in my chest, pleading to be released. We've been spending time together. He's even introduced me to a few of his friends by having dinner with them, but I'm still stunned. My brain stops existing, and I feel like I should say something, but I've lost my tongue.

Zander chuckles. "I am not sure why you're so surprised, love."

"I'm just…" I manage and then return to gaping at him like I'm a fish he reeled in, gills flapping in useless maneuvers out of water.

No.

He takes my hand in his, running his thumb over my knuckles. "Tallie, I like you, being around you."

I inhale through my nose, my chest on fire. Cal wouldn't say that. He wouldn't ask for permission. He'd growl and tell me I was his and I didn't have a choice.

Zander holds my gaze, dropping my hand. He cups my face, his head tilting to the side, and I lick my lips, his sight dropping to the movement, fixating on my mouth.

My heart races, and I stare, wide-eyed until he's too close for my eyes to bring into focus. He lifts my chin, the touch of his lips to mine a foreign, physical pressure. No spark of passion ignites in my chest. That's it, a touch of lips and then Zander pulls away.

"I must go. I'll see you in a couple runes."

"Fine," I say, and watch him turn and walk back up the street. I glance at Luke, who is holding the door open for me while pointedly watching the sky. "Thanks, Luke, but I'm going to get something first."

My feet carry me away from the tower, my body moving without thought. I find a shop, then I find the oldest, most expensive bottle of bourbon I can. I go to pay for the bottle with my phone but hesitate, trying the silver band still locked around my wrist to pay for it.

I expect it to decline, but the reader beeps green, and the man tells me to have a pleasant evening, wishing me to enjoy my selection. For a fraction, I stare at the machine, certain it was an error.

The man lifts his eyebrows. "Is there something I may assist you with?"

Shaking my head, I turn and stumble out the door, pressure building in my chest. It never occurred to me that the cuff would still be active. I wanted to try and then spend Pierre's coin out of spite when it failed. Instead, someone else bought the liquor.

His accounts must have transferred like he said his

contracts would upon death. I have no idea who holds Cal's accounts now, but whoever they are, they bought me ten-thousand-year-old bourbon at the cost of one million, seven-hundred, and ninety-four coin. For the first time since I arrived, my heart hammers with anxiety at the thought of being beyond Izul's gates. Whoever's coin I spent might rip my throat out for it.

Fiddling with the bottle, turning it over and over in my hands, I shuffle all the way to my room. I stand in the middle of the hallway, glancing from my door to Ness's, running my thumb over the label. Each breath I take shoves cotton down my throat and up my nose.

Clearing my throat and blinking, I knock on Ness's door. She doesn't answer, so I send her a message to meet me in my room.

I sit on my bed, staring at the bottle. I inquired about getting an entertainment screen. Zander offered to let me use his whenever we have time. I asked for a phone with access to the communication lines, wanting access to media and the world beyond my routine. All of my requests have been met with warnings of alerting someone to my presence in Izul.

I have nothing beyond Zander and Pierre. Ness has sought refuge in the library, always haunting the rows of shelves and begging me to come see the institution, although never having time to wait for me before slipping into it and being lost to me.

My door opens, and Ness frowns at me from the doorway. We stare at each other. Without a word, I lift the bottle. Ness fixates on it with a desolated hunger, nods, and steps into the room, closing the door.

I hand the bottle to her. She gasps. "Ten-thousand-year aged liquor? Damn girl."

"For Cal."

"And Mass."

I nod, reaching out a hand. My magic extends through the air, picking up my guitar. "For both of them and for us." I take a deep breath. "For what we lost." Sitting on the edge of my bed, I get positioned and ready.

Ness sits next to me, offering the bottle. I take it, then a long drink. I shudder as I hand it back to her. "I know it was Cal's favorite, but I still can't stand that."

"It's okay, you've got..." She gestures at the bottles of vodka. "Why'd you even buy this?"

"It's damn good vodka, but something feels wrong using vodka that Pierre gave me to send off the spirits of Mass and Cal."

"Fair point."

I strum but hesitate. "Need the notebook?"

Shaking her head, Ness takes another drink. "I've got it memorized."

I focus on the guitar and start again. Together, Ness and I sing.

"Deep ruby red beads with stings of sad blue
They meet in shades of dark violet and indigo
The way the shells crack under pressure
They ferment the way this wound will fester
Your darkness tinges the color of my heart
Bleeding to the surface, staining skin torn apart
You know purple has never looked so cruel
Surrounding open skin like a crowning jewel
And still I'm shining just for you

You showed me colors, this wreckage you gave

DIVIDING ILLUMINATION

A world screaming so bright
Wrapped up tight
In your dark blight
Just look at the fool you made

Skin burnished bright shades of noble luxury
Fades to sallow and pink rose petals eventually
The color of delicacy begins to itch and burn
With each tender scrape I begin to learn
Your raw power fractured me, left me reeling
But time is turning your damage to fragile healing
You know soft and pretty has never looked so ugly
This site of carnage that was so bloody
And I'm still shining just for you on the road to recovery

You showed me colors, this wreckage you gave
A world screaming so bright
Wrapped up tight
In your dark blight
Just look at the fool you made

Fresh beginning like delicate frost on my skin
It's purity to the eye, no telling what's within
Stronger now, if not pale innocence and ignorant
This cut has left me marked and different
Your sharp edges hidden under beauty cut too deep
The scar you gave, your last words to keep

321

You know glistening white has never looked so forlorn
A glittering stretch of skin like starlight worn
And I'm still shining just for you, left to yearn

You showed me colors, this wreckage you gave
A world screaming so bright
Wrapped up tight
In your dark blight

Just look at the colors in this wreckage you gave
This forsaken mess you left
Just look at the fool you made
And I'm still shining just for you"

NESS SOBS as she leans into me. I grab the bottle and upend it, gulping down the liquor. It's smoky and sharp, hotter and tangier than vodka. It's Cal in a bottle.

I stop, gulping for air and set the guitar aside, grabbing Ness's hand, forcing her fingers to bend around the neck of the bottle. "Drink, babe."

Ness nods, still blubbering as she starts to guzzle. She doesn't stop until it's gone. Holding the empty bottle aloft, she stares at it, then chucks it to the floor.

We sit on the edge of the bed, silent, staring at the empty bottle until my phone starts to chime. I switch the alarm off and toss it to the side.

Neither of us moves. We don't say anything, either. Ness quiets down, breathing shallow but even. I blink burning eyes, staring at nothing. My heart keeps beating, my Light wrapping in thin strings over my arms in a wasted attempt to comfort me.

I startle at the knock on my door while Ness flinches. I get to my feet, opening the door and frowning at Zander.

His smile fades as he stares at me. "Love?" He scowls, eyes flickering inside the room. "Are you all right?"

I nod.

He steps into the room, takes my face in his hands and tilts my head back to stare down at me with concern. "What's going on?"

"Nothing," Ness snaps with vehemence.

I wrap my fingers around Zander's wrists to pry my face free. "I'm sorry, Zan, but not tonight."

He stares at me, lips together and pressed, eyebrows pushing together, creasing the skin between his eyes. "I really wanted to take you out. We need to talk about things."

"Not tonight."

"Why? What's happening?" His eyes dart to Ness.

She stands, wiping under her eyes. "It's fine. I'm going to go back to the library."

"Are you sure?" I step in her path, wrapping my hands over her shoulders. "I'll cancel in a heartbeat for you."

Ness pushes me away. "This wasn't about me."

I step back, stunned, and Ness shoves past Zander and out of the room.

He glances into the hallway and then back to me. "What am I missing?"

"We were having a moment for Cal and Mass. I wrote a song." I wave a hand at my guitar. "We had a drink."

He pulls me against him. "That was nice of you two to do something for them. It is more than they deserve."

Rage sparkles in my veins, and I shove him away. "Fuck you and your Light righteous shit."

Zander rubs the back of his neck and gives me a half-cocked smile. "I've always let you talk about him, listened, and been polite toward him. I've always respected you, but that's a two-way street. I don't want threats for expressing my opinions."

Looking away, I clamp my jaw. "Just...don't insult Cal again, please."

Tucking my hair behind an ear, he asks, "He didn't deserve something so pure and beautiful as you. Please get ready for dinner."

I roll my shoulders and head for the armoire, grabbing clothes before slipping into the bathroom. Inside, I lean on the counter, staring at myself in the mirror. I drop my gaze, and my eyes fixate on the counter. The memory of Cal touching me after the hunt plays out in my mind, every bit the savage the Light thinks he is in the way he fucked me.

Straightening, I put it from my mind. Zander is waiting, and Cal is dead. If I tell myself that enough times, it might erase the memories. If the memories stop flooding me, the wounds might stop gushing blood, scab over and turn to ugly, jagged red healing before fading to white scars. Maybe then, I would care about something again.

CHAPTER 35
VANESSA

There are a great many things in this world that I don't understand. How Light and Dark mated to create life, why the sky is pink when the suns are low and greenish-blue when they're gone, or how Tallie seems so okay with how things are going.

I shake my head and push the massive door to the library open with both hands on the surface, leaning into it with a grunt. Nothing in Izul is designed for non-Seraphinus. It's a constant reminder of where I am and my shitty little life.

The upside is my toned legs and buttocks. I'm still not slender, but I'm looking fabulous. Between the regular hikes up and down stairs and moving heavy doors, I'm getting stronger.

As I slip inside, familiar faces watch me, drawn with disgust. They always watch and stare, but I learned not to bother trying to talk to any of them. Best case scenario is they ignore me. Some of my attempts were downright humiliating. I cried twice.

I slump past the front desk, heading into the stacks. My tour was quick that felt more like a rushed jaunt. Kazez had seemed very disinterested in showing me around despite being polite. I imagine that it was nothing more than following orders.

I used to eat with Kazez in the morning and Owen in the evening, but then I was set free of chaperone requirements. I'd hoped Owen would be a friend after, but it was in vain. Since he told me I was allowed to wander alone, I haven't seen him again.

Since that day, I have said exactly nineteen words to various Lighters and about three million to myself. The only one willing to speak to me other than Tallie is Aydian, but he's a mystery.

I haven't told her about Aydian yet. Tallie and I only connect every few days, and most times, when we do manage to sync up, Zander and Pierre are quick to intervene or interrupt. It's never the right moment, and Tallie is fading away, our friendship withering.

It's not her fault. They don't give her much option. If I'm fair in the blame game, I've been living in the library, searching for history and knowledge of Mallafic and Beenin, about the Sune, the Sube, and *subtorque*—anything that can explain what was in the codex or a way to legally detach Tallie from Pierre.

There are several options, but no leads that are solid enough for me to wield as a knife sharp enough to sever them. I've read enough to be considered an expert in the Seraphinus, but still empty-handed on what the marks on my torso are or a way out of Izul. It's maddening, and my hope diminishes by the day right along with my will to live.

Taking my phone out, I text her. **"Sorry, babe. Didn't mean to be so harsh."**

I get a response within a fraction. **"I would have told Zander to leave."**

"I know."

"You're always in that damn library. Miss you, babe."

Sighing, I slip the phone into my pocket and climb a set of spiral steps. I've never been so starved for conversation, always preferring books to the company of others, but even I need social interaction on occasion. It's a very sad state of affairs when I miss talking to someone, but this is my life now.

Meandering through the rows of dusty bookshelves in silence, I let myself relax. I'm not sure where the sudden angst and rage came from, and I need to calm down. Being surrounded by dusty tombs and beautifully bound books is a good way to do that, so I walk with no particular section in mind, following my feet as they put one foot in front of the other.

Being ignored does have the benefit of moving unhindered. None of the Lighters care about where I go or the books I pull off the shelf. Not a single eye watches what I do. It brings a fortitude of privacy and the ability to do anything. If only I had something to do.

As I turn away from one section, my chest tingles, spiders crawling across my skin, and I shudder. Swiping at the space beneath my breasts, I stop and glance around. I resume moving, and the sense returns. I fidget, pressing my hands to my lower ribs. I lift my shirt to check for a hair tickling me, brushing over the strange marks and then scowl.

The black marks are shifting, twisting in their figure eight patterns, shimmering as mirages of heat. I run my finger over them. "Stop it, you stupid thing."

Dropping my shirt, I check my surroundings. I've found my way into a new section of the library. A tug spurns me onward, my feet moving of their own accord, but with nowhere to be, I'm content to just walk.

Inhaling deep, I take in the scent of pages bleeding with ink of stories waiting to be discovered. There is nothing like the smell of pressed parchment and paper, lettering stamped into the surface. Aside from Massimo, that is. He always smelled like the most attractive man in my best wet dreams. If I knew what cologne he wore, I'd have made Tallie buy it and sprayed my bedsheets with it. I add that to the list of things I'll never know.

The marks on my sternum and lower ribs start twitching again, setting my heart aflutter. I put my hand over the spot and take a step to the right, turning down a narrow aisle. I don't recall even seeing this section during my tour from Kazez.

Dragging my fingertips along the spines, the old-world construction of exposed bindings intermixing with cold metal clasps over grainy cracked leather comfort me. I stop, turning back as my fingers meet smooth glass, my mind having blacked out to nothingness. Had the texture not jolted my senses, I would have missed the case.

I glance at it, that annoying sense fluttering along my lower ribs with vigor. Two books are encased within, suspended on chains, two running behind, one looped and locked in place. My heart skips, a slight hop before it takes off sprinting. The black scales are still, their edges highlighted.

I start searching the case, needing to reach the Dark codexes within. "Hey babies, hi," I croon, checking around the sides, standing on my tiptoes to see the back. There are no hinges or locks that I can see. "Don't you worry. I'm going to get you out of there."

Grasping the case, I try to lift it, but the glass doesn't budge. Leaning on the shelf, I stare at them, my lips puckering with a frown. The chains attach to dowel rods that erect from the wide base. The wood grain is stained with age and black mold, and a crevice has been carved around the edge for the glass to perch securely.

A glimmer of gold glitter glues the pieces together. I pick at it with a nail, a wisp of black curling from my finger. I pull back, inspecting the pad, checking beneath the nail, and then run my finger over it again. The glint of gold swirls as black seeps from my fingertips.

My heart pounds, excitement and fear commingling as a tonic of shock through my gut. The tendrils of ink writhe across the golden sealant, threading in and out as needle-like shards until the gold bursts in a plume of sparkling dust.

I inhale and cough, whirling away from the case and sputtering.

A hand closes around my arm, a warm breath in one ear. "Are you all right?"

Bobbing my head and gasping for air, I manage. "Yeah." I get a solid inhale in and stand upright. "I'm fine. What about you?" I focus on the speaker, expecting Aydian.

I recoil when I realize it's someone else. I blink at him, a bit stunned. His features are thin and angular, with sharp cheekbones and chin, making a highly attractive ensemble.

The man smiles at me. He's about my height, slenderly built with the white eyes of a Lighter. "Are you certain you are all right?"

I knock a closed fist against my chest. "I'm good. So good."

He turns, focusing his sight on the case. "You broke my magic."

I blink and then face the case. "Your magic?"

"Yes. I am responsible for this section." He turns back to me. "How did you break my magic?"

"I don't know. I was trying to open the case," I say, acting like I'm lifting the case in the air, "and it just…"

He peers at me with mistrust. "Interesting. May I see your hand?" He extends a large palm to me.

I place my hand against his, his pale skin sparkling and black smoky tendrils curling around my fingers.

His hand jerks away, dropping to his side, curling closed. "Dark."

"Magia." I shake my head as I correct him. "Not Dark or Light, somewhere between."

"You are the pet of Pierre's bastard?"

I bare my teeth. "I'm a woman, not a fucking pet."

His hands lift in subtle defense, but he smiles. "My mistake. You have my sincere apology. My name is Aku." He bows.

"Vanessa," I say slowly, leaning back from him to stare down my nose with caution. "Everyone just calls me Ness."

"Ness, it is a pleasure to make your acquaintance. Please." He sweeps the glass case off. "You wanted to see these."

I step to them, reaching out and running a finger over the scales. They pop and hiss, releasing that vulgar stench of decay and death.

Tilting my head, I frown, deciding to play coy. "What are they?"

"You ask difficult questions," he says, rubbing the back of his neck, frowning at the codexes. "These are tombs, and within the seeds of Mallafic are planted."

The lying prick Owen said the myth was nonsense. "Mallafic." I rub between my breasts. "What's that? Like the Sube?"

His face puckers with daft confusion. "The Sube is the seed of all Dark magic, like that which you hold, and yes, relates closely to Mallafic, but no. Mallafic was the first to hold the Sube, a god, the Ancient who fathered the Dark Seraphinus."

I place my palm on one cover. "Sube is just a bad word for the Dark."

"It depends on the translations on how the Sube is defined,

but they all share the similarity that Mallafic used the Sube to create the Dark."

"Beenin used the Sune?"

He chuckles. "Yes. They fought. Beenin won and tore her lover to pieces. The Dark clans collected those pieces, trying to put Mallafic back together. When they failed, they took several pieces, imbuing them within seven codexes, containing his magic in their sacred texts to amass power. These are two of them."

I move my hand from one to the other. Every time I hear information, it changes. It's an obvious flaw in oral myths passed through generation after generation before being recorded in written word. "That's not how I know the myth to go, but I guess, in that version, the smell from these is rotting body parts then."

Aku laughs, the sound, a musical waft. "Perhaps."

"Can I read them?"

"I dare say you will not be able to. They are written in my ancient tongue, Seraphin."

I shrug, paying no heed to the quip. "I read Seraphin."

"If you will allow it, I would like to say you are intriguing."

I laugh. "I'll allow it."

"You are positively ethereal." He chuckles, stepping closer and unlocking one of the codexes from its binding. "I will allow you this one under one condition."

"What's that?"

"All of the books within this section are sacred, holy texts. This is no exception, though it is not of my kind. You are to take extreme care with this, and in return for gifting you the right to lend a book from my section, allow me to take you to dinner. I would like to know more about you."

Accepting the book, I cuddle it close behind crossed arms. "Oh."

"Have I crossed a line?" he asks when I don't answer right away.

"No," I say in a hurry, hoping to avoid offense.

"Forgive me. We have not been properly introduced as society dictates. I have overstepped."

"No, really, you did not. I didn't think anyone in this place wanted anything to do with me. You're honestly the first Lighter to even speak to me willingly. The others were only following orders, and I'm just surprised."

Aku's smile comes slowly, his eyes dropping to the floor, his hands slipping into the front pockets of his trousers. A blush crosses over his high cheekbones. "I do not mean to be forward, but I find such an idea to be elusive. You are enticing, and I think more than what you appear. You have piqued my interest."

I suck in a breath and hold it, finding myself nodding in agreement. Tallie's acceptance of dates with Zander makes sense. It's hard to say no to someone so beautiful flattering me when what I desire is intangible. "I'm always hungry."

CHAPTER 36
NATALIA

Zander pulls my chair out, taking my hand to help me sit, then tucks me under the table. "Thank you."

"You're welcome." He inclines his head, turning to the waiter. "A bottle of rizvor, please."

I shift in my seat, the opulence of the restaurant glittering about me. "This place seems expensive."

He claims his seat and reaches for my hand across the table. "I wanted to treat you to something nice for your birthday."

The urge to spit some twisted sarcasm his way boils up, but I smile, resting my hand on his. Those kinds of remarks aren't appreciated, rewarding me with long stares and lectures of dignified conversation.

I pull my lower lip into my mouth in an old habit, forgetting about the lipstick coating it until I rub my tongue against the waxy gold. I hadn't realized the date. It's felt like an eternity since I came to Izul, but trying to count the weeks is dizzying.

Taking a deep breath, I nod. "It's kind of you, but really, this isn't necessary."

"Love," he smiles, his white eyes crinkling at the corners. "It's your birthday."

I force myself to smile and nod. All I can conjure is the urge to know what Cal would have done for my birthday.

The waiter delivers the bottle and menus, leaving us to decide. I scan the options, twisting a loose piece of my hair around a finger. It's grown past my shoulders, and the longer it gets, the straighter it becomes.

"Tallie," Zander says in a gentle voice, pulling my eyes to his. "You deserve nice. You deserve to be taken care of, spoiled even."

My right shoulder rolls in a slow twitch. "I know. I'm a catch."

"Your sarcasm is unappreciated," he says, holding my gaze. "Yes, you are a catch, as you say, and Pierre has given his blessing."

My mouth goes dry, and I reach for my drink. "What exactly are we discussing?"

"Our relationship has been given full support. Pierre let me know this afternoon after I finished my duties. Our queen has given her blessing should we mate, and even Larles has complimented my choice, deeming you an appropriate mate for my heritage."

"Oh." I blink. "Oh, so, we—the decision was made?"

He nods. "By all those who must give consent."

"I guess that doesn't include me?" Cal asks in my head, then growls. *"Or my fucking host?"*

"We have obtained the right to begin a proper relationship. I want to be afforded your every night, the luxury to sweep you off your feet when I see you, kiss you when I want."

Cal had threatened to put me on his dick for sassing him,

gave me an order I couldn't refuse to sit on his face, then fucked me on a bathroom sink without a word of request, and here Zander is asking for permission to kiss me. Torn between laughter and tears, I gape, my face frozen.

Zander grins. "Tallie, sweetheart, I am asking to begin an intimate relationship."

I pour my drink down my throat. "Oh."

He waits with a relaxed face as I begin to collect my mind to a semblance of order. There is not a single reason I can conjure to say no. Zander is handsome, with high cheekbones and a long face and features. His flared nose is set perfectly centered. It is a face Ness would tell me to sit on, and when I had seduced him after he saved me, it had been a pleasant experience.

Rolling my tongue over my front teeth, I bob my head. Zander is nice, and he can be funny at times. There's no reason I don't want him.

My hands fall beneath the table as I rub Cal's last words. The wound is going to heal, the gash left from where Cal was ripped out of me would seal up. It would be nice to know what it feels like to be loved, and Zander seems to be on track to show me.

My heart cries as I answer him. "A relationship, like dating? Okay. Yes."

Light glints beneath Zander's skin as he perks up. "You honor me." One of his hands slips inside his suit coat, pulling out a dark blue velvet box. He slides it across the table to me. "A gift in turn, although I will not pretend there will be anything I can give you of equal value to your considerations of me as a mate."

I lift a brow, smirking and biting back words of self-deprecating humor. "You bought a gift before I said yes?"

Flashing his teeth at me, he laughs. "I was optimistic, given when we met and the time we've spent together these past few months."

I crack the lid open, the hinges snapping. The white satin interior glistens like pearls, and the air vacates my lungs. A pendant hangs on a silver chain, slivers of diamonds protruding from a center stone. My eyes well up as I blink at the star.

"Little star."

Pain erupts in my heart worse than when Telra embedded a blade in it. A wail builds in my core for Cal, screaming as bile rises in the back of my throat. Fighting to keep the wound from ripping open, a useless attempt to staunch the bleeding from the intangible evisceration in my soul tearing wider, I take a single breath, forcing air into my body.

Tears cling to my lashes as I look at Zander's face of concern. "A star?"

"Are you all right, love?"

"Why a star?"

He tilts his head to the side. "What do you mean?"

"Why are you giving me a star?"

Reaching across the table, he snaps the box closed with a frown. "Give it to me." He drops his hand on the lid, trying to drag it toward himself.

"No." I shake my head, snatching the box up and opening it again.

"You don't like it. I'll get you something else."

Rubbing a sweating palm on the skirt of my dress down my thigh, I say, "I love it, but why a star?"

The lines around his mouth darken, his lips disappearing as he presses them together harder. He relaxes, taking a drink. "As with every other gift I've given you, I saw it and thought of you."

I struggle to maintain composure as he turns to a blurring kaleidoscope. "I remind you of a star?"

His throat bobs. "Your magic. I've never seen another with a Light like yours. Ours is golden. Yours is silver, like starlight."

With my hand in Cal's, I had been a Light wrapped up in his Dark, like a single star in a black sky. Taking another breath, I stare down at the necklace. "It's beautiful."

Zander sighs. "Tallie, please, it was a foolish idea. Allow me to take it back. I will get something else. Something better."

"No." I shake my head. "No, it's perfect." I pull the necklace from within the case.

He stands up, coming around the table. "Allow me to help you."

He moves next to me, pulling the chain from my shaking fingers to clasp it around my neck. The cool kiss of the metal against my skin is a brief flicker reminiscent of Cal's magic slithering over my flesh. I twitch, half-mad enough to rip the thing away and fling it into a corner. Instead, I grip my skirt, balling the fabric in my fists, squeezing until my fingers are numb.

Zander sits, but the expression he wears is grim. "If you are unsure?"

"No," I say, blinking the tears away. "It's really perfect. Thank you." I push my fingers against the star, the sharp edges biting into my skin, and I adjust it to hang centered between the tops of my breasts. As painful as it was seeing it for the first time, I plan to keep the little star close to my heart.

Zander hitches a smile, but it appears as forced as my own. "It looks good on you."

Words fail to fall from my tongue, but he picks up the menu, eyes flickering as he reads, ignorant of the hurricane of agony unleashed in my chest, its epicenter, the very jewel he hung around my neck. With shaking fingers, I pick up my menu to find something to eat, but food is the furthest thing from what I want.

Everything dissolves as tasteless ash on my tongue as we eat in silence. My fingers find their way to the chain and pendant over and over, caressing it through the whole evening.

Zander sits back, smiling and nursing his last glass of wine as the meal is cleared away. "Does a star have meaning to you?"

"A gift of love from the Light to the Dark," I say. "That's what the legends say, right?"

"Yes, the legends are that Adontis, the goddess of Light, wove pieces of herself into her lover, Nehil, the god of nothing. You're quiet this evening."

I shrug, fiddling with the star. "I'm tired. The guy training me makes me do a lot."

He laughs. "I'm sure it's because he thinks highly of your abilities."

"I've had to develop them."

"I understand. You've been through much." He sits forward, setting his drink aside, his hand laying over mine, his thumb teasing over my wrist. "Did you know the Dark has no laws that protect those contracted? The Light does. I'm protected by law from even your father against certain uses. Physical punishments as well, and I am guaranteed certain things, like personal time and protection of my personal affairs."

"I didn't know that," I admit, tucking my other arm close to my stomach. "I didn't realize you were contracted either."

"I am. I'm a worn contract until I enter my sixth century."

I run my fingers up the side of his wrist. "We've never discussed contracts."

"It's not something important for you to know. For now, your standing is still somewhat of a debate in the Light, given your Seraphim nature. Although our queen granted you acknowledgment of the Bordeaux heritage and standing, there are those who feel you should be contracted to your heritage rather than standing on your own. That is the normal conditions for a Seraphim, which eliminates the need for Ritual."

I clear my throat. "About Ritual..."

He holds up his hand with a smile. "Pierre will settle it. Everything we've been working toward is to put you at the full potential of your heritage without endangering you. He's been furious about our queen demanding Ritual take place, and he's been vocal about the abuse of her power. It's causing disruption, but we have concluded that should you and I enter a relationship and find it to our enjoyment, Pierre will petition to break my contract early. This will give me full standing so that I might contract you. If we can arrange this within the next century, there should be no reason you have to face Ritual."

"Wouldn't you have to face Ritual with Larles?"

Zander frowns at the table. "We have. I won. Larles will be contracted to our queen for the rest of his existence. He will not be able to hold his own contracts, nor will he be able to be uncontracted."

My life is planned for me with no regard for my desires. I've endured this before, albeit Zander is a better option than Tony ever was. "What kind of Seraphinus are you? We've never discussed the different breeds of Light."

"Light." He laughs. "We are not beasts like the Dark. We do not shift into animals, although certain heritages have different abilities. My heritage is more electrical, and was the first to smite."

"Neat."

"My heritage is the only one that can smite without building the charge, and unlike most heritages, we can smite on a slight whim as often as we desire."

"Oh." I lift my eyebrows.

Bobbing his head, he grows bashful. "Most heritages can only smite once or twice. Some, such as yours, can manage a five or six, but none match the Fairly heritage in strength and skill. That is why we serve as avengers, bowing to the trinity, reserved to serve the royal family and all other heritage as guardians."

"So, your whole thing is protecting and serving?"

"Yes, although should anything happen to cause the demise of the trinity, my heritage is to take the throne." He bobs his head. "As you already know, the Hallows' heritage has died out, leaving your heritage second in line, next to only the royal family. That moved the Fairly heritage to third in line, but any of our seeds will be deemed as Fairly heritage and forced to serve."

I pick up my wine glass, spinning the clear rizvor liquor in the bottom.

Zander smiles, taking a drink. "The Lamont heritage is more illumination and heat. The Hallows heritage was the first to call on the Light in the suns, harness its power to wield flames."

"Firelight. Yeah, I've got that one."

He jerks back, shock radiating over his features. "What?"

"I've called it a few times. The first time, I didn't even know what I was doing, got covered in the stuff and smited."

His jaw goes slack, his eyes widening. "You did what now? Love, do you know how difficult firelight is to master?"

"I'm not going to say I've mastered it."

"We'll work on it. Well, Pierre will. He wants to take over your training." Zander shakes his head. "The Hallows wielded flames. The Bordeaux heritage can conjure firelight, but that is different than the Hallows. They burned with the flames of suns, but they could ignite air. Firelight is restricted to you, your Light burning on your skin."

Zander pays, and we walk out. He keeps me pressed close, tucked under his arm. I stay there as we walk back through the city, discussing other heritages until we arrive at the flight shaft. He pushes the button and swings me into his arms, flying me up to Pierre's personal floor. He spins me under his arm again as he walks me to my room.

He opens the door for me, and we stare into the room side by side. Twisting to face me, his eyes search my face, the unvoiced question screaming at me from his steady gaze.

I lift onto tiptoes and press my lips to his. They are warm, pressing back into mine, his tongue teasing outward. I open my mouth to him, letting my tongue stroke and twist around his.

Large, warm hands land on my hips, pulling me close against his solid torso. Zander leans forward, dipping me back, and I break the kiss. He grins down at me, shuffling us a few steps into the room, reaching behind him to close the door.

It snaps shut with a soft click of the latch, and my heart rate jacks up, the organ beating wildly. Swallowing, I stand, putting a hand on his chest and stepping back. "Zan."

He pulls me close again, arms wrapping around my waist. "Yes, love?"

"I'm not ready for sex."

His eyes drop to my lips as the bob in his throat dips and lifts with a hard swallow. "It was just a contract between you and Callahan. That's all. Whatever he may have let you believe, it was only ever for his benefit."

I nod, smiling even though my eyes burn. "I know, but I trusted him. It was complicated, and whatever it was, it's over."

"Yes, because he's dead," Zander snaps with a shimmering anger. "You should let me burn out that stupid, useless contract in your arm and forget about him. He used you for his benefit without ever caring for you in the least, I guarantee that."

I rest my forehead against his chest. "I trusted Cal, really trusted in him, and it's going to be a while before I trust someone again. I'm still reeling because I trusted him, and he died. I didn't think it was possible."

"It is," Zan says, his voice twisting to a sneer.

"After everything we went through in the games..." I trail off and shrug.

He gives a curt nod and turns. "I'll be a gentleman, but you accepted this, me. I can give you time, but I will not wait forever. Goodnight, Tallie."

"Don't." I chase him a step to the door. "Don't go. Please. I'm just not ready for..." I wave a hand at the bed.

Without facing me, his shoulders square. His voice is taut. "Then what do you want?"

"Stay," I choke out. "Stay the night with me without fucking?"

He turns, meeting my eyes. "If that's what you want, then I'll stay."

The pulse in my neck jumps at the words, a sad smile stealing my lips. Maybe Zander could be home if I gave him a chance.

Zander unbuttons his shirt. I kick my heels toward the wardrobe and find a t-shirt. I shimmy the dress over my head and lose the bra, tugging the shirt over my head. When I turn around, Zander has lost his belt and shirt and is standing in a pair of dress pants.

He sits on the bed, kicking his legs out straight before him. Cocking his head, he crooks a finger at me. "Come here."

I climb on the other side, scooting over to rest my head on

his shoulder, nestling against him. It's nice. He's solid and warm. Something about that calms me.

He kisses my forehead. "The marks on your back?"

"Magia."

"May I see them?"

Sitting up, I turn my back to him and reach over my shoulder to pull the t-shirt up.

His fingers brush down my spine. "These relate to your Ki?"

"Yes."

"What is Ki? You've never explained much."

"My magic."

"Are you ever going to share your secrets?" He slides his finger down my spine.

"Ki is the magic of the soul."

"So you've said."

"It's...very much like the Light."

"These jade marks, all these lines and symbols, they mean something."

"Yes," I nod. "There are forty-seven pieces. Those who have all forty-seven have completed training."

"They are a show of completion?"

"Yes."

"We need you to tell us how to deal with them. The cities under Dark oppression are fairing better. They seem to lose less than Light cities. Does the Dark have some advantage against the Magia?"

"Not that I'm aware of," I whisper. "They killed Cal, and he knew everything about Ki."

"Mmm, yes," Zander drawls in a hard voice. "He's dead. The Magia killed him, but the other Dark cities aren't experiencing many casualties, even managing to hang several dead Magia as warning to the others."

"I don't know what you want me to say. Maybe Dark are just better at fighting."

Chuckling, Zan moves to my shoulder blade, drawing a line along it with the tip of his finger. "You have no idea how wrong you are. You're developing your wing scars." He leans closer, pressing his lips to my shoulder, and then his arm sneaks around me, tightening around my waist.

Laying us down, he spoons me, pressing little kisses against my neck. I close my eyes, trying to imagine it's Cal at my back. "Is there really no way to turn the fucking lights off?"

"No, much like your use of profanity."

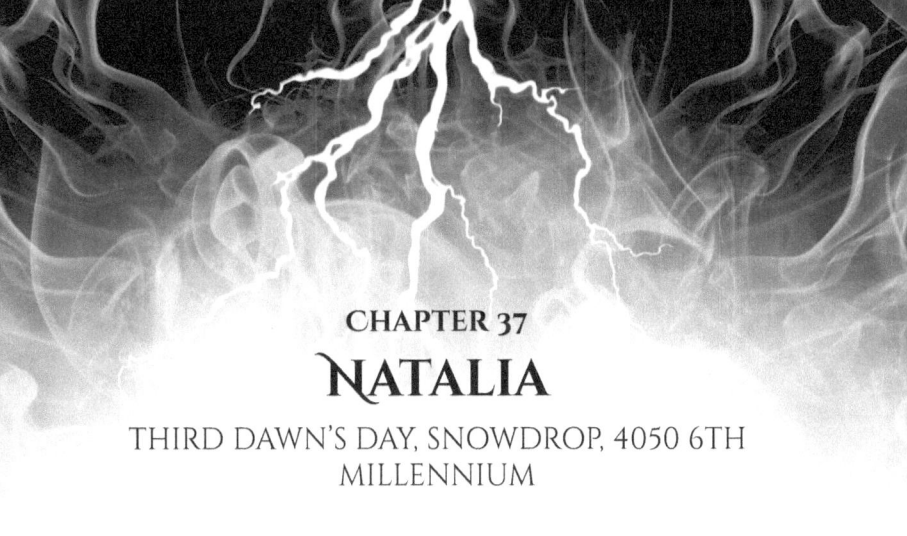

CHAPTER 37
NATALIA
THIRD DAWN'S DAY, SNOWDROP, 4050 6TH MILLENNIUM

Slipping from beneath Zander's arm, I roll myself off the mattress. I stare at him, studying his face with the prominent brow and his long, golden hair loose about his head against the pillow. He'd been lovely last night, with little kisses and small caresses while holding me close. When I closed my eyes and he kept his mouth shut, I could almost forget he wasn't Cal.

That's a problem to end all problems. To Cal, I was a contract, a vassal to jump when it suited him, but it was something else for me. Cal was home. Cal was safe and honest. Cal was a lot of things, including my protector from spiders, but mostly, Cal was my beautiful, wicked Darkling.

He's gone, and I can't keep pretending he's going to walk through the gates of Izul to come get me anymore. I don't believe I'll ever feel home again, but Zander is offering. Most importantly, Zander is alive, and last night had been nice.

Moving on my tiptoes, I cross the room with care to avoid waking Zander. I pick up my guitar and settle in the armchair to curl around it. As I chew on my lip, debating on what comes next with Zander, I trace the letters etched into the surface.

"You're not home."

I lift my hand, feeling for the star hanging around my neck.

"Little Star."

My heart skips a beat.

"You're not home, Little Star."

The guitar shakes in my grasp, my trembling fingers turning clammy and leaving dull streaks across the glossy surface grip, my trembling fingers slipping off the strings.

My Light roars in my skull. *"Find. My. Friend!"*

"He's dead! It's just a coincidence."

My eyes well up, and I slap a hand over my mouth, trying not to bawl. I must make some noise of heartbreak because Zander stirs, turning over.

As he sits up, I panic, starting to hyperventilate.

He rubs his face, peering at me, one eye still half shut. "Tal?"

Blinking dry, tight eyes that burn at the ceiling, I take a deep breath. "I'm fine."

"You're not." He throws the covers back, getting up to walk toward me.

I shake my head, trying to hold myself together, but the seams are stretching against the fine threads I've sewn up my broken heart with. A weak chuckle trickles from the back of my throat, a disguised sob. "It's nothing."

Zander has his hands on his hips, his jaw cocked. The furrow of his brow warns me he's annoyed. "Tal." He kneels before me, pulling the guitar from my lap to lay it on the floor. "Look at me. Look me in the eye and tell me the truth. Are you all right?"

With my face to the floor, I slip off the chair into his lap. His long arms wrap around me, enveloping me in his warmth.

"Yes." I breathe out, low and slow, deflating against him.

Right now, I need something to prop me up and keep me moving forward. Zander is as good a choice as any. "I'm fine."

"What happened?"

I squeeze my eyes shut and shake my head against his shoulder. I can't tell him the truth, the tender threads of my patched-up heart unwinding and snapping in my chest.

"You can tell me anything. I'm here, your future mate."

The words shock me back to reality, and I lean back, blinking my stinging eyes, my eyelashes clumped with tears. "That's more than dating."

His eyebrows push together. "Have you heard of mating?"

"Yeah, Hiro and Thames..." I wave a hand. "Hiro said he mated Thames."

Zander's head tilts to the side like an adorable puppy, almost excited but too befuddled for it to stick. "So, *not* from Cal?"

"No," I sneer, my Light buzzing in my skull.

He nods. "That makes more sense. Yes, mate. When Seraphinus mate with another, a permanent bond is formed between them. It involves your magic, too, rooting the mating bond. I'm ready when you are."

"You're my future mate?"

"Yes. I will make you my mate."

My Light stirs, stretching like a lazy cat. *"I won't mate Pretty Boy. Don't like that stuff. It's too hot and it's too whiny. In fact, tell Pretty Boy to make it stop trying to make me talk."*

I smile at the sound of Cal's cranky tone oozing from my Light. It's so rare that it speaks, only deigning to when it's adamant.

"You need to trust me, and it starts with telling me what this is. What is upsetting you?"

With a groan, I face plant into Zander's chest. "It was...

Cal." Scrunching my eyes closed tighter, I hesitate, not sure of how to explain.

"Tal," he sighs. "What happened between you two that you served with such loyalty? Why do you cry for that dog?"

"He's not a dog!" I slap my hand to his chest and shove away from him.

"He's dead!"

I close my eyes, hanging my head. "I know, and–and..."

"And what, love? I want an answer. Why would you cry for that brute? You were a contract used for his purposes. He never cared about you. Why would you feel sorrow over him?"

"It was a mess," I whisper. "I didn't take orders well. He didn't take my independence well. We were a complete wreck in every sense, but he was mine."

"No, love." Zander tucks hair behind my ear, lifting my chin with his fingers. "You were owned by him as a thing to be used, and he would have used you until there was nothing left of you, then discarded you as waste."

"I trusted him."

"You misplaced your trust."

I meet Zan's eyes, something about his words striking the final blow. The strings in my chest snap, the pieces falling into tattered shambles. I had misplaced my trust in Cal. I thought he could handle anything I couldn't, and I had been wrong.

"You're right," I admit in a hoarse whisper.

Zan sighs. "That's good." His lips press to my forehead. "That is a very good step. How about dinner again tonight? We can talk about it more."

With no reason not to and no other options, I bob my head, unable to speak, afraid of what I would say.

"I have to go." He lifts me to deposit me in the bed again. He gets dressed then kisses me on the lips before walking backward toward the door with a smile. "Contractual obligations, I'm afraid. I have several heritage matters to address today."

"What about training?"

"Pierre is going to begin training you." Zander checks his watch. "In about a rune, but you should have another half rune before you need to get ready."

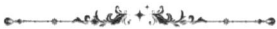

PIERRE STANDS across from me in the training ring. It's odd to see him outside of a suit, but he has donned a t-shirt and athletic pants. His hands are at his hips, a power stance cocked with confidence.

"Zan has mentioned you are comfortable with hand-to-hand combat. Is that correct?"

I cross my arms. "Yeah, the Magia trained me, and then Mass, Cal and I played the games, and Zan and I have been doing drills. Don't bore me to death with more."

Pierre rubs a hand along the underside of his jaw. "I will want to see what you are capable of, but for now, I'll leave it. Our heritage is one of several that can call forth what is known as firelight. It's an effective skill in a battle against the Dark."

"I've called it."

His forehead wrinkles as his eyebrows lift with disbelief. "Most of our heritage cannot conjure firelight until their second century."

"It was on accident the first time, but since then, yeah, I've kind of figured out how to make fire."

"That must have been a grave scenario indeed for your magic to develop in such a rapid manner."

I scoff. "I mean, I was playing a game."

"Your magic must have been fearful of demise."

I stretch my arms in front of me, my fingers lacing together and bending backward to stretch. "Sure. I got dosed with nightmare. That shit sucks, by the way."

"Nightmare is a potent poison and not to be played with."

"I'm aware." I shudder. "That night, Marius and his father both dosed me. Cal was pissed. He said he thought I was dead. I remember being close, ready to let go to the afters, but then I got this spark, and a song popped into my head. I don't really know what happened that night, but yeah, Cal said I covered myself in the stuff and smited."

Pierre appears constipated, a cross between uncomfortable confusion and pissed agony. "You were pushed too far. Your magic shouldn't be so strong at your age, and you shouldn't have been able to accomplish either of those tasks, least of all performing both of them simultaneously. I wasn't able to smite until I was over a hundred."

I shrug.

He sighs, stepping closer. "We'll focus on firelight for now."

"I'd rather figure out how to smite. I've only done it twice, and both times, it was in, like, high-emotion situations."

"Your magic is going to respond to how you feel. It's part of you, like a muscle. Your muscles tense in response to signals from your brain unconsciously when you are afraid or stressed. You'll be able to do more with your Light in those situations, but it is not wise to do that to your magic, being so young and your magic infantile."

"Sure, thought you said I was supposed to control it, though."

"You are, but in those types of situations, it acts on instinct *with* you." He holds his hand out, firelight dancing to life over his palm. "When you can do this, I will consider teaching you how to smite."

I lift my hand, mirror his pose and whisper, "I'll set myself on fire just to keep the demons at bay." Delicate flames twist from my palm, dancing with shimmering heat in a beautiful glow.

Pierre sighs, dropping his hands to his hips again.

I close my fingers over the firelight and let the burn fade. When it's dissipated, I open my hand again to show it's gone.

Someone approaches, and we both turn to Ashely. She scowls. "Teaching her firelight already, Dad?" Her furious gaze turns on me. "How old are you? Your Light isn't even strong enough to handle that."

Pierre holds out a hand, two fingers up to silence her. "Your sister is very young but has been through trauma that caused her magic to respond in a severe way. I need her to be able to master control of her Light and her abilities."

Ashely rolls her eyes, making a face. "She's not my sister."

I lift an eyebrow, turning to lean against the ropes at leisure. Other than our two encounters, I've only seen her in passing, and either Pierre or Zander have kept us well apart when we are within view of each other.

Pierre warns her with a quiet snarl, "She is your sister. She carries our heritage within her, and you need to find a way to be okay with this because Tallie isn't going anywhere."

Ashley throws the bag from her shoulder, kicking it off to the side. "You want me to call her sister? That halfbreed mutt? Fine. Then I call Ritual. She's strong enough to call firelight, so there's no point in waiting for her to get older."

Pierre drags a hand down his face. "I have discussed with you the situation in full disclosure. You are aware of plans being made to ensure the two of you have no reason to fight in Ritual. Neither of you will need to alter your lives as they currently stand."

"That's if our Light Queen even allows several things. She

won't. She's displeased with the idea of another Bordeaux challenging the Lamont heritage for the crown."

"I am aware of our politics, but the laws are on my side. I have found an amicable solution to our queen's distaste. Tallie is your half-sister, not Seraphinus, as we are. She poses no threat to your station and soon will be contracted to the Fairly heritage."

Ashley shoulders past him, saying, "She has wings. She's Seraphinus."

He whips around, grabbing her shoulder. "We don't know what she is, and I don't even know what Tallie is fully capable of. She needs further training and consideration."

"Ritual." Ashley shrugs him off, stepping to me. "We fight until one submits or can't continue."

I laugh, pushing into the ropes and allowing them to spring me forward. "Fine."

"Girls." Pierre shoves between us. "This is not acceptable."

Ashley shoves him out of the way. "Too late, Dad. She accepted. You did this. You get to find a way to deal with it."

"You will not put your hands on me or speak to me in this manner." He crosses his arms, glaring at her. "Now, if you wish to spar with your sister, I will tolerate that as a matter of training. However, under no circumstances is this a Ritual fight."

Ashely squares up to me. "You might want to submit right now and get it over with."

I drop into a half split for a count of three and then switch sides. "I'll figure it out." I stand. "How does this start?"

"Bow."

Eyeing Ashley, I bow. She mimics me and then springs forward, already swinging. I curse, outmatched in both speed and strength. I struggle to dodge and block, catching a blow to the face.

Adrenaline courses through me, the Light sparkling to life

over my skin. I center, taking Ashley's next attack to the fore-arm, using Ki to reinforce my limb, and I get a clear opening to strike with an open palm, blasting Ki to her abdomen.

Ashely stumbles back but recovers quickly, setting on me again. We go swing for swing, blow to blow, but every punch or kick I take heals with a wave of Ki. I tuck and roll, pushing to my feet and whipping around with both hands up. Others have gathered, watching us fight, and Pierre stands in the corner with a scowl.

Engaging with me again, Ashley glows with firelight. It races over me, and I scream, my skin searing. The flames dissolve as I flip her to the mat. She takes my legs out, and we tussle on the ground. Ashley rolls to her feet, and I grit my teeth.

I flip my feet over my head into a backflip, popping up a step away with enough time to send a wave of Ki through me to heal. Electricity zaps around me in the air, and I tense, baring teeth at Ashely. The woman sets on me again, swinging, putting me on the defense.

The hum of current picks up as Ashley gets a clean hook to my face. I stumble, and she leaps back. Bright light flashes, the current ripping through me. The charge burns from my scalp to my toes, screaming into my core as I absorb it.

Swaying on my feet, my limbs shake, an intoxicating sweetness lingering on my tongue. I grin. "Fucking idiot."

I strike at the air before me with an open palm, channeling the smite back at her. Ashley shields, but the strike cleaves clean through the block into her chest. With a shriek, she crumples, lying in a heap.

I hear gasps abound as I stand, swiping at blood dribbling from my nose. Sniffing the fluid into my nasal cavities, I wait. Ashley doesn't stir, her blonde hair a mess about her face.

Huffing, I stomp toward her, flipping her onto her back, but Pierre yells, "Tallie, stop!"

I roll my eyes, slapping a hand to Ashley's chest. The heartbeat within is stuttering and weak beneath clammy flesh.

Pierre storms across the mat. "Tallie, no, it's over. You're breaking the rules of engagement."

I twist my face to him. "If you want her alive, you're going to stay there."

Pierre freezes, and I focus on Ashely. Inhaling, I square my shoulders, my core aligning. Ki pulses through me, a dim glow and fade of Light in my arm as I channel the magic into Ashely until the pulses meet with no resistance.

Ashley opens her eyes, and I pull back, stand straight and stare down my nose at her. "You're welcome."

Pierre grabs me by the arm, dragging me half a step further away from her. "What did you do?"

"Healed her," I say, trying to shove him off, but his grip tightens to the point of pain.

"That is the second time I've watched you survive a smite. How do you do it?"

"Dude, ow. Let go. It's Ki."

Ashley sits up then pushes herself to her feet with one hand. "You cheated."

I gape. "How? I used what skills I have, and you used what skills you have. Mine are just better."

She's red in the face, stomping closer, but Pierre pulls me away, putting himself between us again. "You lost, honey."

"She cheated," Ashley screams. "She shouldn't have survived."

I roll my eyes with a giggle. "You're as stupid as Cal was."

Ashley launches at me. Pierre grabs her, twisting and hooking a foot between her legs in one smooth motion to take her to the mat. "Enough! Or so help you the gods. We have rules of engagement. We are not beasts. We do not act with careless disregard or without honor." He stands, offering a hand to Ashley.

She smacks hers into it, getting to her feet with his help. He says, "Now, I'm aware that Tallie is immune to smites, so I will not consider this another attempt on her life despite knowing you fully intended to kill her."

"It was Ritual."

"I made it clear that Ritual did not apply." Pierre pivots to me. "What is Ki? You will answer me this time. You've kept your secrets long enough."

I raise my eyebrows. "How do you not know this? Like, I don't understand."

"Explain."

"The intermixing of Dark and Light allows us to tap into the power of the spirit. We call it Ki."

Ashley huffs, tossing her hair. "I'm not leaving. That doesn't count, not when she used Ki."

With a sweet smile, I say, "It's my magic."

"Magia magic, not the Light. That's cheating the rules of Ritual."

I lean on my heels, crossing my arms. "You picked a fight you couldn't win. Deal with it like I dealt with you throwing me down that shoot."

Ashley takes a step back, glancing around at all those watching. "I didn't. I never touched you."

I grin. "No, you used your magic like I did."

Pierre turns to the crowd. "All of you leave. Our business is not yours." They scatter in a hurry, it's almost comical the way they rush to flee. He glares at me. "You will watch your words."

"Or what?" I ask with feigned innocence. "You'll smite me? Go ahead, I dare you. I'll put your ass down too."

"Natalia!"

"You'd deserve it for killing Cal's father."

"I did no such thing."

I gape then rock back on my heels, peeling into laughter. "You killed the whole contender list."

"They were the Dark. We are the Light. We snuff them out. You need to learn that and accept it. We don't save the Dark, care about it, or defend it. It's against everything we are." He draws up, breathing deep, his voice lowering. "But I didn't kill a single one of them. That pleasure belongs to that wretched dog you seem to care so much for. He did it. He dragged the blade across his father's throat, not me."

The world spins. "What?"

"He lied to you. He only ever wanted to use you, and he turned you against me to keep you for his use."

"No. He told me before– Before anything to do with you. Cal doesn't lie."

Pierre's face twists with fury, his voice harsh. "He manipulated you. He used twisted facts to suit his intentions to create discord between you and the Light for his own purposes."

"You're lying!" I scream.

"Keep your voice down. There are others, and our burdens are not theirs to carry."

"He told me what you did, and the Dark doesn't lie."

"His goal has always been to capture you for a use. He never cared about you, he's not even capable. The Dark are animals. They are disgusting, parasitic, vile, violent, sadistic, and crude. All of them. Every last mutt including Callahan, and I'm done tolerating this behavior. You are the Light. Act like it."

Cal, Massimo, Hiro, and Thames–they aren't anything like Pierre claims. I grip my fists, cool magic slithering up my forearms as my heart races with putrid fury. "You don't know anything about the Dark. They aren't animals or vile, and I'm done hearing you insult them."

"Natalia," Pierre snaps, his eyes wide and fixed lower on me.

I glance down, seeing black tendrils twisting along my forearms. I lift my hands to inspect the shadows, but they dissolve. My eyes lift to his, shock seeping through me like a blanket of snow coating my mind.

Ashley throws her hands up. "Very good, Dad. You made some kind of Ancient or something. We don't know what she is."

Pierre runs a hand down his face again, frustration sowed into his features. "Ash, she is my daughter, your sister, and her home is here. Ritual does not apply, but maybe you need time to accept things as they are. Perhaps a trip away to find inner acceptance with the discord in your life?"

Ashley stomps to the edge of the mat. "Thanks, Dad." Grabbing her bag and dipping between the ropes, she says. "I'll be going to Kipnop."

Pierre focuses on me, sighing. "Please, go clean up." He rubs at his jaw. "I will collect you for dinner."

"Make sure you tell Zander. He was planning to take me to dinner."

Pierre inclines his head. "I will. I need to consider what you are. Your continual rejection of what you are. Your allegiance to the Dark, this childish infatuation you have with that animal. There is much I need to weigh and discuss with you to determine our next course of action." He rubs his hands together. "I have no idea how he managed to control you."

"He didn't." I shrug, walking away.

CHAPTER 38
NATALIA

I step out of my bathroom and halt, feet sticking to the floor. I blink at Ashley perched on the wide bench at the foot of my bed.

Ashley lifts a hand, standing. "I called Ritual. I lost."

"That's fairly obvious, but sure, enlighten me." I wave a hand across my upper body in a gesture for her to continue.

"I lost Ritual, which means I bow to you." She inclines at the waist in a mock display of respect. "It's why I never wanted you here. However, allow us to dispel our animosity and speak truthfully. You don't want to be here either."

I shy my head to the side, not agreeing or disputing. "I thought you were going to Kipnop?"

Ashley gives a wicked flash of teeth as she smiles. "Yes, dear, I am, but I thought perhaps before I go, you might want to take advantage of Ritual."

"How so?"

"Perhaps you might inquire if Callahan is alive, and perhaps I will have no choice but to answer you."

"Why?" I grip my fists and look to the ceiling. "Why the fuck? Why would I do that?"

She gestures in front of her. "Perhaps you should ask and find out."

"If I do this, will you get out of my room and stop trying to kill me?"

"Oh, honey, I lost in Ritual. I will respect that in every way."

"I don't actually know what that means."

"Hmm, yes, well." She picks at non-existent lint on her skirt. "I may have underestimated you, didn't give credit where credit is due. It's my fault I called Ritual before knowing more about you, and now that I see you as an adversary I should have considered with more care. I feel I owe you a gift in apology for my disrespect." She shrugs, pulling her designer bag higher on her shoulder.

I lean against the doorframe, crossing my arms. "All right, I'll play. But you Seraphinus have the worst fucking games. Is Cal alive?"

"Yes."

"Great, now that—" I spit out half the automatic response I had prepared before her answer sinks in. "Wait. Yes?" I jerk upright, widening my eyes.

Ashley clicks her tongue. "Honey, Callahan is alive."

My heart stops, my ears ringing. I stare at her, and the life returns to my body, fury burning through me. I snarl, "What did you just fucking say?"

"I just thought you should know," she shrugs again and steps to the door.

"You fucking bitch." I fling my hand out, my Ki slamming the door closed in her face. "You fucking come in here because I kick your ass and tell me the most fucked up shit you could spin and expect me to let you walk away?"

Ashley turns wide eyes to me, innocence written in her shock. "No. I came in here to tell you the truth because I know you'll run to him, and I'll get what I want. If you leave and return to him, there is no way our queen will ever accept you into society again, a Bordeaux or not," she says, taking a step back toward me. "I called Ritual. I lost, which means I will no longer be the heir to Bordeaux. That honor will transfer to you. I will no longer have contracts of my own. I have no idea how our father was going to manage that issue, as you are contracted and cannot hold contracts for that reason. However, if you leave, my loss in Ritual will be nullified, and I will be restored to where I belong." She closes the space between us and grips my wrist.

"What are you doing?"

She pries my arm from my body, twisting it so my forearm is in full view, Cal's inky black magic scrawled in my skin. "Are you aware that worn contracts are a piece of the contractor's magic?"

"Yes."

"Then by the gods how are you so damn stupid?" She taps her finger against Cal's words. "Callahan's magic still exists within your skin."

"He said it would default when he died to prevent me from transferring to any who killed him."

"Oh, honey." She giggles. "Defaulting contracts don't transfer, that is true, but when Callahan dies, his magic will die with him. Every single piece in existence will cease to exist." She taps my forearm.

I stare down at it and then shriek, "Are you fucking kidding me?"

Ashley let's go of my arm with a giggle. "Not in the least."

"Why didn't you tell me this sooner? If you wanted me

gone, why push me down the flight shaft, why call Ritual at all?"

She shrugs, rolling her eyes away from me with a *tsk*. "How odious, a Bordeaux serving the Dark. That will forever be an embarrassment to my heritage. Besides..." She sighs with a little smile. "You broke my nose."

CHAPTER 39
CALLAHAN
EIGHTH THISTLE'S DAY, WARMWAVE, 4049
6TH MILLENNIUM

The world is dark, and there's a consistent and subtle drip of water echoing around me. I claw at the thing on top of me, thrashing around at the rubble enclosing me. My spikes scrap and screech with each shove, but I growl, straining to shove debris, lashing out in terror. My claws rake against solid no matter where I reach, and I see naught despite my ability to see without illumination.

I need Natalia—her Light, her voice. I'm buried without my star this time, nothing to stop the anxiety closing my throat and strangling my mind with fear. I have no idea how long I've been stuck, buried beneath rubble in complete darkness.

I've been here before, buried in darkness without ever knowing if I'd taste fresh air again. I'm back in the box my sister buried me in. My heart races and I squirm, sending my Dark in search of a way out. It quivers and ties itself in knots, pissing itself in terror as it tries to find the surface in disorientation.

At least I had shifted as my home collapsed around me. I'm

more durable in this form. I'm not dead yet, which means I fight.

I slam my fist into whatever is on top of me, breaking the pieces apart, but the rubble rains down on me, burying me tighter. I scream in fury and fear alike behind closed lips, and flail in desperation. The rock lightens and I can breathe, shoving again. It lifts and I grunt, sending my magic wrapping around it to force the slab higher.

The weight gives way, and the concrete slab lifts even without my assistance as daylight streams over me.

Two familiar shadow beasts, inky blue and black beasts with leathery blue wings tucked at their back move the slab, grunting as they throw it to the side. Hiro and Thames.

I snarl and squirm to climb out of the broken remains of my prison. The taller turns to me, Thames laughing. "Sorry, baby, took us a while to find you."

I stomp away from the hole, stumbling over broken debris. My tail whips around, aiding me to keep upright until I get onto solid ground that holds steady.

Rage burns in me as I survey the damage. Bright lights strobe and flash on vehicles in the front of what was my house. Humans are streaming over the wreckage, cameras pointed at me, and a helicopter flies overhead. Stomping forward, I growl, batting at a human too close to me.

Leaping over the last fifty feet, I land on my driveway, the cement cracking beneath my feet. "Get off my property."

The humans stare, and one sticks a microphone closer. "Are you the Seraphinus known as Callahan?"

I whack at the reporter with a clawed hand and the cameraman with my tail, sending both sprawling. "Get off my property, and don't ask stupid questions."

Nearby another voice is breathless, "This just in, a massive, unidentified Seraphinus has just appeared from the rubble. Sit tight folks, we may not be rid of Callahan."

Growling, I snap in the direction of the second reporter on all fours. "Get off my property." I stand, lifting a vehicle and throwing it toward the fence.

The humans stand and stare, a camera pointed at me. I snarl, lashing out again at another cameraman, when a man approaches his hands held high. "I'm Officer McClough. We're securing this scene."

"I didn't tell you to. Get that camera out of here and leave."

The man smirks and crosses his arms. "We're just doing our jobs, sir."

"I don't like repeating myself. Get off my property, or I'll have to have someone clean up your blood. Your choice."

"Buddy, someone just knocked you down a couple of pegs. Go sit down, cool off, or the Magia are going to come finish what they started."

I inhale and roar, fire exploding from me. I breathe the flames across every living soul I see, and when I'm out of breath, I start ripping bodies in half, flinging the pieces and vehicles alike toward the front edge of my property.

The humans rush for safety, but I sprint on all fours, closing off their escape route and dismembering any I can find, impaling one with the spike on the end of my tail, whipping it toward the fence to dislodge it.

Breathing hard, my Dark hisses at me with rage mirrored in the strum of my blood. I stalk back toward the ruins of my home. Dozens of figures stand on the pile of destruction, shifted and watching me. My eyes flicker over them, searching for identities. One face is missing.

"Massimo!"

A dark teal figure drops next to me, black leather wings folding to nestle against its back. "Here," Massimo says.

"Is this what you handled?" I turn and advance on Massimo, who shies away. "This is that thing I didn't have to worry about?"

"No."

I stop short, tail snapping back and forth in annoyance. "What was it then?"

"Cal."

I slam my knuckles into the driveway and scream in rage. "What was it?"

Massimo winces, looking away. "Natalia was engaging in sexual acts with a man at the spa."

That sets me on fire with fury. My star was touched by someone else. A red haze creeps over my vision. "Go get her."

Behind me, there's a chuckle, and I whip my tail into the source. It contacts something, and I turn, watching Marius pick himself up, brushing dust off his dress shirt.

We glare at each other, the red fleck in his eye twitching as he contemplates me. Running a hand down his face, he sighs. "Hello, Cal."

I growl. Unlike Hiro, Marius is no friend. Whatever his reason for being here, it's unpleasant. "What the fuck do you want? Can't you see I'm busy?"

Marius holds a hand up. "I am here on behalf of my father, as he is too ill to travel, and I speak for him. Now, sit." He points a finger at me and motions it downward like he's commanding a dog. "As an order of the king."

Crouching on my hind legs, I sit, but my tail and magic are both twitching with contained ire. I stare him down. "Speak."

Marius squares his shoulders, his sharp features set close in his face. "Your house is in disarray. You've been brought down by a ghostly, frail entity, which has made the Seraphinus appear weak. As such, you are hereby disgraced."

I growl through bared teeth. "They blew up my house in the middle of the night, not made me bleed."

Shrugging, Marius crosses his arms. "Have you seen the news?" He glances to the chaos left in my wake from clearing the human vermin from my property. "Given the circumstantial timing and rather interesting gimmick, my father has decided that though disgraced, you will retain your position as contender until the next Gathering Shadows. If he lives that long, you'll be disgraced for life. If you die during the contest, then so be it. You may reclaim good standing once more should you win the throne. All current written contracts you have are absolved as Dark Law states a disgraced may not hold written contracts."

I clench my jaw, claws digging into the pavement as Marius snaps his fingers. It will destroy all contracts bound to me under the authority and magic of their Dark King.

Marius holds his hands up and shrugs. "Not my choice. I am simply the messenger today. Personally? Shit situation, mate. Formally, my father sends his regards and requests you clean up this mess."

"I will," I say with heat shimmering in my breath.

Marius smiles. "Did the lightning bug survive? Now that you're disgraced, I'd love to take her off your hands. She's feisty, would be fun."

"Fuck off."

Laughing, Marius spreads his wings. "Fair enough." He shrugs. "My father won't last until another Gathering Shadows. He's gone fully blind and drools most days. The sickness is in every part of his body."

"Good to know."

He leaps into the air, black and red wings sprouting from his shoulders. He flies higher, gaining height as he leaves.

I watch him grow smaller in the sky, my heart hammering

and then turn to the others watching. I eye them all, a few slinking away to take off, but most stay.

"Those staying, I will remind you, any who are not high-born lineage without a contract, you are in contempt of Dark Law, and I can offer little protection against your death or claiming until I am in good standing again."

My eyes travel over them. A few more flee, but the majority remain motionless, listening and waiting. It pays to breed loyalty.

"Start moving rubble, find me clothes, find me things that aren't destroyed." The three-dozen remaining get to work, and I question how many lost their lives to the Magia. A quandary for another time I decide, and turn to Massimo, snarling. "Go. Get. Natalia."

Massimo takes off, and I stare, breathing hard at the mess. A pair of shadow beasts approach, carrying a man.

Hiro throws it at my feet. "Tough break, but I told you I was buying in and meant it. My loyalty isn't changing. Don't make me regret it."

Thames laughs. "I'll bet on Cal all day, baby, and the king isn't going to last until another Gathering Shadows. What do you want us to do with this?" He kicks at the body. "It's still breathing, found it in the hole we dug you out of."

I eye it, flipping it over with a single talon so its laying face up. I snort through my nose. "Tony. Magia. Keep it, don't use magic. The Magia absorb it, he'll send it back at you, and you can't shield your own magic so its deadly. I'll get answers from it later."

"Fine," Hiro grunts, crossing his arms. "What the fuck happened?"

I snap my tail in ire. "Why are you here?"

Hiro drops his chin toward his chest and glares from the tops of his eyes. "The Magia used the media reports to broadcast that they did this. You were reported as dead early this morning. We were informed, and we came to help you, you entitled ass."

I tip my head back, letting out barks of laughter. "They think they killed me?"

Thames gives a weak smile. "They're using this as a message that they are going to stand up against the Seraphinus, make us answer to their laws."

Tony stirs and sits up. He blinks, looking around and takes sight of me. "Fucking Mother." He scurries back on arms and legs beneath him. "What the fuck are you?"

"Dark Seraphinus and your worst nightmare. You pissed me off."

Hiro reaches down as he laughs, grabbing Tony under the arm. "Up you go, rat."

Tony bares his teeth. "I don't know who the fuck you all are, but if you don't back off, we're going to do to you what we did to Callahan."

I roar in humor. "I am Callahan you useless, annoying, weak speck of dust. You think you killed me? Are your kind really so stupid as to believe that would even hurt me?"

Tony gapes. "You can't be. You should be dead."

"I'm not, but your kind will be very soon."

"No. No, you're just another Darkling fuck, and I'm warning you, back off me, or you're next."

I snap at the air between us. "You survived. Why are you surprised I did?"

"I heal," he yells. "That explosion shattered my bones." He points toward the ruins.

"Not mine." I jerk my head to face Hiro. "Are you returning to Hapsford?"

Tony bolsters. "What the fuck kind of Seraphinus are you? I've never even seen renderings like you."

I slap him with my tail. "You won't. Now shut up. I'm trying to have a conversation."

Thames snickers, inclining his head. "That's where we're headed. We'll take this pig with us though, hold onto him, and you come see us when you're ready."

"Hey," Tony protests. "You can't just– Put me down! You can't do this!" He lets out a shrill scream and his annoying voice ceases.

I crouch and brace with one hand, eyeing the mess. Someone nearby stops. I point, "You, come here." I cock my head. "Who are you?"

"Laz."

"You look nothing like your father."

Laz nods with vigor. "I am aware. I'm small, but I'm not leaving. I'll help every way I can."

"You're high born, so you're safe under Dark Law from the death penalty for not having a contract, but be wary. You're young, so I doubt you realize staying with me while I'm disgraced paints a target on your back. Go." I jerk at the remains of my house. "Find me Thomas. He's Seraphim. I doubt he survived, but maybe."

Laz nods and leaves. I stay put, my heart slowing as I pant like a rabid dog. Time passes as my mind races. Disgraced.

The muscles from my head to the tip of my tail shudder. There are few things worse than being held in disgrace. The only thing that comes to mind is being dead, but I'm not dead yet. I still have a chance at redemption should I win the contest for the Dark Throne.

I've lost all my written contracts, although I appear to have a few loyal who will serve, and I still have the three contracts I wear, not able to be dissolved by the king. The problem with worn contracts was the immediate effects of contempt of the beholden. The contracted had no leniency, no forgiveness, and it can be deadly. The magic required to maintain them is taxing, never ending. I could have wasted all my magic's available power on writing all my contracts for as worn instead of written.

For a moment, I contemplate recalling the third contract I wear: Kowa. I dismiss the idea as quick as it came. I'm not that far-pressed just yet, and he has duties protecting my sister that still require his presence, even more so now that the Barraco name is disgraced.

Marius is right. I still carry the weight and respect of being a contender for the Dark Throne, and that means something. My cities, my loyal, my property and finances would all be up for grabs if I was disgraced under normal circumstances. All I can do is hope the webs of fate favor me and the Dark King dies before the next Gathering Shadows.

Massimo drops to the ground next to me. "We have problems."

I scoff. "We already had problems."

"Natalia and Ness are gone," he says. "There were dead Magia all over. Witnesses state Natalia smited them, so our women are at least safe for the moment wherever they are. Tallie's getting stronger. One looked like Dark took it down. Not sure about that, and human law enforcement is getting involved. You need to see the media reports. I don't like what I heard, and I had to remind them what respect is."

"I heard," I snap, my tail slamming into broken pieces of my house.

"They have a hunt for our women going, too."

"I'll deal with the Magia. They went too far, and they'll bleed for this."

There is no doubt that the world is watching this unfold and disgraced means I'm left with only those who voluntarily stand by me and the worn contracted I have. I have no Council rights, no legal protections, and no Dark King at my back. I am alone and exposed to the Light.

Pierre will see all this. My heart palpitations increase. Pierre will go for his daughter. Someone else touched my star. She is out in the world, unprotected and running. The worn contract is intact, which means legally she is still mine, disgraced or not, but while I'm in disgrace, our contract means nothing to another Seraphinus, and Pierre can ignore it without legal repercussion. She's in danger.

My Light source—my star is at high risk. I slam my fist into the pavement again to release pent up rage and then stand upright. I glare at a wincing Massimo. "Find Natalia. That's your job. It's your only job until she's at my side, do you understand me? I can't lose her."

Massimo nods, turning to the wreckage. "I'll find them. You deal with this. See if—"

"Stop talking. Go find her. I can manage this." I grunt then ask, "Thomas?"

Massimo shrugs, spreading his wings. "Thomas is," he glances around, "somewhere. I got him out of the house before it blew. He was bleeding but should be all right."

I breathe out easier. "Good. Now go."

"I'm sad I'm going to miss the bloodshed. I was looking forward to seeing how many of the fucks I could rip apart."

"Why are you still here talking?"

Massimo leaps into the air, wings flapping, and he calls out with a laugh. "Leave at least one for me."

CHAPTER 40

CALLAHAN

EIGHTH THISTLE'S DAY, WARMWAVE, 4049
SEVENTH MILLENNIUM

All day I spent working with those loyal enough to stay and serve but my numbers are dwindling. Another vassal disappears every time I turn around, more and more abandoning my side, sneaking away without a word. I try not to let that degrade my confidence as a leader. Most are low born, and without a contract are susceptible to losing their life according to Dark Law if they are without contract.

We shifted rubble, bringing organization to the chaos, trying to unbury and salvage anything that survived the explosion. There isn't much, but nothing rips me up inside as much as the loss of my trees. When I uncover the greenhouse, something snaps in my chest. Most are splinters and wood chips, a single tree surviving of the dozens I had curated. I re-pot it, but I don't have a lot of faith that it will take root.

Returning to human-esque form, I evict the humans from the most luxurious apartment building in this city much to their displeasure and my nonchalance at their grumblings. The building is my property, they merely pay to exist within it, and I am reclaiming it for my personal use. The humans mouth-off, yelling until I throw one out a window. The others become much more compliant, obeying my commands in haste.

With the building empty and at my disposal, I set my tree on the windowsill for sunlight and go for a shower. I order what loyal vassals that remain to gather up the remains of my shattered life and bring everything here. It has roof access and I've claimed the top floor, leaving the others to figure out their lodgings at their discretion. I've lost a day of my life to straightening this mess out, and I suspect I will lose more before the dust settles.

Massimo is still gone, which is bothersome. It means my star is still out of reach, and I'm realizing how much I have grown lax, relying on Massimo. I'd gotten comfortable, complacent, even lazy.

I let the Magia live when I should have wiped them out. They were in a room, and I should have bathed the walls in their blood. I didn't.

I stare at my tree on the windowsill as night descends on my building, crossing my fingers and every tendril of my Dark that it will cling to life.

I lost my edge somewhere. Maybe I deserve to be disgraced.

I go floor to floor, checking on my loyal and then head out into the street. I need a drink, more like a whole bottle. I stop in the first store I can find, select a two-hundred-year aged bottle of bourbon, and do the nice thing by stepping into a line of humans.

I'll buy the bottle and head back to the apartment building, sit on the roof, stare at the sky, and count the stars while I wait for my own to be brought back to me.

Waiting behind humans while they finish chatting up the store clerk, I curl my lip and stare at the wall. When they move out of the way, I set the bottle on the counter.

The clerk eyes me and smirks. "Nice to see your kind

paying for something. Must be scared with the Magia out there watching."

I tried to be nice, but as Natalia said, "can't help stupid."

I set my hands on the counter, meeting the young man's eyes. "Scared? You think I'm scared?" I laugh. "I'm not scared. I'm fucking pissed."

He shies away, his bravado faltering. "Yeah, well, you should be. They'll come after you if you don't follow the rules."

I smirk, pick up the bottle and twist the lid free as I stare the human in the eye. I take a drink, maintaining eye contact, and then head for the door.

"You have to pay for that!"

I shrug, pushing open the door.

"I'll fucking report you to them, asshole, and they'll blow you up next."

I halt, letting my hand fall from the glass to my side, the door swinging shut in my face. I pivot, taking another drink, wiping my mouth on the back of my hand as I step back toward the insolent clay pot.

"I'm curious. Are all humans this stupid these days?"

"They blew that asshole Callahan to the burning afters, and they'll do it to the next one of you that steps out of line."

"I am Callahan."

"What?"

"My name," I say, setting the bottle on the counter, swelling up, "is Callahan, and the only thing they sent to the burning afters was my fucking house and my tolerance for them."

The kid goes pale. "They said you were dead."

Leaning in closer, I growl, and the kid leaps back, shaking. I pull upright and chuckle. "Not very tough now, are you? You think the Magia are some kind of saviors? That, they're going to what? Teach me a lesson?" I smirk. "Maybe they did. I showed leniency, let them live, and they taught me that was a mistake, that *mercy* is a mistake."

The kid leans back even farther and lifts his hands. "Sorry, sir, I didn't mean it."

I splay my hands on the counter, my Dark forming elongated shadows from beneath my fingertips, stretching closer to the monkey, hungry to taste its blood. "You didn't mean to step out of line because you think the Magia offer some kind of protection?"

The boy flounders, stammering another apology. The courage he found has cracked, exposing the cowardly, rotten core. If the clerk had maintained the charade, I might have been impressed enough to walk away.

Eyeing the other humans watching, I decide to make use of my audience. "The Magia don't give a fuck about you or the rest of humanity. They're after power, and this little charade, blowing up my house? That they're in control? It's over." Grabbing the human by the front of his shirt, I yank him closer, forcing him to lean over the counter and the smell of piss fills the air. "I could kill you, but I won't, because I want you alive to witness when I tear their heads off and string them on every light pole in my city."

The boy is about to cry, his face splotchy with pink. He nods, trying to maintain composure. "Th–thank you, sir."

I grab his arm and wrench, bones snapping. The male screams at his arm bent backward, and I shove him away. "The next time, mind your fucking mouth."

I grab my bottle and leave, stalking out of the store, spreading my wings and flying to the roof of my building.

Sitting on the ledge, I stare across the city as vibrations of rage ripple through me. I have something else that needs immediate attention. I make a call to my oldest friend, Kowa. He doesn't answer, so I call again and again.

"Whoever the fuck this is, think twice and hang the fuck up, or I find you, and I rip your throat out."

I chuckle. "Good luck."

There's a pause. "Cal?" Kowa's voice is full of shock. "Fuck, what– New number?"

"Phone got blown to the burning afters."

Kowa snickers. "At least you weren't. You couldn't call before now? You left me wondering? Fucking prick."

Grinning, I take a drink. "Love you too."

"Gods," he sighs into the speaker. "Thank the gods you're alive. How bad?"

"I'm disgraced."

"Fuck."

"I'm still a contender," I say and shrug. "If the king dies before the next Gathering Shadows, I can still win the throne and get back to good standing."

"Thank the gods twice."

"Yes. How's Chiara?"

"Your sister is fine. Her words were something like, 'If he didn't survive that, then he deserves to be dead.'"

Rubbing my face, I can't help the grin. "Yes, I'm sure her delicate, bleeding heart was nowhere near as worried about me as you were."

"Or at all."

"Share the message, warn the others. They need to know they're in contempt if they choose to still serve."

"I will. They'll stay, probably, if you have a chance for standing again."

"Pass Chiara my greetings."

"Yes, sir."

Rubbing the side of my neck, I twist my lips to the side. Kowa is my oldest friend and the first contract I ever wore. It passed directly to me upon my father's death as a lineage-bound contract. "Take care of yourself and Chiara. I'll be in touch when I've cleaned this mess up."

"How are you planning to do that?"

"I don't fucking know." I disconnect the call and stare at the night sky.

I drink, the liquor sloshing around the glass, alcohol soothing my ire, but I need to decide on how to proceed.

Something whistles and pops in the sky, and I jerk as brilliant sparks of color shower in brilliant light against the inky back of night. The next one booms, and I tense to fight against a flinch. It pops and fizzles, golden glitter falling across the midnight background. I narrow one eye and chug the rest of the scotch before letting the bottle slip through my grip to the sidewalk below.

Another explosion of brilliant green goes off and I lurch from the wall to solid ground beneath my feet, gaping at the firework dissolving. Something is going on that shouldn't. Approval for this kind of thing needs to be requested and is only granted by me. I need enough time to make arrangements to leave town, and its only allowable when I decide its convenient for me to be elsewhere.

This city thinks I'm dead, or at the very least they believe they don't have to answer to me anymore. My blood begins to boil as I glare at another couple of fireworks exploding in the night sky. My hands begin to shake, so I grip them into fists and cock my jaw. They are dead wrong, soon to be just dead.

The door to the roof slams open behind me. I turn, Thomas and Laz jostling to be the first through the door. "He's here," Thomas yells, waving others through the door.

Laz approaches me, wincing at another firework popping. "It's a display for the Magia."

"What?" Another deep boom rips through the air, all of us making faces of disdain.

Thomas comes closer, leading the pack of my loyal. He grins and nods. "Go."

I narrow my eyes. "What?"

Laz says, "Go to the festival."

We all jump at the loud crack splitting the air. Thomas snarls at the sky, and then scowls at me. "It's fucking sick. They're celebrating your death."

One of my loyal steps forward, Narl cracking his knuckles. "You need to go show them you're alive."

I wave a finger at them all. "I still don't take fucking orders."

Thomas frowns. "Narl's right, so allow me to rephrase. We suggest you go, make a scene, assure them you're still in charge."

Laz steps onto the ledge, his wings spreading as dark tendrils from his shoulders. "Yes. Please do."

I scoff, taking hold of Laz's arm and yanking him to the rooftop. "Where do you think you're going?" I shove him closer to the rest of my loyal. "You and Thomas go nowhere. You couldn't throw a punch to save your life. Literally, had I not realized who you were, had it been anyone else that came round that corner, you'd be dead."

Laz laughs. "We want to see the show."

Thomas bobs his head. "Yes, definitely want to see the show. Please?"

He really is just a child still in every way, and while most of those staying are high born and sheltered from the law, he's exposed and could be put to death for failing to comply with having a contract. It makes my stomach twist.

I cock my jaw, turning as I flinch yet again at a firework. My head jerks to the side at the crack and fizzle. I step onto the ledge, my wings burning through my flesh to illuminate the world as I stare across the city skyline. "Where?"

Narl steps on the ledge next to me. "Gatalian Park, and the festival is being aired, so everyone will see you."

Selene snarls, "Prove to us there's a reason we stayed."

I scoff. "You know why you're here. I'm not killing Magia for any reason other than it will be my pleasure."

My loyal chuckle, but I duck my head into my shoulders at another firework.

Laz gives me a sad smile, his face to the sky. "I get it. That's like the smite Natalia set off." He shivers.

"I don't like smites," I say, curling a lip, "or anything like them that makes me think of them."

Sarina steps to my other side. "Which is why we give approval for this fucking shit and leave before it starts." She nods at me. "We stand with you. Now remind them why we follow."

I step off the edge and fly low between the building, doing my best to grit my teeth at the random booms followed by sparkling light. If the fireworks would just keep going and not stop, it would be easier, but the slow pace and periodic silence isn't helping.

Other figures fly with me as I glide through the city, tracking the source of the fireworks. I wrap my wings around me, falling from the sky. The ground dents beneath me and I snarl, grabbing the man getting ready to set another round off.

My Dark coils tight around him, and I yell, "Who said this was acceptable?"

He lifts his hands. "I'm just doing my job. Don't kill me. Please, don't kill me. My wife just gave birth to our first child—a girl. I have a daughter."

Shoving him away, I sneer. "This stops now. Go." I jerk my chin. "Not another single blip in the sky, or I kill everyone on this site." I lift my voice, glaring at the others milling around. "Do you all understand me?"

A female steps forward. "The city council signed off on this. We're celebrating in honor of the Magia."

"You mean my death?" I spread my arms. "I'm not dead. The Magia didn't kill me, clay pot, and they aren't being fucking honored for blowing up my house in the middle of the night like cowardly rats."

I reach out, my Dark streaking forward as vines to wrap around her. She screams and flails, but my magic fills in her orifices, muting her shrill shriek. Her flesh ripples as it digs through her, beneath her skin. Her lips turn black, her eyes popping from her skull. My Dark retracts into me, her body flopping to the ground, spasming with the onset of death.

I lift an eyebrow at the human and then turn to the others. "Pack it up. Go home." I turn to my loyal. "Yuri, will you stay and make sure they do as they're told? If they don't, kill the rest," I flick my eyes around to the humans gaping. "All of them."

"Will do." Yuri laughs, sticking his arms straight out, fingers laced and bent backward, knuckles cracking. "Can't wait for these fucks to decide they want to ignore orders. You get to have all the fun."

With a smirk, I leap into the air, wings beating as I sail toward Gatalian Park at the heart of the city, where a crowd is gathered. The ground is alive below me, crawling with humans, annoying and fragile, like ants on their hill.

I tip my head back and climb higher into the sky, wrapping my wings around me and plummeting to the ground once more, this time rolling straight into the middle of the foray.

When I land, pavement snaps, a small crater forming beneath me, and I set loose my magic, sending it out to fling and strangle those nearby.

It lashes out, wailing with shrill excitement in my mind as it destroys everything in reach, living or not. Humans and makeshift stalls for vendors are shattered. The clay pots scream and run as I stand, snarling at them. My loyal drop around me, and I stop, taking in the crowd gathering around me like a living ring.

I spin, addressing them all. "Let me make this perfectly clear to all of you ignorant, pathetic, annoying clay fools. I am Callahan Barraco, and I am not dead. This is my city, and you don't get to do anything without my permission, not even exist. So, go home, keep your heads down, keep your mouths shut and know disrespect will not be tolerated."

The crowd stands silent, and I glare at them, warning them not to speak out. There's no reason to kill these humans, and if they bow their heads, there won't be a necessary show of force. I can leave them breathing and collect the money they owe me for existing in my city.

A man shoves forward through the crowd and steps into the circle. I grip my fists, quelling with rage. One stupid human will make an excellent example for the rest.

"Where are they? The Magia?" I spin, slow, meeting eyes, phones lifted for recordings. Perfect. I look at the camera. "Come out, come out wherever you are, filthy rats."

Silence descends. I exchange glances with my loyal. They stand back, giving me room as I scan the crowd in a pivot. "Magia! You wanted to play. You have my full attention now. Let's play. Or are you only capable of hiding in the shadows like the infestation of pests you are?"

I spread my arms. "I'm waiting."

Turning in a quick circle, I laugh at my loyal and shake my head. "No? Fucking cowards." I scoff. "You're like children, throwing a tantrum because I took your toy from you and now afraid of the retribution. I'll wait, and for every fraction of a rune you don't crawl out of the gutters to face me, I kill a human."

There are mutters, and I turn toward the source, the crowd parting. A tall man, jacked up with muscles, comes striding forward. He pulls his shirt off and tosses it to the side. "We're no fucking cowards. We are the Magia, and your kind is going to have a couple hard lessons to learn, but we're going to teach you."

It is comical, the way he jumps and starts moving his limbs. I've never understood the removal of clothes to engage in a fight, and the thought of this overly muscular, practically human teaching me a lesson is downright humorous.

I lift my eyebrow with a smile. "I already have the best you offer, and it's not enough to bring me down."

The man spits off to the side. "Tallie's a pitiful pampered princess who never earned anything you Darkling shitbag. She was handed everything on a silver platter because of daddy, but not me." He takes a stance. "The rest of us aren't here, but I'll take you out myself."

Rolling my shoulders, I turn to my loyal. "I don't want your interference." I step toward the Magia, stopping in front of him to slide my hands in the front pockets of my pants. "I've watched Natalia take down my kind without help, and I believe she just took down several of yours. Do not tell me she is incapable. I doubt you will be able to do the same."

The guy smirks. "You talk too much, cocksucker." He steps into an open palm strike. I step to the side to avoid the shimmering attack, grabbing the male by his wrist, my other hand coming up under his elbow to snap it backward.

He roars with pain as I let go of his wrist, but I grab the back of his neck while he's reeling, forcing his head down to my knee coming up.

Stepping back, I let the man fall, and he's slow to get up. He swipes at a bleeding nose as I chuckle. "Natalia did better pulling her punches."

The Magia gets up, clutching at his broken arm.

I shrug. "Go on, heal. I'll wait."

The man bares his teeth. "That bitch is going to get what's coming to her for betraying us to you."

I tense, fury unfurling at the threat to my little star. My Dark hisses, coiling tighter around me, waiting for my consent to strike. I keep my word though, waiting for the Magia to heal. I am disgraced, but I won't be a disgrace. I'll follow the rules of engagement.

The broken arm snaps straight as it heals, and the man lunges at me, furiously punching. I dodge a couple of strikes, blocking one with my forearm, and using the momentum of yet another to rip the Magia into the center where everyone will be able to see. The man rolls, popping onto his feet.

My loyal back away, frowning but not getting involved. They linger, watching. They know who their alpha is.

The Magia glares, and I stalk toward him. He puts both palms together and then directs them at me. The air shimmers, and I tuck and roll to the side to avoid the hit.

There are screams and a line of humans go down. The Magia gapes, frozen with his jaw hanging. I get on my feet, ignoring the collateral damage and run straight for the Magia. He starts swinging, and this time I swing back.

The man stumbles from a hit I land to the side of his face but regains his senses, and we exchange a few whacks. The Magia counters, landing a strike backed by what I assume is Ki. It snaps my head to the side, the skin over my cheek beginning to pulse with heat.

I snarl, swinging back full force. My fist contacts a block, but the Magia is weak, his block shattering and my fist slams into the side of his head. He rocks, stumbling to the side.

"You're not as tough as you think you are," I roar. "None of you, and I'll rip you all apart."

The man wildly blunders, his arms throwing haymakers, which I duck. I swing and feign, enjoying the way he grows irritated. The man grunts with effort, pulling back and sending an open palm at me. I shield with magic and then lurch at the man.

I take him to the ground, pulling back and throwing my fist into the man's face over and over again. "You fucking cowards blow up my home in the middle of the night and then run and hide? You used detonators and charges. You didn't even fucking face me, and then you fucking tout that I'm dead? That you killed me in slanderous fucking bullshit that you're going to make us answer to you? We don't answer to anyone."

I keep wailing with full force as I roar down at the bloodied man. "We do what we want and be glad we let you fucking clay pots live. Pathetic...sorry excuses of what you once were... You're fucking vermin...cowards...and not one of you can take me down!"

My fist pounds into a pulpy mess of gore that was once a head. I sling my hand to the side to remove the mess of blood, brains, bone, and flesh.

Panting hard, I get to my feet, kicking at the body. I stand still, limbs trembling with fury as I scan the crowd. "Did I not tell you all to go home?" I meet Selene's eyes and jerk my head.

She grins wide, turning and grabbing the nearest human. The rest of my loyal follow, any human in their reach being ripped apart. The rest scream and scatter like cockroaches in the light. I whistle at my loyal, and they stop, not chasing after the fleeing humans. They all turn to me, bowing their heads.

I snarl, still breathing heavily from bashing the head and pure rage. One Magia is a start. The humans scampering into their little holes in fear is a good sign. This little moment is over, but I'm just starting. I'll make sure retribution is paid in full so brutally no one ever dares question me or my kind again.

I scan the faces of my loyal, each smiling. My eyes linger on Thomas, who's grinning ear to ear, bouncing on the balls of his feet. "That was fun!"

Smirking, I say, "It was a start, but we aren't done. This isn't over."

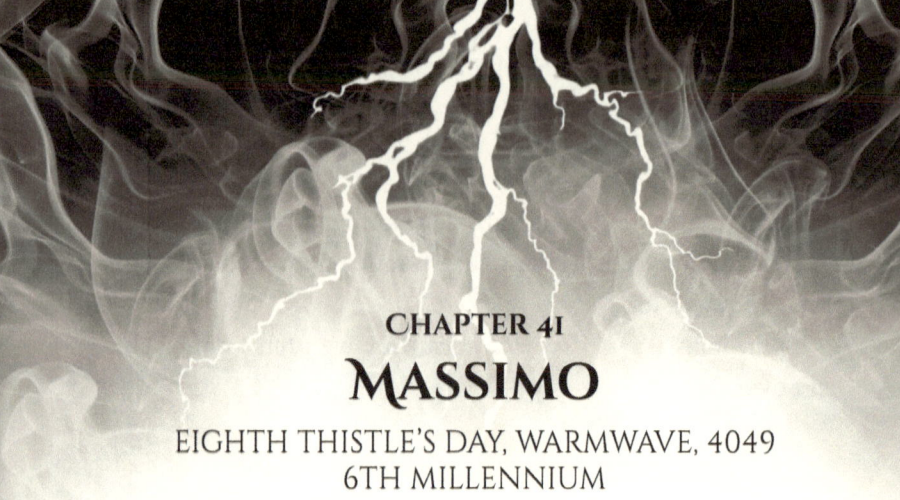

CHAPTER 41

MASSIMO

EIGHTH THISTLE'S DAY, WARMWAVE, 4049 6TH MILLENNIUM

I land in the parking lot, eyeing the two cars with white and red flashing lights as I retract my wings. The right catches and stings as my magic withdraws, the old wound infected by my father lingering for centuries now. If I ever find Tallie, I should ask her about trying to be rid of it once and for all.

I need to find her first, and that problem has become more complicated than I needed it to be. The cuff on Tallie isn't allowing me to switch the tracking function on. The system is reporting an error message and directing me to reset the device. Pulling my phone out, I confirm I'm at the correct coordinates, and then slip it back into the front pocket of my jeans.

Tallie smited the Magia on the spa lawn. Smites are akin to lightning. They hurt, but worse, they're electrical. I have no doubt that she short-circuited her cuff.

She made a charge at this location, so it's somewhat still a tracking device for that reason, albeit it's a terrible version of one. I know she *was* here.

All I can do is make the best of things and hope for luck in this mess. The positives are few and numbered. Vanessa and

Tallie weren't in the house last night, so they're alive. Tallie would have healed, I've seen her take worse and bounce back, but Vanessa might not have been able to recover. So long as they're breathing, I can find them, which means I can get them back.

Thomas is alive, too, and that's a relief. Normally, I hate direct orders from Cal, but I'm grateful for that one. I would have stayed to stand by his side and fight with him if he hadn't forced me to take Thomas. I question if Ness could have survived, but she can heal so it's a coin toss. I know Thomas wouldn't have.

My contract is intact, but it's a weak point. Even without a contract, I wouldn't leave Cal, and the contract means nothing to anyone but me and Cal.

I wrack my brain for another positive, but I'm not seeing one. Cal is disgraced, and our women are in the wind. We've lost everything we have worked to build, and its gut wrenching.

Sighing, I direct my thoughts into focus. This mess is going to be difficult to sort, but Cal will figure it out, and I can help by finding two very important women.

I fixate on the group of young men gathered around the officers. It's as good as any place for me to start.

I walk over, and the officers turn their eyes on me with suspicion. I lift my chin, crossing my arms as I come to a stop. "What's going on?"

One uniform snaps, "This is an official investigation, and you need to leave."

I smile. "I'll ask again. What's going on?"

"Didn't one of your kind just get blown to the burning afters? Shouldn't you be a bit more worried about following the rules now that the Magia are taking you out?"

Cocking my jaw, I consider for a moment. Humans are

forgetting their place. Reaching out, I grab one and fling him into a nearby officer's vehicle. The door dents and the man sprawls motionless on the pavement. I turn back to the other. "The only thing blown to the burning afters was our patience. I will ask one last time. What's going on?"

One of the men in average attire rams his fingers into his hair and grabs a fistful. "That's where I knew them. It was driving me crazy. Dude, they were the chicks on the news."

Another goes pale. "Shit, yeah, they're the two chicks the Magia are after. We're lucky we didn't get murdered."

That's proof I'm in the right place, but I frown. "The two from the news were here? You're certain?"

"Oh, fuck, yeah." One of the guys holds his phone up, displaying pictures of Vanessa and Tallie. "That's definitely them."

The officer scrawls something on his notepad. My Dark snarls, curling around it to dissolve the paper. The officer throws his hands in the air. "Stupid Seraphinus fucking bull-shit. I'm just tryin' to do my job, you know?"

I point a finger at him, my Dark wrapping around my wrist with a whine in my head. It's acting weird, but I don't have time to deal with it. "Anything involving these two women, don't. Don't do anything, or I take your head off." I turn my back on the officer to focus on the group of men. They're young, but all humans look young until they're wrinkled and hairless. "Why are officers here?"

A male groans. "Damn. She was hot—got her number. I thought I had a chance."

I eye him. It doesn't matter which woman he's referring to. "You don't. Where are they?"

"They left. Stole my car. That's why I called the officers." He motions to my back.

I lift my eyebrows. "They stole your car?" I look the men over, scowling that none of them are bleeding. "How?"

The guy shrugs. "Got my keys, I guess. She sat on my lap. The keys were in the way, so I put them on the table, but now they're missing, and so's my car."

Narrowing my eyes, I decide if he touched Tallie, that's a secret to keep from Cal. If it was Nessy, I'll rip his guts out. "Which she? Blonde or black hair?"

"Blonde one."

A secret to keep from Cal then. If he touched Vanessa, I was going to have to go chasing after our women covered in blood. "Tell me what happened."

"We were hanging out, having fun. She said she just had a breakup, and then she tried to drink two drinks at once. She dumped them down her shirt and fell out of my lap."

Another one of the males laughs. "Dude, it was great. You should have seen it. Straight see-through, no bra."

I try not to laugh and fail. That would be a distraction. Cal would be pissed, probably use his magic to dig out the eyeballs of every human who saw the show, but that's funny. "Let me guess, they left right after?"

The male nods. "Yeah, but she gave me her number."

"Probably fake. Toss it." I shrug without care. "Make, model, year of the vehicle they have, now."

"You know..." The officer scratches his head and steps next to me. "I could have just written this all down and done my job while you did your thing."

Baring my teeth, I shove words through them. "I strongly advise you don't do your job. You aren't reporting this." I scan the name on his uniform. "Officer Julius."

"If it doesn't get reported, I can't get any insurance money," the guy says, frustrated, putting his face in his hands and grinding the heels of his palms into his eyes. "Damn, this night keeps getting worse."

Dragging a hand down my face, I sigh. The kid needs a break as much as I do. "Fine, report the theft, but put my name. Now give me the vehicle details."

The officer asks, "What's your name?"

"Massimo Verta," I say without looking from the guy. My contractor's disgrace still doesn't expose me to any comeuppance from humans. Vanessa and Tallie might not understand why humans and their laws don't affect us, but that's not my problem. "Car details, now, or I start killing your friends."

"4047 Silver Yango Droid."

I nod and point at the officer. "Massimo Verta and the girls were never here, or I come for you, got it?"

The officer crosses his arms. "I can't wait for the Magia to—"

My magic and I both snarl, my hand and Dark wrapping around his throat. "The only thing the Magia did was piss off Callahan—piss us all off, and we're going to paint the city with their blood for it. You all need to remember who's in charge. Callahan was in that house when it blew, several of us were, and the only thing we're suffering from is a high level of irritation." I shove the man back. "Now reporting this is going to get back to the Magia, and they're going to hurt those women. So, report it stolen under my name, so the kid gets his money. You all shut your fucking mouths, and I get to go home without blood on me. Deal?"

The boys nod as the officer straightens. He inclines his head but sneers. "Seriously, you were in that house? There's no way."

I tip my head back and laugh. "You want to kill us? Be one of us, and even then, there are some of us that are too strong to be taken down." I turn to the boy. "Plate number, identification number, and how much fuel did you have?"

Entering the information into my phone, I snap pictures of the boys and then the officer, saving all the information I need. "Not one word about the women in any report," I warn the officer again. "Listen to me, not. One. Word. The Magia are hunting for them to hurt them."

He winces. "What's so important about them?"

I smirk and spread my wings. "Think real hard about why a man gets protective over a woman." I clap him on the shoulder.

He stumbles to the side, grimacing. "Really?"

I lift my hands. "Not my fault you're fragile and weak."

Leaping into the air, I scroll through the file to study the information. I've lost countless phones this way, dropping them mid-flight, but time is of the essence. Looking up the vehicle, I determine fuel economy and calculate how far the women can get before another charge hits Cal's account.

There's no way for me to know how far the vehicle can get, given the energy regeneration systems, but I have a guess. For now, all I can work with is where they've been and guesswork. I assume two numbers: one if Tallie is driving, erring on the side of caution, and then a second much lower number if Vanessa is driving. That woman is nuts, and I suspect she drives recklessly.

I plot out possible fueling stations as I glide through the air, aimless until I have a destination to reach. There are too many options for me to search, and waiting for a charge to hit will put me too far behind. I need to know what direction they went.

I make another futile attempt to pull up the location of the tracker, but I get the same error message about requiring a reset. I try to restrain myself from crushing the electronic device in my hand as I scowl. Resetting the cuff is easy but requires the band to be tangible to accomplish. It's inconvenient that the women have funds but no locator. My job would be infinitely easier if it was the other way around.

This situation is developing in the worst possible way. The women are alive. That's the positive I need to focus on. They have funds, which is annoying, but it is a positive. They aren't stranded and easy prey for the Magia also hunting them. The miserably unfortunate downfall of that positive note is that it also means they can run from me, too.

Slipping my phone away before I lose my precious information, I sail through the air at a leisurely pace. I know very little about Vanessa or Tallie. They are Magia, and they both left the organization to serve Cal, each for their own reasons. Mostly, Vanessa followed Tallie, which reminds me that Tallie is likely calling the shots.

Any family or friends the women had were discarded with the Magia, so I'm unconcerned by the possibility of someone helping them. They won't go to anyone who would notify the Magia.

I'd spent a couple of days with Vanessa, the first when I was trying to find a use for her, a reason for Cal to draft a contract for her, and I gave her little heed. The second was the day before I'd bundled them into a car and sent them off to the spa. Vanessa had practically hung off me as I dragged her around the estate to complete my duties, and then again, the other night at the spa, I'd gotten a rune with her. She'd talked about the codex and translating. I'd seen a different side of her, an intelligence I hadn't noticed before as she raved about the Seraphin language.

The complexity of my language is something I'd loathed learning when I was young, but she'd beamed about it. I'd been glad to hand off that project when she signed Cal's contract. She likes history and language and fun noodles. None of that is useful, and she's a distraction.

I focus on Tallie. She's stubborn, hard-headed, willful and independent, and she wanted to burn Cal's contract out, run away and go live on a beach. The coast is to the east, and that's the first useful idea I've had.

With no other viable option that I can think of, I turn and pick up speed, rolling my shoulders with urgency and following the main parkway toward the coast. Doubt creeps into my mind, but I can't conjure another option for the women to take, so I hold fast to my course.

With any turn of luck, I'll catch them on the road or at a fueling station. I can turn them around and bring them home where they belong. Then I'll be back in time to rip the spines out of the Magia that blew up my home before Cal kills them all first.

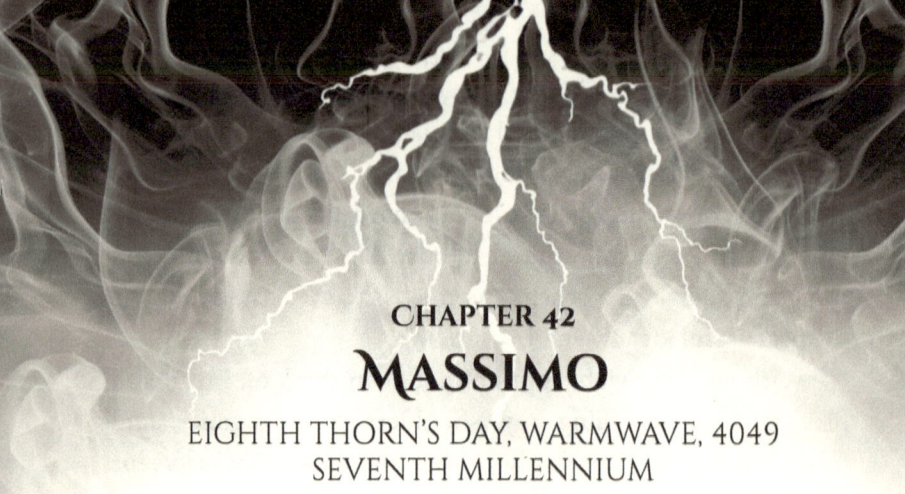

There's been no sign of our women. The make and model of the vehicle are common. It's a crappy, cheap automobile easily purchased by humans. I've destroyed a few trying to get a look at items inside to determine the owner, and I've scared plenty of humans along the way. The first few times were fun, but it lost the entertainment factor and became an annoyance.

I make a quick stop, scarfing a dozen donuts on the roof of a crappy diner while I give my shoulders a moment of rest. Flying all night has left the muscles sore and burning with fatigue, and I've still got runes to go.

Pulling open the photos, I swipe through a few I took of Vanessa. In the kitchen she struggled to reach something on the top shelf. The woman is tall, but she was still on her tiptoes, arm reaching. I smirk, recalling the pathetic, adorable little hop she did trying to reach the snack she wanted. She'd pouted at me after I saved the image, her full lower lip stuck out as she whined about wanting that particular food.

It's a great picture of her butt, her wide hips and full curves on display. The pathetic mewl she gave me wrapped me around her whims. I would have given her anything she wanted at that moment–bent her over the counter and railed her if she'd asked me to.

I was disappointed. It was the only time she hadn't made a request or offer, too busy consuming food with a grin.

I move to the next image of her, sitting on the bed in that spa, legs crossed and a notebook in her lap. She'd been tapping that pen against her knee and chewing her lower lip.

I'd wanted to sink my teeth in it.

She had been absorbed in translating. Her eyebrows are pulled together, the left with a scar through it. The small, rounded nose and her big brown eyes give her an innocent face, but she's got a mouth on her. I curl my lip, recalling her quips about screwing one of the resort employees.

I'm irritated that someone else was letting their hands explore her body. When I get her back under Cal's thumb, I'm going to enjoy accepting her offer of intercourse. I want to know if her brown skin is as soft as it looks, if her black hair is as silky as it shines.

She said she wanted to be the reason I touched myself that night. I hadn't known how to tell her she already was the night before, and the one before that, and–

The tracker app throws an alert. I open it, but it's still presenting an error code. There are new charges, though.

I wipe powdered sugar off my fingers against my jeans and pull up the details of the charges through the bank account. Plugging the fueling station into the search function on the map app, I track where our women are. The station is to the north of Niche.

"Fuck me."

Our women went south. I flew east all night. I figured they

had less than three hundred miles, and they'd gone nearly five hundred.

This is a nightmare. I run my hand down my face and stand, kicking the empty donut box off the ledge to the sidewalk below for someone else to clean up and scowl at the southern horizon of the sky.

Cal isn't going to just kill me; he's going to rip my wings off and peel my flesh. Rolling my shoulders, I drag my fingers along the aching muscles between them. As much as I don't want to, I call Cal.

It rings three times, and then the call connects. "Tell me where you are, and I'll come get her."

Wincing, I turn my face to the sky. "I can't."

Cal's growl comes through clear. "Why not?"

I shake my head. "The tracker is throwing an error. It needs to be reset, but until then, it's not reporting her location. I went with an idea. I was wrong. I need help–don't," I flick my wrist. "Don't yell at me right now. I just need to know where would she go? You've spent more time with her than me."

Cal is silent but even quiet, and through the speaker, I can feel his simmering frustration.

I kick at the stone beneath my feet and sigh. "I need to know so I can go get her–both of them. I'll bring them home where they belong," I say in a quiet voice, ignoring the lump in my throat. "I thought the beach. I went east. I was wrong."

"Which direction did they go?"

"South, they're just outside—"

"Izul."

I laugh at the sky. "No way are they headed to Izul. That doesn't even make sense."

"Talia is headed to Pierre."

"She wouldn't," I yell into the phone. "She doesn't know, she thinks she's—"

"Stop talking. Go fetch." Cal roars. "Now! Before she gets there."

"Think of something else," I snarl. "I'll head south, but that's insanity. She doesn't know what she is, and she doesn't fucking know that bastard is her father."

"You're answer—where she's going?" His voice is lower, but it's dripping with acid. "It's Izul. Stop her. If she goes in, I can't reach her."

"She's not going to Izul." I rub my mouth. "She's not working for him. Stop with the paranoia already. It's not cute anymore."

He chuckles. "My little star is a fucking idiot. She thinks I'm dead. We both know she's capable of killing our kind, and she's believing others are as well. The Magia are hunting for her, and she's looking for a safe place. His magic will call to hers."

"*Similis*," I sigh, glancing around.

"Yes, the call of like to like, and she won't even know it. He offered her a place in Izul. It will be safe from the Magia. That's where she's headed."

"Fuck. I hate that place, even going near it."

"Go get my fucking star!" Cal screams through the phone.

I jerk the phone away from my ear due to his sheer volume. I stare at the screen as the call disconnects. Things are getting worse and worse every rune that passes. All I'm missing is the cherry on top, like burns from a trip to the Light capital. I'll have them soon enough.

Humans like the light and the suns. They go outside to enjoy them. Their skin turns brown. It's weird. My skin is already dark brown, but anywhere near the Light leaves blisters and burns of deep blue. I hate the Light.

I slip my phone into my front pocket and stretch my arms and shoulders. The muscles my magic links to are pulsing at even the slightest movements. As fatigued as they are, they have several thousands of miles to fly, and I'm behind the starting line by hundreds. Jumping into the air, I take flight, lifting into the sky and heading toward the rising suns due south.

CHAPTER 43

CALLAHAN

I hang up, throw my phone to the mattress next to me and stare at the ceiling. My star is on her way to Izul, running straight to Pierre. I'm not going to just lose her. She's going to the Light, to a man who will use her for his gains and give her nothing in return. The Light are a bunch of hypocritical assholes that claim honor and righteousness, staring down on the Dark for our brutal honesty about what we are and want.

The most obnoxious thing about the Light is everything. They're rigid, formal, and grant merit based upon name and age. I've never heard one spit a vulgar word beyond animal in reference to me or my kind, and they preach respect and manners while stabbing each other in the back.

Natalia won't fit in, but they'll cram her into their ways. Pierre will destroy her.

I lift my forearm over my face, frowning at my contract with Natalia ingrained in my skin. It's at peace, so I know she's not in immediate danger. I re-add the line about being home into the contract, but the words puff up and begin to sting. Removing the line, I tuck my arm behind my head.

399

Natalia's too far out of reach for me to change her contract now, or I'd order her to return, but even magic as strong as mine has its limits. If she reaches Izul and goes inside, I'm not sure what will happen to the piece of my magic sealing our contract in her skin. That far from me, it will be weak, and under the Light, it's going to struggle, maybe die.

Light burns out the Dark until it doesn't exist.

"Fuck," I rub my face.

My priority right now is Natalia. My star, my Light source, is not something I can afford to lose. The king has allowed me to remain a contender, and I can only assume his belief that he'll not live until another Gathering Shadows is the reason. Natalia equals necessity. I need her at my side, safe and sound and useable.

Pierre is her father, his heritage carried in her, and the likeness of their magic will call to each other. It's no doubt why Pierre tracked down Natalia's mother to confirm their relation. It's how he knew she was his to begin with.

Natalia turning down Pierre to stand at my side is an intrigue given that fact. Had I been thinking straight a month ago, I would have realized that my star was wound so tight in the Dark with me that she ignored the call of like to choose me.

Natalia had chosen me, and I'd doubted that. To be fair to my temper, Pierre is under my skin in the worst way for what he did.

An overwhelming desire to garner advice from my father grips me, but I'm glad he's not living. I couldn't bear to see his disappointment at my disgraced status. Everything he worked for, I took it and threw it away, destroying his good name.

My father raised me to know if I want something done, use a vassal. If I want something done without the possibility of mistakes, do it myself.

After checking with my loyal, leaving commands with

Thomas to water my tree and that they all spend their time tracking and locating the Magia but not to engage until I've returned, I head to the roof.

Taking flight, I call Massimo.

The call connects, wind rushing past the speaker, Massimo breathing hard. "What?"

"I'm heading south. Give me what you have."

"I can do this."

"I'm not trusting that. I'm not taking chances. I need her back."

There's a pause, and Massimo chuckles on a pant. "Coming from the man who was ready to kill her."

"Don't talk back."

Massimo laughs under his heavy breathing. "I'm not stopping. Your wings are bigger, and you're stronger. You'll catch up. I'll meet you in Harvestend. Tallest roof you can find, call me when you get there." The call disconnects.

I LAND on the tallest roof in Harvestend. I stay in a crouched position, breathing hard as I glare around for Massimo. He's lighter and had a head start. He should have been here before me.

I eye the northern horizon behind me, the sky dark, the suns gone from the world. As much as the muscles in my neck and back are burning, I don't have time to rest or wait for Massimo. It's annoying that he's not here.

Stepping to the ledge, I let gravity carry me down before my wings catch the air. Taking off straight south, I dig my phone out to call Massimo. "I can't wait for you."

"I didn't stop." He pants heavily in my ear. "Our women hit Castler."

"Fuck," I huff for air. "Where are you?"

"Uh," he pants, wind rushing. "Just outside Hapsford? Passed it a few fractions back, I think."

"I don't want 'I think,' I—"

"Shut the fuck up, you pissy bastard. I'm going as fast as I can. I think my wings are going to fall off."

I laugh. "Mine too. I don't fucking care. Just get there. Get my star back for me."

"I'm working on getting them back, but don't get that tone with me. This shit is your fault, and I'm cleaning up your mess again." He stops, breathing hard, and continues in a hissing, breathless snarl, "My fucking body hates me right now, so I want you to take that self-righteous Light-like anger and shove it up your tight ass if you can pull the stick out of the way first because I haven't stopped moving since I saw you last."

I grin. "Baby, talk dirty to me some more."

"You're fucking nuts," Massimo wheezes. "Oh, fuck me."

"Get me Natalia, and we'll talk."

"I get it now."

"What?"

"My thing."

"Yeah, it gets hard, you stick it in something, slam it in and out until it spits." I chuckle through heavy breathing. "Feels good. How old are we, and you're just figuring that shit out?"

"Almost four hundred. We're not having the birds and bees talk. You're not my father."

I snort through my nose and inhale hard. "As if your father ever had that talk with you."

"He did. It was something along the lines of rape women and don't fuck men."

"Sounds about right. What's your thing?" I take an opportunity to try to catch my breath, waiting for him to answer as I begin heading over the Arid Planes.

"It's weird."

"I have a thing too. It's not that weird. Fun to play with. Thought we covered that."

Massimo might be laughing. It's hard to tell. "Nessy's under my skin. Got a thing for her."

"You're into women? Wasn't sure, not sure if you even knew you had a thing or how to use it."

"Like you give me time?"

"So, it's my fault you've never had sex?" I try to ignore the burning, tearing sensations in my back. My shoulders are aching, the muscles threatening to tear.

"I'm ignoring that," Massimo wheezes. "I know I have a dick. I know how to use it."

"You finally realized you have a thing and want to stick it in Ness?" I chuckle and drag in ragged breaths. "You're growing up so fast."

Massimo makes weird breathing noises like he's sucking in hard and struggling to breathe. "Been trying to figure out why. She's fucking nuts. But I get it now. She sounds like you, and that's fucking weird."

"You want weirder? I have a thing for Pierre's Light Seraphim daughter." I get pelted with sand from a dust storm and turn my face to the side. "I'm trying to kill myself to get her back, and I can't figure out if I'm going to hate fuck her, rip her head off, or make her a queen."

"I thought we were passed the killing part."

I grin. "She bought in that I was dead. What the fuck kind of shit is that?" I barrel roll to avoid a pack of birds and push my wings harder, trying to go faster.

"You've got a new reason to kill her? I'll stick her somewhere else till you calm down again. Should I set up a safe house for regular use?"

"Take my star from me again, and you don't get choices this time. I will fuck you into submission."

"It'd be the first time I get off in a decade without using my hand, and we'd finally consummate this shit." Massimo roars with laughter. "Do you even know how to fuck a man?"

I struggle to breathe, laugh, and almost drop my phone. "Can't be hard to figure out. Where are you?"

"Froxton. Want me to tell you what I'm wearing next?"

"No, any new charges?"

The speaker crackles for a minute with the sheer force of wind. Massimo gets back on the line. "Some restaurant. They stopped for food, bought us time."

"They eat more than we do. How long ago?"

"Pending, hit twenty fractions or less ago. Anything over usually clears."

"I'm headed to Izul. I'll demand Pierre's audience, keep him busy while you find them. There's one road in. You hit that."

"Where the fuck are you?"

I scan the horizon, civilization glowing in the distance. "South edge of the plains. Braviot."

Massimo wheezes again through a chuckle. "You've got it bad. I didn't think you'd make it to Harvestend before I hit Castler."

"Pierre's daughter. She's still breathing. Didn't kill the Magia cause they're her family. Tearing muscles trying to stop her from getting to Izul. Need more proof about my weird thing? I'll be fucking willing to suck Pierre off if I have to, to get her out of Izul if we fail."

"You're fucking losing it."

"I mean, I'm disgraced. Why not get on my knees? I'd drag teeth. I didn't say he'd enjoy it, and I'm not swallowing."

Massimo chokes and wheezes. "And we're back to my weird thing where I want to put my dick in a version of you with boobs. I'll see you at the gates."

I slip my phone away, breathing in through my nose and mouth for maximum efficiency of air intake as I leave the plains behind. I have hundreds of miles to clear in very little time. I dig deeper, muscles screaming in protest, but I pick up speed.

PACING, I stare down the guard at the front gates of Izul. My hands are pressed palm to palm, my pointers against my lips. I squint in the brilliant glow emitting from the city and pretend I'm narrowing my eyes in a menacing scowl at the man. He's watching me with disdain, and I mirror the disgust.

I've been waiting over a rune for the guard who was sent to fetch Pierre to return. My patience is wearing thin, my Dark snarling and coiling around me. It's as annoyed as I am with our location and the continuing lack of our personal star. It's hungry.

Massimo drops from the sky next to me. I glower at him sans Natalia, my magic hissing and lashing out at him. It's been far too long since I have fed on Natalia, and I will have to feed soon.

Dodging my Dark, Massimo sneers at me, but I snap, pointing to the road to indicate him doing another sweep.

Massimo pulls his wings away as he crosses his arms. "I've flown it three times now and—"

"I don't fucking care, keep going."

"I decided to get smart and head over to Castler. I checked the restaurant where they ate."

I stop, heart stalling and my Dark whines, tightening around me. Inhaling sharply, I ask in a raw voice, "And?"

His face is grim. "Vehicle is there, all identification matches, but our women are gone. I checked inside. They exited the building two and a half runes ago and haven't been seen since."

Curling my lip, I turn to the captain and snarl. "Go get Pierre."

Pierre's voice calls out with joy, "There's no need to get nasty." He appears from around the corner, approaching the gate with a wide smile. "Hello, Callahan."

I square my shoulders. "Give me Natalia."

Standing on the other side of the gate, Pierre slides his hands into his front pockets and rolls to the balls of his feet, stretching taller. The smugness radiating from him is palpable. "I will grant you an accolade of bravery for coming here and making demands."

"Piss off," I sneer. "Give me what I really want."

Spreading his legs with hands on his hips, Pierre chuckles. "I heard your request for my presence, and I came in person as a courtesy given our history, but I expect the same courtesy in kind."

"Fuck you and your bullshit. I want Natalia," I step closer, gripping my fists. "Now."

"Intriguing," Pierre says, glancing up and rubbing his chin. When he meets my gaze again, it chills my blood. "If she was so willing to serve, why would she take the opportunity to leave?"

"Don't start with me about her stupidity. I'm not in the mood. Go get her. She'll gladly return to me once she sees me."

"I see," his eyes dance with contained mirth as his smile

grows. "You think you hold some kind of charm for her? I doubt that as she took the first opportunity to run from you."

"She wasn't running from me. She thinks I'm dead."

Pierre chuckles. "She believes the reports of your death, yes. I was hopeful of your demise but suspected it as falsehood. As grand as it would have been, I doubted the Magia would be so capable. However my daughter seems to be gullible."

"Yes, she's a fucking moron," I snap. "Go get her."

"I do not answer to you." Pierre's smile turns cold, voice hardening. "Even if we were alike, I would not answer to you, and you would do well to remember that."

My muscles quiver with rage, my Dark thrashing for freedom. I clamp down on it, demanding its compliance, but I'm barely containing it. If it takes control, I'll shift and that will only cause further problems. Pierre will see it as a sign of attack, something I remind my magic as I try to restrain it.

I snarl at it, *"Pierre will use it against us.'"*

It snarls right back, *"Kill him."*

"We need to use our words, not our claws." Unhinging my jaw, I work it back and forth. "She is under a contract, and I have every right to claim her, even take her from you."

Pierre eyes me with disinterest. "Dark Law states once you are disgraced all contracts are void. You are in disgrace, are you not?"

"Written contracts are voided, but Natalia's contract is worn, bound not in ink, but in my magic which cannot be undone. The contract stands."

Pierre shrugs, crossing his arms. "My lessons were long ago, but I believe Dark Law states that while those contracts cannot be broken by your king because of the root in personal magic, they are irrelevant once an individual is disgraced."

Massimo grabs my shoulder and yanks me away as I growl. He uses it to leverage himself closer to the gate, forcing himself between me and Pierre. "There are two women within your gates, and both will want to see us. Please fetch them."

"Manners at last." Pierre waves a hand as he chuckles. "I am impressed that even one of you dogs can manage that. Alas, I'm disinterested in obliging."

Massimo swells up and leans in close. "Let them decide for themselves. Tell Vanessa and Natalia we are here to see them and allow them to make their own choices."

Pierre cocks his head to the side. "As he allowed her to make her own choices?"

The haze of rage diminished, I step next to Massimo. "I have rarely forced Natalia into doing anything. All you have to do is tell Natalia I'm alive and she'll come to me."

"You would think that, but alas, I'm sorry, boys. I'm afraid my daughter is furious with you for not telling her the truth that I am her father."

I laugh. It's unexpected, bursting out of my chest and tearing my throat. "You're a bad liar."

"Fine." Massimo puts a hand on my shoulder. "I simply request you fetch Vanessa."

Pierre's face turns putrid.

Massimo flashes his teeth in faux humor. "She has no reason to be angry with me, and I'll wager she'd be glad to see me."

Pierre studies him and shrugs. "I'll consider passing along your message. You are welcome to wait here, but I don't know how long it will be." He grins as he begins a slow backpedal away from the gate. "I should thank you. Your demands led me to follow the call and find her."

"You fucking Light bat," I yell, throwing fire at the gate.

A shield of black magic blocks the attack, and Massimo grimaces. "Don't," he snarls under his breath. "You'll get called to the Council and there will be no hearing, just death."

I shrug off Massimo and step toe to toe with the gate. "She belongs to me by choice. I hold a contract, and by hiding her from me you are breaking the accords."

Pierre stops his slow gait, crossing his arms. "She is my daughter, and I will protect her, even from herself, if necessary. But as my daughter, she is the Light, and Light belongs here in Izul. I have broken no laws, no rules given your stature, and I have even offered a courtesy to you by answering your visit. I by no means had to do so. I've afforded you luxuries beyond what you are owed, and far beyond what any animal deserves."

I can't win this fight, and despite what I said about sucking him off, I doubt he'd take the offer if I even made it. I'm more likely to bite that part of him off at the moment anyway. I'll do something better.

With a smirk, I say, "Allow me to provide you a courtesy in kind. Do not lie to Natalia."

I know damn well he won't heed my advice. In fact, he'll do the opposite. He'll lie, and I don't know how, but Natalia will learn the truth. The one thing above all else that Natalia hates is being lied to and manipulated.

Pierre smiles. "The Dark is vile and grotesque. Likely any advice you offer is as worthless. Good evening, boys."

He turns and saunters away. I grip the bars harder, the metal creaking as it crumples under my grip. I watch him disappear from sight and then turn to Massimo, who's staring, half hungry, half forlorn, through the bars, lost in contemplation.

My friend has a thing for the first time I can think of, and it's gut-wrenching to realize he is aching, too. Turning my back on the gate, I snap like a dog at the guard, who lurches away, slack-jawed.

His terror almost lifts my spirits, and I push my fist against

409

Massimo's shoulder. "Move. Get out of the Light before it burns you."

Massimo jerks to life, and we walk away from the gates. Together, we come to a halt, staring at the nothingness before us. "Now what?"

"Plan B." I spread my wings and take off.

Massimo joins me in the air, leisurely gliding at my side. "What's plan B?"

"I have no fucking idea."

CHAPTER 44

CALLAHAN

I land on the gravel drive, the wrought iron gate to my back. Massimo hits the ground next to me, standing tall as I eye the expansive estate manor before us.

A female stalks out from the covered wrap-around porch, pacing closer with a raised eyebrow. "Welcome to Haps End of Hapsford."

I peel my eyes from the grand house, gaping at the woman. "It has a name?"

Massimo leans in toward me, whispering, "Why didn't we name ours?"

"Because it was inevitably going to be blown up by cockroaches." I clear my throat and meet the female's eyes. "Is Hiro here?"

She's tall and broad shouldered, her features pinched with mistrust sewn into them. She inclines her head. "Welcome, sir."

As she walks away, I return to inspecting the house. It's built of gray stone, sprawling and grand architecture. I didn't realize how pathetic my home had appeared.

Hiro comes jogging down the steps, followed closely by Thames. He grins but shakes his head as I move to meet him. "About damn time, Cal. Your pig is a nuisance."

I cock my head, ears perking up. "Pig? Oh." I had forgotten about Tony. Maybe he can help. "That thing might be useful. Where's it at?"

"Secured." He waves at the house. "Basement."

"May I?" I ask with glee, pointing at the house.

Thames laughs. "Sure thing, baby. I'll show you the way."

We take a few steps to the house, Massimo stopping next to Hiro. "Beautiful home."

Thames cranes his head to call over his shoulder, "Thank you. It has been in my lineage for ages."

Mass jerks his chin. "Need me?"

"No," I call back, leaving him with Hiro and to their vices.

Inside, I follow Thames to the back of the house, winding through an open floor plan of massive rooms and a single door. The world changes from grandeur to black brick and mortar. The light of day is gone, the air growing dank and damp as we descend. Our footsteps echo on the hewn steps as we slip further beneath the house.

The walls twist and the steps take a turn. Another half set of steps down and we are on level ground, the air full of the dark. The space opens into a massive room. It's a huge square with several black iron doors.

I stop, taking a moment to close my eyes and inhale the dark with my head tipped back. "I need one of these in my life."

Thames laughs. "This one is yours to use at your whim."

"Yeah, but..." I stretch my neck, opening my eyes as I face him. "When I rebuild, I'm definitely adding this on."

Thames jerks his head. "This one, over here."

I step to the door Thames opens. He shakes his head, gesturing inside. "Needed a little extra help holding this one. For a piggy, he's a bit strong. Manipulates our magic, and it heals."

"They're annoying like that, but it's what makes Natalia so effective."

Thames crosses his arms, tilting his head with a frown. "Where is the lightning bug?"

I snap my teeth at him, shoving my way to the other side of the door. My star is locked up in the Light, and it will burn out the web of Dark I wound her in. I rub my contract with Natalia, glaring at the back wall of the cell.

A collapsed form is curled on the stone floor. As I step toward it, chains rattle.

Tony lifts his head, shoving to a sitting position and baring his teeth. "You're supposed to be dead."

I scoff, crouching before him and steady myself with the tips of my fingers. "I want information. I'm not in a good mood, so don't talk and give me an excuse to break you. I'll gladly take it."

Sneering, he tips his head back against the wall. "Where's Nat?"

I reach out and grab him by the jaw, wanting to feel the bone break beneath my fingers, but I hesitate. A human can't speak with a broken jaw, but then again, this filth isn't human. I grip harder, bone splintering beneath my touch.

Tony gurgles in pain, thrashing as I retract. "You don't call her Nat. You call her Natalia or Tallie."

The bones snap, Tony wiggling his jaw as it reforms with nasty crunching sounds echoing around us. His eyes narrow, and he rubs the side of his face, a manacle secured around his wrist, links clinking as he moves. "Fuck you." He spits, a spray of spittle misting my face. "I'm not telling you fuck all, and I'll ask again, where is she? She wouldn't stand for this treatment of me."

"It's cute the way you think she cares about you." I stand, studying the Magia bound in chains, cleaning my face with the collar of my shirt.

Tony scoffs. "She does. She's going to be my wife."

I drop low and swing, my fist colliding with his face. His head snaps to the side, another crack of bone filling the air. "I broke that arrangement as soon as she signed my contract. You're never going to be unioned."

Tony laughs, spitting blood off to the side. "Then why are you so pissed off that I said it?" He chuckles. "You think maybe she'd care about a Darkling piece of shit like you? I'm sure she's repulsed by you."

I grab him by the front of his shirt, thrilled to see the blood leaking from his nose. "I doubt it. She was quick to spread her legs for me."

The chains rattle and pull tight as Tony tries to move. "Fucking liar! She probably begged for it to stop."

I chuckle, "Oh," I lean closer, glee in my voice even as I lower it, "she did, over and over again. Said it was too much, she couldn't take it, but every time I would just fuck her harder, make her come again."

"You're bragging about raping her? That's fucking sick."

I pull back and wail on his face a few times before standing to kick him in the stomach for good measure. "I don't rape women. Everything I did to Natalia she wanted and enjoyed."

Tony groans and rolls over. He pushes up through heavy breathing and then sits up. "You're lying. You forced her into it like you forced her into that contract."

I snarl and kick at him, dropping low to beat on him. "I don't fucking rape women."

Tony pulls at his bonds as if he could fight back. He can't. He's restricted in movement, easy prey.

I swing until my arms are burning, and then shove Tony away before standing and backing up. I breathe ragged through my nose, fists clenched, my fingers numb and aching. My chest burns, my muscles twitching and pulsing with rage.

I pull air through my nose. "The Magia," I say in a hoarse voice. "Tell me everything."

Laughing, Tony shoves up, spitting at me again. "Why are you asking me? Ask Nat. Unless..." He stops smiling. "You lied. She was in that house." Tony makes another attempt to get up.

I growl in my throat. "I don't lie. There's no point, and it's against the honor code."

Tony sneers. "Like your kind has honor."

"My kind?" I roar. "You're the ones who have no honor. You blew up my home in the middle of the night. You didn't face me. You broke the rules of engagement." I kick him in the chest, swinging my full strength behind it, knocking him into the wall. "Falsely declaring I was dead to the fucking world!"

Tony gets to his knees, panting. "Honor? You have me chained to the wall. You won't even face me in a fair fight."

I lift my chin. "I would rip you apart."

"Prove it. Show honor," Tony says. "A fair fight."

Smirking, I ask, "Like you gave me a fair fight? Rats, cockroaches, that's all you are, and you don't deserve honor."

Tony sneers. "I want to see Nat. I need to know you aren't lying."

"I'm not."

"Then why the fuck are you asking me? Why aren't you getting answers from Nat?"

"Because I'm asking you, so give me what I want."

"Give me a fighting chance," Tony says. "Prove you know what honor means."

I narrow my eyes. It really is too easy like this, the rat on his knees. My magic slithers from me, winding around his cuffs and undoing his bindings.

The cuffs fall free, and Tony rubs his wrists. He stands, smiling. "Big mistake, asshole."

He lunges and I counter. We swing at each other. Tony lands a few blows, and I reciprocate. This is better, a fight, a target harder to hit and it swings back. I swing harder, my fists glancing off the pig, my hits struggling to find purchase.

As much as I loathe to admit it, Tony is holding his own. It is glorious. I dodge a punch and counter, catching the man in the gut.

I stand at ease, breathing hard and grinning. "You're not as weak and pathetic as that other rat, I'll give you that."

Tony bares his teeth, a hand to his gut as he straightens, lifting his hands, open palmed. His eyes shift behind me toward the door.

"Oh, I wouldn't."

Tony takes a few steps back, panting. "What other rat?"

"Didn't catch his name. Bulky, arrogant prick that thought Natalia was a pampered princess and fought like a toddler throwing a tantrum."

"Ben?" Tony shakes his head, "Ben thinks Nat was handed her marks. He wouldn't ever shut up about it, refused to accept her as pinnacle, and he's sloppy. What about him? Knocked him down a peg? Good, he needed it. He's not nearly as good as he thinks he is."

I drop my hands on my hips. "You could say I knocked him down. He's dead."

Tony runs at me, pulling back a fist. We go another round, and then I throw him to the ground, putting a foot in the middle of his chest. "Stay down," I say with a smirk, "or not. I'm all for beating on you more."

Tony rolls and grunts, getting to his feet. "I'm done being nice." He throws a palm out, and the blast of Ki hits me in the shoulder twisting me sideways into the wall before I can shield or move.

Recovering, I punch at the air, my Dark streaking straight into Tony. He recoils, taking a step with a guttural noise, and then he looks up with black eyes and a wide grin. He shoves an open palm at me, and I throw myself away from the wall. The attack of my magic cracks the wall, stone chips and dust filling the air.

I catch him as he runs with an arm across the chest. Tony ends flat on his back, coughing.

Staring down at him, I curl my lip. "What happened to a fair fight?" Tony tries to sit up and I slam my foot into his chest, pinning him to the stone. "Magic isn't fair."

"You have magic. I have magic." Tony sneers. "Seems fair to me."

"No." I add weight. "Let's try this again. The Magia, I want to know everything. Now."

Tony inhales and bellows, "Where's Nat? Why isn't she telling you?"

I grip my fists. Rage burns through me, the words erupting out of me. "Because my little star isn't here!" I step off him, bending over to grab him. My hands shake until they're balled into Tony's shirt.

Tony wraps his hands around my wrists, baring his teeth at me. "Where is she?"

"Pierre has her in Izul."

Tony laughs. "Good."

I throw him into the wall. It fractures and the man falls prone. "He's the monster. You have no idea what he's capable of, what he'll do to her. He's the one who will break her, use her without ever caring about her."

I stalk toward him, grabbing him by the shoulder. My fingers have shifted in my fury, black tendrils screaming and wrapping around me. My talons sink into Tony's flesh, and he yells, lifting his eyes to mine.

They shift, turning from rage to panic, and I slam my fist into his face with full force.

Tony goes limp. Dropping the man, I turn and slam my fist into the wall.

I walk out of the cell, meeting Thames's gaze. He stares at me, shying his head back. I grab him by the shoulders to move him out of my way.

Thames calls after me. "I'll take care of the piggy pig then, shall I?"

I stomp up the steps, my mind racing. I get to the door and stalk through the lower floor. Someone approaches, head bowed, to direct me to the back patio.

Massimo lifts his eyebrows. "Anything useful?"

"No. I don't even know what I was hoping for."

Hiro lifts his head. "What's going on?"

Massimo rolls his shoulders. "Our women are in Izul. They think we're dead, and we've got no way of reaching them."

"Izul." Hiro makes a retching noise. "What women?" He turns a dour face to me.

I curl my lip. "Natalia."

Massimo sighs. "And Vanessa."

Hiro shies his head to the side. "Who is Vanessa?"

Massimo grunts. "Like me or Thames for Tallie."

"Mmm..." Hiro glances over his shoulder with a face of concern. "Where is Thames? He went into the basement with you."

Glaring, I say, "He's fine. Taking care of the pig."

"How did they get into Izul?"

I grunt, dropping into a chair and shoving my foot against

the edge of the table. "Natalia is Pierre's daughter. I found out when I reported to the Council. I had Mass put her and Vanessa somewhere so I didn't kill her while I sorted my temper about that little detail."

"Ah, so she is the Light? Not Magia?"

"She's both, and I didn't like that realization."

Massimo rubs his jaw. "The house blew while they were in hiding. It was all over the media stations that we were dead, and they were being hunted by the Magia."

Bobbing his head, Hiro says, "Saw that."

I snarl. "Like called to like, and they ran straight to Izul. Pierre had offered her a place in Izul when he tried to get her from me in Ilbuio. He took her in, knowing she's his seed."

Massimo sits, rolling forward to press his forehead to the table's edge, staring at his feet. "And Vanessa followed Tallie like she always does. That bastard Pierre won't let us see either of them, paraded in our face he has them and will lie to them."

Hiro rubs the back of his neck. "You're having a bitch of a time, Cal."

Snarling, I drop my foot to the ground before I kick the table in fury. "We aren't having fun right now, no."

Hiro rubs his hands together. "Did you call?"

I roll my shoulders. "I took her device and identification when she signed her contractn to keep her where I wanted her. I hadn't gotten around to getting her a new one yet."

"I may have an idea. All you have to do is tell them you're alive, right? They'll want to come back?"

"Yes," I scoff with a snort of derision. "Great plan."

Massimo lifts his eyebrows, wiggling them at me with a grin. "Why didn't we think of that?"

Hiro snickers. "All right, assholes. I meant, go old world with it. Can't call? Can't see her? Write a letter. As far as I know it's still possible to send things through services."

I shake my head. "Anything I send to Natalia Pierre will intercept."

Massimo shrugs. "Worth a try."

I stare at the contract on my forearm. Her name sparkles at me in my skin. "I need a way to communicate with her that won't be cut off by Pierre. I won't risk trying to change her contract while she's in Izul. Even if I am close enough to change it from the front gates, I have no idea what Pierre is doing with her, how much freedom she has. I don't need it killing her if she can't follow the instructions."

Massimo frowns. "What if I reach out to Vanessa? Send the letter to her. Maybe Pierre misses it? Maybe he's arrogant enough to think it won't matter."

Waving a hand, I dismiss the idea. "Vanessa is tethered to Natalia. The Magia tried to use Vanessa. I contracted her. Everyone who knows Natalia knows if they want her, they must possess Vanessa. Pierre will protect her to keep Natalia the same as I did."

Massimo sits back with a groan. "Nessy knows dead languages, and I know every dead language she knows—well, the names of them."

Hiro snickers. "Anything you look up to put in a language, Pierre will have the ability to translate the same way you did."

Massimo groans, tipping his chair onto the back two legs. "That fucking crazy woman is making me nuts. My Dark is whining—*whining*!"

"That's a rough time," Hiro says, pushing his fingers through his glossy black hair.

I need a way to communicate with my little star, something Pierre won't suspect is relevant. I need a way to talk to her, a message only she will know.

There must be something I can send that Pierre might pass off without realizing it's a message. My eyes remain on the contract, the line about being her home still absent. The song, it means everything to her. It comes back to the lyrics, both real and how she changed them.

I grip my fist, watching my muscles move beneath the words. The answer is proving I am her home. I don't need a message. I need a song. That's how I get through to her.

I look to Massimo with a smirk. "I know what plan B is."

CHAPTER 45
NATALIA
THIRD DAWN'S DAY, SNOWDROP, 4050 6TH MILLENNIUM

I stare at Ashley, quivering head to toe. "He's not dead? Cal– Callahan is not dead? He's alive?"

"Alive and in Hapsford. I had him located."

My Light unwinds, stretching in me. *"I want to see my friend."*

Taking a deep breath, I close my eyes, doing my best not to scream, my voice a strangled whisper, "Every single person but me knows Cal is alive, don't they?"

"Well, you and your pet, but yes, we're all aware." She rolls her eyes with a flutter of her lashes. "Pierre was one step ahead, ensuring everyone maintained the illusion and minded their tongues less they revealed the truth. Oh, but believe me, everyone was more than willing to prevent you from ever returning to the service of the Dark. This entire city has been laughing behind your back since you arrived."

I eye her. "You could have told me instead of trying to kill me." She lifts her eyebrows and shrugs. I snap, "You want me gone? Help me get out of this city."

"Mmm." She puckers her lips like she's bitten sour fruit and tilts her head. "In all honesty, I don't feel like it."

"You lost Ritual. You answer to me."

"Yes, but, well, you see, our father did declare that it wouldn't stand as an actual Ritual, and the risks to me for helping you with that detail are far too grave."

I glare. "I'll leave. You'll get what you want."

She scrunches her mouth to one side. "The flaw in your logic is if I'm involved with assisting you to return to that dog, and our father finds out, he'll be furious. If anyone else finds out, it could damage my standing even if you are gone. Beenin forbid, me? A Bordeaux? Helping another Bordeaux to serve the Dark? What would they say?"

Looking around in short, choppy jerks of my head, I try to think of a response.

"Well, I do want to leave Izul..." She puts a finger to her lips, pressing them and drawing her features together in consideration. "Hmm, perhaps?"

"Just say it," I gripe.

"Would you care to come to Kipnop with me? It will take some doing, several days if not weeks yet to convince Pierre we've mended our sisterly bond."

If I found a way to act and speak to please the Light Queen, I can figure out how to convince Pierre I'm the best of friends with Ashley. "Great idea, sister mine," I bat my eye lashes. "Please tell me, when shall we start?"

She laughs. "Oh, you are divine when you need be." She adjusts her purse on her shoulder. "Dinner? This evening? You, me, Akash, Zan, and our father? He will be thrilled with the announcement of your relationship with Zan at a heritage gathering."

My stomach drops. I'm going to have to convince Pierre of

this charade, but worse, I'll have to continue a relationship with Zander still. "H–how long will this take?"

"Oh, honey, you're not worried about maintaining pretenses with Zander, are you?" She giggles.

I want to rip her throat out with my teeth, but lick around my lips and take a breath. She is my way out. "I'll manage," I grind through clenched teeth. "Just play your part, I'll play mine, and we both will get what we want."

She holds her hand out. "Absolutely, honey."

I shake her hand. "Then get me the fuck out of this blinding city."

I PACE IN MY ROOM, my heels clacking against the floor. My heart races, and I check my hair, pulled up in one of the numerous warrior braids I was taught by Weila. It was appropriate to work through the tedious steps. I'm in the mood to fight, even as I turn back and forth in my tailored white dress.

The knock on my door sends my heart into my throat and my stomach into my knees. Tugging at the hem of my dress around my thighs, I open the door, meeting Zander's gaze.

He grins at me, and it takes everything in me not to claw his stupid eyes out. "Love, you are stunning."

"Thank you. I tried a new braid," I point to my hair.

"Excellent job. Had I known I would have put more effort into my hair this evening." He offers me his hand.

I don't want to, but I put mine in his. I won't take his hand for much longer. It will be Cal's hand soon enough, but I need to do what Pierre has wanted since I arrived in this cursed city.

I will act like the Light. I will lie, deceive, manipulate, and stab someone in the back when they think I'm a friend.

As he draws me from my room, I ask, "I thought Pierre was taking me to dinner."

"I am wounded." He feigns injury with a hand to his chest. "I believed you looked so beautiful for me."

Retching in response would be splendid, but I fake a smile. "I may have had suspicions that you'd be joining us."

"Ah." He chuckles. "My assumption is true? You dressed for me this evening?"

"I know your fondness for braids."

He laughs. "I am very fond of them, yes. Pierre is meeting us at the flight shaft. My attendance is still somewhat a debate it seems. He'll want words with you before we leave. What have you done this time, love?"

"Where's the delight in spoiling a surprise, darling?"

"Darling?" He glances down at me, one eyebrow lifted and half a smile.

"Trying something new," I say, looking away in an attempt at indifference.

His lips press to my temple. "I like it. Does this bode well for me? Are you finally coming to terms that Cal was naught but a captor and contractor?"

I clamp my jaw against screaming. I want to tell him to bring Cal into Izul, and we can ask Cal what Cal thinks, but that will dissolve my ploy. Instead, I hum. "I'm beginning to feel more at ease within the Light. It's a start. When I'm comfortable, we can take further steps. I don't want to rush things and spoil our future through forcing things."

"Very good, love," he says as we approach Pierre. "I am anxious to proceed, but I can wait longer."

He can wait until he's in the afters. I'll see Cal again and have him laugh in my face for my fantasies before I ever have sex with Zander.

Pierre lifts his eyebrows as Zander halts before him. "Tallie, you look beautiful, honey."

"Thank you." I lean into Zander. "I put forth more effort than ever before in attempts to begin embracing the Light."

"Very good. I'm glad to hear such." He rests his hands on his hips. "I hope you are accepting that I invited Zan along for the evening."

"Absolutely," I lie through my teeth. "How could I ever be distressed about Zan's company?"

Pierre smiles. "I understand and am delighted." He rubs his chin under his lower lip with a single finger, his features stretched with amusement. "Our plans have shifted as I had an unusual request from Ash."

"My sister?" I beam. "Yes, we had a conversation and came to an understanding. We were hopeful that you would accept our proposition."

Zander tenses, frowning down at me. "You were alone with Ashley?"

"Yes, is that a concern?"

Zander blinks at me, looks to Pierre, then back to me. "She has endangered your future on more than one occasion." He takes my chin in his hand, inspecting my face.

Snorting through my nose, I giggle for real. "Even if she had attacked me, I would have healed in fractions, but she didn't. I am fine, although your concern for me is touching."

Pierre sighs. "What understanding did you achieve?"

"We haven't interacted but twice in rather vulgar displays of selfish behavior, and as we both had a fault, it was agreed that we would forgive the other their's and step beyond those moments. For sisters, that's hardly acceptable, and we have no relationship to encourage sibling adoration."

"Whose idea was this?"

I lick my lips. One wrong word and this whole thing falls apart. "I dare not take the credit from my sister. She apologized beautifully."

He hums. "Very well." Pressing the button to open the flight shaft doors, he says, "Zan, please join my daughters and me for a heritage meal."

Zander bounces on the balls of his feet. "It would be my absolute honor."

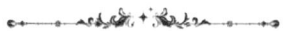

Seated at a table of gold, I smile at Ash.

She winks. "Honey, I would like you to properly meet Akash." She turns to him, her demeanor lifting with love. It's a flagrant display of worship, and my heart tugs. "This is Akash, my brightest light and future mate. He's of the Kimport heritage, an exceptional heritage that possess a rare skill of disintegration. It sounds terrible, but it's quite fascinating."

I incline my head to him, and he does a superior job of bowing while sitting in return. "Tallie," he says, his voice a waft of warm air. "The pleasure of your acquaintance now that you are of the Light is an absolute pleasure."

I duck my head. "My sincere apologies cannot be extended enough in regrets of my actions." With a forced laugh, I look to Zander. "I was rather vulgar when we met."

Zander leans close, stretching his closed lips in a wide smile, his white eyes crinkling at the corners. "I know. Larles told me all about it."

Pierre clears his throat as rizvor and tea are delivered. When the delivery is completed and we are alone, he focuses on me. "Tallie, honey, we need to discuss your behavior this afternoon."

I fit my tongue between my teeth and clamp it down to keep from retorting.

"You have continually rejected what we are and have defended the Dark. You have an abnormal connection to a dog that defiled you and enslaved you."

Zander takes my hand under the table. "Tallie has spoken to me of her contract and the misplaced trust she put in that dog."

Pierre holds up his hand, glaring with a stern expression. "Zan, you will allow her to speak for herself."

I square my shoulders, my words coming easy with honesty. "I value honesty. The Dark doesn't lie, it is part of their honor code. Above all else, I detest being lied to." I hold Pierre's gaze. "I believed in the Dark for their honesty and grew to trust in my contractor for that reason. I was raised as a Magia, neither the Dark nor the Light were a consideration for me, as both were to be my enemy. My *abnormal connection* stems from trust."

Narrowing his eyes, Pierre asks, "Is that so?"

"Yes," I say with disregard. I won't waiver under his inspection knowing I spoke in earnest. I despise handing him this piece of me, but it's a necessary evil. "I trusted him."

Zander gives my hand a squeeze. "However, if I may?" he begins in a tentative drawl, proceeding when no one intervenes. "Tallie and I have spoken of this matter. She has come to her senses, realizing the error she made in that act by misplacing her trust."

"Oh, yes," I widen my eyes and nod. "I have misplaced my trust."

Pierre considers me. "Will you let go of this childish infatuation you possess?"

"That dog is dead." I shrug, my stomach squirming. "I have nothing to hold on to, and I must consider that I am the Light. I have a wonderful man offering to help me find my place in the Light, one I hope to be my possible mate." I look to Zander.

He laughs, glowing slightly. I almost feel bad. I can't decide if his affections are genuine or coerced by Pierre.

Pierre sits straighter, his interest piqued with hope. "You two have decided then? A relationship will be founded between you two?"

Zander nods. "We consented just last evening."

Ashley puts a hand to her chest, gasping. "Oh, how very wonderful! My dear sister, I am thrilled for you. To produce a Fairly seed will be a great honor."

Akash inclines his head. "Indeed, perhaps the highest honor any might possess at this time, as well as remembered fondly in the future for continuing the Fairly heritage."

My mouth waters, my throat constricting as the urge to vomit grips me by the lungs. "Should Zan and I find our arrangement acceptable, it will be my pleasure."

Zander lifts my hand, pressing the back to his lips. "I am delighted to hear it, love."

Pierre chuckles, relaxing in front of me for the first time I've ever seen. "Yes, as am I. Very good, and congratulations. Akash." He waves at the table. "If you will pour the rizvor now, I would like to toast to our heritage's development and my younger daughter's acceptance of her place."

CHAPTER 46
CALLAHAN
SIXTH THISTLE'S DAY, SNOWDROP, 4050 6TH MILLENNIUM

My anxiety increases with each passing day, every desperate gift I send with no word from Natalia ratchets my Dark. My nerves are coiled with tension, threatening to snap. Time is slipping through my fingers. As certain as I used to be that the king would die before the next Gathering Shadows, my belief is wilting. I've stayed busy rebuilding my home and prying information from Tony to determine how I can destroy the Magia, but the weight in my chest and my Dark is mounting.

I returned to Narwal for weeks, ensuring the reconstruction of my home, confirming the architecture designs of my new residence are to my liking, and returning to stores Natalia and I visited to find something else to send to her in Izul. I've run out of ideas on items to send that will convey my continued living status, content to send anything I think she'll enjoy.

Narwal turned frigid. Freezing, wet weather set upon my city with the beginning of the Snowdrop season. Fleeing the bitter cold, I return to Hapsford, which stays warmer being in the south, and is closer to Izul. Two things I desire.

Leaving my home, I bring Thomas with me. Unlike the other loyal staying in my service, he's classified as low born as a Seraphim, and he needs to be contracted for his safety. Hiro consented, letting me breathe easier. If I regain standing, I'll be able to re-sign Thomas with Hiro's blessing. It's one less concern I have.

I arrive just after the suns have risen, sending Thomas with Raz then preparing a meal for myself in the kitchen to the annoyance of Hiro's vassals, but I'm finding excuses to keep myself busy. I can only work out and drink so much.

I carry my sandwich down to the basement for a chat with Tony, having abandoned him to the devices of his mind while I was in Narwal, rebuilding my life.

Dragging a chair into the cell, I set it backward in front of Tony, eating the rest of my breakfast staring at the pig.

He glowers, his stomach gurgling. "You're an asshole for eating that in front of me."

Shoving the last of my meal in my mouth, I lean against the back of the chair, my arms crossed and rested at ease along the top as I chew. Natalia called me an asshole frequently, something I came to adore from her lips as it was often accompanied by a giggle. She has the cutest giggle.

My Dark is becoming unruly, famished in the absence of our star. It hasn't fed since the end of the Warmwave season, and it's pissed at me. I need to feed it again, but I've been holding out for Natalia's return.

The rat stares back at me, lifting a hand and rubbing it down his face. "How long are we going to do this?"

"As long as it takes. The Magia."

"Piss off."

I smirk and ask, "You sure that's what you want me to do?"

Tony scowls, no doubt recalling being pissed on. "No."

"Then start talking, or I start getting creative."

The rat shifts, leaning against the wall. He turns his head, staring at the corner of the ceiling.

I wait. I've incurred physical punishment, beatings and broken bones, but the last time I was down here I gave the pig a golden shower. The scent still lingers, but it hasn't seemed to soften the vermin to my will.

As the silence stretches, I sigh. "There are things I can do that you can't heal. For example, I know if I leave objects within you that you can't heal. Psychological suffering, sodomy, there are plenty of options. I know Magia are stubborn but do yourself a fucking favor for once in your miserable life and crack."

Scoffing, Tony turns his face back to me, his facial features pulled with disgust. "What do you expect me to do here?" He lifts his arms from his sides, chains clinking.

"Tell me about the Magia."

"Buddy, we've been doing this same song and dance for... You know, I don't actually know how long I've been down here."

"It's the beginning of Snowdrop."

"Great, I've been eating cat food and shitting in a pan for months. What is this? What do you want from me?"

Leaning back in the chair, balancing on the two back legs, I consider his inquiry. It's valid, and up until now I've been focused on taking out my aggression on him rather than anything useful.

The pig laughs. "You don't even know, do you? You just keep spitting out the word Magia like it means something."

I sit right, the chair snapping against the stone. "Doesn't it?"

"Sure, but no." Tony tips his head back. "Even smells like shit and cat food down here."

I need two things: Natalia and revenge. I'll start with getting back my star, and then I can use her for information to get revenge. "Do the Magia have a language?"

Tony cocks his jaw to the side, eyes narrowing. The side of my mouth twitches in glee. This little piggy is about to be useful.

The tough guy act drops from Tony, his chin falling toward his chest. "What do I get out of it?"

"Dog food instead of cat."

Tony scoffs, wheezing on an almost chuckle. "That's it? I want a contract."

I tense. "You think you're funny?" I stand and throw the chair to the side.

"If I betray them, they kill me. So I want a contract. I tell you what you want. I get protection from them."

"You fucking blow up my home, think I'm dead, tell me there's no way I fucking survived, and now you beg for my protection?" I roar with laughter. "Fuck you."

Tony rubs his chest, wincing and sitting up. "You want what I know? I want whatever deal you gave Nat–Talia."

It's learning. I turn my back, gripping fists. Expelling air, I face the pig again, crouching to meet his eyes. "You fucks ruined me. Blowing up my home and telling the world I'm dead? The humans believed your little ploy. They think you're going to save them. They're forgetting who they respect, and it cost me everything. Your kind disgraced me."

Tony laughs. "Good. You shouldn't have touched what isn't yours."

"Natalia is mine!" I stand and kick him in the face.

"Then where is she?" He chuckles, nose cracking back into place, straightening even while blood leaks down his front lip. "Contract, or we keep going."

I roar, "I'm fucking disgraced! You and your kind destroyed my standing in society. For me to hold a contract is illegal." I drop to a knee and grab Tony by the front of his bloody, bodily stained shirt. "You blew up any chance you had at that deal."

"That's why Natalia's gone isn't it?" He grins, chuckling. "No more contract so she ran? She knew she was free. You couldn't force her anymore."

Narrowing my eyes, my jaw clamped tight, the muscles in my neck straining and burning, I growl. The pig has the intelligence to wince at the sound, and I snarl. "She was stupid enough to believe the Magia killed me, and she ran from them —the Magia, not me."

Tony blinks, caving in on himself. "I went with their plan so I could find her, save her." His voice is thin. "From you, from them, from everyone. I knew what they'd do when they got her back. It wasn't pretty." He grimaces.

"You want to protect her? Tell me about the Magia language. She ran from them somewhere I can't go, to someone worse than me. If the Magia have a language, I can leverage that. Pierre won't know it."

"Nat's got a way of taking care of herself. No contract, no talking." Tony smirks, settling back with a shrug. "Let's see how creative you are."

I shy to the side, studying the pig down my nose. The miscreant wants a contract, it's a curiosity. "Why a contract?"

"That's what Natalia got. I want the same. I want out of this shit hole, real food, a change of clothes. Fuck, I want a fucking shower." He chuckles. "I know enough to know you treat your servants better than this."

"Natalia's arrangement is unavailable to you. She has uses far beyond your possible skill set." I pause, humor sneaking into my voice. "A contract is an offer of something in exchange for another. You would be required to provide service."

"Yeah, I tell you what you want to know and betray the Magia, you protect me from them." Tony gives me a hard look. "Thought you were smart."

"You don't want a contract, you want protection. Contracts are illegal, but I can make a deal. I'll give you protection as long as you're providing a use to me."

"How do I know that offer is good? I tell you what you want to know, and you throw me out." His shoulder twitches and he winces.

I consider him, head shied and hands on my hips. It's the first chink in his façade of bravado I've seen. "You're afraid of them."

Scoffing, he turns his face away with an expression of pain. "Breaking the laws of the Magia comes with swift retribution."

"Why assume they'd know at all?" I narrow my eyes. "Anything I use that you tell me, you could simply transfer blame by claiming Natalia had already told me."

Tony shakes his head. "No," he groans, rubbing into his closed eyes with the heels of his palms. "The High Assembly has old world magic shit. They can create something that blocks an individual from using Ki, something to force you to speak the truth–they have a whole arsenal of tricks."

"How do you know?"

"It's why Assembly members get training beyond Pinnacle." He looks up at me with desolation haunting the depths of his eyes. "I was supposed to sit on the Assembly after I married Nat."

"Talia."

His chin drops. "They were preparing me, so I know some, but not enough. What I do know is they have a truth serum, and I one hundred percent believe they'd force that on me again if I go home. Even if I run for a while, I have nowhere to go, and I don't know if I'd manage to evade their detection forever. If I chose to just go home, they'll ask questions. If they know I've been here," he picks a hand up, flipping off the wall, "they'll either kill me for anything I say to you, or they'll send me back on some suicidal directive."

"You have my word that if you provide use to me, I will protect you from them."

"Which I'm guessing means nothing from a disgraced." Tony chuckles.

I snap my teeth like a rapid dog, my fingers breaking and shifting to long black talons that I sink into Tony's chest. "It's lost its weight with my kind, but I keep my word. I follow the honor code."

Coughing up blood, the thick dark fluid spilling over his lower lip, Tony wheezes, "And when you run out of questions?"

I dig in harder, curling my talons to widen the wounds. "Then you find another way to make yourself useful, or my protection from the Magia and me ends."

Tony bares his teeth, grunting, "You want to pull yourself out of me, or you going to wait till I bleed out?"

"Be of use, or there's no reason for you to live."

"Deal."

Ripping my talons free, blood splatters across the pig and me alike. My temper abates, my fingers returning to humanesque.

Tony curls over and groans. A moment passes, and he sits up, panting. "Yes, our marks on my back, the geometric runes. It's a language, but that's the extent I know about it."

I sit on the floor, knees bent and rest my arms on them, hands hanging limp. I could find another Magia. They are crawling out of their holes to carry out their derelict ideology. "Does Vanessa know it? She speaks old languages."

Tony shrugs one shoulder, resting back against the wall at ease. "Not that I know of." He lifts and drops a hand, the manacle clinking against links. "Maybe. Ness is weird like that, but I doubt it. The only way the runes play a role is our marks. Even if I knew the words, what they meant, it isn't something we speak."

"Any other codes? Any way you communicate in secret?"

"The Assembly does have some code with other branches in cities across the world."

"The Magia exist in other cities?"

Tony laughs. "You fucks are stupid, aren't you? We're everywhere, and there are more of us than you can even imagine."

Gripping my fists, I cock my jaw. The Magia are half-human. Their lifespans are shorter, but they make up for that with quick breeding and growing. That aspect of Magia never occurred to me. "How many of you are there?"

"A lot," he says, wheezing with a chuckle. "Probably thousands across both continents."

"Do you know the Assembly?" If I can get names and locations, I can take the head off the snake.

Tony sighs, shaking his head. "Which Assembly? Every city has one Assembly, and they collectively answer to the High Assembly. I know every Assembly member in Narwal, but that's only one Assembly, and only one member from each city meets with those that sit on the High Assembly."

"Who is the High Assembly?"

"I don't know who's on the High Assembly or any of the Assembly members outside Narwal."

"You said one from Narwal's Assembly meets with this High Assembly. Who?"

Tony stretches, chains rattling as he gets comfortable. "Don't know. I'm not on the Assembly, so I wasn't given rights to know how it all works yet."

"Fuck." I stand and turn, stalking to the middle of the cell.

This has been a waste of time. Gripping my fists in annoyance, I head for the door.

Tony lifts his voice, shouting at my back, "You're going to let me out of here, right?"

I stop, spinning on my heel with a raised eyebrow. "You wanted protection?" I smile, gesturing to him. "Well, you're safe. I assure you the Magia will not reach you here."

Tony thrashes, and the chains rattling mix with his voice, "Darkling piece of shit!"

Laughing, I tip my head back as I walk to the door, calling out, "Yes, Natalia tried to use my contract against me too, but I never make an arrangement I can't win. We'll see how useful you prove to be, *then* I'll consider giving you more freedom."

I head up the steps to the main level of the mansion. It's time to determine a new machination, but I have something that's becoming more pressing. I need to feed.

I follow voices into the kitchen, where I find Hiro standing at the massive island with two nameless Seraphinus. He waves his hand, dismissing them and turns to me. "Cal."

"Hiro." I cross my arms and lean against the fridge.

"Any progress?"

"The rats are everywhere in the world."

He inclines his head. "We've gathered as much, spread the word as much as possible about the Magia attacking and their weaknesses. Is there anything else I can do to assist?"

"I'll let you know." I rub the side of my face. "I need to head to Capali again in the next day or two."

He stares at me, then frowns. His eyes lower to the floor between us. "You're disgraced."

"As if that matters? I'm going to murder a Light fuck. It's illegal regardless of my standing."

"That's my point. You're too high risk to go poking at the Light. When you had standing, it was dangerous. Now it's deadly. You got away with it once, and you're going to try again?"

"I don't have a choice." I shrug. "I need to eat the Light to survive."

"Showing up at a Light city, though? If one goes missing and someone reports to the Council that you were even there… All some Light fuck has to do is say you sneezed at them wrong, and the Council will issue a death warrant for you."

"I don't have a choice."

"I know Mass is still gone, running your orders, but you can use my contracts. I have fighters."

Shaking my head, I say, "I need it alive."

"Fuck." Hiro turns and braces on the counter. "What can I do?"

I shove away from the fridge. "I'll wait another few days before I return to Capali, and if I don't come back, sign Mass and the others waiting in Narwal or any other city of mine. You can have everything. You've earned it."

"Fine." Hiro bobs his head. "I have Thames setting up Thomas already."

I walk out of the kitchen and head upstairs to my room, to clean up. I wash the blood away and trade blood-stained grunge for a tailored dress shirt and jeans. Checking myself in the mirror, I stare at my eyes, biting down hard and watching the muscles at the corners of my jaw bulge.

It's a face worth sitting on. That's what my little star would say.

I close my eyes and breathe deep. I could use her sass right now, a reason to laugh, some joke that she'd spit to relieve this swallowing hole in my chest. When I get her back, I might tether her to me with my magic so she's never out of arm's reach, where I can feed and put her on my cock any time I want.

There's so much I hate about her being gone, it's hard to believe I lived so long without her. I'm trying to recall all the arguments with my father, the stupid things I said to him, why I was so furious that he'd had a Light of his own. It seems like a different life I lived long ago.

CHAPTER 47

CALLAHAN

The night is cool, but bearable for me to sit outside beneath the night sky as I eat. When I've finished, I shove the plate away and lounge in the chair, tipping my head back to stare at the stars, a gift from the Light to the Dark to eternalize their love from when the world was made. It's the kind of love written about in songs and poetry since language was developed, and it makes me yearn for my star.

I sip my bourbon and stare at the millions of twinkling lights above. There's too much circulating in my mind, my Dark becoming erroneous, throwing a tantrum at the lack of our star, but there's not much I can do about that. I've sent everything I could think of to gain her attention and have received nothing in return.

I stop midway to another drink and glance at Hiro as he takes a seat across from me. I set my glass aside, "Yes?"

"You irritated mine in the kitchens. Kira is fuming about the mess you made." Hiro looks to the plate. "You know how to cook?"

"I made a sandwich."

He smirks. "Let them do their jobs, for fuck's sake. What are you doing?"

I pick up the tumbler, gesture to it, and down the contents. "Drinking."

Hiro shakes his head, flopping back and throwing an arm over the back of his chair. "I can see that."

I run a hand down my face, toying with the empty glass, spinning it around the hard edge of the base on the surface of the table.

Smiling, Hiro turns to stare across his back lawn, the pond shimmering in the moonlight. "I'm throwing everything I have behind you. If you lose, I go back to risking everything I have with a target on my back from the new king."

I set the tumbler flat on the table with a crack. "I don't need Natalia to win. I've been winning games for centuries without her, and if you swear loyalty to the new king and give up a pretty gift while eating your support of me, you'll be fine."

"Brilliant deduction. I don't want that. I want you to win the contest and be my contractor. Your head's not on right, and the contest isn't the games," he mutters, rubbing his chest.

I reach for the bottle and pour another drink. I take a gulp, meeting Hiro's eyes. "And?"

The skin on the bridge of his nose crinkles with disgust. "You're fucking distracted."

I narrow my eyes, the burn of alcohol over my tongue smooth. "Do you have a point?"

Hiro smirks, turning away and shaking his head. "I could lose everything but Thames and still fight. Take Thames and leave the rest, I'd limp around functioning, sure, but no way is my head right."

I throw the whole drink down my throat and reach for the bottle.

He snags the bottle, taking a drink. "You're in love, just

fucking admit it already, then deal with it. Get your fucking head right."

I study him as someone approaches. Thames walks past me, moving to drop into Hiro's lap. Hiro adjusts for him, staring up with adoration.

Thames doesn't seem to notice as he takes a drink from his wine glass and grins at me. "Hello."

Hiro reaches up and grabs the back of his neck. "Come here." He wrenches the man's face down to his, their mouths meeting. Thames flails a bit, reaching to set his glass down on the table.

Curling my lip, I turn away, gripping my glass harder. I scour the night sky, all those stars glittering overhead, and not one of them belongs to me.

I glance at Hiro and Thames, still engaged, set my glass aside with the burning desire to rip them apart and keep them from having what I can't.

Thames pulls back, grinning. "Hi, Honey Pot."

Hiro slides his hand down Thames' chest. "Hi, Sugar Bear."

I scoff. "You two are going to make me throw up all this expensive bourbon, and it's your coin."

Picking up his wine glass by the stem, Thames motions it in little circles, spinning the contents around the basin. "The reports today say a mining town on the other continent was decimated."

Taking a deep breath, Hiro sinks lower in his chair, his arm tightening around Thames. "It's becoming more frequent, but always small towns unclaimed by Seraphinus, and there's only ever children left alive, spouting tales of monsters. I've heard the rumors, but what do you think?"

Shrugging, I say, "There's no way to know if all the Ancients were destroyed in the war. Rumors are bad enough and something I won't disregard no matter how baseless."

Smile fading, Thames asks, "What the fuck is going on?"

Hiro nuzzles him. "Nothing you should be concerned about yet. Let your contractor worry. You just relax and stay my care-free, happy sugar bear." Hiro snuggles him, chin on Thames' shoulder. "That's what I need from you."

Frowning, disappointment weighing his shoulders down, Thames bobs his head. "All right."

Hiro faces me. "You believe it's Ancients?"

I drag a hand down my face. "I don't know, but I can't shake the feeling that the winds are changing again, and I was preparing for the worst-case scenario. I had a codex."

"Codex," Hiro repeats, sitting up and shifting Thames on his lap. "You have a *Dark* codex?"

Hunching forward, I drop my face into my hands. "*Had*. Vanessa was translating it. Mass says she finished, but she's in Izul with Natalia."

Hiro scowls. "You fucked up. They're the most sacred texts of our magic, Dark magic, and you let a vassal walk off with it? And take it to Izul?"

Thames glances between us and throws his hands up. "I don't know what you're talking about."

Jaw dropping, Hiro asks, "How did you even get one?"

I rub the back of my neck, staring at the table. "You'd have to ask my father. He went away for weeks and returned with it. I've tried to find others but never accomplished anything."

Thames sets his wine glass down with a sharp rap. "Someone explain, now, before I throw a tantrum and you both end up bloody."

Hiro clenches his jaw and tips his head back. "Sugar Bear, no. Behave for me. Be my—"

"Don't give me that," Thames snarls. "I'm your partner and mate. I deserve to know things."

Drooping, Hiro wraps his arms around Thames. "How's your mythology?"

I lift my drink, "Mallafic, you've heard of him?"

"I have." Thames sits a bit straighter. "Everyone has. He was the monster that hid under the bed, and according to my mother, he would come eat me in the middle of the night if I didn't eat my tripe." He shudders.

Hiro smiles, nuzzling his ear. "No more tripe, and the only thing eating you in the middle of the night is me."

"Tell me more." Thames brightens and laughs. "What does Mallafic have to do with what you're talking about?"

Bobbing my head side-to-side, I scrunch half my face. "The creation myths aside, Mallafic was real. At worst, an Ancient, and at best, a god. He harnessed the Sube, the origins of our magic."

Hiro says, "Mallafic was betrayed by Beenin, his heart cut out, along with his tongue, eyes, liver, and lungs. They were distributed amongst seven tombs, encased, but they could contain him. His magic bled through, and it created the seven Dark codexes."

Rubbing my jaw, I say, "Don't know about all that myth stuff, but that thing is alive with something."

Thames frowns. "Isn't the story that Mallafic was condemned to live in this world, never to be reunited with Beenin, but imprisoned by being put into books he wrote when he made us?"

I scoff. "Those are two versions of the same myth, and there's never been any evidence to support either tale."

Hiro asks, "If it's alive, and you disregard the myth, what do you think is in them?"

"Something not good." I grimace. "I did not like being around that thing."

Massimo's voice comes from behind me, "I need a fucking drink."

I look up, laying eyes on him for the first time since he left to drop the guitar off to be delivered to Natalia in Izul near the end of the Warmwave season. "When did you get back?"

"Now. All cities aside from Narwal have three vassals—well, uncontracted, willing to work for you—keeping things running. Took some finagling, some moves, did my best to group together appropriate teams, got a lot of push back and requests, and I have a headache to end all headaches." He drops into a chair, leaning his head back. "At times like these, I dream of challenging you...killing you...pissing on your corpse...taking your estate...becoming a contractor..."

I chuckle. "Keep dreaming. I'm disgraced. Killing me doesn't get you much."

"I'm aware. I just took months taking care of your estate to keep it stable." He picks his head up, rubbing his face. "Fuck, I'm exhausted."

"You're done," I say with heat. "You do nothing for a week, and if you needed help, you should have told me."

"I could handle—"

"You still answer to me."

Lifting his chin, Hiro asks, "Do you need anything, Mass? Benefits of being the contracted is we take care of you."

Massimo shakes his head.

"Good timing on your return. Cal only returned this morning."

Picking his head up, Mass frowns at me.

I shrug. "I went back to Narwal. The estate plans are finalized. Construction was started."

He rests back, eyes closing. "Where are we with your plan for the Magia?"

"Nowhere. Still getting information from that rat. He

confirmed they're across both continents and the isles, and he can give a list of major cities he's aware of hosting Magia, but he doesn't know if that's all of them. I can't kill every Magia, so I need something drastic to teach a lesson. Ideas?" I glance at Massimo and then Hiro and Thames.

Thames curls his lip. "Win the contest and then change Gathering Shadows so whoever kills the most Magia are contenders."

Hiro beams at him. "I adore how you think, Sugar Bear."

Slumping back, I rub my face. "All games must be completed by partners within royal grounds."

Massimo says, "We invite them to Ilbuio then."

I widen my eyes and crack my jaw open, wiggling it back and forth. I look to Massimo, lounging with his eyes closed. "I invite them somewhere."

He picks his head up. "I'm too fucking tired to play games. Give me an order if I'm supposed to be doing something."

"Not yet, but it's a thought. Instead of hunting them down, draw them somewhere."

Hiro says, "They aren't going to walk into a setup willingly."

"No," I drawl, "but maybe they'll show to a celebration in their honor."

Shifting, Thames props his head on a hand. "All I care about is that I get to partake."

"Let me figure out the details first, but that's the plan. You'll get advance notice to show if you want."

With a sigh, Massimo asks, "What am I doing?"

I give him a raised eyebrow. "You. Are. Done." Staring at him, I wait for the words to sink in. "I'll take care of it."

His hand drops to his side. "Fine. I'll kick my feet up and drink expensive booze for the next week."

"Is there something else you want to do?"

He grins. "See you crowned the next Dark King. Kill the fucking rats that blew up our house. Get off sometime this decade without using my hand. I've always wanted a fucking trip to the isles. Kipnop is supposed to be relaxing."

"All I can do is hope the king dies before the next Gathering Shadows for the first, so pray he dies soon. Working on a plan for the second. As for the third, if you don't use your hand in some fashion, you're usually doing it wrong, and if you want to go to Kipnop, go. You have a week."

Massimo adopts a contemplative expression. "Usually?"

"Well, there's this fantastic thing when she uses her mouth, and that, my friend, is completely hands-free." I pat him on the shoulder. "I'm sure we can get Vanessa to teach you."

He bellows at me, "I know what a fucking blow job is!"

Sticking a finger in my ear, I wiggle it, laughing at Hiro. "I think he's cranky."

Hiro mocks a frown. "Probably needs a blow job."

CHAPTER 48
NATALIA
EIGHTH EVERGREEN'S DAY, SNOWDROP, 4050 6TH MILLENNIUM

I stand in Pierre's office with Ashley and Ness, who doesn't know the truth yet. She's giving me dirty glances and flicking her wide eyes at Ashley and then back to me. All I do is shrug and look away.

Ashley lounges on one of the cushions before Pierre's desk. She has her head tipped back, her golden locks dangling in perfect curls.

Groaning at the ceiling, she says, "Honey, if this goes wrong, you're on your own."

Turning to me with arms crossed, Ness scowls, "Why are we even doing this?"

I look to the door over my shoulder, "Ash and I have an understanding now, and if we leave, we'll, I don't know, get a room with a light switch."

She flings a hand toward Ashley. "I'm just starting to have a relationship with Aku, and we're going on a trip? Why do I have to go with you two?"

Ashley scoffs.

I rub the space between my eyebrows. "Babe," I twist my

lips, staring at her, scouring my mind for lyrics she'll understand. "I fucking hate boiled leaves at any rate. But I'd drink it on your dime and your time."

Cocking her head, Ness narrows one eye.

Shaking my head, I beg, "Can you just go with it?"

"Go with teatime?" Her eyes open wide enough to show off her full irises. The lyrics appear to register, clearing the baffled haze to her expression. "Oh shit! Yeah, babe."

Ashley has picked her head up, watching with doubt. "What is that? Coded messages? We're not drinking tea right now."

Ness laughs. "Oh, believe me, if I had tea, I'd pour it down your throat."

Swallowing my snicker, I clear my throat, averting my gaze from Ashley. The reference is about poisoning someone, but that's not something Ashley needs to know. "It's a song."

At my back the door opens, and Ashley jumps to her feet. "Hi, Daddy."

"Honey," Pierre says with a smile, stepping next to me. He raises an eyebrow, staring down his nose, "What is going on?"

Ashley steps around the desk, standing in front of Pierre with her hands folded together. "You know my sister and I have been making amends."

"I do. I am beyond delighted."

"Well, I had an idea. My trip to Kipnop was postponed while I made an effort to mend my failures as a sister, but I thought it would be nice if Tallie could come with me to Kipnop."

Pierre stares at her, his lips flinching against humor. "No."

"Dad!"

He eyes me and then laughs at her. "Absolutely not."

"But—"

He holds a hand up, silencing her. He lets the quiet stretch before speaking. "Under no circumstances am I going to trust you with your sister's life after two attempts to end it yourself."

"What? Dad." She rolls her eyes, flipping her hair over her shoulder. "That was ages ago. We've made friends." She holds her hand to me with a smile.

I take her hand, plastering a grin to my lips. "We have, and I'm enjoying having an older sister again."

Ashley nods, pursing her bright red lips. "It has been an absolute delight getting to know her. I feel awful for how I acted previously, and I wanted to take her shopping and to the spa."

Scoffing, Pierre stands with his hands on his hips, smirking at the ceiling. "You can do that within the confines of Izul."

Ashley sits on the edge of the desk, crossing her legs. "It's just a girls' getaway so we can really get to know each other without the prying eyes of others. I'm afraid I did make a spectacle in the arena."

"Mmm." Pierre crosses his arms. "You did, and I'm still not in a forgiving mind for your faults."

She bobs her head. "I know. That is why I immediately began repairing the damage I wrought. This is for my sister and the betterment of our heritage. Akash has agreed to give us a week on our own before he joins us."

My scalp is sweating. Every pore in my skin oozing fear that we might not convince him, but we've spent weeks building up to this. I keep my tone aloof, and curling my fingers tight, I say, "Perhaps you'll allow Zan to do the same?"

Pierre stares at me with a sideways glare. Running a hand down his face, he breathes out in audible frustration. "That I can accept. I will summon Zan. He'll be happy for the time away with you, Tallie and I'll know you," he pauses, staring at Ashley, "aren't going to try anything I'd disprove of."

Shock peels my lips apart, and I find her eyes, gaping at her. Zander would ruin our plan, and her wide eyes tell me she's realizing it as well. Worse, that means we really will have to deal with each other in Kipnop.

"In a week?" I manage before Pierre picks up on our mutual panic. I clear my throat, heart and mind racing. "Akash is staying behind to give Ash and me our space. Zan will be doing the same, yes?"

"I will be sending him with you for the entirety of your trip," he says, drawling the words, his tone dripping with intent.

"It's fine." Ashley flicks her hand at Ness again, "That has no wings, so what do you say to us three driving to Juliquian and then taking a boat to the isles, which will take less than a whole day. We can spend the night in Juliquian and take a boat to Kipnop in the morning. Zander and Akash can fly ahead."

Ness points at her chest. "Ness. My name is Vanessa, and—"

Pierre starts talking over her, "If the two of you are in agreement to this—"

Chirping interrupts him.

He frowns, checks his phone, then sighs. "Ladies, my apologies, a moment please." He answers the call. "Pierre Bordeaux... I understand. When shall I be present?...Very good. I will be on my way."

He disconnects, frowning at the screen. Sliding the phone into his pocket, he turns to me. "I understand you are capable of protecting yourself, but you'll have to forgive a father's urges to protect his seed. I have Council duties to attend to for the next three days, so I will allow this."

"Oh, wonderful!" Ashley beams.

"Tomorrow, you may drive to Juliquian and take a boat to Kipnop while Zan and Akash fly ahead. You will have to check in regularly to prove neither of you is so much as bleeding, and as this is a sisterly getaway, I see no reason Vanessa attend."

I shake my head. "Sorry, Ash, I want to go. I do. But Ness deserves something too."

"I understand." She bobs her head. "I do. We haven't been the most welcoming. I haven't even spoken to her. I was hoping to make full amends to you, including her, given her importance to you, but alas, Father has spoken. Shall we plan a day together upon my return?"

Pierre looks to Ashley in disbelief. "You want to take a vassal?"

Ashley shrugs. "She'll serve as a vassal to all of us while being with friends. The poor thing has only Aku to keep her company."

Pierre tenses. "Aku Drelibu?" His eyes turn furious as they fall on Ness.

She shrinks from him. "I met him in the library."

"Young lady." He squares up to Ness. "You will act as a proper vassal for the duration of your trip, and I will grant your attendance in exchange for a gift in turn. You will not see Aku again."

Ness chews her lower lip, glancing to me.

I nod, straining my eyes at her in a silent command to comply. "She'll do that. Right, Ness?"

"Yeah," she starts nodding.

Pierre glances around with a face full of disbelief, but lifts his chin and says, "Very good. I expect regular check-ins from both of you until I know Tallie is safe with Zan in Kipnop. Tallie, keep your phone with you at all times to call Zan if you have any troubles."

I ask, "How often would you like?"

"Until you are in Kipnop with Zan and I have faith you are safe, I want a message from both of you every half-rune." He comes to stand in front of me. "One more thing. Give me your hand."

I extend my right hand.

"Your other hand."

"Why?"

"The cuff, Tallie. You have access to my accounts through the phone, and this way, I can track you by your spending if necessary, should you find a way around the tracking app on your phone. I've tolerated it long enough, but this is non-negotiable as of now."

I stare at him, unwavering under his gaze. "It's a useless trinket since Cal is dead."

"Then there's no reason for you to wear it." He snags my arm, using his other hand to slip fingers under the metal band. With a sharp yank, he snaps the cuff, turning to throw it on his desk. "Now, ladies, enjoy your evening, and you may begin your trip in the morning. I expect your first check-in when you leave this city."

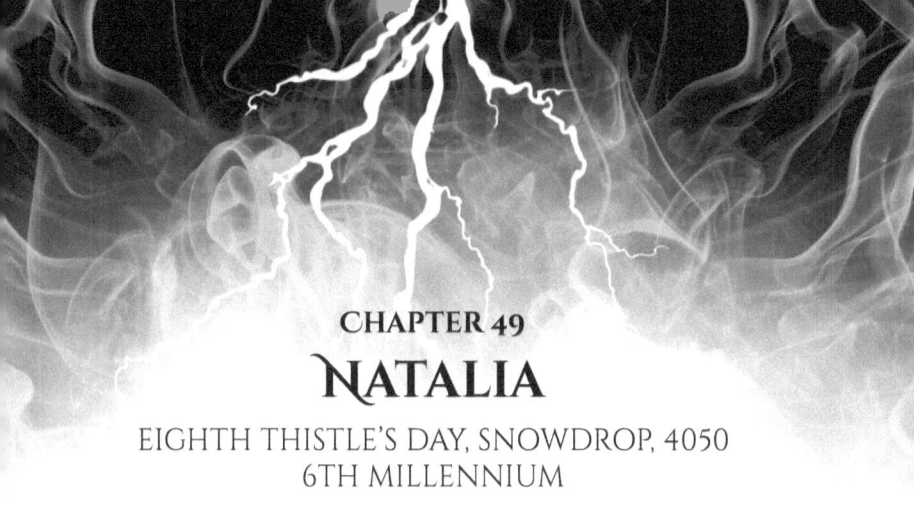

CHAPTER 49

NATALIA

EIGHTH THISTLE'S DAY, SNOWDROP, 4050
6TH MILLENNIUM

It takes every bit of my patience to continue the charade through the evening. Zander helps me pack in the morning, then kisses me before handing his bag to me. As far as he's concerned, I'll bring it with me when I meet him in Kipnop. I allow the illusion, knowing I won't be seeing him again.

"All right," Ness snaps from the backseat as Ashley drives through the city gates. "Out with it, babe, what's going on?"

Holding my phone up at Ashley, I say, "Smile."

She glances over and flashes teeth, and I snap the picture, sending it to Pierre to notify him we've left the city.

I shift in the front passenger seat, turning to grin at Ness. "We aren't going to Kipnop."

Ashley tosses her hair. "I am right after I get rid of you."

Ness throws her hands up. "I knew it. It's a trap."

Giggling, I say, "Sort of, but not for us. We're going to Hapsford."

Unbuckling, Ness moves to the center of the backseat, leaning between the front two. "Why?"

I grin wider. "Cal's not dead."

Ashley makes a noise of disgust. "No, he's not. Gods, how stupid are you two?"

"Excuse you, bitch."

"Haven't you seen the media reports? There were posts everywhere about Callahan. There are several videos of him showing up at a Magia celebration in Narwal. He announced he's still alive and then ripped a bunch of humans apart and shut everything down." She clicks her tongue against her teeth. "While such a beastly display, it was a much-needed act to put them in their place."

I pull my ears back and turn with murder in my soul to Ashley. "I haven't had media access one single day I've been in Izul."

Glancing over, Ashely gives me a look. "Oh, honey, why do you think that was?"

Ness sneers. "Pierre keeping us from knowing the truth."

Ashley taps her nose with a wide smile. "And you," Ashely snaps, pointing at the rear-view mirror. "Absolute idiot, but that's still no excuse for Aku, darling."

Widening her eyes, Ness sticks her head between the seats again. "What about him?"

"You think he was oh so intrigued by a nothing, measly human? Please do tell me you are not that stupid, and it was some misguided desperation for someone, anyone at all, to even deign to talk to you."

Ness glares.

"Oh, no, you really thought...?" Ashley giggles. "He was going to steal your secrets to use them for his benefit, selling them to work his way to higher standing."

Sitting back, Ness mutters under her breath as she sulks.

Clicking her tongue, Ashley says, "You trusting, simple fools. It's been humorous for me, but of all the jokes and ridiculousness of you two, I just can't even believe you two are so moronic to believe a player as big as Callahan could be killed by the Magia. They're a joke."

Ness laughs, but it rings hollow. "Have you ever fought a pinnacle Magia?"

I wave a hand between them. "Stop, and put the claws away, both of you." I warn Ness with my eyes. "We aren't morons. Magia can kill Seraphinus. I've killed multiple, and that list could have included you if I hadn't healed you." I poke her in the shoulder.

Ashley whacks at my hand. "Stop talking. Your breathing annoys me enough. Callahan is alive and I'm taking you to him so I don't have to deal with you anymore. Now, shut up and listen. We need to execute this flawlessly so Pierre doesn't suspect I had anything to do with it."

Ness scoffs, dropping into the backseat. "Sure."

"My life depends on this, so pay attention."

I right myself in my seat, adjusting the seatbelt away from my neck. "Calm down. What are we doing?"

"We are getting our story straight. We got to Juliquian on the coast to catch the yacht, and you took off."

"Fine, what happens when he realizes I'm gone?"

"That's your problem, not mine. I only care that I'm not found out, other than that, do what you will." She tosses her hair again. "We were shopping, I turned around, and you were gone. When I drop you off, leave all your stuff, including your phone."

"A, I'm not leaving my guitar–that's not even believable, and B, no. We stopped for the night, you woke up, and we were gone." I wag my thumb between me and Ness. "That's more believable than you lost me in a store. Drop us in Hapsford, do the check ins until you reach Juliquian, sleep there, sometime in the middle of the night throw the fucking thing in the sea, and then call all panicky in the morning. You're in the clear."

"Hmm." Ashley makes a high-pitched noise of interest, and then glances at me. "Not a bad thought process. Believable that I was asleep when you snuck out, I could claim you drugged me which gives me an excuse for not waking up."

"Sure, I drugged you." I stare out the passenger window at the clear sky, both suns sinking lower. By tonight, I'll be with Cal again. I twist my fingers together in my lap, a cold sweat sprouting along my spine. I have no idea if he'll even care, but I'm hoping he'll be happy to see me.

Ness chimes in from the backseat, "Say we gave you this funny tea we found in Juliquian. They have a large Brishmam population. It's where I'm from—well, my dad, and it's on the edge of the Brishmam rainforest, which is where naliqo grows."

Ashley leans against the center console and stares at me, blinking her false gold lashes a few times, holding my gaze in between each flutter. "Does your pet ever shut up?"

I cock my jaw, ears pulled back to harden my face with malice. "Ness is not a pet. She's a woman, a pretty amazing one, and she's smarter than both of us."

Ness shoves her head between the two front seats. "It's a good plan *but*," Ness stresses the word, holding a finger up, "where would we have gotten drugs? Naliqo tea is potent, its used for ritual, mostly. It puts you to sleep for vivid dreams... mostly."

"You keep saying mostly."

"It's been known to cause hallucinations and heartstops. Also, sleep walking while you're in a trance, like dreaming but you're physically reacting like you're living that dream, and extreme violent behavior, including toward yourself. One guy, killed five people with his bare hands and then clawed himself to death, just shredding his skin and organs with his fingernails."

Gaping with revulsion, Ashley leans away from Ness. "That is disgusting."

She shrugs. "Well, I'm not telling you to actually drink it. Just say we gave you tea."

"Fine, I drink some weird native tea to your stupid human origins, and I saw pretty smoke plumes that glittered and scary things."

I cut my eyes to her. "Nightmare?"

Ashely curls her lip. "Hate those things. By and by they are the absolute worst creatures of the Dark." She shudders.

"Yeah," I sigh. "That venom they have is nasty."

We exchange glances, and then she wiggles in the driver's seat, sitting higher. "Whatever. Three runes then you're no longer my problem."

I smirk, "Nope."

I check on Thomas, making sure he's properly setup with care. He beams and laughs about his duties, happy to serve. I muss his hair with a smirk, reminding him to come to me if he needs anything.

I cross my arms. "This is only temporary, kid."

"I know. I'm delicate." He shakes his head. "You really treat me far better than I deserve. I'm not strong enough to be this much of a burden."

"I can't legally claim you as my son, but between you and me, you're my fucking son."

He winces, with a smile. "I guess I shouldn't say it's a good thing I'm legally not because I'd be a disgrace."

"You're funny, are you?" I lift my eyebrows.

He grins. "I might not have inherited your seed, but I got my jokes from you."

I guffaw, pressing my fist to his shoulder. "Keep your chin up. Show respect."

"I know, Dad. I will. I'll do everything I can to be useful and not a problem."

I go in search of liquor, intruding on Hiro and Thames in the kitchen.

Thames tips his glass of wine and eyes me. "Any word?"

"No, and I'm tired of you asking."

Hiro smirks. "And probably jerking off."

Thames snickers. "Does it make you wish she hadn't killed Telra in that last Gathering Shadows?"

I shudder. Those nights were wild and fun at first, dosed on her venom in a haze. It was like taking a drug that made me high. It cut the ability for me to physically feel in half, driving me half mad, and I'd fuck her through the night chasing a release. The anticipation and waiting made it incredible when I achieved it, but then she started dosing me with more and more. I told her to stop infecting me, no matter the amount, but she ignored me, even infecting me with her venom to have me if I said no to sex.

There's nothing about Telra or getting dosed that interests me. I want to keep control and force my woman to bend to what I want. I want to watch her break in pleasure. I want my little star wrapped up in my magic and calling my name.

Shaking my head, I say, "Fuck no. I'm not sorry that bitch is dead."

Thames huffs. "Honestly, I have no idea how you ever managed her. Like, no idea whatsoever, baby, and no, that's not because she had a pussy, and I don't know the first thing about what to do with one of those."

Hiro puts his arm around Thames, smiling. "They're not hard to figure out." His humor disappears, turning to watch me. "King Basileus is dead."

I take a long drink, staring at Hiro. I set my drink down, splaying my hands on the countertop. Rubbing a hand down my face, I shake my head. "I'll have to face the contest with

Mass." I take a deep breath and then grab the glass, throwing back the contents.

"He's a solid choice still."

"Fuck!" I hurl the tumbler at the wall, my shoulder wrenching, glass shattering and flying around the room. Crouching down and shoving fingers into my hair, I hang my head, voice low, "Fuck."

Thames joins me on the floor, sitting next to me. "Baby, Mass is a good weapon. You'll still win the contest, and she'll come back. I would for Hiro."

I snarl at him. "Of course, you would, you're fucking mated. Talia's just a contract."

"Hmm," he lifts his eyebrows over the rim of his wine glass as he takes a drink. "Are you sure about that?"

One of my eyes narrows in ire, my lips peeling apart, the upper one curling in disgust. "As far as she's concerned, yes."

Thames laughs, tipping back, a hand to his stomach. "Baby, she sang that first song at the games because she got jealous of Telra."

"What are you on about?"

"That light couple dancing." He moves a finger on the floor in circles. "The song about almost love? And we all know you're smitten."

"No." I stand up, meeting Hiro's gaze. "Not smitten."

The word is insufficient. My attachment is woven deep in my soul. If ever I mate, it will be to Natalia.

Hiro crosses his arms. "I told you to stop denying it. It doesn't hurt you. Gave me an edge when I stopped being an idiot. I'll do anything to keep Thames safe, including throwing your ass to the curb if you can't pull your head out of it."

I grab a new tumbler, slamming the cabinet.

Hiro hops onto the counter, staring me down. "I wasted a decade saying Thames was just a contract. He isn't. How long did you spend believing Massimo was just a contract?" Hiro motions toward the open wall leading out of the kitchen, snapping when I don't answer. "Not rhetorical, Cal."

Giving Hiro a dirty glance, I roll my shoulders and pour a drink. Massimo's contract has always been tricky. He fought it at first, then tried to abscond from it. The act stung deep, and I nearly killed Massimo for the betrayal more than for trying to rip out my contract.

I grunt at the ceiling. "Fifty years or so."

Hiro laughs. "Some contracts aren't just a contract."

Thames climbs onto the other side of the island and slides across to put his legs on either side of Hiro's, resting against his back. One of Thames's arms drapes over his lover. "Aw, I'm just your best little vassal."

Hiro tips his head back against Thames's shoulder with a grin, but it looks like a growling animal warning an attacker. "Fuck no."

Grinning, Thames ducks his face into Hiro's neck. I hate them both and dump the liquor down my throat.

"What am I denying? That I'm smitten? I don't even fucking know what that means, but it's not enough. There isn't a word that's enough." I pour myself another drink.

Hiro smirks. "Mate."

"Fuck off and let me drink in peace." Swallowing the drink in a single gulp, I snag the bottle and walk away. I trudge up the steps, my legs heavy and my chest broken.

I knew Natalia was a problem. I figured she'd be the death of me, but this is worse than I expected. The need to seek my father's advice grips me. He'd know what to do.

Thoughts burn in my brain. The memories of my father haunt me like a taunting poltergeist living in my soul. How I'd acted, the fights we had, ultimately what I'd done when he took his last breath.

At the top of the stairs, I take a deep breath at a servant calling my name. "Callahan."

I don't bother turning around. "What?"

"Someone has come to call on you."

Tipping my head back, I glare at the ceiling. I'm in no mood for whatever this is. My Dark ripples, coming out to wrap around me. "Tell them to fuck off."

"My instructions were clear to deliver this one to you upon her arrival."

Another voice speaks, one that ricochets in my ears, spiraling through me like firelight. "That's what you want me to do? Fuck off?" Natalia.

I whirl around, searching for her. I see Vanessa, standing next to a Light fuck.

The Light is poised with perfect posture in a low-cut, white dress. Her face is sharp, her big eyes shimmering with gold makeup.

Stunned, I gape at her, but my Dark snarls, rabid for a taste of her. "Talia?"

"Hello, Cal." She sets a guitar case down, leaning over slightly with bent knees. Upright she smooths her dress and clears her throat, her voice tight. "I can just walk back out the door if you really want me to fuck off?" She twists, waving toward the front of the house.

"Sass? You're going to give me fucking sass?"

Vanessa waves next to her. "Hi boss man." She waves, but her eyes shift away, her head bobbing as she checks around the room. "Where's Mass?"

I drop the glass and bottle, running down the steps in a rush of adrenaline. "I don't know. Go find him."

Ness turns to the vassal. He smiles, and gestures ahead of him. "I will escort you."

I reach for Natalia, needing to put my hands on her, to have solid contact to know she's here. My Dark streaks forward, the shadowy tendrils snaking around her, soaking in her Light with a soft hiss.

I cup her face, scowling as I take in the gold lines around her eyes, the color also painted on her lips. Her white hair is braided or something in a complicated style I can't fathom, and she's not spitting vulgarities at me.

I brush my thumb over her lips. "What the fuck did they do to you?" I ask in a trembling whisper, too terrified to know the answer.

Her eyes well up, her lips tucking under her front teeth as she turns away. "I had lessons in etiquette on how to behave in a proper fashion in order to conform into society."

"Fuck all that." I force her face back to meet her eyes. "I just need you to behave for me. Fuck the others."

My chest squeezes as I stare into her eyes. She blinks her gilded lashes, tears beginning to bubble against her lower eyelids. Her bright eyes well up, drawing a snarl from me, my heart leaping into my throat.

I crush her to me, wrapping her in my arms. My Dark doesn't need encouragement, binding her to us. "I have you, Little Star. I'll fix it."

She pushes against me, mewling and sobbing. "You're not dead. I thought you were dead."

"No, I'm not dead, you fucking idiot." I take her face between my hands. "You believed that would even hurt me?"

She sniffles, gold smearing around her eyes and trailing down her cheeks, her voice warbling. "The contract acted as if I was in contempt. I knew something was wrong, but I couldn't do anything about it and then it just stopped. You said they default when you die."

I grit my teeth, glaring at her. "You fucking idiot. You're a worn contract. It's my magic in you. If I die, it dies with me."

"I didn't know that," she whines, leaning her forehead against my chest, her fingers curling into my shirt in a tight grip. A few fine strands of her Light twist free of her wrists, sliding across my torso, others tangling in threads of my Dark. "I was in contempt, then I saw the news, and Magia showed up and—"

Panic seizes me at the idea of them hurting my star. I yank her face to mine, tasting her.

She shoves at me, then slaps my chest with a limp wrist. "I'm so mad at you. Why didn't you tell me Pierre is my sperm donor?"

I bare my teeth. "You're fortunate I didn't take your head off. Pierre revealed you to be his daughter at the Council hearing. I lost my temper, my fucking sanity."

She hiccups, her eyes widening. "That's why you banished me?"

"You're Pierre's seed, his fucking daughter," I snarl. "I wanted to hurt you, kill you, and drop your carcass in Izul. I didn't trust you. I didn't know if you had been lying to me, playing some game."

"You think I'm the idiot?" Natalia swings before I register her intent. The taste of tangy metal fills my senses.

I growl in the back of my throat as I rub the throbbing side of my face. She must have backed the hit with Ki to have that kind of force.

She sticks a finger in my face. "I told Pierre to fuck off. I burned that contract out of me to save you from yourself and still told him to fuck off, and you thought... You thought I'd..."

I scowl at her tears, the image incomprehensible. Reaching out, I try to wipe a drop rolling down her cheek.

She smacks at my hand and steps back. My Dark screams, the shadowy wisps stretching as she moves further away to stay wrapped around her and knitted with her Light. Using her palm she dries one side of her face, her eyes cold as they lift to mine. "My mistake for ever trusting you."

I laugh, grabbing her and throwing her over my shoulder. She squirms, but my Dark coils tighter in greed.

"Put me down, asshole. You don't get to just pick me up and take me somewhere."

Taking the stairs two at a time I carry her with me, her words full of rage, her little fists slamming into my back.

"I do," I assure her, jostling her for a better grip.

She squeaks like an adorable little mouse and grips the back of my shirt. "No, you don't. Put me down." She slams her elbow into my side.

With a grunt, I jerk in response but keep moving. "You're still my contracted. I get to do whatever I want with you by law."

I shove my bedroom door open and step inside, kicking it shut behind me as I move to the bed. Natalia has returned to squirming, but I throw her onto the bed.

She bounces, "You—"

I fall on top of her, catching some of my weight with hands on either side of her head, pressing my body against hers to force her into the mattress. "Behave."

Wiggling and bracing her palms against my shoulders, she strives for freedom. "Get off me."

"No." I rest my full weight on her, moving my hands to her hips. "Stop."

"Fuck yourself."

I chuckle, nipping at her throat as my Dark purrs, twisting and winding around her to feed again. "Only if I can use you to do it." Dragging my nose along her skin, I follow the chain around her neck, pulling back to trace it with a finger to the pendant. "My little star. If anyone else dared strike me like that I would tear them to pieces."

467

"You deserved it." She scoffs as she arches, trying to push my body down hers. I'm tempted beyond reason to give her what she wants, enjoying the idea of my head between her legs, the taste of her on my lips as I bury my tongue in her.

I smirk tightening my hands around her small waist. I need her to settle down enough for me to pull her clothes off without her running from me. "Maybe."

Her hand smacks against my shoulder, in a playful tap. "How could you even think I would betray you?" she asks, her voice warbling again.

Chuckling, I press my lips to her throat. "I wasn't thinking at all."

"Cal," she moans, tipping her head back to expose the column of her neck for me to open my mouth against her skin, grazing it with my teeth. "There's like a dozen things we need to talk about."

"Later." I press one of my legs between hers, forcing my thigh against her apex. She intakes on a gasp, lifting her hips and I groan, burying my face in the crook of her shoulder as my dick throbs. "I'm going to fuck you until you beg."

"Cal, stop."

I flop to my side with a sigh of frustration.

"You sent me away. I thought I did something wrong, that I wasn't useful."

"You're useful." I adjust my stiff dick for comfort, propping myself up with an arm under me as I stare at the tops of her breasts on display in her low-cut dress. I prefer her in black, but anything that form fitting is fine with me.

"You banished me," she cries, twisting to face me. "I know I'm just a contract to you, but—"

"I didn't fucking banish you," I swell up, snarling with fire and ash in my lungs. "I had Massimo hide you from me so I didn't rip the pretty little head off my future mate in blind fury because I knew I wasn't thinking."

"Mate?"

"You aren't just my contract–a contract–and I have half a mind to tether you to me for what you did."

"What *I* did?"

"You ran to him the moment you thought you were free," I yell at her, pointing at the door.

She twists up to her knees, eyes flashing. "Free?" Her finger shakes as it directs toward her face. "You think I thought I was free? I hated being forced by your contract with all the rules, but I've never felt safer. You never lied to me, and I trusted you."

This is new, the broken voice and tears. I have no idea what to do with her like this. Even my Dark quells, uneasy with her state. We don't do tears.

She sniffs, swiping at her nose. "I felt caged and manipulated by the Magia and I felt trapped and suffocated in Izul. They made me wear beige. Beige!" Her voice cracks, her features crumbling. "I only went to Izul to stay alive, because I didn't know where else to go."

"Fucking idiot," I mutter, reaching for her.

She shoves my hand away. "I felt like I was home every time you held my hand, and you banished me because that asshole came in my mom?"

I hang my head and chuckle. "You have no idea how much I was struggling with that fact, but you weren't banished."

"I don't know what I'm doing. I don't know anything about this Light and Dark shit or what I am, and I trusted you, that you knew, that you'd handle what I couldn't."

Laughing, I scratch at my jaw. "You're a Light Seraphim, and I can handle it."

"I'm not," she says in a shaky voice.

I tip my head back laughing. "You can tell me you're Magia all you want, but you're the Light. You're a Seraphim, Little Star."

"I'm really not." She sucks in air on a wet sob, breathing out slower. "I ha—have wings."

I jerk, my Dark seeping across the bed toward her in search of her in curiosity. "You have wings?"

"Wings." She wipes at her face and then points over her shoulder. "Manifestation of magic that lets you fly." She hooks her thumbs together and flaps her hands, dropping them and rolling her eyes before swiping at her nose. "Fucking wings."

My pulse picks up speed. I'm not sure if it's nerves or excitement coursing through me and knitting my stomach. "Show me."

Her head tips back and the room illuminates, strands of Light stretching out behind her, arranging to flutter like little transparent feathers. She stares at me with an expression I've never seen before, something hollow and lost.

Delicate silver lace swirls over her skin, but her wings are a duller shade. I should say something rather than stare at her with an open mouth, but even my Dark is stunned into immobility, both of us enrapt with her beauty.

As much as I hate her origins, even though she's my natural enemy, I can't stop the tug in my chest. It's like a thread linking between us, a force drawing me to her. My Dark whines, soft and low, slithering to her.

"You take my breath away, Little Star."

"What am I?" The fear in her whisper hitches her breath at the end of her words.

I'm afraid of the answer, but I extend a hand to her, propped up on an arm beneath me as I lay on my side.

Natalia takes my offered hand. "Babe."

"My star," I close my fingers around hers and tug her into

470

me as I smirk. I wrap her in my arms and my Dark alike, tightening around her. "You're beautiful, although your annoyance has far outweighed your usefulness recently."

"I did say I'd try to be more annoying." She rolls to her side, wiggling her butt into my cock. I damn near lose self-control, but she curls in on herself, getting smaller as she sniffles.

"You have no idea how you succeeded." I squeeze her, trying to wrap her up in all of me and my Dark, inhaling her. "I missed you."

"You shouldn't have sent me away."

"That was only the beginning of your annoyances." I push my face into her neck and hair, letting my eyes fall closed as her Light slides across me, warm strings winding around my torso beneath my shirt.

We exist together, wrapped up in our magic. Exhaustion plagues me, my limbs heavier than I can ever recall.

She twists, turning into me. My lips find hers, and she opens her mouth as I roll her beneath me.

Her hand slips up my chest to the back of my neck, her tongue invading my mouth. All my blood rushes lower, my cock pulsing as she stirs my arousal.

"Stay," I tell her, slipping my hands beneath the bottom of her dress to slide along her thighs. "And for one cursed day will you fucking behave for me?"

She giggles, dragging my face back to hers.

CHAPTER 51

VANESSA

Cal runs down the steps, focused on Natalia. That's fine, I have a man of my own to find.

The nice man gestures to me and I follow him away. My babe is crying, but I can't blame her. I'm freaking out, my muscles quivering and my heart racing, high on emotions at the thought of seeing Massimo, and that's from my unrequited, silly crush.

I step into a kitchen at the direction of the man who showed us into this gorgeous home. "If you'll please wait here, I will fetch Massimo."

"Thanks," I say with a nod, and then face a pair of sexy men that have the full black eye of Dark Seraphinus.

One is perched on the massive island counter, the other standing in front of him between his legs. Both have high cheekbones, one face narrow with sexy, tousled fair hair and pale skin. The other has tawny skin with warm undertones, his nose wide, his eyes hooded and inset.

I swallow my nerves and try to smile, knowing no matter how sexy they are, they're able to kill me without effort. "Hi."

The slender one sitting cocks his head, smiling with closed lips. "Hi, baby. I'm Thames, and this is Hiro." He gestures at the dark-haired man standing between his knees. "Welcome to our home."

Hiro drops his chin at me. "Are you one who belongs to Callahan?"

Clapping my hands together, I rub them back and forth. "Yes, I belong to Callahan, but looking for the man they call Massimo right now."

Hiro jerks his chin. "Then welcome to my home. Is there anything you need?"

"Mass." I bob my head, not bothering to disguise the desperation in my voice. I haven't seen him in months, and I'm salivating.

Resting his chin on Hiro's shoulder, Thames asks, "Do you want a drink?"

I rock on my heels. "Does the Mother love?" There's silence as they stare at me confused. "Yes, the answer is yes, and a pain reducer if you have that because I've had a wicked headache for the past few months, and thank the Mother the suns are down, because I have missed the dark. I'd cuddle the shit out of it if I could."

Thames spits out his mouthful of wine over Hiro's shoulder laughing.

Hiro wipes spray from his face with a scowl. "Were you in Izul?"

"Yeah, with Tallie."

"Help yourself." Thames waves his glass at the fridge. "How was the Light capital? And our girl, Tallie? Is she back?"

"Izul is terrible," I say, moving to the fridge, throwing my pack on the island next to them. "Pure fucking misery. The brightness never went off, out, dimmed, just—" I wave a hand in front of my face, opening my eyes wider, "—bright light everywhere. It seriously gave me a permanent migraine. Tallie's here too, already with Cal, so she should be okay now."

I pull a bottle of vodka from the freezer and unscrew the cap. I hesitate, glancing at the men. "Are you like Cal with money to burn and don't care if I drink an entire bottle?"

Hiro's face twists with a smile. "My lineage empire is far greater than Cal's."

"I–Is that a yes? I really don't need to piss off a Darkling. I'll die real quick."

Thames giggles. "You can drink a bottle. You could drink twelve."

"Great." I tip the bottle end up to chug.

The kind man from earlier walks back into the kitchen with a hand flourish and bow. "Sir."

Massimo follows with a glower. "I'm here. What is..." His words die as he fixates on me.

Hiro jerks his head. "You're dismissed, Raz."

I keep chugging, pulse skipping out of rhythm as I stare back. Between the scar from his temple to cheek and all those muscles he looks menacing in the dim room. I pour the liquor into me in long gulps as the silence stretches until the bottle is empty.

Wiping my mouth with the back of my hand, I set the bottle on the counter and try to keep the vodka from coming back out. "Hey, Mass." I give him an awkward, forced smile. "Long time no see."

"Nessy." My name is terse from his lips, no twitch of his face revealing excitement.

"Yeah, so, that's about what I expected." I wince. My fantasies are just that, fantasy. "So, um, what's new?"

He crosses his arms, his shirt flexing to contain him, and I'm in awe of the tinsel strength the fabric must have. "Where's Tallie?"

"With Cal, somewhere, hopefully getting her brains screwed out."

We stare at each other. Despite the sharp sting of grief I felt, there's no reason to suspect he'd missed me in the slightest.

Sighing I step to the counter and unzip the pack. "Here," I yank a codex out and offer it to him.

He steps over and takes it. "You managed to not lose it. Good. Cal will be pleased."

"Mmm," I hum, laying a second on top of it.

"There's two now?" His face goes lax. "Where'd you get another one? How? When?"

I smile and place the last codex on the pile, the one Cal had me translate that had released its magic into me then shriveled. "Three."

"Gods," Thames mutters in a sour tone. "They smell."

I dip my head to the side. "Yes, but you get used to it."

Massimo balances the pile of books on an open palm, lifting the cover of the dead codex with a frown. "What's wrong with this one?"

"Ah, that..." I grimace and drop the notebook with my translations on the stack in Massimo's hands. "Those are the translations for it. That's the one I got from Cal."

"What did you do to it?"

I lean against the counter, my hand on my other hip as I point at it. "Tallie and I were sitting in the parking lot, talking when Pierre and his men–we didn't know it was them at the time—but the Lighters came flying over us and got really close to the car and it freaked. I mean *freaked* out. It started chattering and squealing and then it–like you–your magic." I squint at him and fling my hand out.

"Dark?" He drops his chin and lifts his eyebrows, staring at me with confusion from the tops of his eyes.

"It shot out of the book and attacked me." I rub my sternum with a wince recalling the blistering cold that pierced to my core. "And well." I lift the hem of my shirt to expose the swirls of black lines and runes across my ribcage running under my breasts.

His eyebrows and lips pinch together, one hand extending. The warm pads of his fingers brush over the thin skin of my sternum, and then he pulls back. "What is that?"

"No freaking idea. Hoping I can find answers in one of the other codexes because they aren't in the first. Tallie has some on her too. She tried to grab the book away from me, and she got a mark on her arm." I shrug and let my shirt fall back into place.

Massimo turns to the other codexes. "How'd you get the other two?"

"From the library in Izul," I say. "Let a guy take me to dinner to get the first, and then, you know, let the guy eat for the second." I grin and wink for emphasis.

Massimo inhales, his head jutting forward, eyes narrowed. "I'm done hearing about you spreading your legs for other men."

"Yeah?" I lift my eyebrows. "If it helps, I was thinking about you."

He steps back. "No, it doesn't." He grabs my backpack and shoves the stack of books inside. "Follow me."

I grab another bottle of vodka and wag it at the men on the counter. "Gotta go."

They watch with smiles as I crack the top.

Thames chuckles. "You must be Vanessa."

"That's me. Great house, by the way." I take a drink, wave two fingers, and pivot to follow Massimo.

Out of the kitchen, we head upstairs, down a hall, and up another flight of steps. He opens a door and motions me inside.

I inhale the coolness of the shadows, the curtains drawn to block the moonlight, the only light entering the room from the hall at my back "Oh, fuck me, Mother, I have missed darkness."

I have enough time to see the disheveled bedding and the bottle of golden liquor on the nightstand before the door shuts with a click, submerging me in complete blackness.

"Mass?" I turn and brush against him.

Something thumps as it hits the floor.

"Was that my books? Don't you know how to treat books?"

He snickers. "They'll be fine. I thought you might want to have sex."

"Oh." I draw back, trying to swallow, but my mouth is dry. I take a swig of vodka to settle my nerves, unsure of what to say.

"What? You'll give yourself to Roger and a Light fuck, but not me?"

"Are you fucking kidding me? Until you said that I would have jumped all over you and if I could see you, I'd slap you."

Fingers close around my wrist and the bottle of vodka is taken from me. Massimo shuffles me backward, and I hear the clunk of the bottle setting onto a hard surface just before he lifts my hand to the side of his face. "Does that help?"

I smirk. "Yes, actually." Pulling back, I give him a good crack across the face. Without the ability to see, there's no way to know if it affects him, but it gives me satisfaction.

He chuckles. "Feel better?"

"No, asshole. How do I get out of here?"

His strong arms encircle me. "Can I start over?"

"That's not the kind of thing someone hears and forgets, which is sad. It really is, because I so wanted to sit on your face."

"Still can." He lifts me off the floor with a grunt.

I'm tall and built sturdy with curves, not short and slim

like Tallie. I don't know if I've ever been picked up, but my legs automatically wrap around his waist, ankles locking together. "I heard that. Was that a fat joke?"

"No." His chest rumbles as he snickers, his large hand curling around one of my butt cheeks. "You're flawless."

"Maybe, but my mom says I'm all legs and elbows." I frown. "I'm not going to see her ever again."

"No. The Magia will kill you or try to use you to get Tallie." He leans over, dropping us onto the bed. I damn near orgasm from his body pressing into mine. "Cal will never allow Tallie to be in such danger."

I take full advantage of being beneath this gorgeous sex on a stick, arching into him. "You could have stopped at they will try to kill me."

His face presses against my neck. "I'll never allow them to."

Snorting through my nose, I lift my arms over my head, closing my eyes and pretending like this is a moment before sexy time for personal use later. After giving myself a fraction of a rune to memorize the feeling, I say, "Mass, I'm serious. I'm not sitting on your face after that comment."

"Can I sit on yours?"

Fighting against a laugh, I shake beneath him. "Am I supposed to suck on your nuts?"

"Yeah, try it. Fuck. Please. Let's try that."

I shake my head. "Fuck no. You don't get to... I'm not a slut, and you can't just drag me into your room and expect that I'm going to put out."

He sighs, pushing his weight off me and rolling to the side. "I'm looking for anything you weren't offering."

I pop like a balloon. "Yeah, offering, wanting, practically begging, and you had to go and ruin a good time."

He sighs. "Bad words, love."

I shift to my side, snuggling against him. I slide my leg over him, and one large, warm palm rests on my thigh.

"Nessy," he breathes low.

"Hmm?"

"I want to stick my dick in you."

I dissolve into giggles. "Really?"

"And touch your breasts," he says with a grin to his words.

I cuddle in closer. "Shouldn't have called me a trashy slut and I would have been all over that."

He rolls us, on top of me again. "I was asking if you have something against my kind."

"Your kind?"

"Dark." He nips at my earlobe. "You've told me about a human and a Light fuck."

I run my hands over his shoulder and down his upper arms. Squeezing his biceps. "After Izul, I'm pretty much certain I'm in love with the Dark."

He hums, dragging his lips back and forth across mine.

I inhale sharply, fighting the urge to lift my head and connect our mouths.

His lips curve. "Promise I'll lick until you scream."

I moan, desperate to accept what he's offering. "Buddy, don't tease me. I'm trying to prove I have self-respect."

"I will respect the fuck out of you, woman."

I laugh, but his mouth swallows it, his tongue sneaking into my mouth as his hands draw up my sides to cup my breasts. Arching into his caress, I make a noise of frustration.

His hands slip lower, shoving my shirt up and dipping his head lower. As he kisses down my stomach, he pops the button on my tight khaki's.

I grab at the back of his head, my skin alive with tingling nerves. "Oh, fuck self-respect, I want to know if you taste like chocolate and wine like you look."

"That's what I look like?"

"That and like you can eat gravel and kill dragons with your bare hands."

He grunts, working my pants lower. "Better."

"What's wrong with chocolate and booze? That's what every woman really wants, screw the dragon slaying."

Shaking with laughter, he peels me out of my clothes, his hands and mouth everywhere, a cool slither drawing across my skin that leaves goosebumps in its wake.

I breathe quick and shallow, a coil of tension mounting low in my abdomen. "Mass."

Massimo crushes his mouth against mine, settling between my legs. "What the fuck, woman?"

"Yeah, that's what this is called. Try harder to keep up."

"No, your magic. You have magic?"

"No idea what you're talking about. Less weird words, more thrusting." I rock my hips against his, his hard dick pressing against my leg. "Oh, fuck me, please, please?"

He chuckles, slipping his hand between us, fingers exploring for a moment before finding all the right spots. Throwing my head back, I moan, clenching tighter around his touch.

"It's natural, magic coming out to play," he says. "Feels good, but your magic is as crazy as you are, and I didn't know you had it." He kisses between my breasts.

"I don't know if I do. It's new. It's weird. Don't ruin the mood."

His mouth stays busy, licking down my body, around my belly button, and then my clit. I moan, gripping the sheets and gasping as he teases me to orgasm. Stars explode behind my eyes, and I babble at him in pleasure.

He chuckles, kneeling between my legs as I go limp,

glowing from the inside. Grabbing my hips, he asks, "Is that Brish?"

"Yes, it is. Penis, vagina, now."

He thrusts and I arch, whimpering as my body stretches to accommodate him.

"Oh," I gasp as he pulls back and rams into me over and over, in long hard strokes.

He jerks and twitches inside of me, groaning as he comes. Going still, he curses.

I pick my head up, "Uh?"

"Shut up, woman."

Laughter bubbles past my lips. "Is that the end of this ride?"

"I said shut up," he snaps, hands gripping my hips harder.

"I mean, disappointing compared to my fantasies, but..."

One of his hands wraps around the underside of my jaw. "Stop talking, you crazy woman. I'm not done."

"It's fine. I got an orgasm."

"I'll fix it."

"Sure, but while we wait can I ask, is this normal? Or am I just that hot?"

"Not normal. Maybe normal. It's been..." He sighs. "It's been a while."

"What? How? Why?"

"Cal keeps me busy."

I sit up, wrapping my arms around his neck. He shifts, holding me close, stroking my back as I straddle his hips. "So, this is a one-time giddy up?"

"Depends. Cal is disgraced, and you have no contract. Are you sticking around to serve him?"

"Where the fuck else am I going to go? Tallie's not leaving and the Magia are going to kill me."

He cups the back of my head, bringing my mouth to his. "I won't let them, love," he says, growing with soft throbs.

"Yeah?" I rock in his lap. "Are you going to be my knight in shining armor?"

"No, I'm not wearing anything shiny."

CHAPTER 52
NATALIA
EIGHTH THORN'S DAY, SNOWDROP, 4050
6TH MILLENNIUM

I wake in dim light, long shadows cast across the room from curtains and windows, tucked against solid warmth breathing at my back. A strong arm of tan skin with red undercurrents is draped over my torso, sending a wave of exhilaration through me. I fold my tongue between my teeth, grinning at waking up with the man I want in soft early morning light. I wriggle into him, butt first.

He stirs, shifting to cup my breast. "Mmm, 'ittle Star."

"Cal." I snuggle in again.

"Missed you." He opens his mouth against my neck, drawing a circle with his tongue before dragging his teeth closed.

The admission winds me, and I inhale through my nose trying to catch my breath. He'd said I wasn't just a contract, even dropping the word mate, but I'm reeling at those two words for a second time. "Really?"

He rolls his hips into me, his hard dick pressing into my butt. "The Dark doesn't lie." His fingers skim lower, a gentle brush along my center. "Who's in charge?"

I giggle. "You."

He groans, face against my neck. "Which makes me?"

Shivering in anticipation of the trajectory of his touch, my breath hitches in the back of my throat. "Alpha."

"Yes." He flips me to face him. "My little star."

I push him to his back, straddling him. "You know," I begin, bracing my hands on his chest, gazing down at his cut torso. I bite my lip, lifting my eyes to his. "He asked me how you controlled me." Leaning over, I put my hand to the side of Cal's jaw, kissing him.

He fists my hair, pulling my head where he wants it before dragging his mouth away. "Don't talk to me about that fuck while I'm hard."

Smirking, I reach between us, aligning him and sliding down onto him. He groans, lifting his hips, and I smile, eyes fluttering in pleasure, my words breathless. "You don't control me. You can't, but I'm choosing you."

He groans again, pulling my face back to his and thrusting up. "Mine," he growls.

I ride him, tipping my head back. His Dark slides across my skin, my hair brushing against my back, and I let my eyes fall closed, giving myself to the moment. His hands caress my body, gentle strokes as he moves beneath me.

On the edge, I whimper. His magic lashes tighter, his hands gripping my hips, fingers digging in with brutal force. He thrusts harder, lifting his hips in a quickening rhythm.

A snap of tension gives way to euphoria rippling through my body. "Cal."

I fall forward, panting in little mewls.

His fingers weave into my hair at my nape, tightening into a firm grip. I gasp, going limp in his grip as he speaks in a low, guttural snarl. "This is where you belong—on my cock and in my Dark."

He forces me back up, grinding my hips back and forth, pushing me into delirium.

DRESSED in Cal's sweatpants and sweatshirt, I snuggle the hood with a happy purr as I descend the stairs. His clothes swallow me, but they're soft, warm, and, most importantly, both pieces are black. I'm treading with about six inches of the sweatpants folded under my feet even with the waistband rolled, moving slow to avoid tripping.

My stomach gurgles and clenches, and I glance back at him halfway down. "Can–" My foot slips as I catch the edge of a step. "*Eep!*"

Magic lashes around me, yanking me backward into him. "Little Star," he grumbles like he's still half asleep. "Yes, I'll get you food." Slipping an arm around my stomach, he hoists me off my feet to carry me the rest of the way down the steps.

I grin, tipping my head back onto his shoulder. "Thanks."

He presses his lips to my temple as he sets me back on my feet at the bottom of the stairs. "Next time, walk first, ask second." Smacking my butt, he says, "Now walk."

Giggling, I let him push me forward, and we move through the house. It's not as sleek and bare as Cal's, but carries an old, expensive feel.

Moving out a set of double doors, I step onto a dark wood porch. From a table, two familiar faces turn toward me.

Thames twists up and out of his chair, walking toward me with open arms. "You're a lovely sight, baby."

He wraps me in a hug tight enough I think a couple of my

ribs crack. "Hey, Thames," I wheeze, smacking at him. "Can't breathe."

Thames steps back in a hurry. "My bad, baby. I forget you're human with the way you glow."

I wrinkle my nose. "Not so much human, but okay." Leaning around Thames, I give Hiro a little wave. "Hi."

He gives me a tight smile. "Took you long enough."

Gesturing down my front, Thames shakes his head. "This, no. Cal needs to treat you better."

I laugh, shoving my hands in the front pocket of the sweatshirt. "At least it's black. Everything in Izul was white and gold and beige." I feign a retch.

Thames laughs. "Absolute torture. Come," he grabs my hand and leads me to the table.

Cal drops into the seat next to me. "Hiro, Talia needs food."

Hiro snaps, and a man appears from nowhere, stepping forward. "Sir?"

Hiro gestures at me. "What would you like to eat, Light Bug?"

The man's eyes slide to me, and his lip curls back. "I will not serve the Light."

Pouting, I say, "But I'm so hungry."

Hiro gets to his feet. "Are you refusing to comply with an order, Charles?"

Dark slithers around Hiro, his posture tight, and Charles rocks back on his heels, crossing his arms. "I have complied to every order for the last two hundred and thirty years that you have given me as I swore to you I would do, but I will not serve the Light." He turns and spits. "I can't forgive you for asking me to."

Lowering my eyes to the table, I nod. "Fair enough."

"Damn you." Hiro grabs Charles by the face and slams him down to the deck, Dark magic writhing above the table.

I try to stand but with a hand on my shoulder, Cal forces me back into my seat. "Don't, Talia."

Shrugging and shoving at him, I yell, "Stop! Hiro, stop, please! It's fine."

Cal's fingers dig in my shoulder to the point of pain. "It's a contract. Don't interfere."

"It's not fair. It's not even fair that Hiro asked."

Thames looks up from tracing the rim of his teacup with a sad look. "He refused an order."

"Please," I lift my voice over Charles's shrieking. "I spent months in Izul. I know why you hate the Light."

There's a sickening crunch and Hiro pops to his feet. Glaring at me, he begins to unbutton his bloodied shirt. My blood runs cold, and I blanch, cowering under his gaze as my magic winds in tight vines around me.

Thames shrugs. "We do, but you've earned the right to be served."

"He doesn't know that. He just sees the Light. Hiro, please," I plead. "Please, just, please don't... Let him refuse. I'll serve myself."

Hiro sneers. "He's already dead." He cuts his eyes to Cal, then walks away, shrugging his shirt off.

I check over my shoulder that he's gone, and then cross my arms over my chest, leaning forward with them on the table. I breathe out slow, my stomach churning. "That wasn't right."

Cal runs the back of his knuckles down my upper arm. "He refused an order."

Thames continues running his finger around the edge of his cup. It's the expression I'd have after watching a puppy get kicked. "He knew what was going to happen. It was his choice."

I hang my head, snorting through my nose. "Right, because when I walked into Ilbuio you didn't want me dead because I was the Light, because everyone here doesn't absolutely hate the Light. I was in Izul, I get it. It wasn't fair."

Thames chuckles. "I wanted to watch you die. If the opportunity had presented itself, I would have killed you myself. Ask Hiro. I wanted to draw you and Cal for the sacrifice to send you to the afters myself." Cal snaps his teeth, and Thames laughs with his head tipped back. "It was fortunate we didn't face each other, but then, Light Bug, you pushed him over that line to safety to face the game on your own while he was safe. We all saw. He was going to send you first, but you saved him over yourself. You stunned us all."

Picking my head up, I ask, "Why?"

"You're the Light." He shrugs and sits back with the faint kiss of a smile on his lips. "Light doesn't save Dark, and contract or not I thought for sure you'd find a way to get him killed."

Scrunching my face up, I display my distaste. "No."

"Yes, I know, baby." He picks up his teacup from the saucer as two vassals approach.

I glance at them, but they ignore us at the table as they go about collecting the remains of Charles and carting him away.

A third steps forward, the same man who showed me into the house last night. "I was sent," he says to Thames.

Thames waves his hand toward me with a tight smile. "What do you want, Light Bug?"

Frowning at the man, I consider the shadows curling around him, his strong jawline clamped tight, narrow-set eyes pinched with disdain. Sighing, I flop back, flicking at nothing on the armrest. "What's your name?"

"Raz." There's a stiffness to his words.

I rub the bridge of my nose. "What I want is breakfast, and I'd like it without spit in it if that's possible. Although I'm hungry enough that if you just mix it in really well so I don't notice, that will be fine too, and I want you to make sure everyone here," I lift a finger and draw a circle, "knows I'm not some Light to hate. Can you do that for me?"

Raz lifts his eyebrow, glancing at Thames, who shrugs with an amused smirk. Returning his focus to me, Raz asks, "Why shouldn't we hate you?"

I laugh behind closed lips, exasperated and tired. "I have the Light in me. I'm going to glow surrounded by all of you Darklings, but I spent a few months in Izul, and, let me tell you, I'm not very good at being the Light. I love sarcasm, using the word 'fuck,' and punching people who deserve to be punched."

Raz's features brighten with humor, his up-ticked nose flaring as he grins.

I turn to Cal, Ness and Massimo visible off to the side. Ness is in a black tee-shirt and boxers, winking at me with a wide grin. She must have had as good a night as mine.

Lifting my chin at her, I say, "You know they have a law against punching people? You get a fifty-year sentence for attacking someone. I found that out day one."

Cal frowns. "Who did you hit?"

"Ashley, Pierre's daughter."

Ness sits at the table. "Telling them how you went to jail? Is there food anywhere? I'm hungry."

Raz leans forward, head cocked with intrigue, one side of his mouth pulled up. "You defended Callahan to the Light?"

Cal sneers. "I am not a dog."

I make a face of annoyance. "I broke her nose and screamed at Pierre in front of the Light Queen that I'd be a real savage if they insulted you again. Got myself locked up for fifty days and a shit ton of etiquette lessons to fix my behavior."

Cal twists his lips to the side. "How'd that work for them?"

I shrug. "Well enough that I lied my ass off to make them think it worked."

"No lying. The Dark doesn't lie."

I scrunch my face up. "Well, yeah. Kind of why I love the Dark, but I'm the Light, right? And the Light is a bunch of lying assholes, so you know, do unto others as they do unto you."

Raz tips his head back and laughs, sauntering away. "I will have food prepared."

Ness puts a hand up to her mouth yelling after him, "For me too." She turns to me. "Mother, I'm starving. But hey, look." She points at her chest and then mine. "Black!"

CHAPTER 53

CALLAHAN

Massimo drops a backpack off his shoulder, unzips it and reaches inside. He shoves a stack of books toward me. "Nessy was useful."

Vanessa perks up. "Hey, I was useful." She shoves Natalia by the shoulder. "Hear that, babe?"

Natalia laughs, curling one knee up and relaxing. "Heard loud and clear."

She's smiling again. It's good. Seeing her desolate last night had been difficult, and I had no idea what to do about it.

Pulling the stack of books closer, I rifle through the notebook full of neat print and doodles, then toss it to the side to stare at the shriveled codex. I run my fingers over the scales, ashen and still, the surface no longer black but a decayed gray.

As I lift it for inspection, I realize the other two books beneath are also codexes. I gape at the clicking scales, shock spreading as tingles through my chest all the way to my fingertips.

"I've spent decades trying to find others. How did you

491

manage this?" I peel my gaze from them, gaping at Massimo, then Vanessa.

She beams, proud of herself, but I'll allow it. "Found them in the library at Izul and forgot to return them before I left."

Natalia snorts through her nose. "Or not."

"Yeah, fine, but they didn't belong there. Poor babies were suffocated in a glass case with no room to breathe."

Thames leans forward, lips pulled in a forced frown of disgust. "I understand why. They click, and that odor." His nose wrinkles as he withdraws. "I expect them to be put away when inside my house."

I inspect the codex with curled scales. "They destroyed this one." I thumb through a few pages to determine if they still retain any information. The pages crackle and break apart, disintegrating. "Fuck."

"Actually," Vanessa says in a slow voice and winces. "That's the one you gave me. I translated the whole thing first, thank the Mother, because it's empty now. It freaked near the Light and attacked me."

She stands and pulls the large shirt aside, her attire clearly supplied by Massimo. I'm hoping he'll stop talking about masturbation as I focus on what Vanessa is showing me. Her rich brown skin is marked with black lines across her sternum and lower ribs.

I frown, and Natalia raises her forearm into my line of sight, saying, "And this."

Taking her arm in my hand, I run my thumb over the lines circling her forearm. "What is it?"

"No idea, but, um…" She bites her lower lip, glancing at Thames and then Vanessa and Massimo. "While on the topic of weird, I should tell you I generated Dark."

I lock my eyes on hers, the pulse in my neck skipping. "Dark?"

"Once, and I was pissed, so pissed. Pierre was spouting shit about the Dark again, and you...and, um, said something about your father."

Bile burns as rot gut leaking in my abdomen. I have no idea the story he told her, the lies he would spin.

Vanessa gets excited, chattering on, ignorant of my turmoil. "Me too. I broke magic to get to those codexes, and, babe, give me your hand."

Natalia turns, pressing her palm to Vanessa's. Black twists away from Vanessa, Natalia's Light sparkling brighter.

She withdraws, her voice a thin whine, "What the fuck? You never told me this."

I eye Vanessa, her seat pulled close to Massimo's, his arm draped over the back. If the codex imbued her with magic, she may develop into a useful and sharp tool.

Ness checks her hand before slumping in her chair. "You were always busy."

"You were always in the library."

"Because you were always with Pierre or Zander."

"Zander?" I snarl, the name catching in my ear. He is the Light fuck Natalia spoke of in the maze. The man who fucked her after saving her from drowning. "The *same* Zander?"

Natalia's face jerks in my direction, fear slithering in her wide eyes. "He's Pierre's contracted."

I grab her jaw at the base, my fingers resting against her cheeks as I growl in my chest. As Pierre's contracted, he would have had plenty of access to my star. "Did you fuck him again?"

Vanessa bursts into laughter. "Tallie had every chance to sit on that gorgeous face with the way he was throwing himself at her, and she wasn't interested. Too busy writing songs about you instead."

I focus on Natalia, who has her lips sucked inward, her eyes dancing with mirth. She points a finger over her shoulder. "What she said?"

"I want to hear you say it." I release her face, eyeing her with mistrust.

"I did not have sex with Zander." She wiggles her jaw back and forth, massaging both sides.

I might have pushed too hard. Like Thames, I tend to forget she's not as durable as we are, even with her Magia blood.

"Calm down, jealous prick. I thought you were dead, and I still didn't sit on his face or his dick."

"Hmm." I study her bathed in the daylight, still glimmering like she's covered in thousands of tiny stars. Her hair has grown past her shoulders, the strands straighter about her face.

She smirks, her lips twisting off to one side. "Seriously, Boss-Owner-Master. Stop throwing tantrums." She rubs the side of her face. "It hurts."

Porcelain clinks, and Thames clears his throat. "How did you manage to find your way here?"

"Oh." Natalia laughs at him. "Ashley wasn't thrilled about me being in Izul, so she told me Cal was alive–finally–and helped us get out of Izul. She even dropped us off here."

Thames's eyes take up his whole face, the life draining from his features. "Pierre's daughter knows where my home is?"

"Uh," Natalia winces, "yeah, but I didn't tell her. She already knew."

He shakes his head with a dejected frown.

I ask, "Why did she help you?"

"The Light Queen insisted on Ritual. Pierre was trying to circumvent the whole thing by putting me in a relationship with Zan and having me contracted to him, but Ash went and called Ritual anyway." Natalia rolls her eyes. "She lost, so her only option to avoid the kickback of losing was to get rid of me, and she'd already tried and failed to kill me twice."

My Dark hisses with possessive annoyance. I reach for her hand, pressing the palm to my lips. "You stay with me, Little Star, where I can keep you safe."

Several vassals come forward, delivering trays of food. Plate upon plate of eggs, fruit, bacon, toast, and everything else is set on the table in front of Natalia in quick order. Her stomach grumbles, echoed by Vanessa's.

I shake my head. "You two eat a ridiculous amount of food."

Thames frowns, tapping a finger against the handle of his cup. "Should I stock up?"

I shrug. "Yes, but they're not picky eaters, and they'll want vodka too."

Raz waves the others away and bows to us. "Breakfast without spit in it."

"Thanks." She reaches for bacon, shoving a piece into her mouth, folding it over and over to fit before swallowing it.

I blink, not sure if she chewed.

"My absolute pleasure for someone who defends the Dark to the Light." He inclines his head. "I have reported the news to the others. There should be no one who gives you trouble, but if they do, alert me, Thames, or Hiro with due haste, and we will take care of the concern for you."

The women are shoveling food into their mouths with quick efficiency, washing it down with orange juice.

I jerk my head toward the house. "I'll repeat that when they're done. Interfering with them while they eating might cost you a hand or quite possibly your life."

Thames bubbles with humor, refilling his cup from the teapot. "Did they not feed you two in Izul? I feel as if I'm watching feral malrogs devour bones."

Vanessa lifts her plate to her mouth, opening her lips to shuffle egg from the dish and down her throat with efficiency. The food gone, she starts to fill her plate again, saying, "We're Magia. We have a high metabolism, burn through anything we eat quickly, alcohol too."

Massimo leans over and says something in Vanessa's ear that makes her smile.

Natalia bobs her head. "Magia are human bodies with Seraphinus blood, so, yeah, it burns up our bodies if we don't feed it."

Thames sips his tea and announces, "I want to hear these songs."

My little star's face turns pink in an adorable fashion. "It's really just the one."

"It's rude to refuse a host," he says, slathering jam on a scone. "Don't break my heart."

With a slick move, Hiro steals the morsel from Thames and shoves it into his mouth as he reclaims his seat. "Keep your mouth shut, Lightning Bug. It's my house, so my order to keep."

Natalia shakes her head. "After all that time in Izul, I know why you hate the Light. The way they talk about you? I understand why he didn't want to serve me. It wasn't fair to ask."

"I do not care. I speak, they move. They don't think for themselves, and I expect respect from you. If you were anyone else, you'd be with Charles in the afters."

She shakes her head, looking up and away, her words faint as if speaking to herself when she says, "How about I treat you like a Lighter treats a Darkling, and we'll see how fast you change your mind."

Hiro shifts his chair closer to Thames and pulls the man against him with a sigh. Softening, he blinks at her. "Call me vermin, and you'll find out how quickly I will get my claws out." Shaking his head, he turns his face into Thames, his eyes closing as he embraces his mate. "We aren't animals."

Thames winks at Natalia. "Hiro's an animal in bed, but it's delightful."

Snickering, Hiro musses Thames's hair. "Stop it, Sugar Bear." With a sad smile, Hiro faces Natalia. "Yes, you have the Light within you, and no, the Light doesn't deserve to be treated with respect or served, but I decide what mine do, and I decided they will serve you—you, Tallie, not the fucked Light."

I meet Hiro's eyes. He inclines his head and returns to watching Natalia.

She sighs, staring into her mug. She taps her finger against the handle, and I wait. She's headstrong, and this could spiral into a problem.

Standing, she turns to walk away. "I'll go get my guitar."

Hiro calls out in a cranky tone, "Sit down. I'll send someone."

She keeps walking, and Thames shakes his head. "Not using vassals and ignoring orders... Have you taught her nothing?"

I shake with silent laughter. "Talia doesn't learn."

"Nope," Vanessa says, pushing a cube of pineapple into her mouth. "My babe is stubborn."

I chuckle and take a drink of my coffee. "She doesn't do anything the easy way. Fights orders, barely accepts suggestions, and the only reason I've managed her is her contract. She's beyond stubborn."

Hiro scowls. "Not even that was enough after the maze."

"No. She's too powerful and smart for her own good. Questions everything." I shake my head with a faint smile. "Worst fucking contract I ever accepted."

Natalia sticks her arm in front of me. "Fine, you can take it back then."

I flick her wrist. "No. Behave."

Setting the case down, she pops the hinges and pulls out the guitar I'd sent to Izul. Getting situated with it in her lap, her eyes find mine. She runs her hand down the neck. "It's from you, isn't it?"

"Yes."

She bobs her head, her face low, her hair falling forward to hide her expression. The strands are whiter than I recall, colorless with a sheen. If anything, she's even more beautiful with the silver hair and the longer strands. I have to admit I enjoyed having more to grab.

She sighs, picking her face up to stare at me with a broken expression. "All of them? The guitar, the rabbit suit, the seowolf, the spider spray, the vodka, the sugar scrub, the—"

"Yes." I cut her off, embarrassed at the list of my desperate gifts.

She's silent, her head hung low.

I draw my eyebrows together, pushing her hair away from her face and over the back of her neck. "Little Star, what's—"

"If I ever see Pierre or Zander again, I'm going to wring their fucking necks." Her words carry the rage of a smite and the quiet of the Dark, sending a shiver down my spine.

All my concerns, the late-night workouts and drunken nights because I couldn't sleep filled with dread, had been for naught. It didn't matter how long she was in Izul: they were never going to break her, and they weren't capable of possessing her the way I am.

I run my fingers through her hair, kissing the side of her face. "Do what you will to Zander, but Pierre is mine to dismember."

"The Light has this thing—give a gift, and the receiver owes a gift back that is equal to the gift. That fucker was giving me your gifts and making me pay him back when I didn't owe him fuck all."

I never considered how she was receiving the items I sent. My sole concern had been if she was getting them at all. The realization they were claimed as gifts to be given by another boils in my gut. Worse, they were used against me. I gave him keys to my little star one at a time.

She adjusts her grip on the instrument. Putting fingers to her chest, she toys with the star pendant and turns to me with melancholy. "This was you too, right?"

I lower my eyes to the pendant, the clear stones catching not only the sunlight but hers as well, refracting the Light so that it appears to be a genuine star hanging from her neck. I hadn't imagined that as an effect, but it's fitting.

Rocking forward, I draw my thumb over it, my voice low. "Yes, I picked the stones myself, laid them out, and had it made exactly in that design."

She flinches, turning her face away. "Zander gave it to me," she whispers, "when he asked to start a relationship."

Rage hazes my vision, and my Dark ignites with fury. The world is reeling at my wrath. I long to taste blood.

"I almost started bawling, asked him why a star, and he tried to take it back."

I snap my teeth, shoving words through a clamped jaw. "If I find out you fucked him, that you *lied* to me—"

My little star giggles, leaning over the instrument to put her hands on either side of my face as I pant in short, ragged breaths through my nose. "Babe." She lifts my chin, forcing my gaze to hers as my Dark coils around her wrists. "I lied in Izul. I lied a lot because I had to. I had to convince the Light Queen I was sorry that I accepted your contract so she wouldn't destroy my Light, but I won't lie to you."

I growl, the rumble catching in the back of my throat. "I'm going to fucking rip his Light out of him."

"Music, baby," Thames interrupts. "Sing before Cal loses his temper and he ends up bloody."

Whipping my face out of Natalia's grasp, I snarl at him. "Me end up bloody?"

Hiro smirks, trying to hide it behind a hand. "I'm not sure who would win that fight."

Vanessa gestures to Natalia. "I'd bet on my babe."

Natalia laughs. "Please don't. I might live if we faced on a level playing field, but if he shifted, I'd run." She throws an arm out, pointing into the distance. "As fast and as far as I could until my lungs stopped working."

Leaning in close, I nip her ear, my voice raw. "Not even that would be enough to save you."

Thames lifts his teacup, "Cheers to that. Now, entertain me."

She flips him off. "No. Just no. The way you phrased that gave me flashbacks of the king."

I push her finger down but smile. She said "the king" like she's one of us. "Behave, or we'll find out how fast you can run."

Laughing, Thames takes a drink. "Sing."

Natalia sighs, strumming. A quiet melody unfolds, calling forth melancholy. Her voice is soft as she sings, her voice drifting across my senses, drawing my eyes shut as I inhale her words.

She spins lyrics of bleeding pain, but all I hear is she shines for me, my little star burning bright for me.

I hold back a chuckle, my lips twitching and toying with a smile. She thought herself a fool while I had pined away, sending gifts as a boy with an infatuation, desperate for her attention.

The humor fades, the song spiraling on. The way she was last night comes to mind. Broken. Lost. She'd been hurting.

I scowl, my eyebrows pulling together as she plays notes of music quietly. Natalia's been mine since the moment she took my hand and I pulled her onto my bike. I never questioned that, burying myself in her more than I care to admit, but in all my desire and need, I never considered her wants.

Her contract. She'd thought it was my last words to her. The way she describes it is gutting.

The song spins out a glistening web, lines of pain that weave together to create something delicate and rare. It coils around my throat, closing off my airway. I claim her, own her, every part of her, and I'll never pry my claws free, but I never realized she'd reciprocated the attachment.

As she plays the last notes, my chest is tight, air hard to pull in. She clears her throat, finding a new chord, strumming and following it up with a new song. This time, Vanessa's voice joins in.

They sing and laugh through several songs, the tone of the music changing to an upbeat vibe, but her lyrics keep repeating in my mind. It's left me dazed, stuck in the moment with shock.

I open my eyes to see Vanessa dancing in her seat and Natalia glowing brighter, grinning at her.

As another song ends, Vanessa laughs with a whoop of excitement. "Bring Blood."

Natalia stops, chortling and takes a drink of coffee. "I need a fraction."

Thames is in Hiro's lap, cuddled up, his sight moving to me. "Can we borrow her in the next games?"

Blowing him a kiss, Natalia says, "Absolutely."

I curl my lip. "No, you may not."

Natalia turns with shock.

501

The next time there is a Gathering Shadows, I won't be a player. Either she is their queen, or we'll both be dead. I don't want her to carry the weight of the contest until she must. I'll shield her for as long as I can, so I tap her nose with a forced grin. "Nothing you need to be concerned about right now. Sing your songs."

CHAPTER 54

NATALIA

After breakfast, Cal walks me inside. Hiro and Thames go one way, and Mass sweeps Ness off her feet, carrying her up the steps. She giggles, and I smile after them.

I turn to Cal, hugging his arm and leaning into him. "That's not a problem for you, is it?"

"I don't give a fuck as long as he does his job."

I spin in front of Cal, tipping my head back. "I'm not just a contract?"

His hand rests at the top of my throat, fingers laying against my jaw, his touch and tone gentle. "No."

With a grin, I jump at him, wrapping my legs around his hips as he catches me with a grunt.

He stares at me, something wrong in his features. "Zander."

I sigh, arms around Cal's neck, rolling my head back to stare at the ceiling with a groan. "Fine. We kissed. I really thought you were dead. Don't yell at me. Magia can kill Seraphinus, and you damn well know it. We held hands and slept together a few nights but never fucked. He wanted to and

I said no, I couldn't because... Cal, I–I ..." I meet his eyes, tracing his lower lip with my finger. "You aren't just my contractor."

"And you're not just a contract." He playfully nips at my hand. "He is going to die in the worst possible way I can think of."

Pulling my lips to the side, I tighten my legs around his hips and shrug. "Can I at least punch him first?" I pretend to pout.

"No. He took what was mine and pandered it as his own. He touched what is mine, knowing full-fucking-well it is mine, and he lied to do it."

I touch the necklace, remembering how I lost my breath when I opened the case, but it's like getting punched in the stomach. "Thank you for this, for my guitar..." My words warble.

One of his hands wraps around the back of my head, bringing my face to his, his lips against mine, his tongue swirling inside my mouth. I groan, sagging against him and trusting he won't let go.

Pulling back, he nudges my nose with his. "Never leave me again."

I rub the tip of my nose against his, smiling. "I'll stay."

"Good." He sets me on my feet. "I hated having to hunt for my food again. Come on." He takes my hand, pulling me along.

I skip to fall in step with him, swinging our clasped hands. "Um, A, where are we going? And B, you hate hunting for food?"

"Thames is right, you need better attire, so we are going shopping, and yes, I realized I like having my own personal food source." He lifts our linked hands, his Dark wrapped around my wrist, the end of one tendril caressing my forearm. My Light shines beneath his magic, turning it shades of deep blue.

"Oh," I squeeze his hand. "Right, I'm food."

He opens a door and swings me through it before him with a sly smirk. "Among other things." We pass a few cars, heading straight for a motorcycle. He straddles it and looks to me as he grabs the handles, jerking his head. "On."

Slipping behind him, I slide my arms around his torso, hugging tight, inhaling his strength. Zander might be handsome too, taller even, and lean with muscle, but he can't compare to the raw strength and power Cal exudes. "Don't fucking kill me."

He glances over his shoulder, scowling. "I'm still not sure how I'm going to punish you for being stupid enough to think I could be taken down by the Magia when I know their secrets, running to Izul and Pierre and letting that Light fuck touch you. What else did you do that I don't know about?"

I giggle at his terse tone, kissing his cheek. "I spent a bunch of your money. I didn't realize your account wasn't closed, and I bought a bottle of decade bourbon."

"I'm aware. I was monitoring my account for any activity that you were beyond Izul. That's the one thing I don't care about." He kicks the stand up. "Why did you buy bourbon? You hate bourbon."

"Ness and I toasted you and Mass and sang that song I wrote, kind of a spirit send off the Magia do. It seemed appropriate."

"You sent my soul to the afters before I'm dead?"

"Pretty sure that's not how it works." I swivel my eyes toward the ceiling of the parking garage. "You know, Pierre is going to be furious when he realizes I've disappeared."

Cal flashes his teeth. On the surface, it looks like a faux smile, but the flash in his eyes warns me he's baring his teeth like a predator. "You're my contracted and property by law, even if I am disgraced because you're a worn contract."

505

"You're disgraced?"

Cranking the accelerator, the tires squealing, he speeds out of the garage. I cling to him, burying my face against his back. He's vibrating, and I'm willing to bet he's laughing.

The tires chirp when the bike skids to a stop, and my arms burn with fatigue as I unfurl from him. I smack him between his shoulder blades. "Asshole."

In one smooth motion, he grabs me, twisting me off the bike as he climbs off it, swinging me into his arms to cradle me. "You're alive."

"Thanks, babe."

He turns and starts walking up the street. "You're welcome."

"Going to put me down?" I hook my arm around his neck, my other hand to his chest, hoping he won't.

"You have no shoes."

We both glance at my feet, and I wiggle my toes. "Fair enough." I stare him dead in the eye. "Carry me, bitch."

He stares back for a fraction, and then he cracks, lips twisting to one side like he's trying not to smile, but his voice betrays him. "I still don't take orders."

"You're disgraced?"

The skin on the bridge of his nose crinkles as he curls his lip. "That shit the Magia did humiliated me. After that stunt you pulled in Ilbuio, I was already on thin ice with my standing, and they made me look weak." He stares at me, his eyebrows coming together, the lines of his face deepening as he frowns. "Talia."

I tense at the tone, "I didn't do anything."

"You're not glowing."

Moving my hands from his neck, I hold them in front of me, inspecting the back and front. No trace of my Light is glimmering, no web of silver glistening, no subtle defense shining at all. I stare, concerned that something is wrong, that I've lost my magic somehow.

A rush of humor overcomes me. Several strands of my Light coil through my fingers, one stretching out to twist with a single tendril of shadow from Cal.

His voice purrs in my head. *"It's my friend."*

I blink in confusion. "Oh, it's fine. It just doesn't see you as a threat." I can't breathe as realization dawns. My Light doesn't care about his Dark. It's not defensive or scared.

He's tense, breathing slow, his chest swelling and holding for a moment. "Talia," he says in a strangled whisper. "That's not... Light doesn't..."

Holding his gaze, my eyes stinging, I smile. I slide one arm around his neck, cupping his strong jaw with my other hand to draw his face closer to mine. "*We* trust you, babe."

With a guttural noise, he closes the distance, kissing me. His arms and Dark tighten around me with crushing force.

Grinning, I pull back. "Can we—"

A man knocks into us, Cal stumbling half a step. He recovers, and glares at the two men moving past us on the sidewalk.

The man who bumped Cal turns with a laugh. "Sorry, bud, I—Oh, you're a fucking Darkling."

The other with him is stockier, clenching his fists. "Put her down, Dark shit. Humans aren't your toys."

Cal lifts his chin. "She's mine."

I bob my head. "I'm happy right where I'm at."

The first looks to the second, who cracks his knuckles, with a sneer. "You know the new rules. We see one, we kill it."

Holding a finger up, I cock my head. "New rules?" I move my eyes down them, noticing their cocky stances.

The first steps closer. "Put her down. She doesn't have to get hurt."

I giggle. "What are you? Magia?"

Moron One makes a grab for me. "Yes, and we can help you."

Cal takes a step back, grumbling. "Piss off. I'm not in the mood for a fight. I just want to be left the fuck alone."

Moron One looks at Moron Two, who shrugs and rolls his shoulders and neck like he's getting ready to strike. "They made it clear a loss or two is acceptable."

I center.

Moron Two strikes at the air.

Cal's Dark shields, but Moron One follows suit, too close for his block to help us. I shield from the second attack, but Cal and I reel backward from the percussive shock. We hit the ground with simultaneous groans.

He mutters. "What the fuck?"

"Pinnacle," I manage, squirming as hands latch onto me, trying to yank me away from Cal. "Fucking Mother! Let go, Cal."

He does, and the moron pulls me closer. I throw my legs around Moron's neck, flipping and rolling to take him to the ground.

"What the...?"

I grab his arm, snapping it out of its socket. He shoves his other hand at me, fingers splayed. The air ripples, the force slamming into me.

Grinding my teeth, I absorb it, dropping his dislocated limb. I push my hand to the underside of his jaw, sending his magic back through him. Bone cracks, and he goes limp, his head bent at a revolting angle.

Cal is on his feet, swinging at the other. I detangle from the corpse and watch Cal slam Moron Two to the ground. I smirk, dusting myself off and pulling my clothes in order by kicking my feet up to flip the extra fabric of the sweatpants beneath my soles.

When I look up, Cal is holding a bloody lump in his hand. Only, it's not his hand, but pitch black skin to his elbow, elongated with curved talons. He tosses the mass aside, his claws clicking as he shakes away gore, and then his fingers shorten, his skin fading to a bloodstained tawny color as his hand returns to normal.

I cock my head, pointing. "You can shift just a part of you?"

He inspects his hand, blood staining the wrinkles of his skin. "Yes."

Stepping over the dead body, I ask, "So you could have a tail all the time?"

He glowers, but his whole being pulls in on itself. "Maybe." Swinging me into his arms, he asks. "Why?"

"Because it's cute." I throw my arm around his neck.

His Dark winds around me again, slipping under the fabric of my clothes to caress my skin. "It's useful for impaling things. Balance, too."

"Can I get a snack?"

Chuckling, he moves along the sidewalk through the gaping humans stunned by the action. "If you're hungry."

Laughing, I ignore the rabble as they scurry out of our way. "Always."

I walk next to Cal, my hand in his, my high heels clicking on the cement, the short hem of my new dress brushing against my thighs. We've been wandering in and out of shops all day, and Cal's purchased me a new wardrobe, all to be delivered to Hiro's home. I have a new bracelet, this one engraved with a star, and a phone, both linked to Cal's accounts.

He called Massimo and made him bring Ness to the shop, providing her with a cuff and a phone as well and ordering Mass to get her set up with everything she needs. I adore that he's treating her so well after the abuse in Izul.

We've been here before, this exact day. It's not tense or awkward as we converse, Cal laughing at my jokes with ease, and this time, he didn't disappear when I picked out lingerie, even making requests. It seems like that day was so long ago, and this time, I'm not worrying about how to get out of my contract. Even that is different though, too.

I look to our hands, where tendrils of Dark and Light twist together, interlocking our wrists, but it's the only sight of our magics. "Can I ask you something?"

"Anything you ever want. I'll answer you."

"What's the sound of your heart?"

He blinks at me, cocks his head, shakes it, and scoffs. "I take it back. You can't ask me anything if you're going to ask me stupid questions."

"No, I mean, the answer of your soul."

"My what?" He gapes at me and then rubs his face. "I have no idea what you're talking about."

"That thing that let you connect to your magic? Zander," I say, rewarded with a sharp glance from Cal, "he helped me connect to my Light. I know he said it's highly personal, but..."

Staring down on me, Cal asks, "What the fuck are you talking about?"

"How did you connect to your magic?"

"It talked. I talked back."

"That's it?"

"It exists within me, and it can't live without a host. We have an understanding that we exist together. We do whatever we want within that limitation, and we both get to survive."

I scowl at the pavement. "Pierre and Zander insisted that I

learn to control my Light. If you call it or it comes out when you're not in the arena it's against the law. They insisted I force it to obey, not ever let it act on its own."

The world spins a soft hiss echoing in my skull. I fall sideways, weak and nauseous.

"Talia?" Cal tightens his hand on mine, yanking me into him.

"Mmm?" My head is heavy, throbbing in time with my heart. The illumination of the world goes dim, my vision fading from gray to black.

Brilliant bluish silver comes to life before me, stars that spin and stretch to threads of Light. Cal's voice snarls at me. *"Trust goes both ways. We trust each other to live, or we both die."*

"Talia!"

I blink, panting hard, staring up into Cal's contorted features as he cradles me in his arms.

"What the fuck happened to you?"

I glance around, realizing he's kneeling off to the side of the walkway. "Um…" I droop, breathing him in, shaking like I've been dunked in ice water. "My Light."

Grunting, he lifts me up, starting to move. "That answer thing you were talking about, how you connect to your magic, do you have that?"

"Yeah." I nod, adjusting in his grip, breathing haggardly as I shove my face into the side of his neck for warmth. "Yeah, I have it."

"If you don't," he says in a harsh growl, "your magic is strong, maybe the strongest I've ever seen. It'll strangle your life if you don't have a connection to it."

"It was letting me know that it's not happy with the restrained and obedience thing. Pierre and Zander were both adamant that my Light was too strong, that it shouldn't be so strong and that it needs to be tempered and have complete obedience to me to avoid it overgrowing me."

Cal puffs through his nose. "It will strangle you if you can't control it, yes. Magic that can't be controlled has no connection to the host, and it'll strangle the host. That doesn't mean your magic has to have complete obedience, and how strong your Light is has nothing to do with you as a host. It's not even possible for your Light to outgrow you." Under his breath he mutters, "Fucking idiots."

His laugh echoes in my head. *I will mate this one. It has my friend.*

I pick my head up, beaming at Cal. "My Light likes your Dark."

He glances down at me, lifting his eyebrow. "It does?"

"It calls your Dark it's friend."

Cal laughs. "Does it fucking understand it's friend *eats it*?"

"Yeah, and it's fine with that."

He lifts his eyebrows, closing and opening his eyes in a display of confused disbelief.

"What? You eat me and I like it. Why can't my Light like being eaten by your Dark?"

Shaking his head with mirth on his lips, Cal asks, "What's your answer?"

I close my eyes, going limp. "Trust."

"It's a fucking miracle you can even connect to it then, stubborn fucking woman."

I giggle. "You helped. What you said after I burned your contract out, about trusting you. It..." I shrug, opening my eyes to stare up into his. "It just helped."

A smile creeps across his features, one side of his lips curling up with satisfaction.

"What are you so smug about? You were right, all right? Rub it in my face some more, why don't you?"

"That's *my* use, Little Star. I take care of you. That is being your alpha, and I'm damn proud of it." He shakes his head, shifting me higher in his arms, bringing us face to face. "It took you long enough to accept it."

I press my lips to his, his opening against mine. His Dark slithers around me, comforting ropes of cool shadow whispering against me, binding me to him. I love it, everything about being in his arms and his Dark.

Pulling back, I force a grin, like baring my teeth. "Don't go being an idiot on me. You know I'm still not going to sit, stay, and be a good vassal."

He grumbles under his breath, setting me on my feet. "Then you can walk." He smacks my ass, "Move. You're getting sassy. I need to feed you."

CHAPTER 55
CALLAHAN

Sitting on the back porch as the suns sink low, I languish with a drink, my little star in my lap. My Dark is fat and lazy with her Light, making me woozy. It's still feeding, a glutton if ever there was one.

I snap at it. *"Stop that."*

"It's so tasty, and I was starving."

"Was. Don't kill them."

"It's fine. It's not even weakened. It calls me friend." Elation fills my chest.

I smirk, considering Natalia's Light glinting in a fine web over her skin. While her magic might have deemed me trustworthy, Massimo's proximity is drawing it forth.

Looking to him, I ask, "Mass, have you figured that out yet?" I wave my drink at Vanessa. "Does she have the Dark?"

Mass chuckles, rubbing his face and staring into his tumbler. "She has something."

"Train it. Could be useful," I say. "Especially since the Magia are killing us on sight. I want her to at least be able to protect herself."

He makes a face of disgust. "You need to deal with that."

"I gave orders for arrangements to be made. I'm waiting to hear the results. Soon, though."

Natalia yanks on my shirt. "What're you going to do?"

"Kill them all." I meet Massimo's steady gaze. "I had an idea about inviting them somewhere, and waiting this long will play in our favor."

Massimo darkens, one side of his mouth curling up. "I won't even need an order, just when and where."

She frowns. "Um, babe, kill them all?"

"Yes," I say.

Vanessa sinks her teeth into her lower lip, glancing at Mass and then me. "But my mom's Magia, and she's not bad."

I pull Natalia against me, shifting her for my comfort. "I don't care. I have to make a point, something both the Magia and the humans will..." I trail off, frowning at Raz.

He approaches, moving stiffly with a sour expression. "The Council is here."

I've known this was coming, even desired it, but it doesn't make this easier. "Talia." I fixate on her with hunger, falling silent.

The only reason the Council would be here for me is because the king is dead. My escapades to feed had been written off as Magia attacks, and the Council wouldn't be here because of Natalia. Her contract is legal and binds her to me no matter the fit Pierre throws. If I'm wrong, and this is a pathetic attempt from Pierre, then all the better for her to stand at my side.

She pokes me in the shoulder. "Did you die?"

Standing, I force her to her feet. "You're with me, Little Star." I step to the side, offering my hand, my fingers trembling.

Taking it, she gives me a quizzical glance, but I jerk her to my side and head for the door.

Standing there, I hesitate, swallowing hard.

She nudges me. "You okay, Master-Owner-Boss-Man?"

Shaking my head, I adjust my sweating palm tighter against hers and pull her into the house. I move into the front room, my heart striking harder than hammer strikes in my chest.

A spread of fourteen individuals waits, milling around, some lounging but most standing. Seven linger to one side, wrapped in golden ropes of the Light. I nod at Jacques, who grimaces back, and then glance toward the other half of the Council. One man catches my eye, Pierre Bordeaux.

I was ignorant that Pierre sits on the Council this at present, but watch with amusement as his eyes widen, his features twisting with fury as I approach hand in hand with Natalia. It makes my black heart skip with happiness to witness.

Pierre sneers. "Natalia."

I smirk. "Pierre, what a displeasure to see you again."

He ignores me, taking a step forward. "Tallie, what do you think you are doing?"

She shrugs. "What I want."

He runs a hand down the buttons on his shirt. "Zander is anxiously looking for you."

"Zander is?"

"Ash sent word you drugged her and took off last night, but I've been preoccupied by duty. I received the summons while we were in my office and have been handling my responsibilities since you walked out of my office. Come here immediately." He points at the floor next to him.

My star laughs. "Go fuck yourself."

"Tallie, that is inappropriate language. Now, we will

discuss later why you aren't with Ash, what you did to her last evening, and why you didn't go to Kipnop later. Right now, you will obey me, and we will return to Izul."

I chuckle, kissing the top of her head. "Go ahead, you have free rein." Letting go of her hand, I move to her back, smiling at Pierre. "She's my contracted, and whether or not you deem to abide by the law, this Council will recognize I am, in fact, legally in ownership of her."

"This doesn't concern you, dog."

Half the room bares their teeth. One of the Dark Council members snapping back, "As a member of the Council you are to show respect to both sides regardless of origins and personal feelings. Without that rule we'd never accomplish what this body was designed for."

Natalia scoffs. "Ha, he hates the Dark."

"Tallie, do not say another word."

"How about three? Go..." she says, ticking them off on her fingers, "fuck...yourself."

"That is no way to speak to me."

She takes a half step forward, leaning in to scream, "You lied to me!"

I grab her hips, pulling her back against me. I lift my eyes to Pierre's, speaking slow and clear, "Calm down, *Little Star*." He stiffens, and I grin, continuing on. "I did warn you when I came to fetch her to not lie to her. Perhaps my advice should have been taken instead of disregarded as vile words. I see you were accepting of my gifts to her though, offering them as your own."

She glances back at me. "You came to get me?"

Giving her a gentle squeeze, I nod. "Yes, but Pierre refused to return you to me."

Jacques steps forward. "Pierre is this true?" He looks at the others at his back, and then lifts his voice. "The Council hearing did not ward you possession of her, finding that their contract was not illegal."

Pierre squares his shoulders, hands on his hips. "I returned to Izul, and per the Council's ruling did not pursue the issue further. However, my daughter came to me herself. I had given her my word she'd have a home in the city."

Jacques stares him down with malice. "You knowingly interfered with a contract. That's against every law: Dark, Light, and of this body."

"He is disgraced," Pierre counters, unwavering, his tone aloof. "By my understanding that voids any contractor rights by every law."

I laugh. "A worn contract cannot be negated by the king."

Pierre glances at me and rubs his mouth. "Stay out of this Callahan, this is between my daughter and me. She came to me seeking a home and I provided it. I was not bound by law to do anything for a disgraced dog." He lowers his gaze. "Tallie, you will do what you are told, or things will be a lot harder for you."

Her face twists with a cruel hue. "My answer is now and forever, fuck you."

My black shrewd heart lifts at her words. Natalia belongs to me. My little star isn't going anywhere ever again until I'm in the afters. Even then, I'll chase her down and make sure she stays by my side.

I smirk at Pierre, shaking with contained laughter. "I think that settles this matter." I turn my attention to Jacque. "Why are you here?"

Another Dark steps forward, one I'm not familiar with. "Yes, please, shall we address the reason we are here?" He inclines his head to me. "Callahan, I am Hawthorne. It's a pleasure to make your acquaintance, but I bring grave news for you."

Jacques makes of face of consideration. "Maybe not so bad news for you."

"Maybe. Depends on if I survive." We share a smile, and I step away from my little star. "Let's get this over with."

Natalia frowns, but I fixate on the woman stepping forward. "I am Melina." She opens a small box, two silver rings within on a black velvet cushion.

I roll my shoulders and stretch my neck. The first piece of the contest set. I've read enough texts my father accumulated to prepare for this moment himself. My magic curls around my neck and arms, trepidation spreading through me.

Melina gives an apathetic grimace. "Right for intellect. Left for the mysteries of the heart. Two halves of one whole to decide."

I pick up one, slipping in onto my thumb, and then the other. When both are secure, I hold my hands out level. The rings begin to glow as molten metal, and they warm beyond comfort, heating until my skin sizzles in the quiet.

I clamp my jaw and resist the instinct to pull them off, my hands shaking as the rings turn tarnished. The heat lingers, despite the blackened silver no longer glowing. I drop my hands to my sides, focusing on my breathing.

A petite female steps forward with another box. Eloise presents the box, her honey brown hair is pulled into a ponytail, her small eyes crinkling as she smiles. This one is twice the size, containing the second of three parts.

"Cal." She bows and turns to Natalia. "Hello, Little Light, it is good to see you again."

Natalia stares with parted lips and glazed eyes. "Um, hi, Eloise."

With pursed lips forced into a smile she opens the box. "Three to remind you that it is the strength of mind, body, and magic to rule."

Plucking the small silver balls from within, I hold my left forearm out. I set each orb down in a row. All three begin to glow once they are set, melting into pools, burning into my skin, thin veins connecting one to the other. My arm trembles as I hold it out, showing as the discs cool, turning to the same tarnished silver as the rings.

The scent of burnt skin is heavy in the air, Eloise snapping the boxes closed in the silence. She withdraws, and I clench my jaw.

Hawthorne steps forward, inclining his head and offers yet another box. I rock on my heels, staring down my nose as the lid creeks open.

With a grimace, Hawthorne inclines his head. "The final piece is always the worst." Inside is yet another piece of metal, a thick band formed into an arc. "To bind in service and fealty of our Dark Throne."

I take a deep breath, my chest expanding, then I move in a quick jerk, ripping it from the black cushion and shoving it onto my neck.

I close my eyes, fighting against a scream, my growl catching in the back of my throat. Clenching my jaw, my neck ignites with a blaze of agony, the glow of the metal brilliant behind my eyelids. I twitch, waiting for the searing heat around my throat to cease, trying to clamp my jaw tighter and tighter with each fraction ticking by.

When the heat dwindles, I stretch my neck, rocking it side to side. The flesh screams as it contacts the metal band sealed as a collar around my throat. Breathing out slowly, I open my eyes to those looking on while baring my teeth.

Hawthorne smiles, a genuine expression of humor. "You took it better than the others we've bound thus far. Mattingly was on his knees in tears."

I grunt, not sure if I speak if I'll maintain the mirage that I'm not in agony of the acutest kind.

He closes the box and retreats, Jacques stepping toward me. At least he's empty handed, but this will hurt worse than the contest set. This isn't going to physically harm me, but my stomach is churning at what I'm about to do.

Lifting his pointed chin, he stares at the ceiling. "Cal."

My Dark whines, my chest aching as Jacques cocks his jaw and meets my eyes. His cheek bones protrude, his cheeks gaunt. His flared nose wrinkles with disgust as he pushes his shaggy, blond hair away from his face with one hand. "I cannot fucking believe I have to be the one to do this."

We stare at each other, both of us knowing what happens next. He appears as thrilled as I feel, eyes shifting back and forth, lip curling as if he smells something rotten.

Sighing, his head tips back, and he chuckles at the ceiling. "Perks of the job, I guess."

"Get on with it," I say, my voice shredded and rough.

"You have the right to name a weapon. Any you name is yours to keep should you win and will be destroyed should you fail. Should the weapon be lost, broken or destroyed during the contest you will not be granted another. What do you choose?"

I turn my head to her, to my star and future mate. My heart stalls, my Dark making pathetic whimpers in my mind.

Pierre storms forward. "No."

CHAPTER 56
NATALIA

I gape at Cal. Whatever those metal things are, they have burnt his flesh. We've all stood here listening to it, but he never made a noise, barely flinched, and that was only when the metal sealed around his throat. I'm nauseous from the smell and watching Cal suffer, rooted to my spot in shock, but when Jacques gives him the choice of a weapon, the way Cal turns to stare at me with dead eyes chills me to the bone.

Pierre roars, "No!"

Jacques spins, putting a hand to Pierre's chest, his voice a growl. "You are here as courtesy of the Council in adherence of the accords to allow the Light the right to know the next Dark King, but you will not interfere." He shoves Pierre back. "This choice is Callahan's to make and if he wants to name his lightning bug there is nothing you can do about it. Nothing any of us can do, and believe me, I'd prefer to not face the two of them together."

Pierre turns putrid. He glows from within, his Light shining bright enough to make my eyes water. "Natalia is my daughter and I lay claim to her as my own. As the eldest of my heritage, and in good standing, it is my right to bind any of my heritage in servitude."

I center, straightening my spine and clenching my fists. "You can try."

Pierre sneers, moving closer. "By law I have right to claim you. You have no choice in this matter."

Cal moves to me, squinting at Pierre. "Natalia is already bound in contract negating your claim. That law is not applicable."

"You are disgraced. Your contract is meaningless, without binding foundation. It is nothing but your magic marring her flesh."

"Dark Law dissolves only written contracts, not worn."

"A worn contract bares no weight for a disgraced to any but the holder and contracted," Pierre snaps. "She is my daughter, my heritage, and I have now claimed her. As such she is bound in service to me for life, and any claim you lay gives me the right to dispute in any manner, even death."

Pierre grabs me by the arm, trying to drag me from Cal. I twist, reaching for him.

Cal is quick to grab my outstretched hand, but he just as quickly gasps and releases me. His hands move to the collar around his throat as he wheezes, fingers trying to dig under the band.

I drop my jaw in outrage. "You did not!"

Eloise steps forward, putting a hand against Cal's chest, turning to him. "Cal, it's warning you. You are bound in servitude to the Dark Throne. You cannot turn your back on it and risk your life for this. The laws are on his side. Give in and it will release."

He gasps, bending over with his hands on his knees, hacking like a dog with something in its throat.

Jacques grimaces. "I'm so glad I don't have to wear that stupid thing."

Pierre's grip tightens and he yanks me further from Cal. "No," I whimper, meeting Cal's eyes.

He stares back, his eyes sparking with fury, his magic twisting in black shadows around him, slithering across his body with agitation. He says nothing. He does nothing.

"Oh, fuck you," I snap, twisting toward Pierre as my feet slip across the polished wood floor. I yank free, toppling off balance and hitting the floor. My elbow takes the impact, beginning to throb, and I crawl away from his attempt to grab me again, kicking at him. "Fuck you too."

He makes another attempt to latch onto me, but I roll and pop to my feet. Upright, he drops his hands on his hips. "Tallie, enough. I've made every attempt to indulge your childish infatuation, allowed you freedom to grow into the Light at your own pace, and you have repaid me by spitting in my face and upon the very thing we are."

I glare at him, getting ready to scream, but he reaches out toward me, ropes of gold streaking at me. Caught off guard, I don't have enough time to shield. His magic winds around my throat.

I center to absorb his Light even as the thread restricts, cutting into my skin like cords, cutting off my air supply and blood flow. Spots dance in my vision, and I gurgle.

He stumbles, yanking on the strands. "*Capistro.*"

My core is like a piece of paper ripped in half. The sound, the destruction, reverberating through me. A scream slips up my throat like razor blades, and I hit my knees, falling onto my hands as I pant.

The golden magic recedes from me, and I rub my throat, and then scowl at the back of my hand. There's a distinct lack of silver webbing, and I glare at him. "What the fuck did you do to me?"

"Be silent," he says, pacing forward.

I swipe at the fluid leaking from my nose, a streak of blood left on the back of my hand as I chuckle. "You really don't fucking know me."

He leans over, grabbing my wrist and hauling me to my feet. "You serve me by law, and I have bound your magic."

I whack at him, but my wrist is weak, my hand flopping as muscles quiver. "Unbind it, asshole."

He drags me to my feet. "Lennette, I am leaving. I will be returning to Izul."

"Yes, Pierre."

Turning to Cal, Pierre says, "Release my daughter from—"

"I'm not your daughter," I flail, trying to get free of his grip. "You're nothing but a sperm donor."

Pierre glowers, shaking me. "You carry a seed of my heritage."

"I'm Magia."

He huffs, facing Cal. "Withdraw your magic, Callahan. Renounce you're claim to her. If you maintain your hold, I have the right to kill you."

I kick Pierre in the knee. He grunts, losing balance and his grip on me as he flounders. "If you so much as harm him, I will send you into the afters, and I'll hunt Ashley down and send her to meet you. I will destroy your heritage."

Upright, Pierre sneers at me. "I bound your magic. Your threat holds no weight." His head lifts with his voice, "Now, Callahan."

I turn to him in panic. He'll fix this. He can handle anything I can't.

Cal steps forward, and I breathe out in relief, but it's evaporated by his words. "I will dissolve the contract."

My heart wrenches in my chest, fracturing, "No. Cal."

His face is tight, features pinched with fury. He takes my hand, lifting it and resting his hand over our contract embedded in my forearm.

"Don't." My eyes burn. "Please don't."

Cal wraps his fingers around my arm as he leans in closer to breathe in my ear. "Whatever happens, I promise I will find you in the afters."

"No," I mewl, the word clogged in my throat. I grab at his shirt as he starts to pull back.

His teeth nip my earlobe as he steps away. My fingers lose their grip on him, but he holds my gaze as he walks backward.

Something breaks in my chest, snapping like a rubber band pulled too tight.

I am jerked backward as I sob, grappling with Pierre's cruel grip on me, blinded by unshed tears. "Cal!" I reach for him. "Cal! Please! Please, Cal!"

Pierre shakes me, his voice raised, "You are coming with me. We will return to Izul, and you will not see beyond the walls for the next thousand years that you live. I will bind you to it even in my death. I will see you in a union to Zander, you will continue this heritage I have sired, you will learn respect, serve the Light, and you will die in Izul."

I gape, lips peeled apart with revulsion. The threat to be locked up and surrounded by Light, to never see Cal again rips through me. I had believed once I would never lay eyes on him again. It had broken a part of me. Not my heart, for that was with Cal always, but something deeper and far more tender.

Pierre says the Dark doesn't know love, but there's nothing that is more real than the hunger Cal stares at me with, the heat in his words full of passion, or the way he grabs me without mercy, as if I am his and his alone. A swell builds inside of me, a cry from my heart for Cal, for my hand in his, for home. It's everything I need, my heart's desire, the seed of my soul. I would rather die now than lose his love.

My Light unleashes a wail within me. The crescendo bursts, my skin rippling with my Light flexing to be free. It shatters through my flesh in sparks of cold tendrils and warm heat around me.

I shove Pierre away with hands that glitter silver, Dark tendrils coiling around my wrists and fingers. "You lied to me–manipulated me–planned my whole life without asking me what I want. I won't, and you can't make me. I'm never going to serve you, I'm not going back to Izul, and there is nothing you can do to make me answer to you."

Electricity zaps in the air, Pierre's voice honed to cut. "You are my daughter, my seed, and I decide as the head of this heritage."

"Do it," I whisper. "I dare you."

He lifts his chin, eyeing me down his nose. "Your magic is bound. It will not save you, and I will not kill my own heritage." He latches onto me, his magic curling tight to ensure his grip. "This time, daughter mine, you are going to find I'm far less lenient."

I lower my stinging eyes to my forearm, begging the Mother that Cal's name is still in my flesh. Silver threads lace over my skin, black tendrils wrapping around my arm and petting my skin in a pathetic attempt to comfort, but his name is gone.

I blink, the world sliding out of focus in a blurred haze as tears roll down my cheeks in cool drips. My feet catch the sill of the door as I'm pushed through the opening. I whip around to face Pierre as he closes the door, following me out to the front of the house.

He straightens his shirt, smoothing the buttons down the front. "We are going home, Tallie."

Planting my feet, I take a shaky breath, glaring at him. "I'm not going anywhere. You can get fucked."

He softens, "This sacrilegious attachment to that beast will wither in time. This is for the best."

If he knew the first thing about me, if he knew the real me, if he'd ever bothered to listen to me, he'd know I won't accept this, but he never wanted me. Not *me*. Every gift he exchanged for time with me, every conversation, it was never me that he was talking to. I played my part, and told the lies he wanted, but he's never met Talia.

I draw up straight, breathing in through my nose. "You don't know me at all. I have my own magic."

With a thrust of my palm, I send Ki at him. Light flashes, and he's thrown into the driveway to roll across the gravel.

I stomp after him. "My name is Swan, Natalia Swan, and I am Magia. My mother was Annika. My father's name is Eugene, and you're nothing but a man who came in my mother."

He shoves up to his feet and Light streaks toward me. I flinch, recoiling as it burns through me, and then I hit back, sending his magic toward him. He dives out of the way, popping to his feet and strands of Light wrap around me, binding my arms to my sides.

Pierre sneers. "Continue to annoy me, and that dog will meet the same fate as his father, only this time, there will be no one to release him to the afters."

I grind my teeth, drawing on his magic. Dark tendrils slither across the golden threads, trying to work me free.

"Stop fighting. You can't win, and Callahan won't be coming to save you."

"I don't need Cal to save me." I send a wave of Ki through me, the geometry down my spine igniting with sweet, searing agony as I scream, bursting free of his magic.

CHAPTER 57
CALLAHAN

My thumbs throb, and my forearm sings like a worn contract that I've breached. My neck pulses with raw heat, the weight of the collar suffocating and unforgiving. None of it hurts as much as recalling my magic ending my contract with Natalia, her pleading sobs, or watching Pierre drag my little star away as she cried and called for me.

Frozen blades with honed edges cut through my internals, and I'm helpless to stop it, the collar too much a reminder that I am bound. I must serve the contest and the Dark Throne. To fight for her, risk my life and serve myself would betray my fealty to the throne, and I'd forfeit my life.

It already cut off my airflow in warning at contemplation of fighting Pierre. I must let her go and know I will see her again in the afters for now. There may be a twist in the webs of fate that brings her back to me in the future. It's the best I can hope for.

Hawthorne turns to me, glaring. "You're just going to let him take her?"

Eloise throws a hand at him with an accusatory finger. "Do

not encourage him. I doubt it would take but a word. He is bound to the throne, and if dares fight, he risks his life, and it is not for the throne. The contest set will kill him for it."

Hawthorne laughs. "She is a tool for him to win the throne, that is serving it. Not to mention that power bound to the Dark?"

I grip my fists, every fiber of my being squirming to go after her, my Dark struggling, stabbing at my mind to make me comply, to go after our star. I growl in the back of my throat. "He bound her magic. She's useless to the throne and the Dark."

Jacques glances at the door, rubbing the back of his neck. "I don't want her in this fight. Marius named me his weapon, and I don't think we stand a chance against the two of you, but I'll feel like a cheat if I don't point out that her magic didn't look very bound to me."

Hawthorne scoffs. "It was, for a moment, perhaps, but it didn't last after the fuck told her that horror story about the rest of her life."

I pull my eyebrows together, glaring at the floor. Natalia's Light had gone out for a brief moment, but then she'd burst, brighter than I'd ever seen her. Silver and Dark threads alike had twisted around her.

One of the Light fucks snaps, "This conversation is moot. She belongs to Pierre by law."

"No. I can make a legal claim for my contracted."

"You are disgraced and have no rights to a contracted."

"Worn contracts are excluded," I yell back. "If I have the ability to fight for my contracted then I will. I'm disgraced, not *a* disgrace." I start for the door.

A woman with short honey hair steps in my path, hands up to stop me. "This would be war with the Light. She is the Light and belongs to Pierre by law."

An explosion shakes the manor, the world rumbling. I steady myself, not bothering to reach out and stop the Light fuck in front of me from hitting the floor.

Hiro and Thames come running down the stairs, Thames gaping.

Hiro scans the room. "I'm trying to mind my own but excuse the fuck out of me because you're in my house. What the fuck is happening in here?"

The world rattles again, and I stare at the door, my heart racing. "Talia," I call over my shoulder. "Talia is what's happening." I fling both doors open wide, searching for my star.

She stands on the driveway, glowing bright, wrapped in shadows that glitter, swinging back and forth with Pierre. I freeze in shock, watching them fight.

Jacques knocks into me, breaking me out of the trance. He turns to shove someone else, and asks, "What the fuck is she, Cal?"

Pierre takes Natalia to the ground with a hand around her throat. He slams his fist into her face, bellowing, "You will answer to me."

Natalia screams with laughter. "Go to the afters you fucking prick. I don't answer to anyone."

Dark tendrils stream out of her, sending Pierre rolling across the drive. She gets up, swaying and then she glimmers with a flash and stalks straight toward him.

He kneels, blasting Light into her. She recoils, and he's on his feet, burning with firelight. He throws it at her, and she screams.

I take a step forward, mouth hanging open. I have no idea what to do about this, every law I can think of scrolls through my skull as I try to find one to stop this before it's too late.

Natalia shines, calling firelight in turn, setting on Pierre again. They go blow for blow, swinging at full strength. My little star is outmatched in physical strength, and I'm not sure how long her Ki will last to compete.

I jog down the steps, hesitating at the bottom. The same woman who tried to stop me from following runs past me, sprinting toward the fight, but Eloise tackles her to the ground. They swing and parry with each other, squawking back and forth.

Footsteps smack on the steps at my back, so I turn, catching another trying to interfere with an arm across his chest.

The man flips backward, groaning at me from where he lies prone on the stairs. "That was like hitting a wall."

"This is a contract matter," I say. "It's not for you to interfere with."

The man scowls. "Contracted have no recourse once they are contracted, but this isn't even a contract. She's bound to him in servitude by our laws."

"A contracted can challenge their contractor. If the contractor isn't strong enough to contain the contracted, they forfeit their life and subsequent contracts." I have no idea what Natalia is doing, but the law is real enough. "She knows Dark Law allows this."

Turning my back on the man, I watch Natalia flip through the air to evade Pierre, striking back with an open palm and flash of light. She is fighting. She always does, too stubborn to accept anything she doesn't want. The fate laid out by Pierre had made me sick, and I know Natalia enough to know she's less than thrilled with his choices for her.

I toy with a smile. All that sass and power, and Natalia isn't directing her vitriol at me for once.

Around me, the Council fights amongst themselves, the Dark defending Natalia's right to fight her father on the basis of a contracted challenging their contractor. The Light aren't accepting it, the difference between our laws stark.

My heart hammers against my ribs with powerful strikes as Pierre takes Natalia down and lands on top of her. He swings over and over, Natalia's shield breaking. His fist contacts her face, and he dials back, throwing his weight behind another few swings.

The world begins to dim, and I glance at the black clouds gathering above us. I take a few steps back, gawking at them, the warmth in the air growing stale. Wind picks up, billowing my shirt, chilled air leaving the hairs on my body standing.

Hawthorne snatches Eloise, pinning her to him with one arm while dragging the Light woman by the ankle further away from where Natalia and Pierre are locked together.

Jacques shoves another Light Council member toward the steps as the wind picks up, hail whipping through the air. They all start to rush around me, yelling about finding cover.

Natalia dislodges Pierre, throwing her legs over her head and flipping to stand. She bursts with Light and wipes her face, her mouth moving, but over the howling storm, I can't hear her anymore.

The air pressure drops. The world grows colder. Lightning strikes around the drive in various places, and I flinch, stumbling backward. I trip over the steps, half crawling up them on my back at the blinding streaks of Light.

Pierre reaches out, strands of Light piercing through Natalia. Her scream mingles with the doors of the manor rattling against the house. Others run into the house for cover, a Light woman offering a hand to help me as she heads up the steps. I grab it, shielding her from the wind until we're on the porch. I shove her inside, turning around to watch, afraid of what I'll miss if I go inside.

Pierre's magic entangles Natalia. Hail whips against my face, but I narrow my eyes against it and the stings.

"Cal," Massimo's roar draws my eyes. He waves his arm and points. "Get in here! There's nothing you can do."

Ignoring him, I face forward. Natalia thrashes, tendrils of black mixing with silver and gold. Lightning strikes the ground everywhere. I curl my hands into fists, the cold leaving my fingers and the tip of my nose tingling and numb. The storm might be coincidence, an early Cloudburst gale, but the sudden onset feels like magic. It's magic I'm not familiar with, something I've only heard about in myths.

A man steps to my side under the cover of the porch. In my peripheral, he lifts his chin, his soft voice carrying even over the whistling wind. "How extraordinary she is."

I turn to him, curling my lip. It's not a Council member or anyone I've ever seen before. He's slightly shorter than me with pale skin. His red hair is cropped longer, his straight strands finger length that dance in the wind about his sharp chin. I stare in horror at the man watching Natalia fight, but I jerk to the side as he turns his gaze on me.

"She's very beautiful." He grins, exposing triple fangs, his narrow-set jade eyes focusing on me.

He's not Light. He's not Dark. He's something else that sends fear slithering through me.

The Ancient laughs, turning forward again. "Incredible that others exist. We thought—"

Natalia's scream carries over the drone of everything, stopping his words. "How many fucking times do I have to say it? I'm not one of you!"

A bolt of black strikes down, a brilliant glittering smite born of Dark magic. My jaw drops, and I flinch at the deafening boom, the world trembling.

The Ancient chuckles, reaching out to steady me. "She is not wrong."

Natalia stays on her feet, but Pierre crumples like a soft doll, folding to the ground. She wipes at her face, and the wind stills, the sunlight returning in gradual effect.

The Ancient at my side claps me on the shoulder, and I rock from the force. Our gazes lock, and he smiles, his green eyes crinkling. "I'll see you again."

I blink, and he vanishes. Whipping my head toward Natalia, I see the Ancient standing before her.

CHAPTER 58

CALLAHAN

"Talia!" I race toward them.

The Ancient bows with a flourish. He lifts Natalia's hand to his lips and I'm close enough to see him wink at my star. I collide into her, tackling her to the ground as she squeaks.

I shove up, straddling her on my knees, searching around us for red hair. The Ancient is nowhere in sight, and I narrow my eyes, the hair on the nape of my neck raising.

Natalia slips her hand up my abdomen, breathing hard. "Dude, ow. I got beat up enough by my daddy." She wheezes on a chuckle.

If she's giving me sass, then she can't wait for my attention. My Dark is coating her, turning opaque and ready to defend. "Where did he go?"

"Who? Lucius?"

"What?" I grab her face, scanning her features.

Trails of blood flow from her eyes and nose, but she blinks at me with confusion. "Red head? That guy who came out of nowhere? He scared the piss out of me, but he bowed, said

Lucius, then kissed the back of my hand. Ick, by the way." She glances around.

I groan, pressing my forehead to hers. "Pierre was mine to kill."

"I wasn't going to Izul."

Chuckling, I crush my mouth to hers. I groan as her tongue twists with mine, and then I drag my lips away, rocking to my heels.

I stand, drawing her up with me. "Little Star," I sigh, swinging her into my arms.

Natalia leans her head against my shoulder, her nose against my neck. Her warm breath tickles against my skin as I walk toward the house, but it's the best sensation in this world.

She shifts, "Who was that guy?"

"An Ancient."

"What?" she yells, fingers curling into my shirt and pulling herself closer.

I set Natalia on her feet on the porch, every pair of eyes fixating on us from within the house. I stare back with a grim ache in my chest. Natalia groans, leaning into me, and I wrap my arm around her, hugging her close.

"Jacques."

Jacques sighs, running a hand down his face. "Yeah, I know. Fuck me."

"No," I snicker, "but Natalia is my weapon."

"Blasphemy!" A Light woman stomps forward. "She belongs to the Light, to Pierre. He enacted heritage law as is his right. This will start a war. You have no right to claim her as such."

I lift an eyebrow, knowing that an Ancient stood next to me and claimed her as another one. I can use that. "Natalia is neither Dark nor Light and has the right to decide for herself which laws she will choose to abide by." I twist into her, bowing my head to meet her gaze. "Choose carefully as you cannot change your mind."

The Light scowls. "That law has not been used for millennia, since the times of Ancients. It's antiquated."

Hawthorne scoffs, crossing his arms. "And what do you suppose she is? Her own heritage could not bind her for it's not wholly his to do so. We all saw him attempt to do so and the spectacular failure it was."

A Light male steps forward. "Lennette, we all bore witness. We cannot claim her as the Light after that display."

Lennette wrings her hands. "She is Pierre's daughter, Geoffrey." She drawls his name with a sharp tongue. "She may have Dark magic, but she carries his heritage. Where is Pierre?"

I jerk my head. "Outside. Go find him."

Lennette leads the Light fucks out of the house, and I pry Natalia from my side. "Talia, you stupid, reckless, foolish, stubborn woman. You need to go." I shove her further into the room. "Go, before they come back."

"No. I'm not leaving." Her voice is a muted mewl as she stands there shaking her head.

"Mass?" I scan for my friend.

He steps forward. "Come on, Light bug." He picks her up, meeting my gaze. "Call me?"

Hawthorne shakes his head. "Go. The Light is not going to be happy, but we..." He glances at Eloise and Jacques, motioning to the others.

Meline bobs her head. "Yes, we're in agreement. Natalia will not be handed to the Light and will serve the Dark as Callahan's weapon."

Relief washes through my chest, but I grip my fists. It's not going to be that easy, but it will be easier if Natalia is absent. I glare at Massimo's back as he carries my star further into the house, no doubt going out the back. It's the second time I've watched a man take Natalia away today, and my Dark is furious, attacking me for being complacent both times.

Wincing and jerking my head to the side, I snap under my breath, "Quit it."

Jacques laughs. "It's a bad time when your magic is pissed at you."

Giggling, Eloise puts a hand to her mouth. "Who can blame it?" She focuses on me. "It no doubt feeds on your lightning bug."

"Yes," I say, and then I stumble to the side, almost meeting the floor as my Dark lashes out, leaving my left side tingling and numb. Squinting and rubbing my temple, I stand upright, grumbling at my Dark's thrashing. "Fucking quit it, shadow piss. She'll come back. Don't kill us before then."

With an air of amusement, Jacques covers the lower half of his face. "It's that attached?"

Eloise scoffs. "They're a perfect pair."

"Marius and I are fucked." Jacques fakes a sob.

I smirk, still trying to soothe my Dark. "I'd say it's very attached, but that feels like a lie. What's more than attached?"

Hiro pulls Thames close with a smirk. "Mate."

The collection of Light Council members shuffle in, carrying Pierre which ceases our small talk. All visible skin on Pierre is curdled, black veins prominent at the surface of his flesh as the Light deposit him on the couch.

Thames crosses his arms. "Who's going to pay to clean my furniture?"

"Shut up, vermin."

Hiro steps forward. "You are in my home. You are Council members bound to respect all regardless of origins by duty. You will show respect." He turns, pulling Thames against him, whispering words I can't hear.

Lennette checks Pierre, kneeling next to him. "He's fading. We must hurry."

Geoffrey puts a hand on her shoulder. "There's nothing we can do to heal this."

Movement draws my eyes to Vanessa, stepping between Council members toward the couch. She locks her gaze on mine, chewing her lower lip. Lifting her eyebrows, she points to Pierre. "I can heal."

I curse under my breath, torn between her saving Pierre's life to spare Natalia's for his murder and wanting him dead. He deserves to be in the afters, but I need Natalia in so many ways.

A Light waves her hand. "Do it."

Vanessa looks at me, waiting like a good vassal, and I smirk.

The Light snaps her fingers. "If you have a way to save his life, you are obligated to do so as he is a Council member."

I cross my arms. "Vanessa is Magia. She does not abide by the laws of Seraphinus, and the same can be said of Natalia."

The Light bat sneers. "Natalia is Pierre's daughter, born of Seraphinus and therefore bound by our laws." She points to Eloise. "You are capable of healing. Heal Pierre."

Eloise inspects her nails. "No." Smiling, Eloise shrugs. "Do you think my magic capable of healing the Light? Me, the Dark?"

The woman turns back to me as I'm fighting to keep a straight face. Eloise could heal Pierre, and she hasn't lied, walking the line. It's a gray area, but the Dark won't argue that in this instance.

The Light scowls in my direction. "This is your fault. Order your Magia to heal him."

I drop my chin toward my chest, giving her a long look. "I'm disgraced. She's not a worn contract, and therefore, her contract was dissolved when I was removed from good standing. To your point that this is somehow my doing, I followed the law."

"Natalia did not," Geoffrey says. "She will be charged. She will be executed if he dies, and– Where is she?"

I glance around, crossing my arms and forcing a frown as I pretend to scan for her. "I don't know. I have no contract with her anymore, so she doesn't have to answer to me either."

Geoffrey laughs. "Well played, Callahan."

Lennette is less impressed, fussing as she stands. "This is highly irregular Callahan. You will heal Pierre now and produce Natalia to face charges."

I lift and drop my shoulders. "It's not my magic, but Vanessa's," I say with a nod in her direction, "and as she is Magia, she answers to no one in this room. I dare say you can try to barter with her."

Lennette steps toward her. "Heal Pierre, and you can keep your life."

Jacques stomps forward, putting himself between Lennette and Vanessa. "That is out of line."

I chuckle, "I feel obligated to add I gave her my word to protect her, and though I'm disgraced, I will not break a vow I made."

Vanessa leans around Jacques. "I'll barter. I heard something about charges and execution of my babe, so if I heal this dude," she thumbs at Pierre, "Tallie goes free from everything, any charges whatsoever, or I let him die."

Lennette squeaks and waves her hands around. "Out of the question."

"You may want to hurry," Vanessa says, wrinkling her nose. "He doesn't look so good, and there's only so much I can do."

I grin at her, fighting a chuckle. She's proving to be a wise investment. I am getting more than I ever thought I could from her contract.

The Light Council members converge and converse in hushed tones and then turn to the Dark. Geoffrey speaks for them. "Agreed. Her actions will be denoted as a heritage matter. Pierre's claim to her will stand—"

"Whoa, hold up." Vanessa waves her hands. "This arrogant bat is going to die before I make my babe go back to him."

Throwing her hands up, Lennette screams, "Do as you are commanded."

"How does fuck off work?" Vanessa cocks back with her arms crossed. "I hate this fuck. He manipulated Tallie, and, Izul and you Lighters are a gilded nightmare."

Jacques coughs to cover a laugh. Hawthorne stares at the ceiling and struggles to hold back.

Meline shows her teeth in a disguised snarl. "Well said."

Geoffrey sighs. "Will you agree to heal Pierre if Natalia will not be charged, and Pierre will have to settle his claims with Natalia personally to determine if they stand?"

"I love a good barter," Vanessa says, rubbing her hands together. She turns to me. "Is there a contract to sign or a handshake? Something that makes this official?" Pointing at the Light Council members, she says, "Those are tricky, lying miscreants that will manipulate this."

Jacques peels into laughter, the other Dark Council members following suit. I tip my head back and grin as Lennette shrieks at Vanessa. I didn't need confirmation of what I thought the Light was, but the unbiased description from Vanessa soothes my Dark and heart.

I nod at her. "Heal him, Vanessa."

"Sure thing, boss." She plops down on the couch and slaps her hand over Pierre's head. "Shame you aren't conscious for this, asshole, 'cause it would hurt."

Her eyes close, and she inhales. I wait, expecting her to glow, to see a sign of her using Ki, but there is none.

Lennette stomps her foot. "Are you going to do something or not?"

Geoffrey intercepts her. "Wait. Look, he's changing."

Vanessa starts to convulse, slipping from the couch. Eloise grabs her, stilling her and helping her to sit up. Eloise's Dark wraps around her, likely healing her.

"Shit." Vanessa is pale, her voice hoarse. "It's too much. Dude was dead, I think. He's definitely on the threshold to the afters, and I delayed it, but I'm not going to be able to pull him back."

Lennette says, "Then there is no deal."

I grit my teeth. "If I do something to assist Vanessa, will the deal stand?"

Geoffrey nods. "Yes."

I draw a hand down my face, not sure if I can convince the rat in the cellars to help, but I have to try. Under the bewildered gazes of the others, I storm through the room to the basement.

Slipping into the cell, I kneel before Tony, "I have a proposition for you."

Tony grunts. "Fuck you. I tried that."

"Your freedom."

"How?"

"Heal someone."

Tony scoffs. "Heal a Seraphinus, you mean? Fuck no. I'll rot first."

I frown, standing. "It saves Natalia's life."

Tony lurches. "Nat?"

"Talia," I finish for him.

"Protection from the Magia?"

"You can earn that by being useful to me starting with this, and I'll give you my word it won't be locked in a dungeon."

Cocking his jaw, he hesitates.

"Yes or no, pig?"

"Deal."

My Dark streaks forward, unbinding his chains. I offer my hand, yanking him to his feet when he accepts it. I gag, my eyes water, and I breathe through my mouth at the stench of him. "Follow me."

Tony clomps behind me into the main room. The others turn their noses and back away as he stops by the couch. "This fuck, I suppose? Where's Nat?"

"Tony?" Vanessa gapes. "Gross. What happened to you?"

Tony points at me. "He happened." His finger moves to Pierre. "Dude, this one's already dead."

Vanessa shakes her head. "Not quite. I pulled him back, but you need to hurry. I couldn't, but you can, and this is for Tallie."

"Fine." He moves to the end of the couch, then kneels and leans over the end. After positioning his hands on either side of Pierre's head, Tony closes his eyes. His shoulders square, his back straightening somehow in the position. "This is going to fucking hurt. Nat is going to owe me."

Going rigid, Tony falls silent. The black lines in Pierre's face start to lighten. I hold my breath. Vanessa already failed, and I have no other options unless I summon Natalia.

Tony's face tenses, and he bares his teeth. "Fucking Moth-er," he pants.

Not a good sign. Natalia never speaks when healing. I clench my jaw, my Dark coiling about me with fear.

Fractions tick by, and Tony starts to pant, not moving and not speaking again. The radiating black lines on Pierre's skin fade, turning to smoke-colored, hazy veins that disappear. Pierre's skin turns ashen, then returns to the color of life.

Tony lets go, twisting and falling to the floor with a heavy thump. "Fuck."

Vanessa crawls over to him and pokes him. "How does it feel to be weak?"

"Fuck off," he moans, clutching at his stomach. "That hurt. What happened to that guy?"

"Tallie." Vanessa curls her knees into her chest, leaning over them.

"Makes sense," he says, wheezing a few times in short succession. "She's pinnacle and badass. How far did you pull him?"

"Drained myself."

Tony gurgles, his torso shaking. "How was it still alive?"

Vanessa hums, and the room falls silent. Lennette wrings her hands, and Eloise moves to Tony. She puts her hands on him, and he jerks. "Get the fuck off me."

She shrugs. "I can heal you or not. It's your choice."

"I'm good, Darkling," Tony says, rolling to his side and pushing to sit. "You can't heal what I need. Someone just get me food–real food, not cat shit in a can."

Pierre stirs, sitting up.

No one moves to comply with Tony's demand, but Vanessa groans. "Food. Mmm, yeah."

Rubbing a hand down his face, Pierre's eyes roam the room, settling on me. "Where is my daughter?"

I shrug, crossing my arms and leaning back on my heels. "Not here, but otherwise, I'm unaware of her location."

Pierre lurches to his feet, stopping as if surprised by his spry movements. He recovers and glares. "Produce my daughter."

"You forced me to withdraw the contract. She doesn't answer to me."

"Tallie has never answered to you because of a contract."

Laughing, I admit, "In fact, that is the only reason she ever did anything she didn't want to. She's stubborn and hard to control, especially when she doesn't want to do something. You set her free when you made me dissolve the contract, and she won't answer to me again unless she feels like it. You have no idea the headaches I'll have."

"I claimed her as is my right. You cannot contract what I own."

"You ruined any chance of me coercing Natalia when you made me withdraw my contract. There is nothing I can do to ensure her cooperation."

"You can. You are simply being ornery like a petulant child avoiding consequences."

I stare him down, feeding the full weight of my hatred for him into my words. "Even if I knew where she was, there is not a damn thing I can do to force her to obey me and she made her feelings very clear."

I hold his gaze, taking a step closer. I've already won, just like when he dragged me before the Council trying to condemn me for her contract. The flinching in his face, the rigid tension along his jaw, neck, and shoulders tells me he knows it too.

I smirk. "There's nothing in this world that will make Natalia do what you want. She's chosen me again and again and I will not piss on her loyalty. She is mine. My woman, my star, my weapon, and she'll be my queen."

"No," Pierre snaps, electricity snapping around us as he stands toe-to-toe with me, vibrating with rage. "I will send myself to the afters and take you with me before I ever allow you to desecrate my daughter and corrupt my heritage in that way."

"That is something you'll have to discuss personally with Natalia per the Council." I nod at the grouping of Light. "In exchange for your life. I would recommend against holding your breath as you wait. Natalia is never going to come to you of her own volition."

"There is nothing to discuss."

Spreading my arms out to my sides, I look around. "You know, I think you're right. I don't see Natalia. Do you?"

"Your kind enjoy fetching, yes?" He looks down me and then meets my gaze. "Go fetch my daughter like a good dog."

My hackles raise and my Dark burns with indignant fury. I rock on my heels, clenching my jaw and trying to get a grip on my temper. I'd rather get a grip on him, a solid one, with my claws dug into his neck. "She's not even your heritage. You couldn't bind her magic because it's not yours. She's something else, and we both know it."

"Ancients are nothing but myth."

I flash my teeth in genuine humor. "You're being belligerent."

Vanessa lifts her hand. "As maybe the youngest but most fascinated by history person in this room, the Ancients are real. There is a ton of evidence to support their existence based upon science, and not all of them were accounted for with death certificates your kind issued during the Great War. I wrote my thesis for second-degree graduation on them. Trust me, not myth, or I will bore you with all the details, starting with Ancients is what we call them today, but they are classified as Eternums."

Pierre stares down on her. "I'm not disregarding history, but it is just that. History. There are no more Ancients."

"How Eternums came to existence isn't known," Vanessa replies, ignoring his jab. "All we have are the myths. Not even the Eternums had proof of their origins, citing a blend of Light and Dark. In fact, the creation of the word myth aligns with their very existence, that there was nothing, and we call it Nehil. From Nehil, a single spark ignited, and we call it Adontis. The two were very different, the one enrapt with the other for those differences, and so they mated, the Eternums born of their eternal love."

Linnette holds a hand up. "Stop. We all are aware of myths."

"But no, really, so the whole idea is that there was Nehil, the Dark, and then Adontis, the Light. The Dark and the Light mated to create life. You lot are one or the other. You couldn't even blend the Light and Dark properly. The Arid tribes and the Magia are proof of that, and the Mother only knows how many other attempts the Seraphinus had in creating a new form of Eternum that were complete failures. There's something about the mating, an actual coupling rather than mashing the two together, that has to be responsible for Eternums. Therefore, Magia, a form of Dark and Light mix, and you, the Light, *mated*, which is what is actually needed to properly blend the two together. So, yes, Tallie might actually be an Eternum."

Tony wheezes. "Fucking Mother, Nessy, please, please shut up."

She smacks his shoulder. "You have a stupid truck and a small penis."

He groans. "Wrong on both counts. Where's Nat?"

Pierre squares up to me, glowering. "Yes, where is my daughter? I claimed her as is my right. For you to interfere is grounds for war."

Vanessa sighs loudly and animatedly, tipping her head back to stare at the ceiling. "You Lighters." She shakes her head. "The head of a heritage may claim one of their own, but the law is written in such a way as to protect the heritage from distressed servitude, only to be enacted when there is a threat to the heritage."

Lennette kicks at Vanessa, but Jacques steps between them. "Do it, Light Bat, and I'll fucking put you down. That's against the rules of engagement and she's far too beautiful to wear bruises from you."

She huffs. "Everyone in this room is aware of our heritage laws, and we won't stand for them being twisted to suit some Dark desires."

Pierre snarls down at Vanessa. "I am protecting my heritage as is my right."

Shrugging, Vanessa curls against the bottom of the couch. "Tallie is in no danger from Cal." She flicks her wrist, hand flopping in my direction like a doll's broken arm. "To that point, you aren't protecting her, which should not only nullify your right to use that law, but it's grounds for you to be called before your Queen for disgrace in manipulation of protection laws for personal gain. More importantly, it's not even an option because regardless of Tallie being both Light and Dark as Magia, she's not your heritage based upon three facts. Do you want me to list those and make you an idiot?"

"She is my daughter."

"One," Venessa begins ticking off her fingers, "heritage laws apply only to children of a sanctified union, and you fucked Tallie's mom without a legal union. Two, Tallie is born of a Magia Heiress, her mother, and a Seraphinus, you, which leaves her as an undesirable heritage. I think that's equivocal to the Dark low born status, but either way, not classified as Seraphinus, which means not wholly your heritage. Third—"

"Shut up," Pierre bellows.

Jacques chuckles. "Where'd you learn all this, darling?"

She shrugs. "I love reading, and I had months with nothing to do in Izul but raid the library."

CHAPTER 59
CALLAHAN

A very long and very boring conversation of repetition with Pierre drags on. The only thing that gets him to leave is Vanessa's incessant interruptions, correcting everyone on everything from Eternums to Seraphinus laws. She even corrected me once, and that was embarrassing because she was right and I was wrong.

I'll never admit it, but the time the women spent in Izul was beneficial. Vanessa is a well of knowledge, holding information I've never been privy to about the Light, and Natalia was properly trained by her own kind to wield her magic. I never was well equipped for that task despite my best efforts.

When the Light leave, Pierre warns me to bring Natalia to him the instant I see her. I ignore him along with the rest as they exit the premises.

I step to the couch. "Vanessa?"

She blinks up at me. "Yes, boss?"

"That was incredibly useful."

Jacques steps next to her, introducing himself. "Are you like Natalia?"

Vanessa shakes his hand. "No."

Tony lifts his voice. "No one is like Nat."

Jacques glances at Tony and shrugs. "Shame." He laughs. "You're fun. If Cal doesn't kill me, and you're in need of a contract, I'm sure I can convince Marius he could use you as an adviser."

I bare my teeth and growl. That's Massimo's woman, as far as I'm concerned, and I won't see him lose her a second time.

Jacques flashes his teeth in response. "Can you blame me for trying? Gorgeous and brains? My kind of woman."

Eloise pats him on the shoulder before turning to me. "Both of you have forty days to set your affairs in order, and then you will report to the throne room for the contest."

I nod at her, and the remaining Council members leave. Thames ushers them out with smiles and closes the door behind them. He turns, shaking his head. "This room must be fumigated and thoroughly cleaned. I cannot believe the Light was here so long. They've ruined it."

Hiro steps to him. "It's okay, Sugar Bear. We can throw it out, all of it. We'll replace everything."

Smiling at them, I call Massimo. He answers after one ring, but it's Natalia's voice. "Cal?"

"You can come back now."

"I don't know if I want to," she says with indifference in her voice. "You keep sending me away. I'm starting to think you don't have a use of me. Maybe I'll just stay away."

Narrowing my eyes at Vanessa, I say, "Get your ass back here in less than a rune, or I start dismembering Vanessa."

Vanessa gapes with wide eyes. "Hey, what'd I do? I was useful. Again. That's twice!"

"Eh," Natalia says and hangs up.

I slip my phone away and try to get my fingers under the

metal collar resting at the base of my neck. Giving up, I grimace.

Thames moves to Tony and points down at him. "This. What are we doing with it? It's repugnant."

"We have an agreement. It proves useful, I protect it from the Magia, but I told it, it didn't have to stay in the dungeons."

With a sigh, Thames picks him up and throws him over his shoulder. "Then it gets a bath." He shudders, "Gods, the smell."

Tony grunts. "Put me down. I need food and bourbon, a lot of both. Fuck I just healed a Seraphinus, and seriously, where's Nat?"

Thames carts Tony away, and I turn to Hiro.

He shakes his head. "You really think Tallie's an Ancient?"

I gesture at the door. "Did you see any of that? And that Ancient walking around? Not a rumor anymore, and I have a name. Lucius."

Hiro narrows his eyes. "How do you know that?"

"Because he stood next to me blathering about her, and when she struck down Pierre, he went off and introduced himself to her before he disappeared."

Wincing, Hiro rolls his head back. "Red hair. Saw him next to you on the porch. Thought I was seeing things."

"You weren't. He dropped the word 'we.'"

Hiro laughs. "Well, fuck." He waves a hand at my throat. "Ancients *and* the contest? You're right, the webs are weaving something drastic."

Vanessa gets to her feet, swaying with hazy eyes. "What's with the collar?"

I lean my head from side to side, trying to adjust it. "It binds me in service to the Dark Throne." I try to pull on it again, my skin chaffing and stinging. "I hate this thing already."

Hiro nods. "Better you than me." He claps a hand to my shoulder. "Alcohol helps."

We trudge into the kitchen, Vanessa unsteady on her feet. I remain behind her in case she collapses. Massimo would appreciate it.

She tries a couple of times to hop onto the counter, slumping when she finally gets her butt on the dark blue surface, breathing hard. "That doesn't look comfortable. When do you get to take it off?"

I retrieve the decanter and pour a drink. "When I'm dead."

"Mother, that's brutal. How come?"

I glare at her. "Shut up and let me drink."

I'm on my second glass, and Vanessa is polishing off a bottle of vodka on the floor, having slipped off the countertop, flailing in the occasional weak attempt to get up again. Hiro is working to brew a pot of tea, the only sound in the kitchen.

I start strumming my fingers, draining my drink in a single gulp. When I set the glass down, I start to refill it, but Natalia and Massimo walk into the kitchen.

Massimo stops at the entrance, crossing his arms. "That was quick."

"Vanessa resolved the problem. She bartered Pierre's life for Natalia being free from charges."

Natalia stalks toward me and nabs my drink. "He's alive? Great. Thanks, babe."

"It was that, or they execute you." She toasts with the vodka bottle. "So, anytime, but it wasn't just me. Tony's here, and I drew too deep, on my spirit, almost killed myself."

Massimo rushes to her, dropping to one knee. "You did what, you crazy woman?" He pulls the bottle from her, resting it on the counter as she blinks in shock. He snatches her up, setting her next to it and taking her face between his hands. "What were you thinking?"

Hiro shakes his head as he pours hot water into a teapot then searches the cabinets for something.

Natalia throws back my drink and shudders. "Don't know how you drink that stuff."

"One delicious sip at a time." I say, sneaking my arm around her to draw her to my chest. "You, my little star, are going to stop with the annoyances and behave."

She presses her face against me. "I wasn't going back to Izul."

My stomach clenches and tries to reject the liquor at the plan Pierre has for her. The thought of Zander touching and enjoying what is mine leaves bile in my throat.

She takes a pathetic swing at my side. "You were going to let him take me."

I lower my face to the top of her head. "I am bound to the Dark Throne. I must serve it. If I don't, if I betray my duties to it, this thing takes my head off." I lean away, pointing at the collar. "It slits my throat."

Natalia tips her head back. "Then don't do that."

"Which is why I did nothing. If I would have fought for selfish reasons and risked my life for my desires, it would have been forsaking my obligations to the Dark, and this set would kill me."

She bobs her head and leans into me. I secure her close with both arms, squeezing, remembering not to use too much force to avoid hurting her. Holding her, my Dark rushes forward to wrap her up, warm strands of her Light circling my torso.

I breathe. Fatigue hits me hard, an ache settling in my joints. The world falls away, leaving me safe and content with Natalia. She is the only thing that exists, and the only thing I need.

Footsteps draw my attention and Thames comes slipping

into the kitchen. "Oh, a snogging fest? Me love." He grabs Hiro by the back of his neck. "Come here, Honey Pot."

Their mouths crush together, and Natalia giggles.

I eye Massimo lip locked with Vanessa, jerking my head and muttering, "Guess that's a long-term thing."

"She's been trying to catch that ride since he picked her up from our house."

Tony appears in the doorway, "Nat?"

Hiro scoops Thames up, cradling him. Thames is long and lean, taller than Hiro, but Hiro has no struggle. He smiles at Thames. "I have a better use of our time in mind."

"But you made me tea."

Chuckling, Hiro carries him through the doorway, shouldering past Tony, who frowns after them like he's confused and then shakes his head. "Those dudes are weird."

Thames did a good job at cleaning up Tony, complete with a haircut and shave. Without the hair spilling and growing over his gaunt, pale features his eyes are too big in a shallow face.

"Tallie," I warn him. "Not Nat, or I break bones." I keep an arm around her, claiming her under Tony's watchful gaze.

The man cocks his jaw, eyes narrowing. "What the fuck, Nat?"

I start to unwind from her to hold true to my word, but she clings to me. "Don't," she whispers. "Don't let go of me."

I tighten my arms around her. "Anything for you, Little Star."

She turns to face Tony, and I let her move, but keep her close. "Don't call me that."

"That Darkling has had me locked up for months." He points an accusatory finger, scowling. "He broke shit, pissed on me, fed me canned cat food, and you're," he waves a hand, "whatever this is."

Natalia leans into me, and I pour another drink as she says, "Well, I didn't know any of that. I had no idea you were here, and I've had my own problems, locked up myself."

Dropping his chin, Tony glares from the tops of his eyes. "You? Locked up?"

She shrugs, tipping her head back to look at me. "You peed on him?"

I pinch my lips together. "It was one time. It didn't have the effect I was hoping for. You Magia are stubborn."

Vanessa laughs. "Yeah, we are."

Natalia picks up my tumbler and takes a drink. "Mother, no, ew. Babe, is that bottle empty?"

"Yeah, but Mass can get another." Vanessa laughs, shoving Massimo toward the freezer.

He glares. "Woman, I take enough orders. I don't need them from you."

He opens the freezer, pulls a bottle out and hands it to Vanessa, then fishes for another one, offering a bottle to Natalia.

When she takes the vodka, I lift her into my arms. "Tony, find Raz. Tell him you're mine. He'll get you set up for the evening. I'll deal with you in the morning. Mass?"

He waves me off. "I'll take care of this crazy one," he says, eyeing Vanessa.

He has a thing, and the thing in my chest lifts.

I shift our contract, adding to the fifth line. '*We protect Natalia and Vanessa.*'

I start to move, and Natalia tosses the cap of the bottle to the island. I glare at Tony to move him out of my way as she tips the bottle back.

He crosses his arms. "I want a word with Nat."

"Talia," I finish for him.

She perks up. "Yeah, babe?"

I chuckle. "I'm not talking to you. Move, Tony. Find Raz, and I'll deal with you in the morning. Being a pain in my ass does not constitute a use, so before you talk back or do something stupid, learn that vassals follow orders or get sent to the afters. The choice is yours."

Tony looks away, stepping aside. "In the morning, Tal."

She shrugs, drinking as I carry her to my room.

***

I DROP onto the sofa in my room and pry the bottle from her. I tell her to clean up, dried blood still streaked down her face, and slump on the couch as I wait.

When she exists the bathroom in a towel, I watch. Arousal stirs in my lower stomach as she drops the towel, pulling one of my shirts from the closest. As she shrugs into it, she turns to me, smiling and securing it closed with a button before padding toward me.

My Dark simps and I remain lax as she straddles my lap wearing nothing but my shirt. She has plenty of clothes of her own, but I approve of her choice.

"Heal me."

She takes my face between her hands. "Don't move."

Her small hands are cool, and I close my eyes, leaning my head back, trusting her with my throat. A pulse of energy strums through me, a rush of Light that my Dark drools over. I grunt, trying to control the influx of magic and consume it, but it ceases.

Natalia sighs. "Don't. Whatever it is you're doing, stop it."

"You're feeding me."

"No, I'm healing you, and you need to relax."

Turning up one side of my mouth, I say, "I am relaxed."

"You really need to figure this out." She shifts, and the strum returns.

I command my Dark to be passive, both of us struggling to remain complacent. The energy washes through me then evens out to gentle waves, like low tide against a smooth sandy shore. It stops, and her hands fall to my chest. "Better?"

I make another futile attempt to pull at the collar. My flesh doesn't burn, but the metal doesn't budge. "Yes, but I already despise this thing."

Her fingertips slip beneath the band, brushing against my skin. Her voice is as soft as her touch. "It looked like it hurt."

"It did."

Her hands leave my neck, brushing over my forearm where the discs are embedded. "What is it?"

"The contest set. Every contender gets one. The head and the heart to decide," I say, lifting my thumbs, "the strength of mind, body, and magic to carry out the decision." I look to the metal in my arm. "And the fealty to serve the Dark Throne." I point to the collar.

"The contest for the throne."

"Yes."

Her chin tucks to her chest, cleaning dirt from under a nail. "I'm your weapon?"

"Yes," I whisper.

"Like your partner for the games?"

"Yes," I say. She nods as I run my hands up her thighs. "I told you once, if this was easy, I wouldn't need you, and you wouldn't be here."

She snorts through her nose. "You know, I didn't understand that when you said it. I thought you meant you wouldn't want me if you couldn't use me."

Cupping the side of her face, I lift it. "I would want you, but I wouldn't do this to you if I didn't have to." She bobs her head, and I give her a chagrined smile. "The goal is to not die."

She breaks, laughing. "Right."

I smile, basking in her laugh.

Her smile lingers as she quiets and asks, "You really came to Izul?"

"Yes." I squeeze her butt with both hands. "You're mine."

"I didn't know."

"I will always come for you."

Snorting through her nose, she half-laughs. "So many jokes."

I cup the side of her face, my fingers threading into her hair to push it back and allow me to stare her in the eye, ignoring the sass. This is important. She needs to understand. "I promise you, I will always come for you."

"You'll enjoy it too."

"Talia," I say, holding her gaze, trying to keep my tone serious and not laugh. "I will find you in the afters."

She blinks, her humor fading. "Hiro says that to Thames."

"Yes."

"They're mated."

"Yes."

Confusion flickers across her features. "I'm more than 'not just a contract,' aren't I?"

I press my palm to her throat, resting my fingers along her jaw. "You are mine, Little Star. I am going to keep you, I am going to use you, I am going to make you a queen. I am going to mate you, and when our days have come to an end, I am going to find you again in the afters to keep you by my side for eternity."

Dropping forward, she groans. "So I'm your future mate?"

Kissing the side of her head, I smirk. "You are my guiding star."

She doesn't answer, so I curl my fingers around her hair to clear it away from her neck, opening my mouth against her skin. She shivers as I drag my teeth closed. "You are in so much trouble."

Fake snoring at me, she snuggles in closer, tucking her arms against her chest. "Tell me about it tomorrow."

Smiling against her, I hum. "Pierre won't stop."

"Then I'll kill him."

I press my lips in a trail down her neck. "You drew the Ancient."

"I'll tell him to fuck off too."

I chuckle. "I'm going to use you."

"What exactly is new?"

Grinning, I hold her close by the nape of her neck, whispering, "You want me to use you."

Lifting her head, she narrows her eyes. "I'm not going to agree to that, and I'm not going to disagree to that because yes, I want you to use me to fuck yourself, but no, I don't want to be some weapon or go through more stupid games."

I force her mouth to mine, swallowing her giggle. I slip my hand under her shirt, dragging it up and over her head to reveal the black lace beneath it. Rolling forward, I get to my feet, carrying her to the bathroom. She needs a shower first and then I'm going to put her where she belongs.

The contest isn't games. The Dark Kings who have survived the contest never speak of what transpires. I will be going into the contest blind, without foreknowledge. There is no way to prepare, relying only on my wits and strength, and my little star. That's the most horrifying part. I might extinguish her.

Pierre isn't going to allow me to keep Natalia, but I'll fight to keep her. We are sans contract now, but that is negligible.

We don't require a contract. Natalia is woven into my very core. Mine. I will die before I let Pierre have her. He'd destroy her.

The Ancient's interest is dangerous. Lucius. That might be the most concerning development in our webs of fate, but it is all a problem for another time. Right now, I have a little star to use.

PLEASE LEAVE A REVIEW.

Quick reminder. I am an indie author.

I rely on reviews.

Reviews help others to find a book they might enjoy.

Reviews allow other readers to know if a book is good or not.

Reviews can control the fate of this series.

Please leave a review.

Please?
My day job is killing me.

NATALIA AND CALLAHAN'S STORY CONTINUES...

Converging Contests
Book Three
The Webs of Fate

CHAPTER 60
BONUS CHAPTER
EIGHTH MOON'S DAY, WARMWAVE, 4049
6TH MILLENNIUM
CALLAHAN

Unable to sleep, too anxious to find any rest, I knock on Massimo's door. I'd spent all day making calls and tracking down information. After too much talking, I wrangled the facts I needed.

Natalia is in Izul, beyond my reach, or so Pierre and I both believe. I might not be able to enter the Light capital, but others and other *things* can. Any direct message, an outright declaration is going to be stymied. I must circumvent Pierre's blockade another way. I need to send a message only Natalia will understand, something Pierre won't realize warrants his interception.

Massimo answers my summons, one eye partially open to glare at me. The door swings open and he stands in the doorway in sweatpants. The glossy grayish scars of a smoragon's bite are evident in his left chest and shoulder. I'd nearly lost him the first Gathering Shadows he was my partner.

"I'm going to Molanch."

He grunts. "Got ahold of Sterling?"

"He hasn't responded." I cross my arms and lean one

shoulder on the doorframe. "I'm going to show up and force him to acknowledge me."

Massimo winces and blinks both eyes open. "Am I coming with you?"

"No need."

"Sterling is the one man that could put you down."

I lick along my front teeth. As much as I have an adoration for Sterling, it is for that very fact. "He gains nothing from my death since I'm disgraced. Get your beauty rest."

He lifts his chin and closes the door.

I walk through shadows and exit the manner. Glancing up at the sky, I sigh, my magic burning through my shoulder blades to form wings.

My muscles are still twinging and angry from the mad cross-continent flight I made a couple of days ago while trying to stop Natalia from reaching Izul. Rubbing my face, I jump into the air, heading northwest.

I'll stay close to the isles on my way across the sea between this continent and the next. I'm not sure if I have the strength to make the flight in one trip and I'd prefer not to end up in the sea. Saltwater makes clothes stiff.

When I hit the coast of the continent, I turn north, watching the sky brighten as the first sun rises while I head toward the city of Molanch, where Sterling's primary residence lies. The sky turns a hazy purple, then dull pink, before fading away to sky blue.

Both suns are rising in the sky, my watch indicating it's halfway through Sun's Rune. I land on an island, panting and wincing. My shoulders ache, pulsing with a numb burning that spreads down my spine and through my chest.

Staring at the horizon, I catch my breath. I've got too far to go and no choice but to push onward.

The suns are sinking low before I reach Molanch. My body

hates me, my muscles burning. I'll rest when I have Natalia back.

I take a break on the roof of a tall building, surveying the world from on high. I've never been to this city, and I don't know where Sterling exists within it.

I see a slate gray castle in the distance, sitting on the northern edge of what I can survey. It's as good a guess as any, so I head for it.

I hit the ground and yank the rope dangling from a bell at the wrought iron gates at the front of the massive castle. It's old world, no doubt, from the time of the clans, vines and moss growing halfway up the front, lending an eerie aura to the looming turrets.

This is Sterling's residence. No self-serving and self-respecting Seraphinus would allow this gorgeous relic to be held by humans.

A male stalks toward me from the small hut nearby. He stops short, crossing his arms. "Your presence isn't expected."

"I request to see Sterling. I'm Callahan Barraco."

"I know who you are. We all do now. You made us look weak." The man turns and walks away, heading into the castle through ornate, arched metal doors.

I wait, my Dark coiling around me in reassurance that we've earned our place and respect. We got sucker punched from a blind spot. We did not lose in a fair fight, which means we have the right to request an audience with anyone.

Sterling approaches the gates straight-backed. Tall with brown skin and an arrogant twist to his lips, he moves in a lazy gait across the open expanse.

He stops, facing me through the bars as he slides his hands in his front pockets and rocks to the balls of his feet, stretching up. "Cal."

"Sterling." I nod.

"Fucked situation." He smirks, turning his head to the side, showing his thick, black rope-like twisted locks pulled back. There's a scar on his neck, off to the side and below his jaw. As long as I've known Sterling, that scar has been there. It wasn't earned in the games.

"I got lazy."

He laughs, head tipped back, his shoulders shaking. "Even lazy, you're a contender. That's terrifying."

I shrug. "I said lazy, not weak."

Grinning ear to ear, he says, "I'll confess, I hoped that you being disgraced would give me an easy win."

"Mmm," I grunt, curling my lip. "If the Dark King doesn't keel over soon, you might. Although Chlem isn't that easy to take down."

"It would have been a bit of a disappointment to have that be my most difficult opponent." He snickers. "Other than getting to live, that is."

"In other words, you think I'll win?"

He flashes his teeth, then asks, "You didn't come all this way for pleasantries, so why are you on my doorstep? As I recall, we aren't friends or I might have turned up to help you."

I tense, keeping my face straight. We aren't friends. That's true. I made that point to him. I made it because we could be friends.

I rock back on my heels, lifting my toes and frowning. "I'm disgraced."

Sterling bobs his head to the side. "Keep talking." he lifts a hand, finger extended to draw circles. "You're not one for words, but I'm enjoying this."

I glare at him, narrowing one eye.

He chuckles. "The great Callahan Barraco," he almost sings

my name. It sounds better in his rich voice. "On my doorstep, coming to me for assistance."

I look to the sky. "You're enjoying this too much."

Sterling laughs. "There's no such thing."

"You're usually humbler."

"I'm usually not graced with your presence in my home. Why are you here?"

"I want use of something you own."

Sterling lifts his thick black eyebrows. "One would assume since you showed up on my doorstep."

"You're contracted, Dark Marrow. Are they available?"

His eyebrows come together with confusion, his eyes focusing on the end of his wide nose. His face is long and rectangular, his jaw strong. There isn't an ounce of softness about him, his height and form built for strength that he wears with ease, even if it isn't showcased in his build.

We've known each other for centuries through the games, steadily learning each other through slight interactions and traded quips. I always thought we'd be good friends if life had presented the opportunity. He's an attractive and exemplary man. I can't indulge in friendship, too consumed with the fact that we were both on the list year after year and inevitably one of us would kill the other.

Sterling rubs his lower lip with his thumb. "Of all the assistance I could be to you in your current state of disgrace, that is what you're after? Musicians? You came to me for *musicians*?" he asks, curling his upper lip and staring in horror with an open mouth.

"Yes."

"I'm confused as fuck."

"That's fine." I give him a wry smile.

He laughs.

I lift my chin at his home. "Nice place."

"Been in my lineage for over a million years. Expensive as fuck to keep." Shrugging, he twists to survey it. "Love it, though. You really want musicians?"

"I'm not on my knees begging yet."

He meets my eyes, his amused. "All right, you've piqued my interest." He opens the gate, granting me entry to his property. "Why musicians?"

"Natalia." I step forward. "She's in Izul."

"What the fuck is going on?" His aloof, humorous tone is gone. He turns to me with accusatory eyes and hands on his narrow hips. "Why the fuck is Natalia in Izul? Pierre? Did the fucking Council..." He grabs my forearm, rotating it to glare at my contract with Natalia.

It's there, my Dark spelling out words of duty and service. Her name sparkles silver against my skin below my magic spelling out my servitude to her in return for what she provides. It's giving me reason to hope that my Dark will withstand being in Izul.

He releases my arm, fading a few steps back. "She's still contracted."

Rubbing my face, I take a deep breath. "Do you want to stand here for the whole explanation, or do you want to sit down for it?"

"I'll sit. Hungry?" He twists his lips to the side. "I'll buy you dinner."

Sterling curls his lip at me while holding a tumbler of bourbon and lounging in a carved wood chair. I'm sitting in one too, probably made a millennium ago, like the house, nervous about breaking it. I'm skating on respect but treading a very thin line, and one wrong step will reduce any remaining goodwill I carry with Sterling.

I finish my cappuccino, picking up another scone. He fed me a delicious dinner as I explained the situation. I need the name of his chef for when I'm king. These are the best pastries I've ever had, and his vassals will need a new contractor when he's dead.

His thumb taps on the rim of his glass as he considers me. "I have one question. Why the fuck didn't you kill them all when you had them in a room?"

Looking up and away, I snort through my nose. "When Marius came to disgrace me, he said I was brought down by a ghostly, frail entity. I believed the same. They weren't worth my time." I shrug. "Lazy."

"Idiot. You had the Light bug. You of all of us should have known better."

"*Light bug*. She's Light Seraphim and Magia. They aren't capable of what she is."

"Fair enough." Sterling opens his mouth, closes it, and hides his grin behind his hand, trying to wipe it away. "Hardly a fair fight, if it was a fight at all. What the fuck is Ki-cha?"

I stifle my laugh, rubbing my mouth. "Ki-cha is a Magia thing. They fast for forty-seven days and somehow that makes blood that explodes." I raise my mug. "I do not understand. That shit isn't any magic we know. Natalia made it once, failed to explain a lot, but she mentioned the fast. She claimed she'd never be able to do it again."

He leans forward. "I watched her eat her food and Massimo's at every meal."

"She drinks as much as she eats."

He chuckles. "Not that she shows it. She's small, toned—"

"Mine."

"Perky tits."

I snap my teeth.

He grins. "I'd have to be blind not to notice those tits." Lifting his hand, he checks it. "Probably a good handful."

"Sterling," I warn him, lowering my chin and glowering from the tops of my eyes. "I know she glows, and you like shiny things being a bird and all, but her tits aren't yours to play with...ever."

"They could be."

"She'll be my weapon."

"Depressing." He shrugs. "She's breathtaking, and I don't just mean when she's covered in blood. The raw power she exhibited, the fact that she not only survived our games but seemed to thrive even..." He grins, winking at me. "Shine?"

I laugh. I'd made that same pun. Damn him, I shouldn't indulge this, but he mirrors me in every fashion. "She did."

"I do like shiny."

I choke on my humor. "I know."

Sterling is a flurry, the race created with traits of a bird of prey. We all have our downsides, and he is easily distracted by anything that glitters or gleams. I've used it to my advantage a few times.

The humor fades from him. "I know she glows, and she's more than Magia, but how do you kill her?"

"Natalia? Give her a reason to die, then you might have a chance."

He gives me a long look. "That's less than helpful."

"I'm not telling you the weaknesses of my weapon."

"I'm not after her. I'm after the Magia."

"They are weak when you know their tricks."

"What are they?" His black eyes glitter, his Dark slithering out of him.

I frown, unsure of the sudden display of his temper.

"What are they?" He repeats with a snarl, throwing out a hand with a finger directed to the side. "They attacked two of mine, and one didn't live. I deserve to know because this is your mess."

"You didn't figure it out fighting Natalia?"

He slams a fist on the table. "You are in my house. You come to me for what I have, and you dare—"

"It was an honest question," I yell, staring in ire and confusion alike. "What the fuck?"

He sits back, glaring with pinched lips, breathing hard through his nose. Sterling is every bit the Dark I strive to be, logical, strong, and honest. He's not brutal unless pushed, but he will get his claws out when necessary without hesitation.

He settles, shoulders dropping. "Everything can die. Natalia survived Telra's laced blade to the heart, so I know that won't cut it, but I need to know how to kill them."

Furrowing my eyebrows, I ask, "The Magia attacked?"

"Yes, three against two. One of mine didn't survive. Salvatore reported that the Magia said they will kill on sight. This mess you made is getting worse, and me and mine are at risk because of your mistakes."

I sigh, rubbing my mouth. I almost say they must have got someone important, but all vassals are important. It doesn't matter the name or the job they do. Vassals serve, and in return, the contractor protects and tends. "Who?"

"Salvatore's brother, Diego."

Curling my fists, I grip until they lose color. "The Magia, not all, but if they're fully trained–they call it Pinnacle–they can absorb your magic and send it back. You can't protect yourself from your own magic, but they are weak. Not quite as fragile as humans, but not like us, and they heal quickly. You have to kill them instantly, or they will get back up."

Contemplating the ceiling, Sterling lets the silence stretch.

"You're right, I should have figured that out. I am a fucking idiot."

"You were looking at the Magia like they're Talia. They aren't."

He leans back. "You need to fix this shit." Shaking his head, he stands. "I'll help you get your Light bug back."

"Now I have a question."

He scoffs. "Why? Because I won't cheat by hindering you." He takes a step and stops. "Besides, I like you, baby, and I don't like the idea of the Light possessing her or using her. Fuck those glow bats, they don't deserve her."

I snicker, getting to my feet. "She belongs in the Dark."

"She does, even if she shines. She's nothing like those fucks." He lifts a finger, drawing a circle in the air. "Follow me."

Sterling knocks on a simple wood door, and we wait for it to open. We meet eyes but say nothing.

A man answers, his appearance disheveled, shirtless and wearing wrinkled black jeans with a ripped-out knee. He looks desolate and groggy, but he looks at Sterling and stands straighter, his eyes widening as he clears his throat. "Sir?"

"This is Callahan." Sterling jerks his head at me. "Cal, this is Shawn Gettemeir. He's the lead singer and the songwriter of Dark Marrow."

Shawn is tall, frail, and long-limbed with shaggy black hair that can't figure out if it's curly or straight. He inclines his head. "How can I be of assistance?"

"I want a guitar you have that a fan would recognize."

Sterling says, "You'll give him what he wants if you want to keep your cushy contract this Blooming season."

I glance at him, eyebrow raised.

He shrugs. "They make me money, but I have enough businesses I can manage without him. He's useless otherwise, and if he makes me a cheat, I'll make his life agony for the disgrace."

I press my lips at the insult to his contracted. It's odd. Sterling is rumored to be an amazing contractor.

If I was in standing, I'd offer to take Shawn off his hands for the dig alone, plus Natalia would be delighted to have access to the band.

Shawn sighs. "Yes, sir." He turns, leaving the door open. "I have several options if you'd like to take your pick."

I step into the room and cringe. It's a mess of pages and clothes strewn everywhere. I notice a few vials and a needle next to the bed. One label I can make out: Faeling toxin.

Shawn motions to a wall, a dozen guitars hanging by their necks in an array. "Take your pick."

"They all look the same."

Shawn gapes at me. "Whoa, dude! Are you blind?"

Sterling clears his throat.

"Uh, sir, my bad." He winces, looking at the floor.

I scan the wall, wishing I'd discussed the instrument with Natalia. I'd sent a contracted to purchase the best they could find for Natalia on immediate notice, and she'd seemed thrilled with what I gave to her, but I never took further interest. "Is there one that a fan would recognize as yours?"

"Uh..." Shawn blinks and then frowns at the wall. "Like, what are you after? Most of these I've played at one point or another on stage."

"Do you have a favorite?"

Shawn snatches one off the wall, offering it over with a bleak expression. It's like he's offering to let me slit his throat. "This girl. She's a Dragola, the most expensive I own. There are only a dozen in the world, and I have two of them, but this is the only one I play. She comes with me for every show."

I take it by the neck, staring at it. "There's nothing about this instrument that seems recognizable."

"You don't know shit about guitars, do you?"

Sterling glares. "Shawn. Respect."

He ducks his head. "It's recognizable. For starters, it's old. I bought it centuries ago before I ever had to be contracted."

"Had to be?"

He hesitates, giving me a shy expression. He's not built for anything physical. His ribs are on display, his stomach sucked in. I know Sterling's name carries weight and respect. There's never been a bad word about his abilities as a contractor. Even some who have left him to sign with me were gracious in their words. Not all contractors are given high praise or any praise.

The Dark doesn't lie, and my fellow contractors and I hear more than vassals might think. Sterling doesn't starve his. Sterling doesn't beat his. Sterling treats his with respect, so Shawn's condition strikes odd.

Shawn rubs the back of his neck, staring at the guitars. "My mother was a contractor, but I'm not strong enough to stand on my own. She wasn't either, I guess."

I twist my lips to the side. It happens. I ask, "How much do you want for it?"

Shawn turns to Sterling, his frail body going stick straight. "Sterling, no. I'm not—"

With a single look, Sterling silences him. I can't blame Shawn. That glare would shut me up, too.

Sterling softens, "Pick a number. Cal is taking the guitar. You can be compensated, or you can have shit in return. I give

577

you no tasks. You talk back and forget you are a contracted and offer me no skills of service. You get free rein to live under my protection, to write and sing your songs. You spend more time spending coin to make your music and travel for shows than you spend in my home. The only thing I take is a fair cut of profits as the law demands I take in return for the give."

Shawn sniffs. "My girl isn't for sale."

"The choice is yours."

I inspect the instrument's black surface, tarnished by use with scratches. I don't care what it costs. Shawn has a strong attachment to this guitar, so Natalia will love it.

Shawn wilts, almost in tears. "I bought that centuries ago for eight hundred thousand. In this century, a new Dragola is going to cost me two million."

Meeting Sterling's eyes, I ask, "What's your arrangement?"

"I get two-thirds."

Shooting him a look of disdain, I say, "I don't do arithmetic."

"I'll take six million, and in turn, he," Sterling says, jerking his head to Shawn, "will get the two he needs to replace it."

"Deal."

"Um..." Shawn scratches behind his ear, wincing. "Can I play her one last time before you take her?"

I hold the guitar out, saying, "With a condition."

"Sure." Shawn reaches for the guitar. "Anything you want."

"Play the stay song."

Shawn's features pinch as he frowns.

Sterling asks with force, "Problem?"

Shawn glances at him and then looks at me. It's somewhere between disgust and dejection.

I can't stop the laugh bursting from me. Both men stare.

"You hate that song too."

Shawn turns and sits with the guitar, running a hand down

the strings. "Wrote it on this very girl." He plays a note and then drops his hands. "Don't usually write with her. Break too many strings, and I've destroyed a few in moods." He sighs, staring at the instrument. "Wrote it in a single night, and yes, if you care to know, I do hate that song. Why did you pick that one?"

"Shawn," Sterling says, "you don't question contractors."

I smirk. "He can question me. I'm not a contractor. I'm disgraced."

Shawn stares wide-eyed and then cuts his eyes at Sterling with a sneered expression. "He's disgraced, and you're still making me sell my best girl? What the actual fuck?"

"I don't owe you an explanation."

"He's out of standing, and he had to have fucked up bad to get disgraced. Why the fuck are you helping him?"

Sterling chuckles. "First, you're addressing your contractor without respect. Second, you're in the presence of Callahan Barraco. You are ignorant of the weight he has, the strength, his honor, and the respect he's earned, but I am not. I know what happened, and he doesn't deserve to be disgraced."

I laugh. "Talia burned out my contract after the maze in front of our king. I'm surprised I wasn't disgraced then and there."

Sterling rolls his shoulders back, smiling at me. "I was already done, waiting to see who was and wasn't coming back. Natalia might have destroyed her contract, but she made her point. She was choosing you and no one was going to take her from you. I wasn't shocked in the least that Basileus didn't disgrace you, nor that you remained a contender."

Screwing my face up, I ask, "Are you fucking joking? I wasn't strong enough to stop her."

"You were strong enough to claim her and sign her in the first place. You earned her loyalty within very little time. It wasn't the contract that made her answer to you. Without a contract, she could have run, accepted Pierre's offer, anything she wanted. She didn't. You, Cal, you are what she had accepted as an alpha. To have won the respect, loyalty, and service of something as strong as she is speaks volumes to your character and strength. No, I wasn't surprised by either choice."

I look away, trying to hide my wince. When he puts it in that perspective, I can't find fault with the king's choice either.

Shawn plucks at the strings, and I answer his original question. "I want to hear your version of the song 'I'll Stay.'"

"My version? My version is the song. You can listen to it on any music service."

"There's another version." I shrug.

"There aren't other versions. I wrote the fucked thing, and *no one* gets to cover my songs. I've killed anyone who did without permission."

Sterling swells, and I hold out my hand to him with a chuckle. "I doubt he's calling me a liar. He's unaware of what I know."

Sterling's voice is tense. "I won't tolerate mine showing disrespect to you."

Shawn asks, eyes narrowed, "What other version?"

"Natalia's."

"Who the fuck is Natalia?"

With head cocked, Sterling asks, "Was her version one of the songs she played in the game?"

I twist my lips to the side. "No. She first refused to play the song as I requested, and at the order of the king, she played my request second but decided to perform the original version." I gesture at Shawn. "His version. I wasn't even aware of its existence."

"She's hard to control, isn't she?"

I laugh, maybe for the first time since I have seen Natalia. "I'd be fucked without a worn contract."

"I assumed you were fucked."

"Yes," I say, not sure how Sterling will take my admittance of sexual activities with the Light.

I shouldn't care. I don't know why I care.

"We all know it." He shakes his head, crossing his arms. "Can't blame you. She looks tasty."

"She is."

Sterling smirks. "Lucky bastard. I almost had her in the restaurant."

"Just be grateful she didn't kill you. Jeza tried to steal her while I was busy with the smoragon and ended up in the afters."

"I was pissed Chelm summoned that thing. It caused too much havoc."

"You never stood a chance. I'd already sunk my claws in her."

"Ah." Sterling rubs his chin. "That makes more sense. She didn't fight you."

Looking between us, Shawn asks, "She played my songs at the games?"

Sterling nods. "She performed two songs."

Shawn's face is one of disbelief. "Marrow songs?"

I shrug. "The stay song."

"It's '*I'll Stay*.'"

Sterling glares. "You're pushing it today."

I smirk. "Natalia gets annoyed when I say it wrong, too. 'I'll Stay' and then another. "Almost love" was said a lot."

Frowning, Shawn says, "Solid Pairing." He mocks a deeper frown, eyes widening a bit as he stares at nothing. "Good to know my songs were played well enough to keep someone from getting their head lopped off. What do you mean you didn't know the existence of my version? It's the only one."

"Not how she originally played the song for me, and it's a lot less kill yourself to meet your mate in the afters."

Shawn scoffs. "What the burning afters did she do to my song?"

"In her words? Made it a beautiful lie."

He's staring at me with pain and fury alike. "Do you know why I wrote that fucked song?"

"No."

"I was contracted to Yanri. She was, too. We had our thing, and one night, she told me she loved me. So, I fucking mated her, and right after, the bitch started crying because she was trying to tell me she was taking a contract with another contractor and leaving me behind but didn't have the fucking courage to say it. Instead, she let me fucking mate her because she wanted to–and I'm fucking quoting her–keep a part of me when she left."

I stare with wide eyes. My stomach squirms, my balls sucking up and invading its space. Of all the possible torturous things in the world, that might be the worst thing imaginable. I might vomit at the concept based on my knowledge of mates. "Did you kill her?"

"Should've, could've." He sighs. "Didn't." Looking away he winces.

Sterling sits on the couch, forlorn lingering in the lines of his face. "I wasn't aware."

"You never asked, it never came up, and my shit isn't your burden."

Sighing, Sterling says, "Under our Dark tenets, no, your problems are not mine to share."

I scoff. "The tenets are–"

"However," Sterling says, staying focused on Shawn, "as a contractor, it's my duty to take care of mine."

A ripple moves across Shawn's face, snarling then settling into a scowl. "That bastard didn't think so."

I drag a hand down my face. "Not all contractors understand the responsibility is shared between the contractor and contracted."

"No," Sterling says with a sour look. "At least that makes a difference in society these days."

I move to a nearby piano, settling on the bench. It's true that the relationship of contracted and contractor does carry weight, but not enough. There are still contractors who take the idea of contracted being property too harshly. I protected as many as I could, but I couldn't sign them all and still care for mine to the high level I demand from myself.

Sterling looks to Shawn. "Yanri is well known to be abusive."

I bare my teeth. "He's got a special place in the burning afters."

Startled, Shawn gapes. "You know him?"

I laugh. "Yanri's a contractor, which means he's a player at Gathering Shadows. We all know him," I say, lifting my chin at Sterling. "He's slippery and hard to kill, or I would have already, on principle. He's alive because I hold back on killing his partner. That pathetic asshole Yanri sacrifices his partner Oscar every fucking time to save himself."

Sterling drags a hand down his face. "We all have tried to kill him. I've extended an offer of a contract to Oscar several times for when his contract with Yanri is over but never receive any word in return."

Shawn glances between us with daftness. "Yanri trapped him in a worn contract. Oscar negotiated the contract, a written contract, and signed. Yanri put it on his skin as he laughed. Oscar never had a chance."

I stare, livid. When I signed Natalia to her original worn contract without her knowledge of what the contract was, she hadn't negotiated for a written contract. I used her ignorance against her. Oscar knew and played by the rules. Yanri knew and disregarded the rules.

Sterling scowls. "Why hasn't Oscar gone to the king?"

"Beyond Oscar telling me he can't because of the contract? It's Oscar's word against Yanri's, and as a contracted–"

"Oscar is fucked." I turn away, crossing my arms to keep from breaking something. "Sterling, make an agreement with me. If either of us wins the contest, that gets fixed."

Sterling laughs at me, genuine glee twisting his face. "Absolutely. We all know Yanri is a sick bastard. I'm convinced if contracts weren't mandated by law, he'd have none."

Shawn hangs his head. "We get desperate, and most contractors that are good are hard to sign with."

"If your mate was running from him, give me a name, and I'll find her. I can support another vassal and reunite you two."

Sterling is everything a Dark should be.

Shawn shakes his head. "If that's an offer, fuck no, and if that was an order, I still say no, and you can send me right to the burning afters for all I fucking care." He takes a deep breath. "My contract had been up previously. I was going to find another contractor, but she begged me to stay, so I signed again. Then she pulled that shit."

I wince.

"I could have gotten better, gotten away, free–fuck, I could have had a contractor that just fucking fed me." His voice raises in volume while descending into the snarl of a rabid animal. "But I didn't. I fucking stayed–for her. I starved, took the beatings, every fucked thing he put us through, and I did it for her–

to not abandon her to suffer the torture and misery alone, and then she fucking let me *mate* her and ran off, leaving me in that place?"

He takes a deep breath and lowers his voice. "If she would have just left?" His words start to fracture, "I'd have been pissed but gotten over it. If she would have told me the truth about her intentions? I wouldn't have mated her, and I'd have moved on. But no, that fucking bitch stole from me, and I hate her for that–for letting me mate her because she did that, knowing full well what it would do to me. She doesn't deserve a contractor as good as you. She doesn't deserve my forgiveness."

Resting a hand on Shawn's shoulder, Sterling asks, "Is there anything I can do to help your situation?"

Shawn shakes his head. "No," he croaks, blinking a few times. "No one can break the mating bond. That bitch damned me. My Dark hurts, and it doesn't want to work with me anymore. It whines constantly. It's dying without our mate. I know it is."

"Would bringing her closer help you? I do have dungeons."

Shawn swipes at his nose with the heel of his palm. "No. I crave her, and if she were close..." Looking away, the muscles in his jaw clamp. "I haven't seen her since that night 'cause she'd already signed and was leaving in the morning. If I ever see her again, I'll kill her and give myself a reason to live without my mate, only this time it'll be my choice."

My Dark folds in on itself, hugging itself tight inside of me. We only have read or heard things about the mating bond. I've witnessed the bond between Hiro and Thames. The sick agony of what Shawn is saying is a concept and still more grotesque than I can stomach.

Shawn sniffs, breathing out hard. "I never–she walked away from me right after while I was too weak to chase after her. She left in the morning. I remember her scent, but that's it. I never even had a fucking chance to experience anything else. I'm stuck with this mating bond and never even got the chance to enjoy it."

Sterling says, "The offer is outstanding should you change your mind, but it is your choice. I'd never force perversion or pain on one of mine." He adds with a slight smile, "Even one who is a pain in my ass and forgets respect too many times to count."

Shawn shakes his head. "Problems with signing the child of a contractor." He sighs. "I tend to forget my place. Bad habits are hard to quit, and all."

Chuckling, I cross my arms. "Play that song for me and any other you want," I say, getting comfortable. "I'll take it when you're done."

"Other fucking version," Shawn mutters under his breath, getting ready to play. He glares at me. "What's this other fucking version? I deserve to know."

"If I get Natalia back, I'll introduce you. She'd be thrilled, and I'll have her play it for you."

Shawn scoffs, sneering and then focuses on the instrument. "That fucking bitch is still ruining my shit and fucking up my days and doesn't even know it." His eyes swivel to me with his head low. "My mate, not Natalia."

Grinning, Sterling drops a hand on his shoulder, giving him a slight shove. "He didn't take offense, or you'd be laid out already."

Lifting my chin, I say, "He's right, and it's safe to assume anytime bitch comes out of your mouth, I'm correlating it to your mate."

"Good choice."

"Play so I can take that guitar. I need it."

Sterling asks, "Are you sure it will work?"

"No, but I'm limited on avenues I can take." I pull my phone out. "Where do I send payment?"

Sterling stands. "I'll fetch my account number, and I expect an extra payout to Salvatore on your behalf for the loss of his brother and the strain that will put on him as the sole remainder of his lineage in compensation for my generosity."

Coin I have, and it's my weakness that started this mess. I incline my head. "Have him pick a number."

INDEX

THE LIGHT

The Light Queen
HONORIFIC TITLE

The Light Queen is a title given in honor for their god, Beenin. It does not revert to King even when a male holds the throne. The first Light Queen was Renave, and she established the trinity of leaders from the most powerful heritages: Lamont, Hallow, & Bordeaux.

The Lamonts have ruled the Light since the foundation of Light Society without exception.

The Light Queen is responsible for ruling the Light, settling disputes within their rank and managing the society. They act with an iron fist and unforgiving rule to maintain their ways.

The Light Queen is undeniable and is uncontested rule. As the crown is hereditary, each upcoming Light Queen is taught extensively on law and etiquette from a young age until the Light Queen expires, then being crowned.

The Light Queen still answers to the Council if they incite conflict with the Dark.

The Light King
HONORIFIC TITLE

The Light King is the unioned partner to the Light Queen.

The Light King has limited authority. The Light King is not equal to the Light Queen.

Magistrates

The Light Queen has nine magistrates that are tasked with carrying out their rulings and decisions. The Magistrates will run interference, blocking subjects from reaching the Light Queen unless truly necessary or of high enough rank to deserve a direct audience.

Magistrates are the only contracted to the Light Queen. It's seen as an honor to serve the Light Queen, and magistrates have significant influence within society, enjoying benefits.

THE LIGHT SOCIETY

Emulating Beenin, the Light Serphinus strive for what they believe Beenin to be, what she told them she was: eloquent, simple beauty, graceful, and beyond reproach.
They believe they are the best, they are right, and they are without fault, exactly like Beenin.

THE FOUR PILLARS OF ETIQUETTE

Respect

Harmony

Tradition

Honor

ETHICAL CODE OF CONDUCT

Be mindful of others. One is not more important than the many.
Conform and be part of the many. If all succeed so will the individual.
Generosity is a gift and deserves a gift in turn.
There is beauty in simplicity, let not the individual be overly exaggerative of deeds or display.
Participate & perform. In return, the individual receives belonging, protection, & purpose.
Above all else, place heritage. An individual does not exist without the ancestors and will cease to exist without future generations.
Respect your elders for they have come before you and have taught you. Rank and seniority are to be respected.
Do not be overly assertive as it is a gateway leading to aggression and acts of violence, the ultimate ignorance.
Carry kindness and compassion in the heart. Keep the mind sharp and the tongue soft. Allow the illumination of Light to glisten brightly for beauty is grace.
The Light is a precious treasure to be respected and honored but temperance in all things. Do not allow the Light to control your actions. The host is to be in command.
Act with dignity, not as beasts. In all the individual does, act with intensions of honor, integrity, and respect. Bring about harmony through unity and diligence.

THE TRINITY LINEAGES

These three heritages make up the ruling faction of the Light. At the top, sitting on the Light Throne is the Lamont heritage.

	HERITAGE NAME	RACE
	LAMONT	(VIOLET)
	HALLOW	(IGNIS)
	BORDEAUX	(CALIGLIO)

HERITAGE RANKING

PRESTIGIOUS
Prestigious heritages can hold contracts and be contracted. They answer only to the Light Queen and are the ones selected to be magistrates or granted audience with the Light Queen. These are city owners and the wealthiest of all heritages.

STANDARD
Standard heritage can be contracted but cannot hold contracts. They answer to the prestigious heritages, magistrates, and the Light Queen. They get audiences with the magistrates. These heritages are business owners and wealthy.

Majority of society

UNDESIRABLE
Undesirables cannot be contracted or hold contracts. They must petition for an audience with a magistrate and are never granted rights to speak to the Light Queen. These heritages are mostly working class and have little wealth, most often used for paid services to the Prestigious and Standard heritages, including the Throne or Queen of Light.

LIGHT LIFE
"WELCOME AND BE WELCOMING"
Life for a Light Seraphinus is as structured as their society.

FIRST MEAL
Every Light begins their day with a jejinn in a vescor.

"VESCOR"	word derived from the words food & entertainment	establishments serving traditional first & second meals within the light
"JEJINN"	word derived from Beenin's love of an early meal	traditional meal comprised of five portions served with a choice of tea

Vescors do not serve alcohol. They open Dawn's rune and close at Evergreen rune.

SECOND MEAL
Every Light enjoys a second meal during Evergreen rune.
They will eat at a cafe or grab a meal from a velkeno.

"VELKENO"	translation: quick eat.	Establishment offering pre-made meals that can be enjoyed within the cafe or taken elsewhere

EVENING MEAL
Evening meals are enjoyed at restaurants.
On special occasion meals will include rizvor.

"RIZVOR"	translation: fizzy	A carbonated liquor made from fruit Delicacy made exclusively for the Light

RANK
Rank determines everything from suited company to who an individual can speak to or if an individual can even speak in certain company.

The lowest ranked individual speaks for the group and will serve the group, serving highest rank to lowest rank (themselves last).

Standard greeting: "Welcome and be welcoming"
Standard reponse: "I/We are welcomed and welcoming"

All interactions begin with a show of due respect (if necessary) and the standard greeting.

APPEARANCE
Individuals must always appear their best; to radiate from within and emulate Beenin's grace. Warbraids are common hairstyles for men & women. Clothing must be tailored and only in shades of whites, beiges, and golds.

ADDITIONAL LIGHT SERAPHIN WORDS

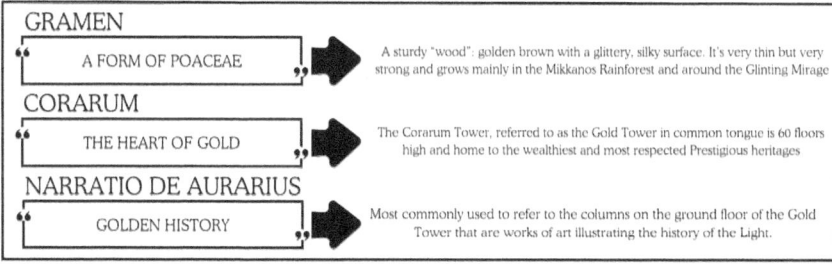

GRAMEN
"A FORM OF POACEAE"
A sturdy "wood": golden brown with a glittery, silky surface. It's very thin but very strong and grows mainly in the Mikkanos Rainforest and around the Glinting Mirage

CORARUM
"THE HEART OF GOLD"
The Corarum Tower, referred to as the Gold Tower in common tongue is 60 floors high and home to the wealthiest and most respected Prestigious heritages

NARRATIO DE AURARIUS
"GOLDEN HISTORY"
Most commonly used to refer to the columns on the ground floor of the Gold Tower that are works of art illustrating the history of the Light.

RITUAL

A CEREMONIAL FIGHT BETWEEN SIBILINGS

Ritual was initiated in the time of clans when death rates were higher.
Siblings would face in combat to determine which would be active in society.
The victor was determined to be the strongest with the highest survival chance.
The defeated would be sequestered to ensure their safety and the continuation
of the lineage/heritage.

RITUAL LAWS

The younger/youngest sibling will call the Ritual
fight to ensure a fair fight.

The defeated will contract themself to the victor.

LINEAGE LAW
Ritual contracted follow Dark Contractual Law

HERITAGE LAW
Ritual contracted are to be cannot perform
society duties.
The contracted are still viewed as an extension
of their heritage for rank purposes.
Ritual contracted must have approval for union
contracts from the victor.

Operation in society is determined by the victor,
and any loss or gain of standing achieved by the
victor extends to Ritual contracted.

Ritual combats are excluded from legal
accountability in terms of murder.

*IN PRESENT DAY IT'S PRACTICED ONLY BY DARK CONTRACTORS
& PRESTIGIOUS OR STANDARD HERITAGES OF LIGHT

ACKNOWLEDGMENTS

Thank you, dear reader, for taking the time to read my book.
I must thank my husband, Eric, for indulging my obsession
with this story.
To my beta readers Renee and Amanda, the beautiful women
who took the time to read this story, I cannot offer enough
appreciation for your time and feedback.
Thank you to Cover Craft – Fantasy Covers by Julie for the
gorgeous interior artwork. Julie is nothing short but amazing.
Thank you to Gina Casto – KillingItWrite, my fabulous editor.
She's beyond thorough and helpful.
And last, but certainly not least, thank you to my lovely,
invaluable street team! Instagram handles for anyone who
would like to check out their bookstagrams:
Simplyjustbooks
4articleally4
Chey_chapterss
Courtneythebookdragon
Booksbydanielle
Dani.ellereadsbooks
Debeeofficalbooks
Hannahsprettybooks
Jinxxysbookcorner
Lamiaslibrary
Mariereads_romance
Cheekichibishay

www.ingramcontent.com/pod-product-compliance
Lightning Source LLC
Chambersburg PA
CBHW022232020726
47496CB00004B/861